William Wyatt Gill, Friedrich Max Müller

Myths and Songs from the South Pacific

William Wyatt Gill, Friedrich Max Müller

Myths and Songs from the South Pacific

ISBN/EAN: 9783337180324

Printed in Europe, USA, Canada, Australia, Japan

Cover: Foto ©Andreas Hilbeck / pixelio.de

More available books at **www.hansebooks.com**

MYTHS AND SONGS

FROM THE SOUTH PACIFIC.

NEW BOOKS.

THE CHILDHOOD OF THE WORLD: A Simple Account of Man in Early Times. By EDWARD CLODD, F.R.A.S. New Edition. Crown 8vo. 3s.

"Likely to prove acceptable to a large and growing class of readers."—*Pall Mall Gazette.*

"The book is one which very young children could understand, and which grown-up persons may run through with pleasure and advantage."—*Spectator.*

"Its style is simply exquisite, and it is filled with most curious information."—*Christian World.*

"I read your book with great pleasure. I have no doubt it will do good, and hope you will continue your work. Nothing spoils our temper so much as having to unlearn in youth, manhood, and even old age, so many things which we were taught as children. A book like yours will prepare a far better soil in the child's mind, and I was delighted to have it to read to my children."—(*Extract from a Letter from Professor* MAX MULLER *to the Author*).

THE CHILDHOOD OF RELIGIONS: Including a Simple Account of the Birth and Growth of Myths and Legends. By EDWARD CLODD, F.R.A.S. Crown 8vo. 5s.

"His language is simple, clear, and impressive. His faculty of disentangling complicated masses of detail, and compressing much information into small space, with such felicitous arrangement and expression as never to over-tax the attention or abate the interest of the reader, is very remarkable."—*Examiner.*

"The style is very charming. There is something in the author's enthusiasm, something in the pellucid simplicity of his easy prose, which beguiles the reader along."—*Academy.* ·

THE LIFE AND GROWTH OF LANGUAGE. By W. D. WHITNEY, Professor of Sanskrit and Comparative Philology in Yale College, New Haven. Second Edition. 5s.

"We commend Mr. Whitney's book as being a clear and concise summary of all that is known of the still infant science of language."—*Hour.*

MISSIONARY LIFE IN THE SOUTHERN SEAS. By JAMES HUTTON. With Illustrations. Crown 8vo. 7s. 6d.

This is an historical record of mission work by the labourers of all denominations in Tahiti—the Hervey, the Austral, the Samoa or Navigator's, the Sandwich, Friendly, and Fiji Islands, &c.

"The narrative is calm, sensible, and manly, and preserves many interesting facts in a convenient shape."—*Literary Churchman.*

A YACHTING CRUISE IN THE SOUTH SEAS. By C. F. WOOD. Demy 8vo., with six Photographic Illustrations. 7s. 6d.

The author has spent considerable time in Polynesia, and his work is a description of the islands and the manners and customs of the natives as they exist. Much that is interesting from a scientific and ethnological point of view will be found in the volume.

MYTHS AND SONGS

FROM

THE SOUTH PACIFIC.

BY THE

REV. WILLIAM WYATT GILL, B.A.,

OF THE LONDON MISSIONARY SOCIETY.

WITH A PREFACE BY

F. MAX MÜLLER, M.A.,

PROFESSOR OF COMPARATIVE PHILOLOGY AT OXFORD; FOREIGN MEMBER
OF THE FRENCH INSTITUTE.

HENRY S. KING & CO., LONDON.
1876.

PREFACE.

HAVING expressed a strong desire that the collection of Myths
and Songs from the South Pacific, which the Rev. W. Wyatt Gill
brought home with him from Mangaia, should not be allowed to
lie forgotten, or, like other valuable materials collected by hard-
working missionaries, perish altogether, I could not well decline
to state, in a few words, what I consider the real importance of
this collection to be.

I confess it seemed strange to me that its importance should be
questioned.   If new minerals, plants, or animals are discovered, if
strange petrifactions are brought to light, if flints or other stone
weapons are dredged up, or works of art disinterred, even if a
hitherto unknown language is rendered accessible for the first time,
no one, I think, who is acquainted with the scientific problems of
our age, would ask what their importance consists in, or what they

are good for. Whether they are products of nature or works of man, if only there is no doubt as to their genuineness, they claim and most readily receive the attention, not only of the learned, but also of the intelligent public at large.

Now, what are these Myths and Songs which Mr. W. W. Gill has brought home from Mangaia, but antiquities, preserved for hundreds, it may be for thousands of years, showing us, far better than any stone weapons or stone idols, the growth of the human mind during a period which, as yet, is full of the most perplexing problems to the psychologist, the historian, and the theologian? The only hope of our ever unravelling the perplexities of that mythological period, or that mythopœic phase of the human intellect, lies in our gaining access to every kind of collateral evidence. We know that mythopœic period among the Aryan and Semitic races, but we know it from a distance only, and where are we to look now for living myths and legends, except among those who still think and speak mythologically, who are, in fact, at the present moment what the Hindus were before the collection of their sacred hymns, and the Greeks long before the days of Homer? To find ourselves among a people who really believe in gods and heroes and ancestral spirits, who still offer human sacrifices, who in some cases devour their human victims, or, at all events, burn the flesh of animals on their altars, trusting that the scent will be sweet to the nostrils of their gods, is as if the zoologist could spend a few days among the megatheria, or the botanist among the waving ferns of the forests, buried beneath our feet. So much is written just now, and has been written during the last fifty years, on human archæology, on the growth and progress of the intellect, on the origin of religion, on the first beginnings of social institutions; so many theories have been started, so many generalizations put forward with perfect confidence, that one might almost imagine that all the evidence was before us, and no more new light could be expected from anywhere. But the very contrary is the case. There are many regions still to be explored, there are many facts, now put forward as certain, which require the most careful inspection, and as we read again and again the minute descriptions of the journey which man is supposed to have made from station to station, from his childhood to his manhood, or, it may be, his old age, it is difficult to resist a feeling of amazement, and to suppress at almost every page the exclamation, Wait ! wait !

There are the two antagonistic schools, each holding its tenets with a kind of religious fervour—the one believing in a descending, the other in an ascending, development of the human race; the one asserting that the history of the human mind begins of necessity with a state of purity and simplicity which gradually gives way to corruption, perversity, and savagery; the other maintaining with equal confidence, that the first human beings could not have been more than one step above the animals, and that their whole history is one of progress towards higher perfection. With regard to the beginnings of religion, the one school holds to a primitive suspicion of something that is beyond—call it supernatural, transcendent, or divine. It considers a silent walking across this *jhúla** of life, with eyes fixed on high, as a more perfect realisation of primitive religion than singing of Vedic hymns, offerof Jewish sacrifices, or the most elaborate creeds and articles. The other begins with the purely animal and passive nature of man,

---

* " So, on the 12th of August, we made the steep ascent to the village of Namgea, and from there to a very unpleasant *jhúla*, which crosses the foaming torrent of the Sutlej. In this part of the Himálaya, and, indeed, on to Kashmír, these bridges are constructed of twigs, chiefly from birch trees or bushes, twisted together. Two thick ropes of these twigs, about the size of a man's thigh, or a little larger, are stretched across the river, at a distance of about six to four feet from each other, and a similar rope runs between them, three or four feet lower, being connected with the upper ropes by more slender ropes, also usually of birch twigs twisted together, but sometimes of grass, and occurring at an interval of about five feet from each other. The unpleasantness of a *jhúla* is that the passenger has no proper hold of the upper ropes, which are too thick and rough to be grasped by the hand; and that, at the extremities, they are so far apart that it is difficult to have any hold of both at the same time; while the danger is increased by the bend or hang of the *jhúla*, which is much lower in the middle than at its ends. He has also to stoop painfully in order to move along it, and it is seldom safe for him to rest his feet on the lower rope, except where it is supported from the upper ropes by the transverse ones. To fall into the raging torrent underneath would be almost certain destruction. The high wind which usually prevails in the Himálaya during the day, makes the whole structure swing about frightfully. In the middle of the bridge there is a cross-bar of wood (to keep the two upper ropes separate) which has to be stepped over; and it is not customary to repair a *jhúla* until some one falls through it, and so gives practical demonstration that it is in rather a rotten condition."—Andrew Wilson, "The Abode of Snow," p. 197.

and tries to show how the repeated impressions of the world in which he lived, drove him to fetichism, whatever that may mean, to ancestor-worship, to a worship of nature, of trees and serpents, of mountains and rivers, of clouds and meteors, of sun and moon and stars, and the vault of heaven, and at last, by what is called a natural mistake, of One who dwells in heaven above.

There is some truth in every one of these views; but they become untrue by being generalized. The time has not come yet, it probably never will come, when we shall be able to assert anything about the real beginnings of religion in general. We know a little here, **a** little there, but whatever we know of early religion, we always see that it presupposes vast periods of an earlier development.

Some people imagine that fetichism, at all events, presupposes nothing: they would probably not hesitate to ascribe to some of the higher animals the faculty of fetich-worship. But few words are so devoid of scientific precision as *fetichism*, a term first rendered popular by the writings of De Brosses. Let us suppose that it means a kind of temporary worship of any material object which the fancy may happen to select, as a tree, a stone, a post, an animal:—can that be called a primitive form of religion? First of all, religion is one thing, worship another, and the two are by no means necessarily connected. But, even if they were, what is the meaning of worship paid to a stone, but the outward sign of a

b

pre-existent belief that this stone is more than a stone, something supernatural, it may be something divine, so that the ideas of the supernatural and the divine, instead of growing out of fetichism, are generally, if not always, presupposed by it? The same applies to ancestor-worship, which not only presupposes the conceptions of immortality and of the ideal unity of a family, but implies in many cases a belief that the spirits of the departed are worthy to share the honours paid to divine beings.

To maintain that all religion begins with fetichism, all mythology with ancestor-worship, is simply untrue, as far as our present knowledge goes. There is fetichism, there is ancestor-worship, there is nature-worship, whether of trees or serpents, of mountains or rivers, of clouds and meteors, of sun and moon and stars, and the vault of heaven ; there is all this, and there is much more than all this, wherever we can watch the early growth of religious ideas : but, what we have to learn is, first of all, to distinguish, to study each religion, each mythology, each form of worship by itself, to watch them during successive periods of their growth and decay, to follow them through different strata of society, and before all, to have each of them, as much as possible, studied in their own language.

If language is the realization of thought and feeling, the importance of a knowledge of the language for a correct appreciation of what it was meant to convey in the expression of religious thought and feeling, requires no proof. I have often insisted on this, and I have tried to show—whether successfully or not, let others judge—that much of what seems at first irrational and inexplicable in mythology, and in religion also, can be explained by the influence which language exercises on thought. I have never said that the whole of mythology can be explained in that way, that all that seems irrational is due to a misunderstanding, or that all mythology is a disease of language. Some parts of mythology I have proved to be soluble by means of linguistic tests, but mythology as a whole I have always represented as a complete period of thought, inevitable, I believe, in the development of human thought, and comprehending all and everything that at a given time can fall within the horizon of the human mind. The Nemesis of disproportion seems to haunt all new discoveries. Parts of mythology are religious, parts of mythology are historical, parts of mythology are metaphysical, parts of mythology are poetical; but mythology as a whole is neither religion, nor history, nor philosophy, nor poetry. It comprehends all these together under that peculiar form of expression which is natural and intelligible at a certain stage, or at certain recurring stages in the development of thought and speech, but which, after becoming traditional, becomes frequently unnatural and unintelligible. In the same manner nature-worship, tree-worship, serpent-worship, ancestor-worship, god-worship, hero-worship, fetichism, all are parts of religion, but none of these by itself can explain the origin or growth of religion, which comprehends all these and many more elements in the various phases of its growth.

If anything can help to impress upon students of religion and mythology the necessity of caution, the advantage of special research, and, above all, the necessity of a scholarlike treatment, it is a book like that of Mr. Gill,—an account of a religion and mythology which were still living in the island of Mangaia, when Mr. Gill went there as a missionary twenty-two years ago, and which, as they died away before his eyes, he carefully described to us from what he saw himself, from what the last depositaries of the old faith told him, and from what was recorded of it in sacred songs, which he gives us in the original, with literal translations.

It is true that the religion and mythology of the Polynesian race have often been treated before, but one of their greatest charms consists in the very fact that we possess them in so many forms. Each island has, so to say, its own religious and mythological dialect, and though there is much that is common to all, and must therefore be old, there is at the same time much local and indi-vidual variety. Again, the great advantage of Mr. Gill's collection is that Mangaia has kept itself freer from foreign influences than almost any other of the Polynesian islands. " The isolation of the Hervey Islanders," he says, " was in favour of the purity of their traditions, and the extreme jealousy with which they were guarded was rather an advantage than otherwise." When we find strange coincidences between the legends of Mangaia and Jewish, Christian, or classical stories, we need not suspect that former European travellers had dropped the germs of them, or that missionaries had given, unconsciously, their own colouring to them. Mr. Gill has been specially on the guard against this and other sources of error. "Whilst collecting my myths," he says, "I put away from me all classical mythology, being afraid that unconsciously I might mould these Polynesian stories into similarity with those of Greece and Rome.

On my making inquiries whether the Polynesian tradition about Eve (Ivi), which I had discussed in my "Science of Religion" (p. 304), was to be found in Mangaia, Mr. Gill informed me that it was not, and that he strongly suspected its European origin. The elements of the story may have previously existed, and we see some traces of it in the account of the creation current in Mangaia, but Mr. Gill suspects that some of the mutineers of the *Bounty* may have told the natives the Bible story, and that it became incorporated with their own notions.

The jawbone, too, with which we are told that Maui, the great solar hero of the Polynesians, destroyed his enemies, is absent in Mangaia. When I inquired about it, Mr. Gill informed me that he never heard of it in the Hervey Group in connection with Maui.

Such things are extremely important for a proper treatment of

mythology. I hold no longer to the rule that when two mythologies agree in what is irrational or foolish, they must have had
the same origin, or must have come into contact with each other
at some period of their history. If there was a reason for the
jawbone to be used as a weapon in one country, the same reason
may have existed in another. But, even if there was no reason,
a fact that happened or was imagined to have happened in one
place may surely have happened or have been imagined to have
happened in another. At first, no doubt, we feel startled by
such coincidences; and that they often offer a *primâ facie* pre-
sumption in favour of a common origin cannot be denied. But
as we read on from one mythology to another, our sensitiveness
with regard to these coincidences becomes blunted, and we feel
hardened against appeals which are founded exclusively on such
evidence.

At first sight, what can be more startling than to see the
interior of the world, the invisible or nether world, the Hades of
the Mangaians, called *Avaiki*, Avi*k*i being the name of one of the
lower regions, both among Brahmans and Buddhists? But we
have only to look around, and we find that in Tahitian the name
for Hades is *Hawai'i*, in New Zealand *Hawaiki*, and more
originally, I suppose, *Sawaiki;* so that the similarity between the
Sanskrit and Polynesian words vanishes very quickly.

That the name of the Sun-god in Mangaia is *Ra* has been
pointed out as a strange coincidence with Egypt; but more really

important is the story of Ra being made captive, as reminding us of similar solar legends in Greece, Germany, Peru, and elsewhere.*

Who can read the Mangaian story of Ina (the moon) and her mortal lover, who, as he grew old and infirm, had to be sent back to the earth to end his days there, without thinking of Selene and Endymion, of Eos and Tithonos?

Who again, if acquainted with the Vedic myth of the *Maruts*,† the strikers, the Storm-gods, and their gradual change into the Roman god of war, Mars, can fail to see the same transition of thought in several of the gods of the storms, of war and destruction among the Polynesians, though here again the similarity in the name of *Maru* is purely accidental.

In some of the Polynesian islands the Deluge is said to have lasted exactly forty days. This, no doubt, is startling. It may be the result of missionary influence. But, even if it were not, the coincidence between the Polynesian and the Jewish accounts on that one point may be either purely accidental, or may be founded on rude meteorological calculations which we have not yet detected. I do not like to quote coincidences from American traditions, because we know that we are never safe there against

* Chips from a German Workshop. 2nd Edition, vol. ii. p. 116.

† Rig-Veda-Sanhita, The Sacred Hymns of the Brahmans. Translated by F. Max Müller. Vol. i. Hymns to the Maruts, or the Storm-Gods. London, Trübner and Co. 1869.

Spanish by-notes; otherwise the account of the Toltec deluge, and the statement that the mountains were covered to the depth of "fifteen cubics," might be quoted as another undesigned coincidence.* According to the Chimalpopoca MS., the Creator produced His work in successive epochs, man being made on the seventh day from dust and ashes. Why, we may ask, on the seventh day? But others, without even insisting on the peculiar character of the seventh number, may simply ask, Why not? There is much similarity between the Hindú account of the Deluge and the Jewish; but no one who has read the numerous accounts of a deluge in other parts of the world, would feel much surprised at this. At all events, if we admitted a common origin of the two, or an actual borrowing, then to explain the differences between them would be extremely difficult. The only startling coincidence is, that in India the flood is said to begin on the seventh day after it had been announced to Manu. Considering, however, that the seventh day is mentioned in the "Bhâgavata-Purâna" only, I feel inclined to look upon it as merely accidental. It might, no doubt, have been borrowed from Jewish or even Mohammedan sources; but how can we imagine any reason why so unmeaning a fact should have been taken over, while on so many other points, where there was every temptation to borrow, nothing was done to assimilate the two accounts, or to remove features of which, at that time, the Hindus might well be supposed to have been ashamed? I mention all this for the sole purpose of

* Bancroft, Native Races, vol. v. p. 20.

preaching patience and caution ; and I preach it against myself quite as much as against others, as a warning against exclusive theories.

On every page of these Mangaian legends there is evidence that many of them owe their origin to language, whether we adopt the theory that the Mangaians played on the words, or that their words played on them. Mr. Gill himself fully admits this ; but to say that the whole of the Mangaian mythology and theology owed its origin to the oxydizing process to which language is exposed in every country, would be to mistake the rust for the iron.

With all these uncertainties before us, with the ground shaking under our feet, who would venture to erect at present complete systematic theories of mythology or religion? Let any one who thinks that all religion begins with fetichism, all worship with ancestor-worship, or that the whole of mythology everywhere can be explained as a disease of language, try his hand on this short account of the beliefs and traditions of Mangaia ; and if he finds that he fails to bring even so small a segment of the world's religion and mythology into the narrow circle of his own system, let him pause before he ventures to lay down rules as to how man, on ascending from a lower or descending from a higher state, must have spoken, must have believed, must have worshipped. If Mr. Gill's book were to produce no other effect but this, it would have proved one of the most useful works at the present moment.

But it contains much that in itself will deeply interest all those who have learned to sympathize with the childhood of the world, and have not forgotten that the child is the father of the man; much that will startle those who think that metaphysical conceptions are incompatible with downright savagery; much also that will comfort those who hold that God has not left Himself without a witness, even among the lowest outcasts of the human race.

F. MAX MÜLLER.

Oxford, *January* 26, 1876.

INTRODUCTORY REMARKS.

THE writer of the following pages has been for twenty-two years a missionary in the Hervey Group, a small cluster of islands in the South Pacific, lying between the 19° and 22° parallels of S. latitude and 157° and 160° of W. longitude.

He has sought to reproduce, as nearly as possible, the traditionary beliefs of a small section of the widely scattered Polynesian family. On them the hopes and aspirations of many past generations were founded. We correctly call the entire system a "mythology;" to them it was a "theology,"—the true doctrine of the visible and the invisible world. The actual working of these false ethics was unceasing and pitiless war, unbridled and unblushing profligacy. Correct knowledge of these "mysteries" was possessed only by the priests and "wise men" of the different tribes. By them the teachings of the past were embodied in songs, to be chanted at their national festivals. These songs possessed great fascination for the native intellect, and tended to the preservation of the ancient faith. The writer's object is simply to aid the student of ethnology in his researches.

While there is much that is puerile and absurd in this heathen philosophy, there are evident glimmerings of primeval light. The

Polynesian name for God expresses a great truth. The continued existence of the human spirit after death is implied in their "laments" and in the beautiful allegory of Veêtini. The cruel system of human sacrifice is but a perversion of ancient truth. The common origin of mankind is taught in the contrast between "the fair-haired and fair-skinned children of Tangaroa," and "the dark-haired and dark-skinned children of Rongo;" both the offspring of Great Vātea. There is an undercurrent of yearning after the True God in some of their songs; *e.g.* as when Koroa sings (p. 215) :—

> Oh, for some other Helper!
> Some new divinity, to listen
> To the sad story of thy wasting disease!

As the result of many years' inquiry into the ancient faith of Polynesia, the writer most heartily endorses the remark of Professor Max Müller : " Wherever there are traces of human life, there are traces also of religion." *

A large portion of what is contained in this volume was derived from Tereavai, the last priest of the shark-god Tiaio. Some links in the system were irrecoverably lost by the slaughter of his father Tuka, at the battle of Araeva, not long before the landing of the first Christian teachers. Nothing but the cordial reception of the new faith could have induced Tereavai to yield up to the stranger the esoteric teachings of the priestly clan. The writer throughout has been greatly indebted to the sagacity and unwearied patience of Sadaraka (grandson of the poet Koroa), who is allowed by his own countrymen to be the best living critic of his own language. Each island in the group had a dialect, a history, and a worship of its own. The language of ancient Polynesian

---

* Science of Religion, p. 118.

song is not that now spoken; bearing the same relation to the living tongue as the Greek of Homer does to that of Xenophon. The myths and prayers (karakia) are believed to be of great antiquity. The dirges and clan-songs are modern, but are doubtless echoes of older compositions. Should the present volume meet with acceptance, a collection of " Prehistoric Sketches," with illustrative clan-songs, may hereafter appear.

W. W. GILL.

Lewisham, *January*, 1876.

CONTENTS.

MYTHS AND SONGS

FROM THE SOUTH PACIFIC.

CHAPTER I.

MYTHS OF CREATION.

THE BEGINNING OF ALL THINGS.

THE universe of these islanders is to be conceived of as the hollow of a vast cocoa-nut shell, as in the accompanying diagram. (See next page.)

The interior of this imaginary shell is named Avaiki. At the top is a single aperture communicating with the upper world, where mortals (*i.e.* Mangaians) live. At various depths are different floorings, or lands, communicating with each other. But at the very bottom of this supposed cocoa-nut shell is a thick stem, gradually tapering to a point, which represents the very beginning of all things. This point is a spirit or demon, without human form, and is named Te-aka-ia-Roê,[1] or *The-root-of-all-existence.* The entire

---

[1] Roê = thread-worm. The idea is of a quivering, slender, worm-like point, at which existence begins, *i.e.* the extremity of the thread-worm.

fabric of the universe is constantly sustained by this primary being.

Above this extreme point is Te-tangaengae, or Te-vaerua; that is to say, *Breathing*, or *Life*. This demon is stouter and

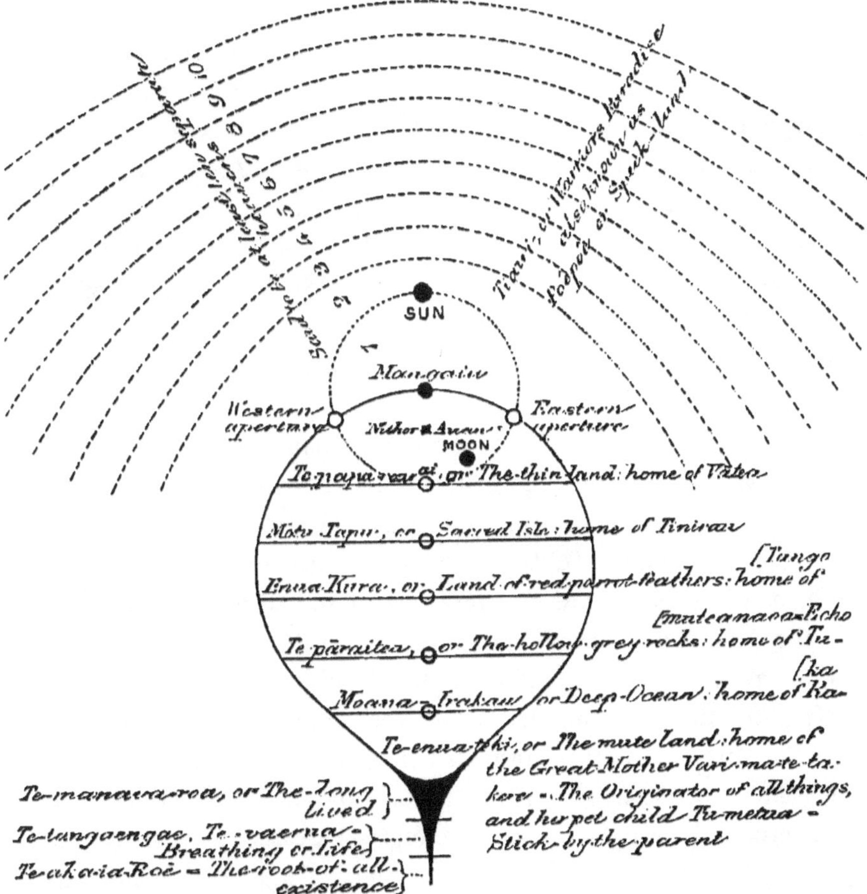

This diagram will suit the mythology of many other islands; substituting, for instance, "Tahiti" for "Mangaia," as the land where egress and ingress to Avaiki exist.

stronger than the former one. But the thickest part of the stem is Te-manava-roa, or *The-long-lived*, the third and last of the primary, ever-stationary, sentient spirits, who themselves constitute the foundation, and insure the permanence and well-being of all the rest of the universe.

We advance now to the *interior* of the supposed cocoa-nut shell. In the lowest depth of Avaiki, where the sides of the imaginary shell nearly meet, lives a woman—a demon, of flesh and blood—named Vari-ma-te-takere,[1] or *The-very-beginning*. Such is the narrowness of her territory that her knees and chin touch, no other position being possible. Vari-ma-te-takere was very anxious for progeny. One day she plucked off a bit of her *right* side, and it became a human being—the first man Avatea, or Vātea (the elision of the *a* in Avatea is compensated by the elongation of the second vowel).

Now Vātea, the father of gods and men, was half man and half fish, the division being like the two halves of the human body. The species of fish to which this great divinity was allied being the taairangi (*Cetacea*), or great sea monsters, *i.e.* porpoises, whose sides are covered with pure fat, and whose home is the boundless ocean. Thus one eye of Vātea was human, the other a fish-eye. His right side was furnished with an arm ; the left with a fin. He had one proper foot, and half a fish-tail.

But there is another, and probably far more ancient, account of Vātea, or Avatea, which means *noon* in all the dialects of Eastern Polynesia.[2] Vātea is a man possessed of two magnificent eyes, rarely visible at the same time. In general, whilst one,

---

[1] Literally, *The-beginning-and-the-bottom* of the hollow cocoa-nut shell.

[2] Vātea is the *Wākea* of the Hawaiians, with a similar meaning and history.

called by mortals the sun, is seen here in this upper world, the
other eye, called by men the moon, shines in Avaiki.   (A contra-
dictory myth represents the sun and moon as living beings.)

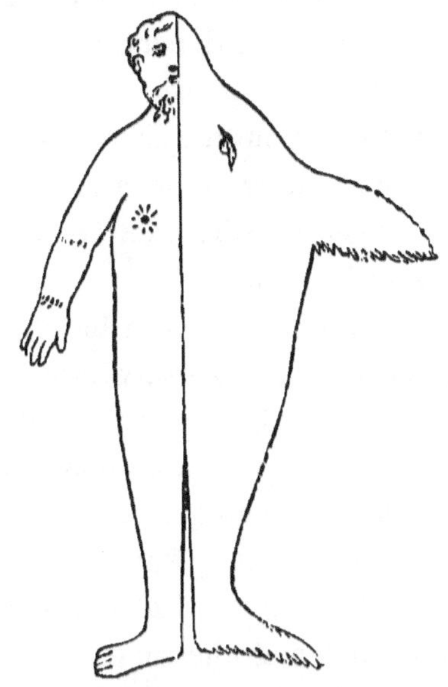

IMAGINARY REPRESENTATION OF VĀTEA.

Compare with this a remarkable picture of a fish-god, from Layard, in Smith's
Dictionary of the Bible, p. 381 (central picture).

The land assigned by the Great Mother to Vātea was Te-
papa-rairai, or *The-thin-land.*   Another designation for his home
was Te enua mārama o Vātea, or *The-bright-land-of-Vātea*, implying the perfect contrast between the brightness of *noon-day*,
or Avatea, and the utter gloom of Po, or *night* which is
equivalent to Avaiki.

On another occasion Vari-ma-te-takere tore off a second bit
from that same right side, and it became Tinirau, or *Innumerable*, who, like his brother, had a second and fishy form.

The sort of fish which composed his half fish body was of the *sprat*-kind. The Great Mother gave him the land of Motu-Tapu, or *Sacred Isle* as his own domain.[1] There were his celebrated ponds full of all kinds of fish. Tinirau was lord of the finny inhabitants of the sea, from the shark downwards.

Another day Vari-ma-te-takere took a bit off her *left* side, and it became Tango, or *Support*, who went to live at Enua-Kura,[2] or *The-land-of-red-parrot-feathers.*

A fourth child was produced from a bit of the same left side, and was named Tumuteanaoa, or *Echo*, whose home was Te-pārai-tea, or *The-hollow-grey-rocks*. Echo is represented as a female.

A fifth child originated from a bit of that same left side of the Great Mother, and was designated Raka, or *Trouble*, who presides, like Aeolus, over the winds. Raka found a congenial home in Moana-Irakau, or *Deep-ocean*. Raka received from Vari-ma-te-takere a great basket in which the winds were hidden; also the knowledge of many useful inventions. The children of Raka are the numerous winds and storms which distress mankind. To each child is allotted a hole at the edge of the horizon, through which he blows at pleasure.

Vari, or *The-very-beginning*, finding that her left side had been more injured than her right, resolved to make both sides alike by taking a third bit from the *right* side, and named this, her last child, Tu-metua, *Stick-by-the-parent*. Now, this sixth and most beloved child, as the name implies, lives with the Great Mother in

---

[1] At Ngatangiia, Rarotonga, there is an islet, covered with cocoa-nut trees, so named. This is, of course, a modern identification. *The* " Sacred Isle " is supposed to be in the shades.

[2] Manuae, or Hervey's Island : yet mystically the scene is laid in Avaiki.

that narrow strip of territory constituting the very bottom of Avaiki, and which is designated Te-enua-te-ki, or *The-mute-land.* Do what you may to the attached mother and daughter, you cannot provoke an angry reply; for the only language known in The-mute-land is that of signs—such as nods, elevated eyebrows, grimaces, and smiles.

It is to The-mute-land that Potiki, temporal lord of Mangaia, circa 1790, referred in a fête song :—

E enua parere i Avaiki	In Avaiki is a land of strange utterance,
E enua mu matangi ē !	Like the sighs of the passing breeze ;
Kua īe Tautiti nei	Where the dance is performed in silence,
Aore e kite i te tara ē !	And the gift of speech is unknown.

Tu-metua is usually shortened into *Tu*, a principal god in most of the Polynesian mythologies, to whom the fourteenth night in every " moon " was sacred. On Cook's second visit to Tahiti, he found the king to be Otoo, ancestor of the present Pomare. Otoo should be written *Tu*, the *O* being a mere prefix to all proper names. This mythological name was adopted in order to secure for its owner the superstitious reverence due to the gods which are unseen by mortals. Tu was the tutelar goddess of Moorea. On Mangaia Tu was invariably linked with her nephew Tangaroa ; but was little regarded. The second islet of Hervey's Island is known as " the kingdom of Tu " (au-o-Tu).

At Raiatea Tu-papa = *Tu-of-the-lowest-depths* (the same as Tu-metua) becomes the wife of Rā, the Sun-god, whose too frequent visits to her home required to be checked by Māui.

It was deemed by Vari very unseemly that Vātea's land, which originally was immediately above her own, should be underneath, and so to speak invaded by, his younger brothers'. The-very-beginning, therefore, altered the relative position of The-thin-land,[1] placing it directly under the opening from this upper world ; so that the law of primogeniture was established, the lands of all the younger brothers thus lying *underneath* the territory of Noon-day.

Vātea in his dreams several times saw a beautiful woman. On one happy occasion he succeeded in clutching her in his sleep, and thus detained the fair sprite as his wife in his home in Te-papa-rairai. Another account asserts that on Vātea's waking from sleep he could discover no trace of the fair one. He searched in all directions for her—but in vain. At length it occurred to him that her home might be in some dark cavern communicating with a land lower than his own, from which the fair one was in the habit of ascending to The-thin-land to pay him nocturnal visits. To test the correctness of this supposition, Vātea scraped a quantity of cocoa-nuts and scattered handfuls down all the chasms in his territory. Some time afterwards he found that from the bottom of one cave, named Taeva-rangi, or *The-celestial-aperture*, the rich white food had entirely disappeared. A fresh lot of the same dainty food was now thrown down, whilst Vātea from behind a projecting crag cautiously peered down. It was not long before a slender hand, very unlike his own, was slowly extended towards the coveted morsels. Vātea at once concluded that this must belong to the woman he had

---

[1] It was from The-thin-land that Potai sagely conjectured that Captain Cook had come. "Era, e te matakeinanga, no raro i Te-papa-rairai i Vātea " = "*Surely, friends, he has climbed up from The-thin-land, the home of Vātea.*" How? By breaking through the solid sides of the vast cocoa-nut shell.

seen in his dreams.   With a favouring current of wind, he descended to the bottom, and caught the fair thief.   His visions were realized; this lovely one confessed that she had again and again ascended to his house above in The-thin-land in order to win him as her future husband.   She correctly guessed that Vātea would never rest until he had discovered the whereabouts of the fair coquette, and made her his wife.   She informed her lover that she was Papa, or *Foundation*, the daughter of Timātekore, or *Nothing-more*, and his wife Tamaiti-ngava-ringavari, or *Soft-bodied*.   The famed Papa thus became the cherished wife of Vātea; both ascended by another eddy of wind through the chasm to The-bright-land-of-Vātea !

DRAMATIC SONG OF CREATION.

FOR THE FÊTE OF POTIKI, CIRCA 1790.

Call for the dance to begin with music.

Noo mai Vari i te āiti,	The home of Vari is the narrowest of all,
I te tuturi i te memenge	Knees and chin ever meeting—
E Rongo ē, a kake !	It was reserved for Rongo to ascend.[1]

Solo.

Taipo ē !	Go on !

Chorus.

O Vātea kite i tena vaine ;	'Twas in the shades Vātea first saw his wife,
I moe ana paa i reira e !	And fondly pressed her to his bosom.

Solo.

Aē !	Aye !

---

[1] Rongo often came up from the shades to this upper world ; Vari never.

Chorus.

Te ui a te metua i anau ai

    Ia Timātekorē !

When asked who was her (Papa's) father,
She said Timātekore! (Nothing more).

Solo.

Ia Timātekorē !
Aore o tatou metua, ua tu e,
  I Vari ua mai ē !

Most truly, Timātekore.
But WE have NO[1] father whatever :
Vari alone made US.

Solo.

   Noo mai Vari ē !
   I te āiti aē !

That home of Vari is
The very narrowest of all !

Chorus.

Noo mai Vari i te āiti ;

E tuarangi kai taro mata
I na turanga pure ē !
O Vātea metua e pua ua ake.

Vari's home is in the narrowest of spaces,
A goddess feeding[2] on raw "taro"[3]
At appointed periods of worship !
Thy mother, Vātea, is self-existent.

Solo.

  Pua ua o Vātea,
  O Papa i te itinga,
  O Vari-ma-te-takere
  I tapākāu ana ē !

Vātea sprung into existence.
Papa is bright as the morn.
Vari-the-originator-of-all-things
Sheltered her (Papa) under her wing.

FINALE.

Call to begin.

Ie taia ia Maukurautaroa
Te rua i te matangi, e Vātea ē !

Let the storm be restrained
In favour of Vātea, O thou god of winds !

---

[1] Papa could boast of father and mother ; but the children of Vari were simply moulded out of bits of her own body.   An allusion is intended to the belief that the three original tribes are descended from the three *illegitimate* sons of Tevaki.

[2] As a matter of fact, however, Vari and Vātea had no altars and no separate worship ; but the grandchildren of Vari had.

[3] Arum esculentum.

<table>
<tr><td></td><td align="center">*Solo.*</td></tr>
<tr><td align="center">Taipo ē !</td><td align="center">Go on !</td></tr>
</table>

<table>
<tr><td></td><td>*Chorus.*</td></tr>
<tr><td>Taotao matangi na Ina
   Te kumutonga.</td><td>Awake the gentle breeze of Ina
   That bare her to her lover.</td></tr>
</table>

<table>
<tr><td></td><td>*Solo.*</td></tr>
<tr><td>O nai matangi riki ē
Ka arara'i oki toku tere
   Ki raro ē !</td><td>O for a soft zephyr to bear me (Vātea)
   Prosperously on my way
   To the shades !</td></tr>
</table>

<table>
<tr><td></td><td>*Solo.*</td></tr>
<tr><td>A taia e te matangi.</td><td>Be lulled, ye winds.</td></tr>
</table>

<table>
<tr><td></td><td>*Chorus.*</td></tr>
<tr><td>Taia e te matangi
O Tukaiaa te tai mākoako.</td><td>Aye, they are lulled.   No storm
Now sweeps o'er the treacherous sea.</td></tr>
</table>

<table>
<tr><td></td><td>*Solo.*</td></tr>
<tr><td>Koakoa ē o tei po
Kai matangi rueke ē !</td><td>Ye inconstant winds of nether-land
Bear me down to her gloomy abode.</td></tr>
</table>

Tangaroa and Rongo were the twin children of Vātea and Papa. These boys were the first beings of perfect human form, having no second shape.

Tangaroa should have been born first, but gave precedence to his brother Rongo. A few days after the birth of Rongo, his mother Papa suffered from a very large boil on her arm. She resolved to get rid of it by pressing it. The core accordingly flew out: it was Tangaroa ! Another account, equally veracious, says that Tangaroa came right up through Papa's head. The precise spot is indicated by " *the crown*," with which all their descendants have since been born.

Vātea's third son was Tonga-iti, whose visible form was the white and black spotted lizards. Under the name of Mata-rau, or *The-two-hundred-eyed*, *i.e. The-sharp-sighted*, Tonga-iti was an object of worship in the Hervey Group. The fourth son of Vātea was Tangiia; the fifth and last son was Tane-papa-kai, or *Tane-piler-up-of-food.* Both Tangiia and Tane were principal gods of Mangaia.

The home of Rongo was Auau (afterwards named Mangaia) in Avaiki. As an individual consists of two parts, viz. body and spirit, so this island has a sort of essence, or *spirit*, the secret name of which is Akatautika, *i.e. The-well-poised*, only used by the priests and kings of ancient days. When in after times the earthly form, or *body*, of Auau was dragged up to light, there remained behind in the obscurity of nether-world the etherial form, or *spirit*, of The-well-poised.

Now, Tangaroa was altogether the cleverest son of Vātea; he instructed his brother Rongo in the arts of agriculture. Their father wished to make Tangaroa lord of all they possessed; but the mother Papa objected, because as parents they dared not taste the food or touch the property of Tangaroa, the eldest *by right.* The mother had her own way. Hence, when a human sacrifice was offered to Rongo,[1] the refuse, *i.e.* the body when thoroughly decayed, was thrown to his mother, who dwelt with Rongo in the shades, in order to please her.

Government, arrangement of feasts, the drum of peace, *i.e.* all the fountains of honour and power, were secured to Rongo, through the selfish craft of Papa.

Nearly all sorts of food, too, fell to the share of the younger

[1] On Rarotonga only the reeking *head* of the victim was offered to Tangaroa, their tutelar divinity : the body might be devoured by the captors. On Mangaia the *whole* body was laid upon the altar.

twin-god.   The division was made on this principle : all the RED on earth or in the ocean became Tangaroa's ; the rest, *i.e.* the great bulk, was Rongo's.   Thus of the numerous varieties of taro, only one—a reddish sort (kakā kura) was Tangaroa's ; the rest being sacred to Rongo.   Amongst the multitudinous varieties of " meikas,"[1] only the plantain was the property of Tangaroa's, on account of the *redness* and *uprightness* of its fruit.   The very name, " the upright-fruit " (uatu), testifying to the dignity of the eldest of the gods.   Bananas of all sorts belonged to Rongo. The plantain, being the kokira, or head, of the great "meika" family, does not bend its head ; just as Tangaroa is the kokira, or the first in the family of the gods.

Of three kinds of chestnuts, but one, the red-leafed, is sacred to Tangaroa.   Of the two sorts of the indigenous yam, the red is Tangaroa's.   Of the double variety of cocoa-nuts, one belongs to Tangaroa.   *All* bread-fruit was sacred to Rongo.

In regard to the wealth of the ocean, Rongo was decidedly the gainer.   But four sorts of fish—all scarlet, besides lobsters, fell to Tangaroa.   The silvery, striped, spotted, and black were all Rongo's.

Thus Rongo became very rich ; Tangaroa comparatively poor.   The twin gods made a grand feast, each collecting only his own food, to which Vātea and Papa were invited.   Tangaroa made one great pile of red taro, yams, chestnuts, cocoa-nuts ; the top garnished with red land-crabs and all the red fish he could find in the sea, etc.

Rongo's pile was immensely greater.   The treasures of earth and ocean were there.   The parents declared that Tangaroa carried the palm for *beauty ;* whilst Rongo excelled in *abundance.*

[1] The term " meika " includes bananas and plantains.

Upon the same principle all fair-haired children (rauru keu) in after ages were considered to be Tangaroa's (the god himself had sandy hair) ; whilst the dark-haired, which form the great majority, are Rongo's. Now Rongo's hair was raven black, as became E atua po, or *God-whose-home-is-the-shades.* Now and then a stray child might be claimed for Tangaroa, whose home is in the sky, *i.e.* far beyond the horizon ; the majority of his fair-haired children live with the fair-haired god in distant lands. Very few natives have light hair, a colour greatly disliked amongst themselves, but in their view suitable to foreigners. To this day a golden-haired child is invariably addressed in playful allusion to this myth, as "the fair-haired progeny of Tangaroa." Hence, in the ancient legend about Tarauri, the prince of reed-throwers, this famous son of Tangaroa is represented as being, with his brother, *fair-haired.*

Chorus.

Tarauri i te puti angaüa e Pinga	Tarauri, the waif brought up by Pinga,
Ei uke i te mate ē !	Avenged the disgrace of his brother.

Solo.

Taipo ē !	Go on !

Chorus.

Anau keu a Tangaroa,	The fair-haired children of Tangaroa
Kua piri paa i te ao.	Doubtless sprung from dazzling light.

Hence, when Cook discovered Mangaia, the men of that day were greatly surprised at the fair hair and skin of their visitors, and at once concluded that these were some of the long-lost fair children of Tangaroa !

It was but natural that Tangaroa should be displeased at the preference always shown to his brother Rongo. He therefore collected a vast quantity of red food of all kinds, and set out on a voyage in search of some other land, where he could reign alone. He made a long journey, and touched at many islands, scattering everywhere the blessings of food piled up for the purpose in his canoe. Finally, he settled down on his beloved islands, Rarotonga and Aitutaki, leaving Auau, or, as it was afterwards designated, Mangaia, in the quiet possession of Rongo = *The Resounder.*

In winter tree-fruits disappear; whereas taro, bananas, etc., are in season all the year round. The reason for this is, that the former belong to Tangaroa, who merely permits his gifts to be seen and tasted here in the land of Rongo on their way (in winter) to realms where he reigns undisturbed.

On this account these fruits were not regarded as private property, but as belonging to all the inhabitants of the district in which they grew.

Ro(ng)o or O Rō was the chief object of worship at Tahiti and most of the Leeward Islands. His seat was the *marae*,[1] or sacred grove, at Opoa, on the island of Raiatea; whence this worship extended to all the neighbouring islands, and throughout the Paumotu Group. Human sacrifices were continually offered to the great Polynesian god of war, to obtain success in their cruel enterprises.[2]

---

[1] These *maraes* were planted with *callophylla inophylla*, etc., etc., which, untouched by the hand of man from generation to generation, threw a sacred gloom over the mysteries of idol-worship. The trees were accounted sacred, not for their own sake, but on account of the place where they grew.

[2] At Atiu Te-rongo, = *the* Rongo, the Rongo of Mangaia, was represented as a *son* of Tangaroa. At Raiata Oro was in like manner regarded as a *son* of the great Tangaroa. At Samoa Longo is represented as the *son* of Tangaroa by Sina.

When Captain Cook visited the Sandwich Islands, he was regarded as the incarnation of Rongo, or, in their dialect, Orono, or Rono, and accordingly received divine honours. An ancient prophecy asserted that Rongo, or Rono, who had gone to Tahiti, would return to Hawaii in a canoe of a remarkable shape. This seemed realized in the visits of Captain Cook with his two wonderful vessels from Tahiti. The great navigator counted forty-nine skulls on the marae of Oro at Tahiti, and witnessed the placing of the fiftieth. When he himself received divine honours at the Sandwich Islands, he was not aware that it was as the blood-stained Rongo, whose home was supposed to be in these southern islands, and at whose shrine those fifty reeking heads had been offered during a single generation. On Mangaia it was Tangaroa that was expatriated, without hope of return ; Rongo was regarded as being in possession,[1] although resident in the shades. His marae is called O-Rongo, and was first set up on the eastern side of the island, but was ultimately removed to the west, where the great navigator held communication with these islanders. It is singular that the " Voyages " do not allude to his great stone image, the secondary representation of Rongo, which must have been visible from the boat of the *Resolution.* Reference *is* made to the residence of the shore king, the guardian of the great national idol.

The principal god of Rimatara was Rono or Rongo, to whom human sacrifices were offered.

The wife of Rongo was Tākā, who bare a daughter named Tavake. In the course of time Tavake grew up and gave birth

---

[1] The word is often used as equivalent to " *deadly hate :* " " Kua noo Rongo i roto " = " Rongo (*i.e.* deadly hate) fills his heart ; " in allusion to his being the author of bloodshed and war.

successively to Rangi, to Mokoiro, and to Akatauira—all illegitimate.   Rongo wished his three grandsons, who were also his sons,[1] to live with him in Auau, in the shades.   But Rangi was resolved to pull up this land Auau, afterwards called Mangaia, from Avaiki.   This was a most arduous task; but, with the assistance of his brothers, the brave Rangi succeeded in dragging up the little island to the light of day.   Rangi, Mokoiro, and Akatauira took up their permanent abode in this upper world. Thus the three brothers were the first inhabitants of Mangaia, and in the course of years gave rise to the original tribes which peopled this island.   Three small rocks, united at the base, close to the marae of Rongo and the altar for human sacrifice, are pointed out as symbolizing the threefold lords of the soil.

Rongo continued to live in Avaiki, in the invisible or nether Auau, of which this island was asserted to be but the outward expression![2]   He directed Rangi to offer bleeding sacrifices on

---

[1] That these children of Tavake were Rongo's is attested by the well-known couplet :—

Tai anau kakaoa	The three royal bastards,
Na Rongo paa ïa tama e !	Offspring of the god Rongo !

Ngariu's fête, circa 1790.

[2] The Hervey Group consists of seven inhabited islets. Each is supposed to be the *body*, or outward form, to which a *spirit*, bearing a distinct name, located in Avaiki, belongs.

BODY.	SPIRIT.
1. Rarotonga = *Western Tonga,* *i.e.* in loving memory of Western Tonga, or Tonga tapu.	1. Tumutevarovaro = *echo.*
2. Auau = *terraced* (The later name, Mangaia, means *peace.* Mangaia-Nui-Neneva = *Mangaia-monstrously-big*).	2. Akatautika = *well-poised.*

his marae in the upper world, from time to time—the decayed corpse to be invariably thrown in the bush to his mother Papa.

Mangaia now for the first time emerged to the light of day, and became the centre of the universe. Its central hill was accordingly designated Rangimotia = *The centre of the heavens.* The inhabitants of Mangaia were veritable *men* and *women*, as contrasted with the natives of other outlying islands, who were only tuarangi, or evil-spirits in the guise of humanity.

Vātea, or Avatea (= *noon-day*), was thus "the father of the gods and men,"[1] the three original tribes being regarded as the direct offspring of Rongo; all subsequent settlers and visitors were regarded as interlopers, to be, if possible, slain and offered in sacrifice.

3. Aitutaki = *God-led.*	3. Araura = *fragrant wreaths for dancing.*
4. Atiu = *eldest-born* (name of first settler).	4. Enua-manu = *land of birds.*
5. Mauki = *land of Uki* (the first inhabitant).	5. Akatoka =. *stony.* Some say, Te-rae o-te-pau = *the lip of the drum.*
6. Mitiaro = *face of the ocean.*	6. Nukuroa = *vast host.*
7. Manuae = *home of birds.*	7. Enua-Kura = *land-of-red-parrot-feathers.*

It is said that the "spirit" name of Tahiti is "Iti," *i.e.* "*iti* nga" = *sun-rising.* Tahiti simply means "east," or "sun-rising," from *hiti* (our *iti*) to "rise:" *ta* being causative. That island was known in the Hervey Group by the name Iti or "east:" it is only of late years the full name Tahiti has become familiar.

[1] Yet the great Vātea possessed no marae, had no wooden or stone representation, nor was any worship ever paid to him.

In song, the gods are called " te anau atea," *i.e.* " te anau a Vātea " = " children of Vātea."   The same shortened phrase is in use at Rarotonga : at Aitutaki and Atiu the full form " Avatea " is used, *e.g.* " kia kakā te mata o Avatea Nui " = " when the eye of Great Avatea (= noon) is open ; " in other words, " when the sun is in its full glory ; " still in contrast with the darkness and gloom of Avaiki, or Nether-world.

The ocean was known as Rauaika Nui, or *The-vast-out-spread-plantain-leaf;* [1]—that leaf being the largest in the world.   The ocean was sometimes designated " the sea of Vātea ; " at other times " the sea of Tane."

Above was the blue vault of solid stone, sustained originally by the frail props of Rū on the central hill of Mangaia, but afterwards permanently raised to its present height by the tremendous exertions of Māui.   In all, there were said to be *ten separate heavens*, rising one above the other into immensity.   These constituted the Elysium of the brave.   Here, too, was the home of Tangaroa, the scarcely worshipped god of day.

Upon the brow of a hill, facing the setting sun, and near the great marae of the war-god, it is asserted that there once existed a deep, gloomy chasm (long since closed up), known as Tiki's hole (Te rua ia Tiki).   This constituted the regular road to Avaiki, *like the single aperture at the top of a cocoa-nut.* Through it the three brothers descended to Avaiki, or ascended to the light of day, at pleasure.

The three brothers are always described as joint " kings," or " Nga ariki."   The entire body of their descendants were there-

---

[1] A plantain leaf lying before me is eleven feet long and three broad.

fore called by the shorter form "Ngariki." To Rangi Rongo gave "the drum of peace ;" to Mokoiro, the direction over food of all kinds ; to the pet—the youngest—Akatauira was given the "karakia," or "prayers," and the sway over his brethren.

Rangi, Mokoiro, and Akatauira were probably veritable persons, chiefs of the first settlers on Mangaia. Their wives were respectively named Tepotatango,[1] Angarua, and Ruānge. Then came Papaaunuku, son of Tane-papa-kai, or Tane-giver-of-food. When Tane died he was worshipped by his son, who was sent for by Rangi as his priest. But Rangi was not pleased with Tane, as he spake only as a man, without frenzy, through his son Papaaunuku. His grandfather Rongo lived only in the shades ; Rangi wished for a god who would live with him in this upper world. He therefore sent to Rarotonga to ask Tangiia, a renowned warrior-king of that island, to send him over one of his sons "who had grown up under the sacred shade of the tamanu leaves" to be his god. Rangi's wish was gratified, and Motoro was fixed upon by his father for the purpose.

Tangaroa had *one* marae, and that almost neglected, the only offering ever presented being the first-fruits of all newly-planted cocoa-nut groves—the tiny buds, which eventually become nuts. This was simply a recognition of his primogeniture. But the island was supposed to belong to Rongo and Motoro : the one god ruling the dead ; the other the living.

Doubtless the worship of Tangaroa, Rongo, Tane, and possibly the Lizard god of Tongaiti, represented a much earlier and more widely-diffused system of idolatry than prevailed

---

[1] Bottom of Hades.

here in historical times, when the children of Tangiia were deified.

The heathen intellect has no conception of a Supreme Being creating a universe out of nothing. At Mangaia the idea of divinity was pared down to a mere nothing. Whenever the gods make anything, the existence of the raw material, at least in part, is presupposed.

The primary conception of these islanders as to spiritual existence is a *point.* Then of something *pulsating.* Next of something greater, *everlasting.*

Now comes the Great Mother and Originator of all things. For the first time we meet with the ideas of *volition* and *creation.* Vari is represented as a female, on account of fecundity, she being the original of all the gods, and, remotely, of mankind. The arrangement of various lands in Avaiki, and the apportionment of the different functions of air, earth, and sea, are hers. The ninth night of every moon was sacred to her. Yet Vari is incapable of speech, and lives in darkness, her solace being the constant society of an affectionate daughter.

In the description of her first-*made* (*not* born) son, *Bright Noon* (Avatea, or Vātea), one of whose eyes is the sun, we gain the first idea of *majesty* as associated with divinity. The ocean is his; his children, born like ourselves, are the great gods who direct the affairs of the universe, and are worshipped by mortals. To them belong the maraes and idols; they receive offerings of food and listen to the prayers of mankind.

And yet, strangely enough, associated with these original gods are the deified heroes of antiquity, in no wise inferior to their fellow divinities.

Birds, fish, reptiles, insects, and *specially inspired priests,* were reverenced as incarnations, mouth-pieces, or messengers of the gods.

The gods were supposed to have distinct functions; their quarrels were reflected in the wars of men. But *none create*, in the proper sense of that term. The Great Mother approximates nearest to the dignity of creator; but when she *makes* a child, it is out of a bit of her own body. *She herself is dependent* on three prior existences destitute of human form.

The earth is not made, but is a thing dragged up from the shades; and is but the gross outward form of an invisible essence still there. At least ten heavens are built of azure stone, one above another (to correspond with the different lands in Nether-world), with apertures for inter-communication; but the stones were pre-existent.

The principal words used by the ancient sages in speaking on this subject are—

1. Vari = *Beginning.* This important word is used when describing the commencement of any new order of things. The Great Mother herself is *Vari*-ma-te-takere.

Strangely enough, at the sister island of Rarotonga this word no longer means "beginning," but "mud;" agreeing, however, with the sense of the Mangaian reduplicate "varivari" = *muddy*.

Evidently, then, apart from their mythological views, these people imagined that once the world was a "chaos of mud," out of which some mighty unseen Agent, whom they called Vari, evolved the present order of things.

2. *Pua* ua mai = *Bud forth, or blossom,* as of a tree. Evidently here is no fit conception of creative power.

In seeking for an equivalent for בָּרָא, the first missionaries chose the word "anga" = *made*. Undoubtedly this is the best word ; its original narrow sense being enlarged by the constant perusal of the Bible, etc. The magnificent conception of real creation is as unattainable to a heathen sage as the sublime conception of a Supreme Deity.

CHAPTER II.

DEIFIED MEN.

DERIVATION OF THE POLYNESIAN WORD FOR GOD.

SOME five hundred years ago there lived on Tahiti two powerful chiefs : the younger named Tangiia, the elder Tutapu.   Now the lands of the younger adjoined those of their only sister, and it chanced that one or two branches of a bread-fruit tree of hers, growing close to the boundary line, extended themselves over the soil of the irritable Tangiia.   As is frequently the case with this tree, one half of this bread-fruit was almost barren, whilst the branches extending over the land of her brother were heavily laden with fruit.   Tangiia claimed the fruit as his, as it grew on his side of the boundary line : naturally enough the sister felt herself to be harshly dealt with.

The elder brother Tutapu hearing of the quarrel interfered on behalf of their sister.   Thenceforth the brothers became deadly foes ; and after many angry words, Tutapu resolved to collect his dependants, and upon a certain night to make a final end of his brother and his family.   Tangiia, obtaining timely notice of his intention, fled with wife, children, and friends to the neighbouring island of Huahine ; but was pursued by the irate Tutapu. Tangiia was chased by his brother throughout the Leeward Islands, until finally finding that there was no rest for him in that group, he committed himself to the trackless ocean.   Fortunately for him, he reached Atiu, where he stayed awhile.   But the insatiate Tutapu followed him even to Atiu, many hundreds of miles from Tahiti.   Tangiia again took flight—this time to Rarotonga, which was destined to become the home of this renowned chief.

Tutapu remained a considerable time on Atiu.   Children were born to him ; some of his descendants afterwards reached Mangaia in a drift canoe, founding a tribe devoted to furnish human sacrifices.

Hearing that Tangiia was prospering on Rarotonga, Tutapu again manned his large double canoe, which is said to have had three masts, and to have carried 200 warriors, and started off once more in quest of his brother.   Upon entering the harbour at Rarotonga, which bears the name of Nga-Tangiia,[1] the brothers prepared for a final encounter.   In the conflict which ensued, Tangiia, assisted by Karika's party, defeated the invaders, and slew Tutapu-aru-roa = *Tutapu-the-relentless-pursuer*, whose body was eaten by the victors.

Tangiia himself never landed on Mangaia, the island which is so intimately associated with the history of several of his children. It is needful to distinguish this Tangiia, who is unquestionably an historical character, from the mythical Tangiia descended from Vātea, and one of the gods of Mangaia, whose iron-wood form is deposited in the museum of the London Missionary Society.

---

[1] = Ngati-Tangiia, *i.e.* the tribe of Tangiia.

The sages of Rarotonga erroneously assert that Mangaia was first discovered and inhabited by the famous brother of Tutapu. This is foreign and new. Unquestionably, Rangi and his friends were the first settlers on Mangaia from Savai'i. Other canoes came. In the presence of the new comers, the children of the original settlers, wishing to establish their pre-eminence, boldly asserted that Rangi, etc., came "up," *not*, as in truth, from the sun-setting, but *out of the earth*, from (S)avai(k)i, the original home of men and gods, a land in some places much like this, in others filled with horrors. It was, in their opinion, self-evident that all drift canoes were mere waifs predestined to destruction in the presence of a race who grew, as it were, out of the soil.

The *Karika* family at Rarotonga expressly state that their ancestor came from Manu'a, the easternmost island of the Samoan Group. The family marae of the Makea tribe is therefore named *Rangi-Manuka*, or " Manu'a (= Manuka) in the skies ; " as *we* say *New* Britain, *New* Caledonia, *New* England, etc., etc. They even state that Karika's great canoe, in which he performed his wonderful voyage, had " two masts," and carried 170 people (okoitu).

It has been already stated that Rangi [1] requested the invincible warrior Tangiia to send him one of his sons as a god. Accordingly Motoro was sent, with two of his brothers, Ruanuku

---

[1] The " Ruanuku " of Mangaian mythology is the " Uanuku " of Rarotonga. Uanuku is represented by their " wise men " as the *eldest* son of Tangiia.

" Motoro " signifies " to approach to (a woman) ; " so that it is equivalent to Ἔρως, in the sense of *libido*. He was so called by his father Tangiia, in allusion to his own passionate love for his wife Moetuma. Tangiia in his wanderings married two Mauke girls, Moetuma, and her younger sister Puatara.

and Kereteki. Utākea, the third son of Tangiia, started for
Mangaia some time after his brothers. *Motoro* was the fourth
and best beloved son of the great Rarotongan chief. When the
three brothers—Ruanuku, Kereteki, and Motoro—were halfway
on their voyage to Mangaia, a violent quarrel sprang up, the
two elder brothers united in throwing Motoro into the sea, where
he miserably perished. The fratricides safely landed opposite
to the marae of Rongo, and were pleased to see a deep hole in
the reef, through which the fresh water from the interior is poured
into the ocean. It is surprising to find a large body of pure
spring water gurgling up in the midst of the sea. Here they
resolved to refresh themselves with a bath after their adventurous
voyage. But as the aperture in the sharp coral will not admit of
two large men bathing together, the point was hotly contested,
who should get in first. It was finally settled that the first-born
should enjoy the first bath. The instant Ruanuku's head was
under water, his long hair was firmly grasped by Kereteki, to
prevent him from raising it again. After a time Kereteki dragged
ashore the dead body of the murdered Ruanuku, and buried it.

At a well-known spot on the south of the island afterwards
landed Utākea, who lived peaceably with his brother Kereteki.
Both lived and died on Mangaia. Very strangely indeed, the
cruel Kereteki, twice a fratricide, and his brother Utākea, were
worshipped as gods in the next generation. As if in penitence,
Kereteki set up the marae sacred to his slain brother Motoro.
Here the *spirit* of Motoro was supposed to reside ; and down
to the destruction of idolatry, in 1824, this spot was regarded as
being the most sacred *in the interior ;* as the marae of Rongo was
the most sacred *on the sea-shore.* A flourishing plantation of
plantains now occupies the place of the idol grove.

It was well-known that Motoro's body was devoured by sharks; but then it was asserted that his *spirit* floated on a piece of hibiscus [1] over the crest of the ocean billows until it reached Mangaia, where it was pleased to "inhabit" or "possess" Papaaunuku, and driving him into a frenzy, compelled him to utter his oracles from a foaming mouth. This was just the sort of divinity that Rangi, the first king of Mangaia, wanted. Motoro was at once recognized as the great chief's own god, and Papaaunuku and his descendants as the *priests* of the new divinity. As Rongo lived and reigned in the "night," or the shades, so Motoro should live and reign in the "day," or this upper world. The three original tribes—and the kings, invariably worshipped Rongo *and* Motoro; but many are said to have disapproved of the new worship, correctly regarding Rongo as the great original heathen divinity of Mangaia. Until 1824 both were conjointly worshipped as the supreme deities of this island, Rongo taking the first place.

The family of the first priest of Motoro was named the Amama, or *the open-mouthed*, to intimate that they were the mouth-pieces of that divinity. To this day this appellation is kept up, although but few know the reason for it.

Makitaka, the last priest of Motoro, embraced Christianity, and died in 1830. The idol itself has long reposed in the museum of the London Missionary Society.

The worshippers of Utākea and Kereteki were, in later times, offered in sacrifice to Rongo and Motoro.

Motoro was proudly called Te io ora, or *The-living-god,*

---

[1] The sacred men assert that this is the reason why *au* (hibiscus) comes also to mean "reign," or "rule."

because he alone of " the gods of day " would not permit his
worshippers to be offered in sacrifice.   The other divinities were
styled " io mate," or " dead-gods," as their worshippers were ever
eligible for the altar of dread Rongo, who lived in the shades.

The word " io," commonly used for " god," properly means
" pith," or " core " of a tree.   What the core is to the tree, the god
was believed to be to the man.   In other words, the gods were
the life of mankind.   Even when a worshipper of Motoro was
slain in fair fight, it was supposed that the enraged divinity would,
by some special misfortune or disease, put an end to the offender.
Most appropriately and beautifully do the natives transfer the
name Io ora, or *The-living-god* to Jehovah, as *His worshippers*
NEVER *die !*

Motoro, Kereteki, and Utākea were represented by iron-wood
idols in the god-house of the king.   On entering that rude reed
hut, the dwelling-place of the chief divinities of Mangaia, the first
idol was Rongo, in the form of a trumpet-shell ; next came the
honoured Motoro, the guide of daily life ; then came Tane and
ten other objects of worship, amongst which were Kereteki and
Utākea.

The iron-wood idol called Tane merely, was asserted to
represent the fifth son of Vātea; and yet was only third in order
of dignity.   Tangiia, the fourth son of Vātea, was the last in
regard to dignity and order.   Of the innumerable objects of fear
and worship, only thirteen were admitted to the honour of a place
in this rude Pantheon as national gods.

TIAIO, KING AND GOD.

The history of this sovereign of Mangaia is well known. A body of invaders from Atiu was utterly routed by the warlike chief Tiaio. To this day the natives of Atiu make pilgrimages to the spot where their countrymen fell in the olden time.

Tiaio became deservedly famous for this exploit. But some years afterwards his pride led him " to defile the sacred district of Keia," the favourite haunt of the gods, by wearing some beautiful scarlet hibiscus flowers (kaute) in his ears. Now, anything red was forbidden in that part of the island, as being offensive to the gods ; the redness of the flower being emblematical of the shedding of blood. Even the beating of native cloth was forbidden, lest the repose of the gods should be disturbed by the noise.

A hot dispute took place about this mark of disrespect to the gods, in which Mouna, priest of Tane-the-man-eater, slew the king with a blow on his head. The blood of Tiaio mingled with the waters of the brook running past the marae of Motoro, and eventually mixed with the ocean. Thenceforth that stream was held to be sacred, and it was fabled that a great fresh-water eel— Tuna—drank up the blood of the murdered king, whose spirit at the same time entered the fish. Tuna made its way to the dark deep fissure running underneath the rocks into the sea. The indomitable spirit of Tiaio, having thus succeeded in reaching the ocean, forsook the form of the eel and took possession of the large white shark, the terror of these islanders. The new divinity had a little marae set apart for his worship, close by the more sacred grove of Motoro, and but a few yards from where he fell by the hand of the jealous priest.

The Mautara, or priestly tribe, gave up their ancient divinity, Tane, in favour of this new god. The greatness of Tiaio marks the political supremacy of that warlike clan, which is of recent origin. Tiaio was a " food-eating " god, generally associated with Motoro. His oracles invariably ended with demands for a feasting. This jolly-tempered divinity's last priest was Tereavai, who died a valuable deacon of the church in 1865. A few cocoa-nut trees now mark the site of Mārā, the deserted marae of the shark-god.

Rori's life was spared by Manaune, expressly that he might carve the rough iron-wood representation of Tiaio, which, with the rest, now quietly reposes in the Society's museum.

Koroa refers to this in his " crying " song for his friend Ata, recited at the " death-talk " of Arokapiti, circa 1817.

Kua tae paa i te tiangāmama	Cruel misfortune has again o'ertaken
Ia Teakatauira e kotia ;—	This royal tribe.
Kotia O Ata O Tukua raua	Ata and his father Tukua have fallen !
O Turou O Mouna O Tane-kai-aro,	E'en as once Turou and Mouna, in-spired
Kai-aro ra ia Mārua.	By Tane-the-man-eater, struck down
E tainga taito ia ne'e, ia kora atu,	Tiaio the king in the olden time.
I tai paū o Tiaio i te toru, ua tutua ē !	Long, long ago was that great man slain.

TANE-NGAKIAU.

That is, Tane-*striving-for-power*. This pretended god was a brave warrior, who gave important assistance to Rangi in the first battle ever fought on Mangaia, in which the invaders from Tonga were defeated with great loss. As his reward he received the chieftainship of Ivirua. After his death his family deified him, and erected in his honour the famous marae Maputū, which stands a lasting memorial of cruelty. The entire centre was filled with reeking human heads cut off in cold blood to mark his canonization. It was asserted that whenever this detested divinity took up his abode in any individual, it was made evident by his skin assuming a blood-red colour, and the dying man would, with supernatural strength, fight imaginary foes, or rather unseen demons.

This uncomfortable god had a carved iron-wood form, and was one of the thirteen principal gods of Mangaia now in the museum.

TEKURAAKI.

This god was introduced by Tui from Rarotonga. So long as "the royal Tama-tapu," the chief of "*the-red-marked-tribe*," maintained their supremacy, this divinity was popular. For some generations prior to the introduction of Christianity, this tribe was almost extinct, and the separate worship of Tekuraaki almost unknown. Yet the carved iron-wood idol remained in the Pantheon until 1824, when it was surrendered to Messrs. Williams and Platt.

SONG OF THE SHORE KING, HIGH PRIEST OF RONGO.

COMPOSED BY VAIPO FOR RAOA'S FÊTE, CIRCA 1815.

Mariu te tapu o Motoro,	I lay aside the sanctity of Motoro
Te taka ra i Vairorongo	Ere bathing in this sacred stream.
I te koukou anga vai ē !	'Twas here his spirit landed,
O turuki o Rongo i kake ei.	On this pebbly beach devoted to Rongo.

Kua kake atu au ra i te pa,   It landed on this narrow shore,—
E atua noo ata i te kea,   A god whose shade ever rests
   E tau ariki nei.   On the sandstone sacred to kings.

Ariki Tamatapu i noo i Marua   Tamatapu once spent a night at Marua,
Taea 'i Aupi i te vai   When the entire valley was flooded.
O nga ariki e puipui aere,   Such was the might of that king!

Mariua Rongo te tapu i tai e !   I lay aside the sanctity of the shore-dwelling Rongo.

Thus it is evident that many of their gods were originally men, whose spirits were supposed to enter into various birds, fish, reptiles, and insects; and into inanimate objects, such as the triton shell, particular trees, cinet, sandstone, bits of basalt, etc., etc. The greater gods alone had carved images for the convenience of worshippers; the lesser were countless, each individual possessing several. The gods were divided into two orders, "dwellers in day," and "dwellers in the shades, or night." All the thirteen principal gods, save Rongo, were "dwellers in day," *i.e.* were continually busy in the affairs of mortals; moving, though unseen, in their midst, yet often descending to "night," or to Avaiki, the true home of the major divinities. In like manner those who "dwelt in night" were supposed frequently to ascend to day to take part in the affairs of mankind, but generally preferred to dwell in spirit-land. A few were supposed to remain permanently in the obscurity of Avaiki, or "night."

The "dwellers in day" were believed to hover about in the air, hide themselves in unfrequented caves, besides taking frenzied possession of men and women. These were the divinities of recent human origin.

The lowest depth of heathen degradation is unconsciously

reached in the worship of phallic stones, such as still exist in Tinian, one of the Ladrone Islands. The scene was one of great interest—a natural grotto converted into a heathen temple, outside of which these degrading rites were performed. The original significance of this embruting form of idolatry is lost, although its symbols are still preserved.

DERIVATION OF THE POLYNESIAN WORD "ATUA," OR GOD.

The great word for God throughout Eastern Polynesia is "Atua" (Akua). Archdeacon Maunsell derives this from "ata" = *shadow*, which agrees with the idea of spirits being *shadows*, but I apprehend is absolutely unsupported by the analogy of dialects.

Mr. Ellis [1] regards the first *a* as euphonic, considering "tua" = *back*, as the essential part of the word, misled by a desire to assimilate it with the "tev" of the Aztec and the "deva" of the Sanscrit. Occasionally, when expressing their belief that the divinity is "the essential support," they express it by the word "ivi-mokotua" = *the back-bone*, or vertebral column; *never* by the mere "tua" = *back*.

That the *a* is an essential part of the word is indicated by the closely allied expressions "atu" ("fatu" in Tahitian and Samoan) and "aitu;" in the latter the *a* is lengthened into *ai*.

A key to the true sense of "atua" exists in its constant equivalent "io," which (as already stated) means the "*core*" or "*pith*" of a tree.

Analogically, God is the pith, core, or *life of man*.

[1] Polynesian Researches, vol. ii. p. 201.

Again, " atu " stands for " lord, master ; " but strictly and primarily means " core " or " kernel." The core of a boil and the kernel of a fruit are both called the " atu," *i.e.* the hard and essential part. (The larger kernels are called " katu.") As applied to a " master " or " lord," the term suggests that his favour and protection are essential to the life and prosperity of the serf. By an obvious analogy, the welfare of mankind is derived from the divine " Atu " or " Lord," who is *the Core and Kernel of humanity.* In the nearly related word "Atua" = *God,* the final *a* is passive[1] in form but intensive in signification, as if to indicate that He is " the VERY Core or Life " of man. A person who at a critical moment has lost courage is said to be " topa i te io," *i.e. forsaken by his god,*—that divine something which imparts courage to fight or to endure. At Rarotonga the 13th phase of each moon is called " Maitu ; " at Mangaia, "Atua" (see calendar).

The word " rimu " means *moss;* " rimua " = *moss-grown,* the final *a* as in the word " Atua," being intensive. Thus it comes to pass that "*eternity*" or "*for-ever*" is expressed by the phrase " e *rimua* ua atu "—the essential part of which is " rimua." The idea is of a lofty tree covered all over with moss, the growth of untold ages. So that the phrase might be rendered "*until covered with the moss of ages,*" *i.e.* for ever and ever.

" Tupu " means *grow, happen.* In the phrase "mei *tupua* roa mai " (the essential part of which is " tupua ") the sense is "*from the very beginning,*" *i.e.* from the time when things first began to " *tupu* " = *grow* or *happen.*

A very comprehensive designation for divinities of all kinds is " te anau tuarangi " or *the-heavenly-family* (" tu-a-rangi " = *like-*

---

[1] All nouns may be converted into verbs by means of suffixes.

the-heaven-or-sky). Strangely enough, this celestial race includes rats, lizards, beetles, eels and sharks, and several kinds of birds. The supposition was that "the-heavenly-family" had taken up their abode in these birds, fish, and reptiles.

A common and expressive name for God is "tatua manava" = *loin-belt* or *girdle*, as giving strength to fight.

A HUMAN PRIESTHOOD NEEDED.

The gods first spake to man through the small land birds; but their utterances were too indistinct to guide the actions of mankind. To meet this emergency an order of priests was set apart, the gods actually taking up their abode, for the time being, in their sacred persons. Priests were significantly named "*god-boxes*" (pia-atua),—generally abbreviated to "*gods*," *i.e.* living embodiments of these divinities.

Whenever consulted, a present of the best food, accompanied with a bowl of intoxicating "piper mythisticum," was indispensable. The priest, throwing himself into a frenzy, delivered a response in language intelligible only to the initiated. A favourite subject of inquiry was "the sin why so and so was ill;" no one being supposed to die a natural death unless decrepit with extreme old age. If a priest cherished a spite against somebody, he had only to declare it to be the will of the divinity that the victim should be put to death or be laid on the altar for some offence against the gods. The best kinds of food were sacred to the priests and chiefs.

Although unsuited for the delivery of oracles, birds were ever regarded as the special messengers of the gods to warn individuals of impending danger; each tribe having its own feathered guardians.

Of their many priests the leading place ever belonged to the
" mouth-pieces" of Motoro.   These men, significantly known
as " the Amama," or " open-mouthed-tribe," in reality ruled the
island from the time of Rangi downwards : first as priests of
Motoro, and latterly by right of conquest.   The two districts
belonging to this tribe are the only ones which have not changed
hands.

From the gluttonous habits of these priests is derived the
phrase, " to gormandize like a god " (kai Atua).

DEDICATION OF INFANTS.

As soon as the child was born, a leaf of the gigantic taro plant
(*arum costatum*) was cut off, its sides carefully gathered up, and
filled with pure water.   Into this extempore baptismal font the
child would be placed.   First securing with a bit of *tapa* the
part of the navel string nearest the infant, the right hand
of the operator *longitudinally* divided the cord itself with a
bamboo knife.   The dark coagulated blood was then carefully
washed out with water, and the name of the child's god declared,
it having been previously settled by the parents whether their little
one should belong to the mother's tribe or to the father's.   Usually
the father had the preference ; but *occasionally*, when the father's
family was devoted to furnish sacrifices, the mother would seek to
save her child's life by getting it adopted into her own tribe, the
name of her own tribal divinity being pronounced over the babe.
As a rule, however, the father would stoically pronounce over his
child the name of his own god Utākea, Teipe, or Tangiia, which
would almost certainly insure its destruction in after years.   It
was done as a point of honour ; besides, the child might *not* be

required for sacrifice, although eligible. The bamboo knife would be taken to the marae of the god specified, and thrown on the ground to rot. If a second god's name were pronounced over the child, the bamboo knife would go to one marae and the name of the babe only be pronounced over the second marae. The removal of the coagulated blood was believed to be highly promotive of health, all impurities being thus removed out of the system. Hence the common query in heathen times: "I taia toou pito noai?" = "What divine name was pronounced at the severance of thy navel string?" In other words, "Who is thy god?"

A deacon, still living, told me that his god was to have been Teipe, but when halfway to the marae of that unfortunate god, his father resolved to break his promise to his wife, and actually turned back and presented the knife to Motoro—his own god. "Had my father not done so, I should long since have been offered in sacrifice, and should not have heard of the one great offering on Calvary," said he with evident feeling.

At Rarotonga, when a boy was born a collection of spears, clubs, and slinging stones was made. When the sun was setting a great taro leaf filled with water was held over these warlike weapons, and the navel string was treated as above described. The idea was that the child should grow up to be a famous warrior.

On the birth of the first-born son of the reigning king Makea, a human victim previously fixed upon was slain. The royal babe was placed upon the dead body for the purpose of severing the navel string, thus indicating the absolute sway he would exercise over the lives of his subjects upon succeeding to the throne of his father.

It is often said to an ill-tempered person, " E pito raka toou "

= "The name of a *devil*[1] was pronounced over *thy* severed navel string,"—the phrase having outlived the custom.

NAMING OF CHILDREN.

At convenient intervals the principal king of Mangaia, as high-priest of *all* the gods, assisted by the priest of Motoro, summoned the young people to their various family maraes to be publicly "named." Some might be verging on manhood or womanhood, whilst others were scarcely able to walk. Standing in a half circle, two or three deep, the operator dipped a few leaves of a beautiful species of myrtle (*maire*) in the sacred stream flowing past the marae, and sprinkled the assembly ; all the while reciting a song or prayer to the particular god at whose shrine they were worshipping, and who was supposed to be the special protector of those present.

At certain pauses in the song the king, as "pontifex maximus," gently tapped each youngster two or three times on the head or shoulders, pronouncing his or her name.

The idea evidently was to secure a public recognition of the god and clanship of each of the rising generation—for *their own* guidance in the ceremonial of heathen life, and for the guidance of *priests and chiefs* afterwards. The greatest possible sin in heathenism was "ta atua," *i.e.* to kill a fellow worshipper by *stealth*. In general it might be done in battle. Otherwise such a blow was regarded as falling upon the god himself; the literal sense of "ta atua" being *god-striking*, or *god-killing*. Such

---

[1] Whilst their gods were nearly all malicious, some being more mischievous than others, the Hervey Islanders had not the idea of one supreme evil spirit corresponding to our Satan.

crimes were generally the consequence of ignorance : to prevent the priests and chiefs from such blundering, these occasional "namings" were appointed. In the event of war, and a consequent redistribution of lands, the favour of all the principal gods must be secured by favours shown to their worshippers— at least to a selection of a few to keep up the worship of each idol. A great feasting invariably succeeded this ceremony of naming.

CHAPTER III.

ASTRONOMICAL MYTHS.

A CHASE THAT NEVER ENDS.

THE only children of Potiki were twins : the elder, a girl, was named Piri-ere-ua, or *Inseparable;* the younger was a boy. These children were naturally very fond of each other : whatever the sister wished the brother agreed to. Unhappily, however, their mother, Tarakorekore, was a scold, and gave them no peace. One night the mother went torch-fishing on the reef. The tide, rising at midnight, put an end to her sport; but not before she had obtained a basket full of small bony red fish, called kūkū. Upon arriving home, according to invariable native custom, she woke her husband and cooked the fish. Four divisions were made ; the parents eating their portions at once. The mother would not agree to her husband's suggestion to wake the children to partake of the warm and savoury midnight feast. However, she carefully put away *their* portions into their baskets.[1]

---

[1] Throughout the islands each member of the family has a separate food-basket, so that if hungry at night he should only take his own share, and not encroach upon his neighbour's.

Now, Inseparable and her twin-brother were all the time awake, but did not let their parents know the circumstance. In vain they waited for their mother to fetch them to share their good things. Potiki and Tarakorekore enjoyed a thorough good supper, but their children were not to get a taste until morning. The twins wept in secret. As soon as their parents were soundly asleep, Inseparable proposed to her brother that they should flee away for ever. At first the boy hesitated, but eventually agreed to comply with his sister's wishes. Cautiously opening the sliding door of their house, they started on their journey. Upon reaching an elevated point of rock, they sat down and again wept, each filling a little natural hollow in the rock with their parting tears, without, however, in the least relenting in their purpose. At last they leaped up into the sky, Inseparable holding on to the extremity of her brother's girdle.

As soon as the morning star became visible, the mother went to rouse the children, so that they might eat their fish and taro ; but they were gone. Their little bed of fragrant dried grass was cold, though moist with tears. Hastily summoning her husband, a strict search was made. The path taken by the twins was traced by their tears. The little hollows filled from their eyes revealed the spot where they had last rested on earth. But no further trace could be discovered. In utter perplexity the now sorrowful and repentant parents looked up at the sky, where the sun had not yet risen, and, to their great surprise, saw their beloved children shining brightly there. Vainly they called on Inseparable and her brother to return. To stay longer on earth without these dearly loved, though ungrateful, children could not be thought of : so then father and mother leaped right up into the heavens in hot pursuit of the " Twins." But the children had got the start of their parents, and made the best of their way through the azure vault. This strange chase is still going on; for the parents have never yet succeeded in overtaking their truant children. All four shine brightly: the parents Potiki and Tarakorekore, being larger, exceed their children in brilliancy. Brother and dearly-loved sister, still linked together, pursue their never-ceasing flight, resolved never again to meet their justly enraged parents.

SONG OF THE TWINS.

Eaa te ara i ooro ai nga tamariki a Tarakorekore?

Wherefore fled the children of Tarakorekore?

Noa riri paa i te ai kūkū na Potiki;

Anger at the cooked fish of Potiki.

I tu ai i ooro ai; i tu ai i ooro ai!

They stealthily rose, and ran and fled for ever.

Ua vaia au i teia e, ei ta ua taana e!

Alas! that a mother should thus ill-treat her children.

E kore au e ta; o te ui maie ua atu,

Such was not *my* (father's) wish; and when I intercede,

Ua kore ake oi ē!

She will not relent.

Ka akakutu ta ua'i; ka akakutu ta ua'i.

She thrashes them,—is always at it.

I moe ana au i Karanga; i moe ana au i Karanga.

If one sleeps at Karanga or elsewhere,

I tau metua vaine: kore ua ka rerua koe ikona ē!

Still there is no peace—only threats and blows.

These lines were composed by Reinga for a fête held circa 1815. A play is intended on the mother's name "Tarakorekore," which means "never-speak-at-all."

Inseparable and her brother are the double star μ^1 and μ^2 *Scorpii*. The irate parents are the two bright stars v and λ *Scorpii*.

The Rev. W. Ellis, in his "Researches," erroneously calls them Gemini, or "The Twins," vol. iii. p. 172, second edition.

I once heard a native preacher say, that Christ and the Christian should be like these twin stars, ever linked together—come life, come death. The allusion was happy, and was perfectly understood by all present, the story being a favourite one throughout the islands.

MATARIKI, OR PLEIADES.

These stars were originally one. Its bright effulgence excited the anger of the god Tane, who got hold of Aldebaran (Aumea) and Sirius (Mere), and chased the offender. The affrighted fugitive ran for his life, and took refuge behind a stream. But Sirius drained off the waters, thus enabling Tane to renew the chase. Finally, Tane hurled Aldebaran bodily against the exhausted fugitive, who was thereby splintered into six shining fragments. This cluster of little stars is appropriately named Mata-riki, or *little-eyes*, on account of their brightness. It is also designated Tau-ono, or *the-six*, on account of the apparent number of the fragments ; the presence of the seventh star not having been detected by the unassisted native eye.

Reinga thus sings of the wars of the star-gods :—

Ua riri paā Vena ra ia Aumea,	Vena [1] was enraged against Aumea, (Aldebaran),
Noa kite ake i te kakenga.	On account of the brilliance of his rising.
Noa ui atu i te ara i pao ai Matariki ma	She demanded if he recollected the fate of the Pleiades,
E Mere ma ē !	Shivered by Sirius and his friends.
Tuārangi maiti ! Tuārangi maiti !	Alas ! ye bright-shining gods! Bright-shining gods !

---

[1] Vena was a goddess, represented by the star Procyon (*Canis Minor*).

This beautiful constellation was of extreme importance in heathenism, as its appearance at sunset on the eastern horizon determined the commencement of the new year, which is about the middle of December. The year was divided into two seasons, or *tau :* the first, when in the evening these stars appeared on or near the horizon ; the second, when at sunset the stars were invisible.

The re-appearance of Pleiades above the horizon at sunset, *i.e.* the beginning of a new year, was in many islands a time of extravagant rejoicing.

We have already seen that the sun was known as " the eye of Avatea, of Vātea (*noon-day*)," *i.e.* the *right* eye : the *left* eye of Vātea being the moon.

Venus, as the *morning* star, was called Tamatanui, *i.e. the eye of Tane.* The *evening* star was regarded as a different planet. being known as Takurua-rau. Jupiter was often mistaken for the morning star.

The rainbow was designated "the-girdle-of-Tangaroa," by which the eldest of the gods was accustomed to descend to earth.

The Magellan clouds are known as " nga māû," or the upper and lower *mists*.

THE SUN AND MOON.

A curious myth obtained in the now almost extinct Tongan tribe relative to the origin of the sun and moon. Vātea and Tonga-iti quarrelled respecting the parentage of the first-born of Papa, each claiming the child as his own. At last the infant was cut in two. Vātea, the husband of Papa, took the upper part as his share, and forthwith squeezed it into a ball and tossed it into the heavens, where it became the sun.

Tonga-iti sullenly allowed his share, the lower half, to remain a day or two on the ground. Seeing the brightness of Vātea's half, he resolved to imitate his example by compressing his share into a ball, and tossing it into the dark sky during the absence of the sun in Avaiki, or nether-world. Thus originated the moon, whose paleness is attributable to the blood having all drained out and decomposition having commenced.

This myth was rejected by the victorious tribes; *not* on the ground of its excessive absurdity, but on account of its representing Tonga-iti as a *husband* of Papa, instead of being her third *son.* By this account the almost extinct tribe of Tongans should take the precedence of their hereditary foes, the descendants of Rongo.

The origin of this myth seems to be this :—

Day (Vātea) and Night alternately embrace fair Earth (Papa). Their joint offspring are the sun and moon. The cutting of the babe in two was invented in order to account for the paleness of the moon.

THE WOMAN IN THE MOON.

The eldest of Kui-the-Blind's four attractive daughters was simply named Ina. Marama (Moon), who from afar had often admired her, became so enamoured of her charms that one night he descended from his place in the heavens to fetch her to be his wife. The goddess Ina became a pattern wife, being always busy; of a clear night one may easily discern a goodly pile of leaves, known as " te rau tao o Ina," for her never-failing oven of food; also her tongs of a split cocoa-nut branch, to enable her to adjust the live coals without burning her fingers.

Ina is indefatigable in the preparation of resplendent cloth, *i.e. white clouds.* The great stones needful for this purpose are also visible. As soon as her tapa is well beaten and brought into the desired shape, she stretches it out to dry on the upper part of the blue sky, the edges all round being secured with the large stones. Ina smoothes out every crease with her own hand, and finally leaves it to bleach.

The cloth manufacture of the goddess is on a much grander scale than any seen in this world; consequently the stones required are of a monstrous size. And when the operation is completed, Ina takes up these stones and casts them aside with violence. Crash, crash they go against the upper surface of the solid vault, producing what mortals call *thunder.*

Occasionally the goddess first removes the stones from the part of the tapa nearest to her fair person, and then hastily rising empties out, as it were, the whole lot at once. The concussion produced by these ponderous stones falling together is termed by mankind a *terrific thunderclap.*

Ina's cloth glistens like the sun. Hence it is, that when hastily gathering up her many rolls of whitest tapa, flashes of light fall upon the earth, which are designated *lightning.*

The great antiquity of this myth is attested by the circumstance that throughout the Hervey Group the only names for "moon-light" and "no moon" refer to Ina. Moonlight is expressed by Ina-motea = *the-brightness-of-Ina;* "no moon," by Ina-poiri = *Ina-invisible.* In the Samoan "Ina" becomes "Sina;" the word mā-*sina* = *moon,* embodies the name of the goddess. In the Tahitian "Ina" becomes "Hina."

At Atiu it is said that Ina took to her celestial abode a mortal husband. After living happily together for many years, she said to him, " You are growing old and infirm. Death will soon claim you, for you are a native of earth. This fair home of mine must not be defiled with a corpse. We will therefore embrace and part. Return to earth and there end your days." At this moment Ina caused a beautiful rainbow to span the heavens, by which her disconsolate aged husband descended to earth to die.

ECLIPSES.

Tuanui-ka-rere, or *Tuanui-about-to-fly*, a demon from the *east*, is at times subject to excessive fits of rage, in which he thinks nothing of swallowing up the *moon* whole. Affrighted mortals exclaim, " Alas ! a divinity has devoured the moon !" and very anxiously wait to see whether the useful luminary will be restored or not.

Tangiia-ka-rere, or *Tangiia-about-to-fly* a demon from the *west*, was the ill-mannered god who devoured the *sun* in his anger. It was very comforting to find that in every instance sun and moon were vomited forth whole again, and resumed their old duties, apparently none the worse for what they had endured.

No offerings were made at Mangaia to these demons, as was the invariable custom at Rarotonga, when the irritated Tangaroa was *there* believed to have done what at Mangaia was attributed to Tangiia and Tuanui.

The upshot, however, was a very serious matter ; for the anger of these demons having been vainly exercised against the heavenly bodies, must occasion the death of some man of distinction, to assuage their ire, and as a sort of payment for giving back to mankind those luminaries.

Note the inconsistency of this with the former myth.

A CELESTIAL FISH-HOOK.

The tail of the constellation " Scorpio," consisting of eight stars, two of which are double, is here known by the curious designation of " *the great fish-hook of Tongareva.*"   The monstrous myth associated with it is as follows :—

Vātea, the father of gods and men, whose home was in a part of Avaiki, or nether-world, called The-thin-land, one day went fishing in the deep blue ocean.   He carried with him a great fish-hook, which he baited with a *star* (doubtless an allusion to the bright star, the last in the tail).   Notwithstanding this brilliant bait, he caught nothing.   Vātea now resolved to imitate the conduct of his mother, Vari-ma-te-takere, *i.e. The-very-beginning ;* accordingly, he pulled a piece of flesh off one of his own thighs and baited his big fish-hook afresh.   This time he found that he had got a prize, but it was extraordinarily heavy.   Fortunately, however, the line attached to the hook was the strongest known, consisting of many strands of cinet cord plaited round.   Vātea pulled away lustily at this line, and was rejoiced at seeing a large dark round mass slowly rising to the surface.   This proved to be the island of Tongareva, which had till then lain at the bottom of the deep blue sea.   Vastly pleased with this achievement, Vātea hung up his great fish-hook in the sky.   Hence its name, " the great fish-hook of Tongareva."

In some islands this constellation is known as " the fish-hook of Māui, with a somewhat similar myth to account for it.

It is not a little remarkable that this group of stars was so called on Mangaia long before any European had discovered the island in question.   When found, it was designated in the charts as Penrhyns, without its native name, Tongareva, being known until a schooner, in 1853, had the misfortune to go ashore there.

When discovered, the inhabitants of Penrhyns knew of the existence of Auau (or Mangaia), and asserted that Tāvai, the erring wife of their great ancestor Mahuta, was a native of that island.

A DAY SONG FOR MAAKI'S FÊTE.

BY TANGATAROA, 1820.

Chorus.

E aparangi	Like the outstretched heavens
O te kauā peau nui ka rere.	Are the spread wings of the warning bird.
	'Tis the incarnation of a god.
E uoa mai na e taae,	One shakes with terror
E mataku paa taua ē !	At the long curved bill.
E roroa ua na ngutu ē !	

Solo.

E roroa ua na ngutu e, e kauā,
   E manu no tai enua ē !
   Oi au ikitia te manu
   E tei taraka aē !

Ah, that long curved bill !
'Tis a bird from some other land.
I am the chosen bird
That comes to warn thee.

Chorus.

   Oi au ikitia te manu
   I taraka, e tai rau, e Tanē !
Paoa i te kaki aro, e pauru kauā.

We are all chosen birds,
Messengers of Tane, to save you,
Our bills are long and dangerous.

Euea te mata o te mārāngi nui
    Tamatakutaku ē !
Omai tai turama ia Mangaia
   mārama ē !
E tamatanui aengata ua ao ē !

Reveal thy face, lovely full-moon,
    Whom all adore.
O for a torch to illumine Mangaia,

A bright morning star, harbinger of day.

Solo.

   Ie tutu ake ki runga ē !
   Nga manu taae, noea koe ?
No nunga au, no ua reia e te
   matangi,
   Ua viriviri i te arorangi,
    Ra rôi mai !

   Pray stand erect,
Ye divine birds.   Whence came ye ?
From the sunrising, driven about

Through the expanse of heaven,
   We come to you.

Chorus.

Tena oa te anana kauā !

Hail flock of warning birds !

Solo.

Ua ana mai nei koutou ?

Ha ! ye have arrived.

E

Chorus.

Nako nei maira !	Welcome to our midst !
Koki, koka Tangaroa,	In the heavens Tangaroa
Akarongo koumu i te tua o Vātea	Listens to the whispers of Vātea.
Kokiia te rangi.	Awake, ye winds !
Tāpai ïa te rangi.	Sweep o'er the skies.
E rere i te itinga.	Fly east (ye warning birds),
E rere i te opunga.	Fly west.
E kapakapa te manu e tau ra.	What a flapping of wings when resting !

FINALE.

BY TIKI (1820), IN FULL CHORUS.

Na verovero o te rā	See yon rays of light
I patia i Avaiki,	Darting up from spirit-world
O Rongo Nui Maruata	(Where Great Rongo reigns),
E puta i te rangi.	Piercing the heavens.
Ko verovero o te rā	The rays of light are lengthening ;
Ia iti pakakina te etu,	The stars still shine ;
E mâu te marama	The moon is full-orbed.
O Rongo te atua tupu a taae,	Rongo, thou fiercest of gods,
E tupiti i te moe	Arouse all sleepers, e'en those
O Tavare-moe-roa.	As profound as Tavare of old.
E ara ! E ara !	Awake ! Awake !
E ara, e Tane, i to mata katau,	Open, Tane, thy brilliant right eye.
Aue ē ! kua kata te anau Atea	Ha ! all the divine offspring of Vātea
I te rara varu !	Laugh at our brave diversion.
Kua itirere i te popongi.	Day is at hand.
Kua ao ē !	'Tis dawn.
Ruru i te tere ia Tiki,	The fête of Tiki is over.
Ka aere ei !	We part.

Six men in masks represented the warning birds. As incarnations of Tane they come from "the sunrising." The "brilliant right eye" of Tane is Venus.

"Tavare" is the lengendary sound sleeper (the mother of Moke), who passed each winter in unconsciousness.

CHAPTER IV.

THE EXPLOITS OF MĀUI.

—◆—

THE FIRE-GOD'S SECRET.

ORIGINALLY fire was unknown to the inhabitants of this world, who of necessity ate raw food.

In nether-world (Avaiki) lived four mighty ones : Mauike, god of fire ; the Sun-god Rā ; Ru, supporter of the heavens ; and lastly, his wife Buataranga, guardian of the road to the invisible world.

To Ru and Buataranga was born a famous son Māui. At an early age Māui was appointed one of the guardians of this upper world where mortals live. Like the rest of the inhabitants of the world, he subsisted on uncooked food. The mother, Buataranga, occasionally visited her son; but always ate her food apart, out of a basket brought with her from nether-land. One day, when she was asleep, Māui peeped into her basket and discovered cooked food. Upon tasting it, he was decidedly of opinion that it was a great improvement upon the raw diet to which he was accustomed. This food came from nether-world; it was evident that the secret of fire was there. To nether-world, the home of his parents, he would descend to gain this knowledge, so that ever after he might enjoy the luxury of cooked food.

On the following day Buataranga was about to descend to Avaiki (nether-world), when Māui followed her through the bush without her knowing it. This was no difficult task, as she always came and returned by the same road. Peering through the tall reeds, he saw his mother standing opposite a black rock, which she addressed as follows—

Buataranga i tona rua, e rarangatu koe.
 E anuenue i akarongoia atu ei.
  Opipiri,[1], Oeretue-i-te-ata e !
Vāia, vāi akera i te rua i Avaiki, nga taae !

Buataranga, descend thou bodily through this chasm.
The rainbow-like must be obeyed.
As two dark clouds parting at dawn,
Open, open up my road to nether-world, ye fierce ones.

At these words the rock divided, and Buataranga descended. Māui carefully treasured up these magic words; and without delay started off to see the god Tane, the owner of some wonderful pigeons. He earnestly begged Tane to lend him one ; but the proffered pigeon not pleasing Māui, was at once returned to its owner. A better pigeon was offered to the fastidious borrower, but was rejected. Nothing would content Māui but the possession of Akaotu, or *Fearless*, a red pigeon, specially prized by Tane. It was so tame that it knew its name ; and, wander wherever it might, it was sure to return to its master. Tane, who was loth to part from his pet, extracted a promise from Māui that the pigeon should be restored to him uninjured. Māui now set off in high spirits, carrying with him his red pigeon, to the place where his mother had descended. Upon pronouncing the magic words which he had overheard, to his great delight the rock opened, and Māui, entering the pigeon, descended. Some assert

---

[1] Names for the two clouds which are parted by the rising sun.

that Māui transformed himself into a small dragon-fly, and perched upon the back of the pigeon, made his descent. The two fierce guardian demons of the chasm, enraged at finding themselves imposed upon by a stranger, made a grab at the pigeon, intending to devour it. Fortunately, however, for the borrower, they only succeeded in getting possession of the *tail;* whilst the pigeon, minus its beautiful tail, pursued its flight to the shades. Māui was grieved at the mishap which had overtaken the pet bird of his friend Tane.

Arrived at nether-land, Māui sought for the home of his mother. It was the first house he saw : he was guided to it by the sound of her cloth-flail. The red pigeon alighted on an oven-house opposite to the open shed where Buataranga was beating out cloth. She stopped her work to gaze at the red pigeon, which she guessed to be a visitor from the upper world, as none of the pigeons in the shades were red. Buataranga said to the bird, "Are you not come from 'daylight?'" The pigeon nodded assent. "Are you not my son Māui?" inquired the old woman. Again the pigeon nodded. At this Buataranga entered her dwelling, and the bird flew to a bread-fruit tree. Māui resumed his proper human form, and went to embrace his mother, who inquired how he had descended to nether-world, and the object of his visit. Māui avowed that he had come to learn the secret of fire. Buataranga said, "This secret rests with the fire-god Mauike. When I wish to cook an oven, I ask your father Ru to beg a lighted stick from Mauike." Māui inquired where the fire-god lived. His mother pointed out the direction, and said it was called Are-aoa = *house-of-banyan-sticks*. She entreated Māui to be careful, "for the fire-god is a terrible fellow, of a very irritable temper."

Māui now walked up boldly towards the house of the fire-god, guided by the curling column of smoke. Mauike, who happened at the moment to be busy cooking an oven of food, stopped his work and demanded what the stranger wanted. Māui replied, "A fire-brand." The fire-brand was given. Māui carried it to a stream running past the bread-fruit tree and there extinguished it. He now returned to Mauike and obtained a second fire-brand, which he also extinguished in the stream. The third time a lighted stick was demanded of the fire-god, he was beside himself with rage. Raking the ashes of his oven, he gave the daring Māui some of them on a piece of dry wood. These live coals were thrown into the stream as the former lighted sticks had been.

Māui correctly thought that a fire-brand would be of little use unless he could obtain the secret of fire. The brand would eventually go out; but *how to reproduce the fire?* His object therefore was to pick a quarrel with the fire-god, and compel him by sheer violence to yield up the invaluable secret, as yet known to none but himself. On the other hand, the fire-god, confident in his own prodigious strength, resolved to destroy this insolent intruder into his secret. Māui for the fourth time demanded fire of the enraged fire-god. Mauike ordered him away, under pain of being tossed into the air; for Māui was small of stature. But the visitor said he should enjoy nothing better than a trial of strength with the fire-god. Mauike entered his dwelling to put on his war-girdle (ume i tona maro); but on returning found that Māui had swelled himself to an enormous size. Nothing daunted at this, Mauike boldly seized him with both hands and hurled him to the height of a cocoa-nut tree. Māui contrived in falling to make himself so light that he was in no degree hurt by his adventure. Mauike, maddened that his adversary should yet breathe, exerted his full strength, and next time hurled him far higher than the highest cocoa-nut tree that ever grew. Yet Māui was uninjured by his fall; whilst the fire-god lay panting for breath.

It was now Māui's turn. Seizing the fire-god he threw him up to a dizzy height, and caught him again like a ball with his hands. Without allowing Mauike to touch the ground, he threw him a second time into the air, and caught him in his hands. Assured that this was but a preparation for a final toss which would seal his fate, the panting and thoroughly exhausted Mauike entreated Māui to stop and to spare his life. Whatever he desired should be his.

The fire-god, now in a miserable plight, was allowed to breathe awhile. Māui said, "Only on one condition will I spare you;—*tell me the secret of fire. Where is it hidden? How is it produced?*" Mauike gladly promised to tell him all he knew, and led him inside his wonderful dwelling. In one corner there was a quantity of fine cocoa-nut fibre; in another, bundles of fire-yielding sticks—the "*au*,"[1] the "orongā,"[2] the "*tauinu*," and particularly the "*aoa*,"[3] or banyan tree. These sticks were all dry and ready for use. In the middle of the room were two smaller sticks by themselves. One of these the fire-god gave to Māui, desiring him to hold it firmly, while he himself plied the other most vigorously. And thus runs—

THE FIRE-GOD'S SONG.

Ika, ika i taku ai ē !   Grant, oh grant me thy hidden fire,
  Te aoaoaoa.   Thou banyan tree !

---

[1] The lemon hibiscus.   [2] Urtica argentea.   [3] Ficus Indicus.

Tutuki i te pupu ;	Perform an incantation ;
Ka ai i te karakia.	Utter a prayer to (the spirit of)
Te aoaoaoa.	The banyan tree !
Kia ka te ai a Mauike	Kindle a fire for Mauike
I nunga i te pāpānga aoa e !	Of the dust of the banyan tree !

By the time this song was completed, Māui to his great joy perceived a faint smoke arising out of the fine dust produced by the friction of one stick upon another. As they persevered in their work the smoke increased ; and, favoured with the fire-god's breath, a slight flame arose, when the fine cocoa-nut fibre was called into requisition to catch and increase the flame. Mauike now called to his aid the different bundles of sticks, and speedily got up a blazing fire, to the astonishment of Māui.

The grand secret of fire was secured. But the victor resolved to be revenged for his trouble and his tossing in the air, by setting fire to his fallen adversary's abode. In a short time all nether-world was in flames, which consumed the fire-god and all he possessed. Even the rocks cracked and split with the heat : hence the ancient saying, " The rocks at Orovaru [1] (in the shades) are burning."

Ere leaving the land of ghosts, Māui carefully picked up the two fire-sticks, once the property of Mauike, and hastened to the bread-fruit tree, where the red pigeon " Fearless " quietly awaited his return. His first care was to restore the tail of the bird, so as to avoid the anger of Tane. There was no time to be lost, for the flames were rapidly spreading. He re-entered the pigeon, which carried his fire-sticks one in each claw, and flew to the lower entrance of the chasm. Once more pronouncing the words he learnt from Buataranga, the rocks parted, and he safely got back

---

[1] Equivalent to saying, " The foundations of the earth are on fire."

to this upper world. Through the good offices of his mother the pigeon met with no opposition from the fierce guardians of the road to the shades. On again entering into light the red pigeon took a long sweep, alighting eventually in a lovely secluded valley, which was thenceforth named Rupe-tau, or *the pigeon's-resting-place.* Māui now resumed his original human form, and hastened to carry back the pet bird of Tane.

Passing through the main valley of Keia, he found that the flames had preceded him, and had found an aperture at Teaoa, since closed up. The kings Rangi and Mokoiro trembled for their land; for it seemed as if everything would be destroyed by the devouring flames. To save Mangaia from utter destruction, they exerted themselves to the utmost, and finally succeeded in putting out the fire. Rangi thenceforth adopted the new name of Matamea, or *Watery-eyes,* to commemorate his sufferings; and Mokoiro was ever after called Auai, or *Smoke.*

The inhabitants of Mangaia availed themselves of the conflagration to get fire and to cook food. But after a time the fire went out, and as *they* were not in possession of the secret, they could not get *new* fire.

But Māui was *never* without fire in *his* dwelling: a circumstance that excited the surprise of all. Many were the inquiries as to the cause. At length he took compassion on the inhabitants of the world, and told them the wonderful secret—that fire lies hidden in the hibiscus, the urtica argentea, the " tauinu," and the banyan. This hidden fire might be elicited by the use of fire-sticks, which he produced. Finally, he desired them to chant the fire-god's song, to give efficacy to the use of the fire-sticks.

From that memorable day all the dwellers in this upper world used fire-sticks with success, and enjoyed the luxuries of light and cooked food.

To the present time this primitive method of obtaining fire is still in vogue; cotton, however, being substituted for fine cocoa-nut fibre as tinder. It was formerly supposed that only the *four* kinds of wood found in the fire-god's dwelling would yield fire.

"Aoa" means banyan-tree; for intensity and for rhythm the word is lengthened into "aoaoaoa." The banyan was sacred to the fire-god.

The spot where the flames are said to have burst through, named Te-aoa, or the *the-banyan-tree*, was sacred until Christianity induced the owner to convert the waste land into a couple of excellent taro patches.

Often when listening to the story of this Polynesian Prometheus, the question has been proposed to me, "Who taught *your* ancestors the art of kindling fire?"

At Rarotonga Buataranga becomes Ataranga; at Samoa Talanga. In the Samoan dialect Mauike becomes Mafuie.

THE SKY RAISED; OR, THE ORIGIN OF PUMICE STONE.

The sky is built of solid blue stone. At one time it almost touched the earth; resting upon the stout broad leaves of the *teve* (which attains the height of about six feet) and the delicate indigenous arrow-root (whose slender stem rarely exceeds three feet). The unique flattened-out form of these leaves, like millions of outspread hands pressing upwards, is the result of having to sustain this enormous weight. In this narrow space between earth and sky the inhabitants of this world were pent up. Ru, whose usual residence was in Avaiki, or the shades, had come up

for a time to this world of ours.   Pitying the wretched confined
residence of its inhabitants, he very laudably employed himself in
endeavouring to raise the sky a little.   For this purpose he cut a
number of strong stakes of different kinds of trees, and firmly
planted them in the ground at Rangimotia, the centre of the
island and of the world.   This was a considerable improvement,
as mortals were thereby enabled to stand erect and to walk about
without inconvenience.   Hence Ru was named "The sky-sup-
porter."   Wherefore Teka sings (1794) :—

Tuperetuki i te rangi,	Force up the sky, O Ru,
E Ru e, ua mareva.	And let the space be clear !

One day, when the old man was surveying his work, his graceless
son Māui contemptuously asked him what he was doing there.
Ru replied, "Who told youngsters to talk?   Take care of yourself,
or I will hurl you out of existence."   "Do it then," shouted Māui.
Ru was as good as his word, and forthwith seized Māui, who was
small of stature, and threw him to a great height.   In falling Māui
assumed the form of a bird, and lightly touched the ground
perfectly unharmed.   Māui, now thirsting for revenge, in a moment
resumed his natural form, but exaggerated to gigantic proportions,
and ran to his father saying :—

Ru tokotoko i te rangi tuatini,	Ru, who supports the many heavens—
Tuatoru, ka ruatiaraurau !	The third, even to the highest, ascend !

Inserting his head between the old man's legs, he exerted all his
prodigious strength, and hurled poor Ru, sky and all, to a tremendous height—so high, indeed, that the azure sky could never get
back again.   Unluckily, however, for "the-sky-supporting-Ru," his
head and shoulders got entangled among the stars.   He struggled
hard, but fruitlessly, to extricate himself.   Māui walked off well

pleased with having raised the sky to its present height ; but left half his father's body and both his legs ingloriously suspended between heaven and earth.　Thus perished Ru.　His body rotted away, and his bones, of vast proportions, came tumbling down from time to time, and were shivered on the earth into countless fragments.　These shivered "bones of Ru" are scattered over every hill and valley of Mangaia, to the very edge of the sea.

"The district" (said my narrator) "where Ru's bones are supposed to have fallen is on the northern part of the island, and derives its name from this circumstance.　It belongs to me."

It is true that what is universally known in these islands as "*the bones of Ru*" (te ivi o Ru), is found all over the island in small quantities.　Upon repeated careful examinations these "bones" proved to be *common pumice stone.*　The largest "bone" I have ever seen on the island is about the size of a man's fist. The peculiar lightness and bonelike appearance of pumice stone doubtless suggested the idea that it was the veritable remains of a famous hero of antiquity.　The younger natives now know pretty well the volcanic origin of these mythical "bones."

In 1862, when at Pukapuka, or Danger Island, where two years afterwards the first *John Williams* was wrecked, the natives brought me a large collection of idols of secondary rank. They piled them up in a heap before me.　My curiosity was aroused by seeing an old man, formerly a priest, carrying what seemed to be a large lump of *coal* with evident ease.　Upon carefully looking at it, *this god proved to be merely pumice stone* blackened by long exposure to rain and wind.　Of course it had drifted from some other island.　It was known as Ko te toka māmā *i.e. the-light-stone,* and was regarded as the god of the wind and the waves. Upon occasions of a hurricane, incantations and offerings of food would be made to it. Such worship will be made no more; for it is now deposited with the other gods in the museum of the University of Sydney. Pumice stone was not regarded as being sacred in the Hervey Group.

THE SUN MADE CAPTIVE.

Māui had secured fire for the advantage of mortals, had elevated the sky; but there remained one great evil to be remedied—the sun had a trick of setting every now and then, so that it was impossible to get through any work. Even an oven of food could not be prepared and cooked before the sun had set. Nor could a "karakia," or incantation to the gods, be chanted through ere they were overtaken by darkness. Māui resolved to remove this great evil.

Now Rā, or the Sun, is a living creature and divine; in form resembling a man, and possessed of fearful energy. His golden locks are displayed morning and evening to mankind. Buataranga advised her son not to have anything to do with Rā, or the Sun, as many had at different times endeavoured to regulate his movements, and had all signally failed. But the redoubtable Māui was not to be discouraged. He resolved to capture the Sun-god Rā, and compel him to obey the dictates of his conqueror.

Māui now carefully plaited six great ropes of strong cocoa-nut fibre, each composed of four strands, and of a great length. These wonderful cords of his were named by the inventor Aei-ariki [1] *i.e. royal nooses.* Māui started off with his ropes to the distant aperture through which the Sun climbs up from Avaiki, or

[1] = Taei-ariki.

the land of ghosts, into the heavens, and there laid a slip-noose for him. Further on in the Sun's path a second trap was laid. In fact, all the six ropes were placed at distant intervals along the accustomed route of Rā, or the Sun.

Very early in the morning the unsuspecting Sun clambered up from Avaiki to perform his usual journey through the heavens. Māui was lying in wait near the first "royal noose," and exultingly pulled it ; but it slipped down the Sun's body, and only caught his *feet*. Māui ran forward to look after the second noose, but that likewise slipped.   Luckily, however, it closed round the Sun's *knees*. The third caught him round the *hips ;* the fourth, round the *waist ;* the fifth, *under the arms*. Still the Sun went tearing on his path, scarcely heeding the contrivances of Māui.   But happily for Māui's designs, the sixth and last of the "royal nooses" caught the Sun round *the neck !* Rā, or the Sun, now terribly frightened, struggled hard for his liberty, but to no purpose.   For Māui pulled the rope so tight as almost to strangle the Sun, and then fastened the end of his rope to a point of rock.

Rā, or the Sun, now nearly dead, confessed himself to be vanquished ; and fearing for his life, gladly agreed to the demand of Māui, that in future he should be a little more reasonable and deliberate in his movements through the heavens, so as to enable the inhabitants of this world to get through their employments with ease.

The Sun-god Rā was now allowed to proceed on his way ; but Māui wisely declined to take off these ropes, wishing to keep Rā in constant fear.   These ropes may still be seen hanging from the Sun at dawn, and when he descends into the ocean at night. By the assistance of these ropes he is gently let down into Avaiki, and in the morning is raised up out of the shades.

Of course this extravagant myth refers to what English children call " the sun drawing up water ; " or, as these islanders still say, " Tena te taura a Māui ! " = " Behold the ropes of Māui ! "

It is interesting to note that the great Polynesian name for the Sun-god is Rā, as was the case in ancient Egypt—entering into the composition of the regal title " Pharaoh," etc. The rule of each great temporal sovereign was indifferently called a " mangaia "[1] = *peaceful reign*, or a " koina-rā " = *bright shining of the sun*, the sovereign chief, of course, being the sun. Sometimes he was called " the man who holds the Rā (sun) ; " at other times " the Sun(Rā)-eater." At death, or the transference of the supreme temporal power, it was naturally said, " the Rā has set."

Rā was the tutelary god of Borabora.

Such are the three great achievements of Māui. Nothing more is related of him in the Hervey Group, save that he was driven away by Rangi for setting the rocks on fire.

A husband is lovingly called by his wife her " rua-rā " = *sunhole*, in allusion to the preceding myth, as *from him comes the light of her life*. The husband gallantly calls the wife his " are-rau," = *well-thatched house, — where his affections repose*. These are standard expressions in hourly use.

THE WISDOM OF MANIHIKI[1] (KORERO MANIHIKI).

On the island of Rarotonga once lived Manuahifare and his wife Tongoifare, offspring of the god Tangaroa. Their eldest son was named Māui the First, the next Māui the Second. Then fol-

---

[1] Manihiki, Rakaanga, and Tongareva are situated about 600 miles north of Rarotonga.

lowed their sister Inaika = *Ina-the-Fish*.   The youngest was a boy, Māui the Third.   Like all other young Polynesians, these children delighted in the game of hide-and-seek.   One day Inaika hid her pet brother, Māui the Third, under a pile of dry sticks and leaves, and then desired the elder boys to search for him.   They sought everywhere in vain.   Inaika at last pointed to the pile, and naturally expected to see her little brother emerge from his hiding-place, as the sticks were scattered to the right and left.   The heap had disappeared, but no Māui was to be seen.   What had become of him ?   But after a few minutes they were astonished to see him start up from under a few bits of decayed wood and some leaves which had been thoroughly searched a few seconds before.   This was the first intimation of Māui the Third's future greatness.

This wonderful lad had noticed that his father, Manuahifare, mysteriously disappeared at dawn of every day ; and in an equally mysterious way came back again to their dwelling at night.   He resolved to discover this secret, which seemed to him the more strange as, being the favourite, he slept by the side of Manuahi-fare, and yet never knew when or how he disappeared.   One night he lay awake until his father unfastened his girdle in order to sleep.   Very cautiously did Māui, the Younger, take up one end and place it under himself, without attracting his father's notice.   Early next morning, this precocious son was roused from his slumbers by the girdle being pulled from under him.   This was just as he desired ; he lay perfectly still, to see what would become of Manuahifare.   The unsuspecting parent went, as he was wont, to the main pillar of his dwelling, and said—

O pillar ! open, open up,
That Manuahifare may enter and descend to nether-world (Avaiki).

The pillar immediately opened, and Manuahifare descended.

That same day the four children of Manuahifare went back to their old game of hide-and-seek. This time Māui the Younger told his brothers and sister to go outside the house, whilst he should look out for some place to hide in. As soon as they were out of sight, he went up to the post through which his father had disappeared, and pronounced the magic words he had overheard. To his great joy the obedient post opened up, and Māui boldly descended to the nether regions. Manuahifare was greatly surprised to see his son down there ; but after saluting (literally, " smelling ") him, quietly proceeded with his work.

Māui the Third went on an exploring tour through these unknown subterranean regions, the entrance to which he had luckily discovered. Amongst other wonderful things, he fell in with a blind old woman bending over a fire where her food was being cooked. In her hand she held a pair of tongs (*i.e.* a green cocoa-nut midrib, split open). Every now and then she carefully took up a live coal, and placed it on one side, supposing it to be food, whilst the real food was left to burn to cinder in the fire ! Māui inquired her name, and, to his surprise, found it was Inaporari, or *Ina-the-Blind*, his own grandmother. The clever grandson heartily pitied the condition of the poor old creature, but would not reveal his own name. Close to where he stood watching the futile cooking of Ina-the-Blind grew four *nono* trees (*morindo citrifolia*). Taking up a stick, he gently struck the nearest of the four trees. Ina-the-Blind angrily said, " Who is that meddling with the *nono* belonging to Māui the Elder ? " The bold visitor to nether-world then walked up to the next tree and tapped it gently. Again the ire of Ina-the-Blind was excited, and she shouted, " Who is this meddling with the *nono* of Māui the Second ? " The audacious boy struck a third tree, and found it

F

belonged to his sister Inaika. He now exultingly tapped the fourth and last *nono* tree, and heard his old grandmother ask, "Who is this meddling with the *nono* of Māui the Third?" "*I am Māui the Third,*" said the visitor. "Then," said she, "you are my grandson, and this is your own tree."

Now when Māui first looked at his own *nono* tree, it was entirely destitute of leaves and fruit ; but after Ina-the-Blind had spoken to him, he again looked and was surprised to see it covered with glossy leaves and fine apples, though not ripe. Māui climbed up into the tree, and plucked one of the apples. Biting off a piece of it, he stepped up to his grandmother and threw it into one of her blind eyes. The pain was excruciating, but sight was at once restored to the eye which had so long been blind. Māui plucked another apple, and biting off a piece of it, threw it into the other eye of his grandmother—and lo ! sight was restored to it also. Ina-the-Blind was delighted to see again, and, in gratitude, said to her grandson, "All above, and all below "(= all on earth and all in spirit-land) " are subject to thee, and to thee only."

Ina, once called the-Blind, now instructed Māui in all things found within her territory ; that as there were four species of nono, so there are four varieties of cocoa-nuts and four of taro in Avaiki, *i.e.* one for each child of Manuahifare.

Māui asked Ina, "Who is lord of fire ? " She replied, " Thy grandfather Tangaroa-tui-mata," (or *Tangaroa-of-the-tattooed-face*). "Where is he ? " inquired Māui. "Yonder," rejoined his grandmother ; "but do not go to him. He is a terribly irritable fellow : you will surely perish." But as Māui persisted, the grateful goddess Ina said, " There are two roads to his dwelling. One of these is the *path of death;* whoever unwittingly approaches the

Great Tangaroa by this path, dies. The other is the 'common,' or 'safe' (*noa*) road." Māui disdained to choose the path of safety. Knowing his own prowess, he boldly trod the path of death.

Tangaroa-of-the-tattooed-face, seeing Māui advancing, raised his right *hand* to kill him—that hand which as yet had never failed to destroy its victim. But Māui, nothing daunted, lifted *his* right hand. At this Tangaroa, not liking the aspect of Māui, raised his right *foot*, for the purpose of kicking to death the luckless intruder. But Māui was prepared to do the same to the lord of fire with *his* right foot. Astounded at this piece of audacity, Tangaroa demanded his name. The visitor replied, "I am Māui the Younger." The god now knew it to be his own grandson. "What did you come for?" "To get fire," was the response of Māui. Tangaroa-of-the-tattooed-face gave him a lighted stick, and sent him away. Māui walked to a short distance, and finding some water, like that dividing the two islets collectively called Manihiki, extinguished the lighted stick. Three times this process was repeated. The fourth time all the firebrands were gone, and Tangaroa had to fetch two dry sticks to rub together, in order to produce fire. Māui held the under one for his grandfather; but just as the fine dust in the groove was igniting, the impudent Māui blew it all away. Tangaroa, justly irritated at this, drove Māui away, and summoned a "kakaia," or tern, to come to his assistance to hold down the lower piece of wood, whilst Tangaroa diligently worked again with the other stick. At last, to the infinite joy of Māui, fire was obtained. It was no longer a mystery. Māui suddenly snatched the upper stick, one end of which was burning, out of the hand of Tangaroa. The patient bird of white plumage still firmly clutched with her claws the under fire-stick, when Māui purposely burnt either side of the eye of the bird. The indignant tern, smarting at this ill-requital, fled away for ever. Hence the black marks, resembling a pair of eyebrows, on either side of the eye of this beautiful bird to this day. Tangaroa reproached his grandson with having thus wantonly deprived him of the valuable services of his favourite bird. Māui deceitfully said, "Your bird will come back."

Māui next proposed to Tangaroa that they should both fly up to day-light through the hole by which the bird had escaped. The god inquired how this could be accomplished. Māui at once volunteered to show the way, and actually flew to a considerable height like a bird. Tangaroa-of-the-tattooed-face was greatly delighted. Māui came down to the ground, and urged his grandfather to imitate his example. "Nothing," said Māui, " is easier than to fly." At his grandson's suggestion, Tangaroa put on his glorious *girdle*, by mortals called *the rainbow*, and, to his immense delight, succeeded in rising above the loftiest cocoa-nut tree. The crafty Māui took care to fly lower than Tangaroa, and getting hold of one end of the old man's girdle, he gave it a smart pull, which brought down poor Tangaroa from his giddy elevation. The fall killed Great Tangaroa.

Pleased with his achievement in getting the secret of fire from his grandfather and then killing him, he returned to his parents, who had both descended to nether-land. Māui told them he had got the secret of fire, but withheld the important circumstance that he had killed Tangaroa. His parents expressed their joy at his success, and intimated their wish to go and pay their respects to the Supreme Tangaroa. Māui objected to their going at once. "Go," said he, " on the *third* day. I wish to go myself to-morrow." The parents of Māui acquiesced in this arrangement. Accordingly, on the next day Māui went to the abode of Tangaroa, and found the body entirely decomposed. He carefully collected the bones, put them inside a cocoa-nut shell, carefully closed the tiny aperture, and finally gave them a thorough shaking. Upon opening the cocoa-nut shell, he found his grandfather to be alive again. Liberating the divinity from his degrading imprisonment, he carefully washed him, anointed him with sweet-scented oil, fed him, and then left him to recover strength in his own dwelling.

Māui now returned to his parents Manuahifare and Tongoifare, and found them very urgent to see Tangaroa. Again Māui said, "Wait till to-morrow." The fact was, he greatly feared their displeasure, and had secretly resolved to make his way back to the upper world he had formerly inhabited whilst his parents were on their visit to Tangaroa.

Upon visiting the god on the morning of the *third* day, Manuahifare and Tongoifare were greatly shocked to find that he had entirely lost his old proud bearing, and that on his face were the marks of severe treatment. Manuahifare asked his father Tangaroa the cause of this. " Oh," said the god, " your terrible boy has been here ill-treating me. He killed me; then collected my bones, and rattled them about in an empty cocoa-nut shell; he then finally made me live again, scarred and enfeebled, as you see. Alas ! that fierce son of yours."

The parents of Māui wept at this, and forthwith came back to the old place in Avaiki in quest of their son, intending to scold him well. But he had made his escape to the upper world, where he found his two brothers and his sister Inaika in mourning for him whom they never expected to see again.

Māui the Third told them that he had made a grand discovery —he had obtained the secret of fire. He had found a new land.

"Where is it situated?" inquired they. "Down *there*," said Māui the Younger. "Down *where?*" they demanded. "Down *there*," again shouted Māui. The fact was, they were not aware of the secret opening in their house leading to Avaiki. At the earnest solicitation of Māui, they all consented to follow him. Accordingly, he went to the old post of their dwelling, and said as before :—

> O pillar ! open, open up,
> That we all may enter and descend to nether-world.

At these words the wonderful pillar at once opened, and all four descended. Māui showed them all the wonders of spirit-world, and when at length their curiosity was perfectly satisfied, he conducted them back to the upper world of light, to which they all properly belonged.

MĀUI ENSLAVING THE SUN.

Food was now *cooked* by the inhabitants of this upper world, whereas formerly it was eaten raw. But the Sun-god Rā used to set in mad haste, ere the family oven could be properly cooked. Māui considered how he could remedy this great evil. A strong rope of cocoa-nut fibre was made and laid round the aperture by which the Sun-god climbed up from Avaiki (nether-world). But it was in vain. Still stronger ropes were made; but all to no purpose. Māui fortunately bethought himself of his beloved sister's hair, which was remarkably long and beautiful. He cut off some of Inaika's locks and plaited it into rope, placed it round the aperture, and then hid himself. The moment the Sun-god Rā emerged from spirit-world in the east, Māui quickly pulled one end of the cord and caught him round the throat with the slipknot. The hitherto unmanageable monster bellowed and writhed in his vain efforts to extricate himself. Almost at the last gasp, he begged Māui to release him on any terms he pleased. The victorious Māui said that if he would pledge himself to go on his course at a more reasonable rate, he should be released. The promise was readily given by the trembling captive, and hence it is that ever since the inhabitants of this upper world have enjoyed sufficient sunlight to complete the duties of the day.

THE SKY RAISED.

Originally the heavens almost touched the earth. Māui resolved to elevate the sky, and fortunately succeeded in obtaining the assistance of Ru. Māui stationed himself at the north, whilst Ru took up his position in the south.

Prostrate on the ground, at a given signal they succeeded in raising a little *with their backs* the solid blue mass. Now pausing awhile *on their knees*, they gave it a second lift. Māui and Ru were now able to stand upright ; *with their shoulders* they raised the sky higher still. The *palms of their hands*, and then the *tips of their fingers*, enabled these brave fellows to elevate it higher and higher. Finally, drawing themselves out to gigantic proportions, they pushed the entire heavens up to the very lofty position which they have ever since occupied.

But the work was not complete, for the surface of the sky was very irregular. Māui and Ru got a large stone adze apiece, and therewith chipped off the roughest parts of the sky, thus giving it a perfectly oval appearance. They now procured superior adzes, in order to finish off the work so auspiciously commenced. Māui and Ru did not cease to chip, chip, chip at the blue vault, until it became faultlessly smooth and beautiful, as we see it now !

MĀUI'S LAST AND GREATEST ACHIEVEMENT.

A native of Rarotonga, named Iku, was a noted fisherman. He was accustomed to go out to sea a great distance, and yet safely find his way back with abundance of fish. The obvious reason of this was that Iku knew the names and movements of the stars; and by them he steered his course at night.

Upon one occasion this Rarotongan fisherman, at a great distance from his home, discovered a vast block of stone at the bottom of the ocean. This was the island of Manihiki. Iku made sail for Rarotonga to tell what he had seen.

The three brothers Māui heard Iku tell his story of this submarine island, and determined to get possession of it for themselves. Accordingly, without giving the discoverer the slightest hint of their intentions, they sailed in a large canoe to the north (a distance of 600 miles) in quest of the sunken island. Many days passed in weary search, ere they were rewarded with a sight of the great block of coral at the bottom of the sea.

Māui the Elder now baited his large hook with a piece of raw fish, and let it down. The bait took; and Māui the Elder pulled hard at the line. As the fish drew near the surface, he asked his brother whether it was a shark or a kakai. They pronounced it to be a kakai.

Māui the Second next baited *his* hook, and like his brother caught only a kakai.

It was now Māui the Younger's turn to try *his* luck. He selected as bait the young bud[1] of the cocoa-nut, which he had brought with him for the purpose. This he wrapped up in a leaf

[1] The size of a filbert.

of the laurel tree. A very strong line was attached to the hook, and then let down. Māui soon found that he had got hold of something very heavy, and he in his turn asked his brothers what sort of fish was on his hook. They sapiently assured him that "it was either a shark or a kakai."

Māui found his prize to be intolerably heavy, so he put forth all his hidden strength, and up came the entire island of Manihiki ! As the island neared the surface, the canoe in which the three brothers were, broke in two with the mighty straining of Māui the Younger. His two brothers were precipitated into the ocean and drowned. Luckily for Māui the Younger, one of his feet rested on the solid coral of the ascending island. At length Manihiki rose high and dry above the breakers, drawn up from the ocean depths by the exertions of the now solitary Māui.

Māui surveyed his island possession with great satisfaction, for this he regarded as his crowning achievement. There was, however, one serious defect,—there was no canoe passage. Māui at once set to work upon a part of the reef, and made the excellent opening for canoes which distinguishes Manihiki above many other islands.

Not long afterwards Iku came back to his favourite fishing-ground. Great was his surprise and indignation to find Manihiki raised up from the ocean depths by the efforts of Māui, and already inhabited by him. Iku resolved to slay Māui for doing this. He got ashore at the passage which his adversary had so conveniently made, and fought with Māui. In this fight Māui retreated to a certain spot, stamped his foot with great violence, and so broke off a part of what now constitutes one extremity of the sister islet of Rakaanga.

Iku feared not this exhibition of the prowess of Māui, and

again pursued him with intent to kill him. Māui now ran to the opposite side of Manihiki, and again violently stamped the earth with his foot; and thus it was that the originally large island of Manihiki was cleft into two equal parts, one of which retains the ancient designation Manihiki, the other is called Rakaanga. A wide ocean channel (of twenty-five miles) separates these twin coral islands. Finally, Māui ascended up into the heavens and was seen no more.

On the island of Rakaanga visitors are shown a hollow in a rock near the sea, closely resembling a human foot-print of the ordinary size. This is called "*the foot-print of Māui*,"—where his right foot rested when the canoe parted, and he had almost sunk in the ocean. Close by is a hole in the coral, said to be the place where Māui's fish-hook held fast when he pulled up the island from the bottom of the ocean. It is asserted that Māui carried with him to the skies the great fish-hook employed by him on that occasion. The tail of the constellation "Scorpio" is to this day called by the natives of Manihiki and Rakaanga "*the fish-hook of Māui.*"

Iku lived alone on Manihiki for a time. One day he saw a cocoa-nut floating on the surface of the ocean. He brought it ashore, and then planted it. Thus grew the first cocoa-nut tree on Manihiki.

Iku returned to Rarotonga to fetch his sister Tapairu and her husband Toa. All three safely reached Manihiki and settled down in their new-found home. Five daughters were born to Toa ; but no son was given to him until he married his youngest daughter. From Toa and Tapairu, a single family, all the present inhabitants of Manihiki and Rakaanga are descended. In after times Mahuta and his clan migrated to Penrhyns; thus the Penrhyn Islanders, the natives of Manihiki and Rakaanga, are all descended from the Rarotongan Toa and his wife Tapairu.

Such is "the wisdom of Manihiki." Few myths are so complete, and few islanders have been so free from foreign admixture as the natives of Manihiki and Rakaanga. They wonderfully resemble each other; so that to have seen one Manihikian is to have seen all.

A close parallel runs between their version of the exploits of of Māui and that which obtains elsewhere. Some particulars are wholly dissimilar; for instance, I can find no account of "the *bones* of Ru."

Mangaian tradition represents Māui as being driven away by Rangi to Rarotonga, for setting the island on fire. The "wisdom of Manihiki" represents Māui as living at Rarotonga, and starting thence on his wonderful voyage in search of Manihiki.

The tail of "Scorpio" is on Mangaia known as "*the great fish-hook of Tongareva*," *i.e.* Penrhyns. The myth respecting it is similar to the preceding, but refers to Tongareva, or Penrhyns, not to Manihiki. Vātea takes the place of Māui.

The story of Toa and Tapairu is simple history, well known at Rarotonga. That Mahuta, accompanied by his wife Tavai, emigrated to the hitherto uninhabited island of Penrhyns is undoubted truth. A second canoe, piloted by the son of the renowned Mahuta, followed and succeeded in making that extensive but most barren of islands, Tongareva.

In July, 1871, I visited Rakaanga. We rowed in a flat-bottomed boat without a keel, built of cocoa-nut timber neatly *sewn together* with cinet. Yet these adventurous islanders think nothing of traversing the twenty-five miles of ocean between Rakaanga and Manihiki in such frail barks.

The king pointed out to us the foot-print of Māui, and the rock in which his fish-hook caught. He next took us to the uninhabited islet (where now they keep their pigs), to show us the ancient road to spirit-land. We could perceive no hole or special depression in the ground; but were assured that, *if we dug deep enough*, we should be sure to find it.

Māui once, standing upon this spot, overheard a confused murmuring of voices beneath. In a low voice he inquired who these imprisoned spirits were. Those underneath shouted out their names in the form of a song, which our guide repeated. Said he, "Our fathers assured us there they still are; only earth has been piled upon the aperture." These spirits are said to be "like soldier crabs, boring down and hiding in the bowels of the earth."

CHAPTER V

TREE MYTHS.

THE MYTH OF THE COCOA-NUT TREE.

INA-MOE-AITU,[1] or *Ina-who-had-a-divine-lover*, daughter of Kui-the-Blind, once dwelt at Tamarua, under the frowning shadow of the cave of Tautua, so like the entrance of a gigantic edifice. A sluggish stream, abounding in eels, ran near her dwelling, and finally disappeared beneath the rocks. At dawn and sunset Ina loved to bathe near a clump of trees. On one occasion an enormous eel crept up the stream from its natural hiding-place under the rocks, and startled her by its touch. Again and again this occurred; so that Ina became in a measure accustomed to its presence. To her surprise one day, as she fixed her eyes upon the eel, its form changed, and the fish assumed the appearance of a handsome youth, who said to Ina, " I am Tuna (eel), the god and protector of all fresh-water eels. Smitten by your beauty, I left my gloomy home to win your love. Be mine." From that day he became her attached admirer in his human form, always resuming the eel shape upon his return to his proper haunts, so as to elude notice. Some time after he took his farewell of the

[1] Aitu = god.

lovely Ina. "We must part," said Tuna ; "but, as a memorial of our attachment, I will bestow on you a great boon. To-morrow there will be a mighty rain, flooding the entire valley. Be not afraid, as it will enable me to approach your house on yon rising ground in my eel form. I will lay my head upon the wooden threshold. At once cut it off, and bury it : be sure daily to visit the spot to see what will come of it."

Ina saw no more of her handsome lover ; but was that night roused from sleep by rain falling in torrents. Remembering Tuna's words, she remained quietly in her dwelling until daylight, when she found that the water, streaming down from the hills, had covered the taro-patches, and had risen close to the entrance to her hut. At this moment a great eel approached her, and laid its head upon her threshold. Ina ran to fetch her axe, and forthwith chopped off the head, and buried it at the back of her hut on the hill-side. The rain ceased, and in the course of a day or two the waters were drained off by the natural passage under the rocks —the true home of Tuna.

According to her promise to her lover, Ina daily visited the spot where the enormous eel's head was buried ; but for many days saw nothing worthy of notice. At last she was delighted to find a stout green shoot piercing the soil. Next day the shoot had divided into two. The twin shoots, thus gradually unfolding themselves, were very different from other plants. They grew to maturity, and sent forth great leaves, exciting the wonder of all. After the lapse of years flowers and fruit appeared. Of these twin cocoa-nut trees, sprung from the two halves of Tuna's brains, one was red in stem, branches, and fruit; whilst the other was of a deep green. And thus came into existence the two principal varieties of the cocoa-nut; the red being sacred to Tangaroa, and the green to Rongo. In proof of its being derived from the head of Tuna, when husked on each nut is invariably found the two eyes and mouth of the lover of Ina.

The white kernel of the cocoa-nut is commonly called " te roro o Tuna," or *the brains of Tuna.* In heathenism it was unlawful for women to eat eels; and to this day they mostly turn away from this fish with the utmost disgust.

The extremity of a great cocoa-nut leaf, termed the " iku kikau," and comprising ten or twelve lesser leaves, when cut off and neatly bound with a bit of yellow cinet by " the priest of all food," constituted the fisherman's god. Without this Mokoiro, as the divinity was called, no canoe would venture over the reef to fish.

The same device was used in inviting great chiefs to a feast; the sacred cinet, however, being omitted.

The principal taro patch in each district was analogically designated the " iku kikau," as its possession indicated chieftain-ship.

All " raui," or taboo restrictions, were and are still made by means of an entire cocoa-nut leaf plaited after a certain ancient pattern.

The preceding myth is evidently designed for the glorification of the Amama, or priestly tribe, who were worshippers of Tiaio under the double form of shark and eel. In the year 1855, at the very place indicated in this story, an enormous eel, measuring *seven* feet in length, was caught by daylight in a strong fish-net. In heathenism this would have been regarded as a visit of Tiaio, and the dainty morsel allowed to return under the rocks unmolested.　As it was, it furnished several families with a good supper.

In a figurative sense, Rongo's cocoa-nuts are *human heads*. Hence the common phrase respecting the beginning of war, "Kua vā'i i te akari a Rongo" = *the cocoa-nuts of Rongo have been split open;* in other words, men have been clubbed.

The mass of the people, chiefs included, never struck off the top of a cocoa-nut in order to drink; but were content to *suck* the refreshing liquid through the hole which nature provides.　The cocoa-nuts of the priests were invariably struck off (tipi take) when drunk by them, symbolical of the fact that with them lay the power of life and death.　Chiefs and warriors were merely instruments of their vengeance.

TAHITIAN MYTH OF THE COCOA-NUT TREE.

A king named Tai (sea) had a wife named Uta (shore) who was anxious to visit her relatives.　But Tai did not like her to go without a present.　He therefore inquired of the oracle what would be most suitable.　The god directed him to send his wife to the stream to watch for an eel; that she should cut off the head of the first that presented itself, and deposit it in a calabash and carefully plug up the aperture.　The eel was then to be thrown back into the water, and the calabash carried to the husband.

Upon Uta's return from the stream, the king inquired whether she had been successful.　The wife joyfully said yes, and laid the well-plugged calabash at his feet.　Tai now advised her to start on her intended journey, and present the precious calabash to her parents and brothers, "for there is a wondrous virtue in it."　He told her that it would grow into a cocoa-nut tree, and would bear delicious fruit never before seen. He enjoined her on no account to turn aside from the path, nor to bathe in any tempting fountain, not to sit down, nor to sleep on the road, and above all not to put down the calabash.

Uta gladly started on her journey. For a while all went well; but, at length, the sun being high in the heavens, she became very hot and weary. Perceiving a crystal stream, she forgot her promise to her husband, put down the calabash, and leapt into the inviting waters. After luxuriating for some time in this manner, she cast a glance at the calabash; but, lo ! it had sprouted—the eel's head had become a young tree with strange leaves ! Grieved at her own folly, she ran to the bank and strove with all her might to pull it up; but could not, for its roots had struck deep.

Uta wept long and bitterly. Perplexed now what to do, with joy she perceived a little messenger-bird from her husband directing her to return. She went back to the king with shame and fear, and related to him all that had befallen her. Tai sadly said to her, "Go back to the place where thou didst see the eel whose head was cut off and deposited in the calabash. Seek for the living, wriggling tail. When found, get a stick and kill it : then come back and tell me."

Uta did as she was desired; but as soon as she entered their dwelling her husband expired in expiation of her sin.

THE IRON-WOOD TREE.

The iron-wood tree (*casuarina*) was originally introduced by the Tongans, and planted in a deep sequestered valley at Tamarua, named Angaruaau. In the course of years it attained to a great size, and the fame of this graceful and stately exotic spread over the island. Oārangi and his four friends, hearing of its various uses in other lands, resolved to appropriate it to themselves, and thus to gain a superiority over the rest of their countrymen. In a secret conference about the matter, some advised Oārangi to have nothing to do with the tree, as it was an impersonation of an evil spirit named Vaotere. Oārangi, however, resolved that the famous tree should come down, in order to furnish him new and better weapons of war.

Thief-like, they started by night on their ill-starred expedition, each provided with a sharp stone axe and a candle-nut torch. Arrived at the hill-side, they easily found the tree, so utterly unlike all others, in its long slender branches and wiry leaves, and towering above all its companions. It had four gigantic roots, gnarled and twisted in fantastic shapes. The torches were placed on the ground around the tree, making the night light as day. The four woodmen zealously set to work upon the four great roots, whilst Oārangi sat at a little distance to watch their progress. From time to time they changed all round, as some made cleaner and deeper cuts than others. But curiously enough, when each returned to the root which had nearly been severed, he found it restored to its original condition, as if no axe had ever touched it. The astonished men desisted awhile to consult with Oārangi, who, resolved to attain his object, advised that each should keep to his own root until entirely severed. Again they plied their axes, and carrying out the advice of Oārangi, they eventually succeeded in their endeavours. At dawn the tree fell to the ground, with a tremendous crash. By full daylight the top had been lopped off, and the ponderous trunk lay on the soil. They had triumphed. They resolved now to return home to rest; to-morrow they would come back to finish their task.

At this moment the four men were taken ill, and began to vomit blood—the redness of the blood answering to the redness of the inner bark of the iron-wood tree which had been so injured by them. They staggered to the stream which winds through the valley, and sought relief in its waters, but kept on vomiting until two of their number died, and their unburied bodies were left in the tall fern.

Oārangi and the two surviving woodmen went off with heavy hearts. Upon reaching the crest of the hill overlooking the scene of their midnight toil, to their utter astonishment they saw that the great tree they had so recently felled was growing as stately as ever. They retraced their steps, in order carefully to note this wonderful phenomenon. There was no mark whatever of an axe on the resuscitated tree ; even the chips all around had disappeared. The tree was restored to its former condition, with this difference, however—the trunk, branches, and leaves were now all of the brightest red : as if resenting the treatment it had received, it bled at every pore.

They slowly wended their way homewards, but ere long the two surviving woodmen fell dead in the road. Oārangi, greatly annoyed at his failure, resolved that his next attempt should be made by daylight, in the hope of better success. With a number of friends he returned one day to the valley in quest of this tree. Upon arriving at the summit of the hill, where the tree could first be seen, their eyes became totally blinded. With difficulty they descended to the bottom of the valley, and wearied themselves in searching for the tree. But after wandering about all day in its immediate neighbourhood, they groped their way homewards at nightfall without having found it at all.

Oārangi had done his utmost, but had been foiled by the

malicious demon of the iron-wood tree, and soon after died.   But was there no one who could overcome Vaotere, and render the wood of the tree useful to mankind?   Ono came from the land whence this tree was originally derived, and had in his possession a remarkable iron-wood spade, named Rua-i-paku = *the-hole-where-it-must-fall*, given to him by his father Ruatea, ere he set out on his voyagings, for any dangerous emergency.   This talisman was very valuable as a club.   Armed with Rua-i-paku, he resolved to do battle with the demon Vaotere.   Upon reaching the shady valley of Angaruaau, he carefully surveyed the coveted tree, and began his operations by digging up the earth about the roots, being careful, however, to avoid injuring any of the main ones. Day after day, entirely unassisted, the brave Ono persevered in his arduous task in pursuing the roots in all their deviations over the valley and hill-side.   Upon their becoming small and unimportant, although exceedingly numerous, he fearlessly chopped them with his famous spade.   The chips flew in all directions, over hill and vale, under his mighty blows.   After many days' toil all the surface roots were bared and severed at their extremities, so that the tree began to totter.   The tap-root alone remained. Ono dug to a great depth into the red soil, and then, at a blow, divided it.   At this critical moment, the head and horrid visage of the evil spirit Vaotere became visible, distorted with rage at being again disturbed.   His open jaws, filled with terrible teeth, prepared to make an end of the impious Ono, who, perceiving his danger, with one well-directed blow of his spade-club luckily succeeded in splitting the skull of Vaotere.

The victorious Ono now leisurely removed the four great gnarled roots which were, in sooth, the arms of the fierce Vaotere, and afterwards divided the enormous trunk—the bleeding body of the demon—into three unequal portions: one to furnish a quantity of long spears, another to be split into *araâ*, or "skull-cleavers;" the third to furnish *aro*, or wooden swords. All this was accomplished by the versatile qualities of Rua-i-paku, which was used first as a spade, then as a club, and now as an axe.

The thousand chips from the small roots of this wonderful tree falling everywhere over hill and valley and sea-shore, originated the iron-wood trees now covering the island : but, happily, Vaotere can no more injure mankind.

Until a few years ago this was believed to be the true origin of all the iron-wood on the island. It is not surprising that the heavy wood which in past times furnished all the deadly implements of war, should have been regarded as the embodiment of an evil spirit. The possession of land and the slaughter of men were alike the result of the use of this famous tree. "Toa" signifies indifferently "iron-wood," and what most resembles it, a "warrior."

A series of songs on the exploits of Ono once existed. They are believed to have been several hundreds of years old. Such compositions are called "pee manuiri," *i.e.* "songs relating to visitors." They are known to be the oldest extant.

The following fragment relates to the preceding myth :—

ONO FELLS A FAMOUS TREE.

TUMU.	INTRODUCTION.
Kotia rai te toa i Vaotere	The iron-wood tree of Vaotere is felled :
Kua aka-inga.	It lies low on the earth.
Tu e tauri te rakau e !	Once it stood erect ; now it is prostrate.

<table>
<tr><td>

PAPA.

Uriuri ana rai
Kua kotia ïa rakau
Uriuria o te vao

Tu e tauri te rakau e !

</td><td>

FOUNDATION.

Turn the log over and over,
The tree thus laid low.
Formerly it was the glory of the
 valley,
Once it stood erect ; now it is pros-
 trate.

</td></tr>
</table>

WANDERINGS OF ONO.

<table>
<tr><td>

TUMU.

Rupitia ra Ono e te matangi,
Tau akera i tai motu.
O te rorongo i kauvare a Iva e !

</td><td>

INTRODUCTION.

Ono tossed about by a tempest,
Eventually reached this isle.
Alas for the haunts of loved Iva !

</td></tr>
<tr><td>

PAPA.

Kua nui ua rai ;
Kua tokarekare rire.
Ka ara Ono iaku nei
 Kauvare a Iva e !

</td><td>

FOUNDATION.

How terrific the ocean !
The waves covered with foam !
A punishment for the sins of Ono.
 Ne'er more will Iva be seen !

</td></tr>
<tr><td>

UNUUNU TAI.

Ka ara ra koe ra iaku nei e !
 Iaku nei e !
E enua tauria e te manu
Kua kai ana i Ono e,
O te ua o te pitai
Kura ra i motu e !
 Kauvare a Iva e !

</td><td>

FIRST OFFSHOOT.

How great must be thy sins
 Against the gods !
This isle is but the home of birds.
Ono is driven to satisfy hunger.
With wild fruits and berries
Growing, ruddy, over this isle.
 Ne'er more will Iva be seen !

</td></tr>
<tr><td>

PAPA RUA.

E ua te matangi
E te matangi tere ariki
 Kauvare a Iva e !

</td><td>

SECOND FOUNDATION.

Through rain and fierce winds,
On a peaceful errand we sail.
 Ne'er more will Iva be seen !

</td></tr>
<tr><td>

UNUUNU RUA.

Tei te matangi tere ariki e,
Nai ariki no Ono e,
Ka araara i Iva nui
E taia e Murake.

</td><td>

SECOND OFFSHOOT.

On a peaceful errand we come,
Ono, denied his regal honours,
Still longs for Iva the Great.
Alas for those slain by Murake !

</td></tr>
</table>

Ka eva ra Ono-kura	Ono the Handsome chants mournful songs
I te puka maru.	Under the shade of the laurel trees.
Kauvare a Iva e !	Ne'er more will Iva be seen !

This song is complete in itself, and is an introduction to the narrative of his exploits and sorrows. The style is very unlike that of later times, when the art of song-making became a national passion. There is no reference to the known history of Mangara. The " Iva " referred to is believed to be Nukuh*iva*.

It was under the rule of the Mautara tribe that the poetical faculty of these islanders was most highly cultivated ; *i.e.* during the past 150 years of their history.

CHAPTER VI.

INA, THE FAIRY VOYAGER.

INA'S VOYAGE TO THE SACRED ISLE.

THE only daughter of Vaitooringa and Ngaetua was Ina, whose brothers were Tangikūkū and Rupe. The parents of Ina were the wealthiest people in the land of Nukutere, boasting as they did of a rich breast ornament, abundance of finely braided hair, beautiful white shells worn on the arms, and—more precious than all these —a gorgeous head-dress, ornamented with scarlet and black feathers, with a frontlet of berries of the brightest red.

Early one morning the parents for the first time left their home in the care of Ina; the mother charging her to put these treasures out to air; but should the sun be clouded, be sure to take them back into the house. For Ngaetua knew well that in the bright beams of the sun the arch-thief Ngana would not dare to come ; but if exposed on a lowering, cloudy day, the envious foe would not fail to try his luck.

In a short time the sun shone brightly ; not a cloud could any-where be seen. The obedient Ina carefully spread out these treasures on a piece of purest white native cloth. But the arch-foe

Ngana was on the watch. Very cautiously did he approach through the neighbouring bushes in order to get a good sight of these much-coveted articles. He forthwith used an incantation, so that the sun suddenly became obscured. Ngana now fearlessly emerged from the thicket and endeavoured to grab the long-wished-for ornaments. But Ina was too quick in her movements to permit this. Ngana now with affected humility begged permission to admire and try on the various ornaments, for her to see how he would look in them. Ina was very loth, but after great persuasion, consented that Ngana should put them on *inside* the house. To prevent the possibility of his taking away any of these treasures, she closed the doors. The crafty Ngana now arrayed himself in these gorgeous adornments, excepting the head-dress, which Ina still held in her hand. Ngana, by his soft words, at length induced her to give *that* up too. Thus completely arrayed he began to dance with delight, and contrived to make the entire circuit of the house, careering round and round in hope of seeing some loophole through which he might escape with his spoil. At last he espied a little hole at the gable end, a few inches wide, through which, at a single bound, he took his flight, and for ever disappeared with the treasures. Ina at first had been delighted with the dancing of her visitor ; but was in utter despair as she witnessed his flight, and heard the parting words :—

Tamu tamu tai tara	Beware of listening to vain words,
E Ina e tou reka.	O Ina, the fair and well-meaning !

Not long afterwards the parents of Ina came back in great haste, for they had seen the arch-thief passing swiftly and proudly through the sky, magnificently attired. A fear crept over them that all was not right with their own treasures. They asked the weeping girl the cause of her tears. She said, "Your choicest possessions are gone." "But is there nothing left?" demanded the parents. "Nothing whatever," said the still weeping Ina. The enraged mother now broke off a green cocoa-nut tree branch and broke it to pieces on the back of the unfortunate girl. Again and again Ngaetua fetched new cocoa-nut branches and cruelly beat Ina. The father now took his turn in belabouring the girl, until a divine spirit ("manu") entered and took possession of Ina, and in a strange voice ominously said—

E kiri taputapu taua kiri ;	Most sacred is my person ;
E kiri akaereere tauá kiri ;	Untouched has been my person ;
E kave au i Motu-tapu	I will go to the Sacred Isle,
Na Tinirau e ta ta i taua kiri.	That Tinirau alone may strike it.

The astonished father desisted : her younger brother Rupe cried over his beloved sister. After a while Ina got up, as if merely to saunter about ; but no sooner had she eluded the eyes of her parents, than she ran as fast as her legs could carry her to the sandy beach. When nearly there, she fell in with her elder brother Tangikūkū, who naturally asked her where she was going. She gave an evasive answer ; but fearing lest he should inform her parents of her flight, she snatched his bamboo fishing-rod, broke it in pieces with her foot, and selected one of the fragments as a knife.[1] She now said to her brother, " Put out your tongue." In an instant she cut off its tip. Tangikūkū vainly essayed to speak ; so that Ina was certain that he could not reveal the secret of her sudden departure. She kissed her maimed brother and pressed on to the shore, where she gazed long and wistfully towards the setting sun, where the Sacred Isle is. Looking about for some means of transit, she noticed at her feet a small

---

[1] The only knife known in these islands formerly, save red flint.

fish named the avini. Knowing that all fishes are subjects to the royal Tinirau, she thus addressed the little avini[1] that gazed at the disconsolate girl :—

Manini tere uta koe i teia manini?	Ah, little fish ! art thou a *shore*-loving avini ?
Manini tere tai koe i teia manini?	Ah, little fish! art thou an *ocean*-loving avini ?
Oro mai takitakina atu au	Come bear me on thy back
Ki taku tane ariki kià Tinirau,	To my royal husband Tinirau,
Matoto atu au i reira.	With him to live and die.

The little fish at once intimated its consent by touching her feet. Ina mounted on its narrow back ; but when only halfway to the edge of the reef, unable any longer to bear so unaccustomed a burden, it turned over, and Ina fell into the shallow water. Angry at this wetting, she repeatedly struck the avini; hence the beautiful stripes on the sides of that fish to this day, called " Ina's tattooing."

The disappointed girl returned to the sandy beach to seek for some other means of transit to the Sacred Isle. A fish named the paoro, larger than the avini, approached Ina. The intended bride of the god Tinirau addressed this fish just as she had the little avini; and then, mounted on its back, started a second time on her voyage. But like its predecessor, the paoro was unable long to endure the burden, and dropping Ina in shallow water sped on its way. Ina struck the paoro in her anger, producing for the first time those beautiful blue marks which have ever since been the glory of this fish.

Ina next tried the api, which was originally white, but for upsetting Ina at the outer edge of the reef was rendered intensely *black*, to mark her disgust at her third wetting.

[1] " Manini " is an old form of " Avini."

She now tried the sole, and was successfully borne to the edge of the breakers, where Ina experienced a fourth mishap. Wild with rage, the girl stamped on the head of the unfortunate fish with such energy that the underneath eye was removed to the upper side. Hence it is that, unlike other fish, it is constrained now to swim flatwise, one side of its face having no eye !

At the margin of the ocean a shark came in sight. Addressing the shark in words very like those formerly used, to her great delight the huge fish came to her feet, and Ina mounted triumphantly on its broad back, carrying in her hand two cocoa-nuts to eat. When halfway on the dangerous voyage to the Sacred Isle, Ina felt very thirsty, and told the shark so. The obedient fish immediately erected its (rārā tua) dorsal fin, on which Ina pierced the eye of one of her nuts. After a time she again became thirsty, and again asked the shark for help. This time the shark lifted its head, and Ina forthwith cracked the hard shell on its forehead. The shark, smarting from the blow, dived into the depths of the ocean, leaving the girl to float as best she could. From that day there has been a marked protuberance on the forehead of all sharks, called " Ina's bump."

The king of sharks, named Tekea the Great, now made his appearance. Ina got on his wide back, and continued her voyage. She soon espied what seemed to be eight canoes in a line rapidly approaching her. When near they proved to be eight sharks resolved to devour Ina. Ina in an agony cried to her guardian shark, " O Tekea! O Tekea !" " What is it ? " inquired the shark. " See the *canoes?* " said the girl. " How many are they ? " " Eight," replied Ina. Said her guardian shark, " Say to them, ' Mangamangaia, mangamangaia aea koe e Tekea Nui ' = ' Get away, or you will be torn to shreds by Tekea the Great.' "

As soon as Ina had uttered these words the eight monstrous sharks made off. Delivered from this peril, Ina again went on her long voyage to the Sacred Isle. But one more danger threatened her: what seemed a fleet of ten canoes, but which proved to be ten ground sharks, started off from the very shores of the Sacred Isle to make an end of Ina. Again they were driven away by the fear of the king of sharks. At length the brave girl reached the long-sought-for Sacred Isle, and Tekea the Great returned to his home in mid-ocean.

Upon going ashore, and cautiously surveying her new home, she was astonished at the salt-water ponds, full of all sorts of fish, everywhere to be seen. Entering the dwelling of Tinirau (= Innumerable), the lord of all fish, she found one noble fish-preserve inside. But strangely enough the owner was nowhere visible. In another part of the house she was pleased to find a great wooden drum, and sticks for beating it by the side. Wishing to test her skill, she gently beat the drum, when to her astonishment the sweet notes filled the whole land, and even reached to Pa-enua-kore (= No-land-at-all), where the god Tinirau was staying that day. The king of all fish returned to his islet dwelling to discover who was beating his great drum. Ina saw him approaching, and in fear ran to hide herself behind a curtain. Tinirau entered and found the drum and sticks all right, but for a time could not discover the fair drummer. He left the house, and was on his way back to No-land-at-all, when the coy girl, unwilling to lose so noble a husband, again beat the wonderful drum. Tinirau came back and found the blushing girl, who became his cherished wife. Ina now discovered that it was the might of Tinirau that inspired her with a "manu," or strange spirit, and then provided for her safety in voyaging to his home in the "sacred islet."

In the course of time Ina gave birth to the famous Koromaū-
ariki, commonly called Koro. Besides this boy she had a girl,
named Ature.

Her younger brother Rupe wished much to see his sister Ina,
who had long since disappeared. Rupe asked a pretty karau-
rau (a bird of the linnet species) kindly to convey him where
Ina lived. The bird consented, and Rupe, entering the linnet,
fled over the deep blue ocean, in search of the Sacred Isle,
where his beloved sister had her home.

It happened one morning that Ina noticed on a bush near her
dwelling a pretty linnet, just such a one as she used to see in her
old home. As she complacently gazed upon it, the bird changed
into a human form. It was Rupe himself! Great was Ina's
delight ; but after a brief stay Rupe insisted on going back to tell
his parents of the welfare of Ina. They were rejoiced to hear of
their daughter, for whom they had long grieved. A feast was
made, and the finest cloth prepared for Ina and her children.
Mother and son now entered two obliging linnets, and laden with
all these good things, flew off over the ocean in search of Ina.
Arrived safely at the Sacred Isle, mother and daughter embraced
each other tenderly; the past was forgiven. Three whole days
were spent in festivities on account of Koro and Ature, the children of Ina. The visitors returned to their home over the sea,
and Ina was left happy with Tinirau the king of all fish.

"Sacred Isle" is an islet in the harbour at Ngatangiia, Rarotonga. "No-land-at-all" is the residence of the chieftainess Pa,
on the mainland.

This very popular legend seems designed to support shark-worship. It is expressly said to be an account of the origin of *tattoo*, although another myth refers *that* to Rongo's ill-treatment of his brother Tangaroa. It is, however, true that the tattooing of this island was simply an imitation of the stripes on the avini and the paoro.

"Tinirau" literally means "forty millions." Doubtless it stands for "*Innumerable*," referring to the impossibility of counting the small fish-spawn supposed to be under his special care at the Sacred Isle. Tinïrau was second son of Vari, The-very-beginning.

This heroine is known as "Ina, daughter of Ngaetua," to distinguish her from the four Inas born of Kui-the-Blind.

SONG OF INA.

TUKA'S CONTRIBUTION TO AKATONU'S FÊTE, CIRCA 1814.

Call for the music and dance to begin.

E manini au na Ina ē !	Here are we, Ina's little fish,[1]
A ta te reu o Tautiti	On whom the *tattoo* was first performed
E paoro ina i te apainga ē !	As we bare her on her voyage.

Solo.

Taipo ē !	Go on !

Chorus.

Riunga atu na ia Tinirau	On her way to Tinirau
Na Ina Tekea i ta ē !	Ina invented *tattooing*.

---

[1] Literally, "Here are we, Ina's *avini* and *paoro*, from which mortals—*i.e.* Mangaians—derive their *tattooing*."

"Te tatau a Rongo,"—*i.e.* "the tattooing of *Rongo*," as opposed to that of *Ina*,—means the bloody marks inflicted by spears in war.

<table>
<tr><td></td><td>*Solo.*</td></tr>
<tr><td>Manini tere uta !</td><td>Ah, thou shore-loving little fish !</td></tr>
<tr><td></td><td>*Chorus.*</td></tr>
<tr><td>Eiā Ina tata ïa i te reu ē,
Motu te tatau ra ē ?</td><td>When did Ina imprint so distinctly
Those lines on thy body?</td></tr>
<tr><td></td><td>*Solo.*</td></tr>
<tr><td>Takitaki atura na te manini aē !</td><td>As I, a little fish, bare her on my back.</td></tr>
<tr><td></td><td>*Chorus.*</td></tr>
<tr><td>Takitaki atu na te manini</td><td>Brave fish that bare her to her husband,</td></tr>
<tr><td>Anau tama it te akatapungā
Tautiti e Koro ē !</td><td>So that she became the happy mother
Of the dance-loving Koro !</td></tr>
</table>

FINAL STANZA OF THE DAY-SONG FOR TENIO'S FÊTE.

BY KOROA, CIRCA 1814.

<table>
<tr><td></td><td>*Solo.*</td></tr>
<tr><td>Ua pururu ua te etu
I maunga Opoa</td><td>The stars have all set
Behind the western hills.</td></tr>
<tr><td></td><td>*Chorus.*</td></tr>
<tr><td>Purui tataka i te ara
Era vaine taia e te matangi.
Tarotaro Ina i te pa ika,
Oro mai ana tatakina 'tu au,
E Tekea, i tau tane ariki
Ia Tinirau i te moana.</td><td>Like a tall solitary tree is the fairy
Who committed herself to the winds.
Ina invoked the aid of many fish
To bear her gaily on their backs ;—
The lordly shark to convey her safely
To the royal Tinirau o'er the sea.</td></tr>
<tr><td>Vāia te upoko, tipitake te akari</td><td>Alas, the bruised head of the angry monster,</td></tr>
<tr><td>I te pane o mango,</td><td>Who hitherto had obeyed the trembling maid,</td></tr>
<tr><td>I te mimi o Ina ia takaviriviri,
Ia tae au i Motutapu.
Titi kaara na Ina.</td><td>Who opened a cocoa-nut
On her voyage to the Sacred Isle.
Softly she beats the drum.</td></tr>
</table>

Ua rongo Tinirau   Tinirau is enchanted
Ua kanga Unga ē ōi !   By the music of the lovely one.

Ka uraura pia ; e ura te tere o Our sport is over : the visit of Tautiti is
  Tautiti,   ended,
E numi te tere o Avaiki ka aere ! The guests from spirit-world are gone !

THE VOYAGE OF INA.

FOR A FEMALE REED-THROWING MATCH, CIRCA 1814.

BY KOROA.

Solo.

Patutu i Tekea Nui   Tap gently the head of the shark king,
Ei tarotaro na Ina ē !   And invoke his aid, fair Ina.

Chorus.

Tena Tane-ere-tue   Here comes Tane-the-fierce
Te apai atu na i te anau ika Driving along shoals of young fish,
I uta i te naupata kura   To cover the white sandy beach
I Motutapu e ia Tinirau   Of the " sacred islet " of Tinirau.

Solo.

Tinirau taua tanē !   Yes, Tinirau, my future husband.

Chorus.

Aore au e keu i to Iva tangata. I will be no bride to the men of Iva.
Ua ii i te kare i te matangi. My feet are wet with the ocean waves.
I te moana i Rangiriri—   Foam-sprinkled I press on to Rangiriri,[1]
I Rangiriri te aroaro ariki. To Rangiriri, the home of my royal
            husband.

Solo.

Aroaro ariki i kakea ē !   At the home of my husband I land.

Chorus.

Oro mai tapoki ake au.   Come, throw a garment o'er me.
Te āni maira Ina Paenuakore ; Ina has reached No-land-at-all ;
Pou enua tapu i taea mai nei. A sacred spot attained by few.

---

[1] The name of a place at Rarotonga, near the Sacred Isle.

THE TAAIRANGI, OR PORPOISE.

Vātea, the elder brother of Tinirau, lived in The-thin-land, and was lord of the ocean ; whilst Tinirau, whose home was the Sacred Isle, was king of all fish—from the shark to the tiniest minnow. The taairangi, or porpoise, was not counted with other fish, as it is covered with pure fat or blubber. How came this to be so ? Why, Vātea himself, half fish and half man, imitating the conduct of their great mother Vari-ma-te-takere, *i.e. The-very-beginning*, tore off a portion of his own person, and made it into a porpoise. Thus the porpoise is of necessity unlike all other fish. Whales were often seen but never tasted on Mangaia in heathenism. Had they been obtained, these islanders might have learnt that other fish besides the " sky caught " are covered with pure fat.

As the ocean was the undisputed property of Vātea, it soon became alive with taairangi sporting about in it. Tinirau became jealous of this magnificent ocean fish-pond, seeing that his own subjects were in danger of dying in the too contracted, though very numerous, fish-ponds of the Sacred Isle. So he craved his brother's permission to let some of his small fish go into the great sea. Vātea would consent only on one condition —that Tinirau would add a portion of *his* own territory of the Sacred Isle to the land of Vātea. With immense difficulty this was accomplished—the two brother gods had to get under the Sacred Isle, in order to break off a part of it. This done, Tinirau liberated a portion of his finny population, and thus the ocean became swarming, not only with the great half-divine taairangi, but with fish of all sorts and sizes.

THE FINNY SUBJECTS OF TINIRAU.

BY TEREAVAI, FOR HIS FÊTE, 1823.

Call for dancing and music to lead off.

Vaia mai i te akeke i Aitutaki

Throw open the fish-ponds of Aitu-taki [1]

O te pa ika na Tinirau e Koro ē !

Where sport the fish of Tinirau and Koro.

Solo.

Taipo ē !

Go on !

Chorus.

Vaia mai te tino ika nei, e Vātea,

Tear off part of the half-fish body of Vātea,

Ei taairangi, e Tanē !

That it may become a porpoise, O Tane.

Solo.

Aē !

Aye.

Chorus.

E utu oki i te kava rauriki,
E roaka mai ai.

Pour out a libation of " *kava*,"
To win the favour of the gods.

Solo.

Vaia mai ē i te akeke aē !

Yes, throw open the fish-preserves.

Chorus.

Vaia mai i te akeke ;
Tei te moana te ikatauira a Tanē.

Throw them all open, O Tane,
That the little fish may sport in the ocean.

Solo.

Aē !

'Tis done.

Chorus.

Takave mai i te uru kare

See, they are borne on the crest of the billows,

Na Tane-ere-tuē,
Ka aere e tauri atu i te akau.

Driven by Tane-the-Fierce,
And are lying in shoals on the reef.

---

[1] The Sacred Isle is here confounded with Aitutaki, both lands apparently lying in the vast unknown.

NUMERATION AND THE ART OF FISHING INVENTED.

Vātea prepared an enormous net which he entrusted to six fishermen, the first of their order. But the subjects of his brother Tinirau were too crafty to be easily caught. Day after day the finny tribes were hunted in vain. At length the aid of Raka, the god of winds, was invoked to make the surface of the ocean rough, and thus to hide the great net of Vātea from the sight of the fish below. Their younger brother, Raka, willingly lent his aid, and the net was completely filled ; but it was not in the power of the six fishermen to hold the net. Tane, son of the great Vātea, came to the rescue, and resolutely held on to the captive fishes. Eight days and nights the finny prisoners raced through the wide ocean, carrying the net with them. At last they became exhausted, and Tane exultingly dragged the rich spoil to the feet of his father. Vātea turned out the fish one by one, pronouncing for the first time the various names by which each kind has since been known; and thus, also, originating the useful art of counting. At last, utterly wearied with reckoning, he gave up the remainder as being in truth innumerable. The exhausted inhabitants of the ocean lay in heaps on the reef and sandy beach until the rising tide carried them out again to their proper element, none the worse for this first experiment in fishing.

THE ORIGIN OF DANCING.

Tinirau and his son Koro, whose proper home was at the Sacred Isle, occasionally lived on the northern part of Mangaia. The son had repeatedly noticed that his father disappeared by night, and remained away from their home two or three days at a time.   Where the sire went was a mystery.   One thing greatly attracted the admiration of Koro; whenever his father came back, he was adorned with a fresh necklace of fragrant pandanus seeds, yellow and red.   Determined to solve this mystery, one night Koro craftily hid away Tinirau's girdle, and then lay down to sleep.   Not long afterwards the old man sought everywhere for his girdle—but in vain.   At last he woke up his boy, who rose and gave it to his father.   Koro pretended to go to sleep again, but, in reality, was narrowly watching his father's movements. Tinirau having adjusted his royal girdle, went outside; and in a short time Koro slipped out unperceived, and hid himself in the shadow of the house.   The old man now passed over his ankles some strong bark in the usual fashion, and climbed a cocoa-nut tree.   But to the great astonishment of Koro, he used only his right hand, and did not even permit his chest to touch the tree itself.   Tinirau twisted off the ripe nuts one by one, and throwing them on the ground descended, as he had gone up, with the assistance of *only one hand.*   On reaching the ground, still with one hand, he husked the nuts, clave them in two, and scraped out their contents upon the broad leaf of a variety of gigantic taro [1] called "pongi."   This finely grated cocoa-nut was then carefully wrapped up in the same great leaf, and secured with bark string, was carried by Tinirau to the sea, a distance of a mile, over rough rocks, by a narrow path overhung with lofty trees.   On reaching the beach, he took up his station on a point of rock, still called Akatangi, or *the-calling-place,* and which runs into the waters of the reef.   Koro hid himself in the low bushes growing out of the sand a few yards behind his sire.   " The king of all fish "

---

[1] Arum costatum.

now liberally scattered the scraped cocoa-nut over the waters whilst chanting a long incantation to his finny subjects. Koro quickly caught up the words, and treasured them in his memory for his own use at some future period. To the infinite delight of the son, the smaller inhabitants of the reef at once obeyed the call of their lord, and came to taste the food provided for their entertainment. At length the voice of Tinirau was heard by the larger fish in the great ocean, who hurried to the feet of their sovereign. Ere the incantation ended, the Sacred Isle itself came bodily from its proper place to the edge of the reef! Thus the entire throng of Tinirau's obedient subjects assembled on the moving Sacred Isle, and changing their forms into a partial resemblance to human beings, came dancing to meet their lord— who, being himself in his true attributes, half man and half fish, gladly united with them in their dance, which was of the famous sort called "Tautiti," in which hands and feet all move at the same time. The subjects, like their sovereign, were all arrayed in necklaces of sweet-scented pandanus seeds, which grow plentifully over the native home of Tinirau. The Sacred Islet, king, finny subjects and all, started off, and were speedily lost to sight in the distant ocean. Koro returned home to the interior, satisfied as to the real cause of his father's frequent disappearance in past times.

A day or two afterwards Tinirau returned to his son, all fragrant as before, with a pandanus fruit necklace, but entirely ignorant that Koro had witnessed his proceedings on his last visit to the Sacred Isle. It was some time ere "the king of fish" started off again on a midnight expedition; but when he did so he did not escape the vigilance of his watchful son, who was anxious to perfect his knowledge of the necessary invocations.

Again with a single hand the old man climbed the tree, threw down the nuts, and descended to the ground. Again he traversed the lonely path to the sea by moonlight, carrying with him a great quantity of finely scraped cocoa-nut. At the projecting piece of rock overlooking the ocean he scattered food for his marine children. The invocation over, fish, islet, and all came again to the feet of the mighty Tinirau, who exultingly joined his merry subjects in their favourite employment of dancing by moonlight. Koro gained his object : he had learned the magic words, and therefore went home well satisfied with himself. On the following night he, in his turn, climbed a cocoa-nut as his father had done, and then carried the finely scraped kernel to "the calling place" where Tinirau had performed his wonderful feats. Now was the time to test his own powers as the son of the king of all fish. Reciting the prayers, he scattered the rich food on the waters, when, to his delight, the fish obeyed the summons, swimming in shoals to his feet. The Sacred Isle, too, with all its vast preserves of fish, soon hove in sight. Amongst its finny inhabitants he had the joy of recognizing his own father, Tinirau, in the merry throng of moonlight dancers. Koro at once joined this novel assembly, when his father greeted him thus : "Son, this, then, is why you hid away my girdle."

Arrayed like the rest in beautiful necklaces of fragrant pandanus berries, father and son that night, and ever after when so inclined, enjoyed the pleasure of a prolonged midnight dance with their finny subjects on the Sacred Isle. It was the renowned Koro who conferred on the inhabitants of Mangaia the favour of planting the first pandanus tree close to the spot (Akatangi) where he was accustomed to summon his scaly friends. He instructed the inhabitants in the mysteries of dancing. His time was spent half at the Sacred Isle and half on the northern shore of Mangaia, which is thence named Atua-Koro,[1] *i.e. the land of the divine Koro.*"

A SONG FOR TENIO'S FÊTE.

BY VAARUA, CIRCA 1814.

Call for the dance to begin.

Tautiti au ē !	I am Tautiti.
O te ara ra i Taipau, e Tanē !	O Tane, the fragrant pandanus on the beach is mine.

Solo.

Taipo ē !	Go on !

Chorus.

Tanumia te ara i te Atuakoro ē !	That fragrant tree was first planted by the divine Koro.

Solo.

Aē !	Aye !

Chorus.

Tautiti rava ki tonga makatea oopu.	Tautiti's favourite wreaths grow in yon gullies.

Solo.

Nai makatea oopu ē !	Yes, in those gullies grow
O te ara kura o Tautiti ei mai ē !	Red pandanus berries to adorn the dance.

---

[1] Every return of March shoals of bream (ature) find their way to Atua-Koro. The name of Tinirau's daughter is *Ature.* Of course there is a play upon the name of the beautiful silvery fish which every year visits that part, *and that only*, of the island, *as if* the sister and her attendants were paying a visit to the chosen home of her brother Koro.

<table>
<tr><td align="center">UNUUNU TAI.</td><td align="center">FIRST OFFSHOOT.</td></tr>
</table>

	Solo.
E māu te ara ē tei Taipau aē !	Groves of pandanus cover yon sandy beach.

Chorus.

E māu te ara i Taipau,
No Tautiti kake mai ē !

Yes, groves of fragrant pandanus
For Tautiti, whenever he may come up.

Solo.

Aē !   Aye.

Chorus.

Tere maira te ara no tai tuamotu ē !

This famous tree came from some other isle,

Patiki io i te kea ē !

To grace the sacred sandstone.

Solo.

Patiki io i te kea ē !
O te ara ra i Taipau, e Tanē !

Yes, to grace the sacred sandstone.
O Tane, the fragrant pandanus on the beach is mine.

Solo.

Taipo ē !   Go on !

Chorus.

Tanumia te ara i te Atuakoro ē !

That fragrant tree was first planted by the divine Koro.

Solo.

Aē !   Aye !

Chorus.

Tautiti rava ki tonga i makatea oopu

Tautiti's favourite wreaths grow in yon gullies.

Solo.

Nai makatea, oopu ē !
O te ara kura o Tautiti ei mai ē !

Yes, in those gullies grow
Red pandanus berries to adorn the dance.

UNUUNU RUA.   SECOND OFFSHOOT.

Solo.

E te opu, e te opu !   Entwine sweet-scented fern-leaves.

Chorus.

Eaa ra ?   Eaa ra ?   What is going on yonder ?

Solo.

Tei tai !   Tei tai   At the margin of the sea ?

Chorus.

Ae !   Ae !   Aye !   Aye !

Solo.

A kitea !   A kitea !   The god reveals himself !

Chorus.

Tautiti kake mai.   Tautiti himself has come up (out
                                        of nether-world)

Solo.

Kitea mai, e Tane ē !   O Tane, he stands revealed !

Chorus.

Maniania, o maau tara mea.   Pleasure thrills through my body.

Solo.

Maaraara 'i au ē !   I would I were
O te iva taumara a te rā ē !   A dragon-fly exulting in the sun
                                        beam.

CHAPTER VII.

MISCELLANEOUS MYTHS.

A BACHELOR GOD IN SEARCH OF A WIFE.

AMONGST the thirteen principal gods of Mangaia which at the establishment of Christianity were surrendered to the missionaries were four bearing the name of Tane.[1] They were simply pieces of iron-wood carved roughly into the human shape, once well wrapped up in numerous folds of the finest native cloth. Of these four Tanes three—Tane Ngakiau, Tane-i-te-ata, and Tane Kió—were considered to be inferior to the first, who was usually called Tane, sometimes, however, Tane Papa-kai, *i.e. Tane-piler-up-of-food.* In order of rank Tane came after Rongo and Motoro, the chief deities of Mangaia. Tane was said to be the fifth son of Vātea, born in Avaiki, or nether-world. The following is the extravagant myth of Tane's exploits when in search of a wife.

At Ukupolu there lived a woman named Tekura-i-Tanoa, *i.e. The-ruddy-one of Tanoa*, possessed of uncommon attractions.

---

[1] Tane = husband, or the generative principle in nature. Tane is equivalent to בַּעַל. Innumerable modifications of this dance-loving god were worshipped throughout eastern Polynesia.

But she had one sad defect,—her right foot was afflicted with elephantiasis. The chief Ako was violently in love with her; but the fair one disdained his advances, saying, "If it had been *Tane,* she would have thought favourably of the proposition." Now Ako was a great friend of Tane's; so that he at once paddled off to Avaiki to fetch Tane, who cheerfully consented to accompany him. The two friends started for Ukupolu, each in his own canoe. A day or two after their arrival Ako confessed to Tane the real motive of getting him to pay a visit to Ukupolu, and earnestly entreated his assistance in winning The-ruddy-one of Tanoa. Tane good-humouredly promised his aid.

Ako had two sisters, to whom he applied for two garlands for the neck, of sweet-scented flowers—one for himself and one for his friend, against their projected visit to the inexorable beauty. The sisters were to arrange it so that the fragrant garland intended for Ako should have numerous sprigs of myrtle intermixed with the flowers; whilst Tane's should be spoiled by the admixture of offensively smelling leaves. When tastefully arranged, these garlands were carefully enclosed in a thin white layer of the banana stalk, according to the invariable custom of the olden times. A mark was set upon the outside, so as to prevent mistake. Now Tane was a god, and was not to be deceived in this way. Accordingly, when these friends, now become at heart rivals in love, were both arrayed in their best garments, and their hair glistening with sweet-scented oil, Tane took out the fragrant garland of flowers and put it on. Ako, to his dismay, perceived that his crafty friend had by some means got possession of the best garland: being thus outwitted, he declined to put on his own, lest Tane should twit him with his ill-faith. Off these rivals started to the dwelling of The-ruddy-one of Tanoa. Tane first entered, bearing in his hands a gift consisting of several highly-scented garments ; the rich perfume filled the house. Ako now made his appearance. Each pleaded his suit with great earnestness, for Tane was at first sight smitten with the charms of the fair girl. But the capricious Tekura-i-Tanoa accepted the advances of Ako, and Tane retired in disgust. He resolved to return at once to Avaiki. With this purpose in view he walked to the sandy beach to launch his canoe and start for his home ; but upon examination found a large hole in its bottom made by his treacherous friend Ako. Tane sat down and loudly bewailed his misfortunes in these words :—

Kua viivii e ! Kua vavaiia ra tañ vaka e Ako	Unhappy me ! My canoe has been destroyed by Ako.
I tua o Avaiki. Ringiringiia toku nei roimata	How shall I return to Avaiki ? I will rain down my tears.

Tane fell musing what he had best do. Upon looking up he now for the first time noticed a gigantic *bua* tree (*beslaria laurifolia*) spreading forth its noble branches. In a trice Tane got up the trunk of this tree and clambered to the extremity of one of the longest branches. Tane gave the far-stretching limb on which he sat a mighty jerk, and thus swung himself fairly into another land, Enuakura, *i.e. The-land-of-red-parrot-feathers.* After walking about this newly discovered land, he came upon an old woman named Kui-the-Blind, who was busy cooking yams on a fire. In all she had ten yams cooking ; at her side were ten calabashes of water. After awhile the old blind woman took a yam off the fire and scraped it clean with a cockle shell. She then devoured the entire yam, washing it down with a calabash of water. But Kui-the-Blind did not know that the moment she took up a yam, Tane helped himself too, and at the same time emptied a calabash of water.

The old woman had no sooner finished her first yam and her first calabash of water, than she carefully counted the remainder with her fingers, when to her amazement she found a yam and a calabash missing. She angrily exclaimed, " What thief has come here ? Had I my sight I would devour him."

Having thus vented her indignation, she ate another yam and drank another calabash of water; Tane helping himself in silence as before. Again the old woman counted the remaining yams and calabashes with her fingers, and found that only six of each remained. Once more she gave vent to her anger against the unknown thief. Tane uttered not a word to reveal his presence. In this way the ten yams and ten calabashes of water disappeared. Each time Kui-the-Blind missed a yam and a calabash of water her anger grew hotter. At last her meal, but half the usual quantum, was finished, and she resolved upon immediate vengeance. Accordingly, she rose and entering her house felt in the accustomed place for her *great-fish-hook*, which she had never yet used in vain. Whilst adjusting the long line she slowly chanted this ominous couplet :—

Oi au ka rave, ka rave i te tautai a Kui matapo.
Aā poiri i te ika a te tupuna e ! Ara tatia

Here am I about to fish. It is the angling of Kui-the-Blind.
The old woman must have her *fish* (*i.e.* human victim). Here goes for it !

As she uttered these last words she violently swung round the dreadful sharp-pointed fish-hook. Tane, prepared for this, held in his hand a banana stump to catch the hook, which he retained for a second, deluding Kui into the belief that she had caught the struggling thief. The malicious old creature pulled vigorously at the line, hoping to get a victim to eat, when she grasped a miserable banana-stalk. Chafing with indignation at her failure, she disengaged the stump and again whirled the hook, uttering the same words. This time a low bush, bearing edible red berries, was used by Tane to tease the old woman. Kui pulled away at her hook with great satisfaction, but found only a bush. Her anger now knew no bounds, having never before missed her victim. A third time she threw her hook, using the old formula. This time Tane allowed himself to be caught. Kui was delighted that she had at last secured the thief. She grabbed him tightly whilst demanding his name. He calmly said, " I am Tane." Kui instantly forgot her anger, and exclaimed, " Why, you are my own grandson Tane ! Stay with me."

Some time afterwards Tane, again feeling very thirsty, asked his old grandmother for some water to drink. Kui-the-Blind said, " There is no water in this country, save in the nuts of yonder tall cocoa-nut tree. But you had better not attempt to climb it, or you will surely die. You will be slain by my children, the guardians of the tree, viz. the lizard, the centipede, the beetle, and the mantis." Tane resolved to climb the tree, whose top seemed to reach the sky. Kui said to the fearless Tane as he began to ascend, " Do not injure my children who live in this tree." This solitary cocoa-nut tree, the property of the blind grandmother, was remarkable for the wonderful profusion of fruit on it, and for a great accumulation of dry branches underneath the green limbs. In these withered branches were hidden the fairy guardians of the fruit, excepting the mantis, who kept watch on the under side of the green leaves. Their duty was to see that no one stole any of the fruit. At the sight of the intruder Tane climbing up the tree, a large *lizard* advanced boldly from its hiding-place to drive him away. Tane caught the lizard, tore it in two, and threw the pieces down. Tane now began to clear off the dry branches and cloth-like coverings, when a great *centipede* came out wrathfully intending to sting Tane to death. But the brave grandson of Kui deliberately killed this foe also. The dry branches were falling in all directions, and the work was nearly completed, when a feeble *beetle* came forth to defend the precious fruit. But the beetle speedily shared the fate of the lizard and centipede ; and Tane climbed up into the great living fronds and sat down to rest awhile. At this moment a *mantis*, of unendurable smell, assailed the intruder, spreading out its gay red wings ; but Tane served the mantis as he had already served the others. Thus he had conquered all foes. With great admiration he viewed the vast clusters of nuts on every side. Plucking two or three of the nuts, he husked them on the "rōrō," or unopened sheath,[1] containing the young flowers and fruits.

Tane leisurely slaked his thirst. Then violently swinging this lofty cocoa-nut tree until its top hung over the very land where Tane's home was, he shook off all the nuts as food against the day of his return. But Tane still kept his place at the top of the wonderful tree, which, rebounding, resumed its former position in Enuakura, The-land-of-red-parrot-feathers. There remained on the tree only two tiny nuts, each about the size of a small pebble. Tane plucked them, and descending to the ground, said to Kui, "Turn your face towards me." The old woman

---

[1] It is an interesting fact, of which thieves do not fail to avail themselves in seasons of scarcity, that it is quite practicable to husk the hardest cocoa-nut and pierce the eyelet upon the point of the closed sheath referred to, without descending to the ground. Ordinarily a sharp stake is fixed in the earth near the foot of the tree for the purpose of husking the nuts that are thrown down ; but nature has provided a sharp-pointed stake at the top of the tree, where the nuts grow, and the climber finds a sure foothold for cases of emergency.

did so, when she received a smart blow on her *right* eye from one of the nuts. She cried out in agony; but in a second found her sight restored.

Tane again said to Kui, "Look at me." Upon doing so, she received a blow on her *left* eye from the remaining nut. Her anguish was extreme; but the reward was great, for she could now see well with *both* her eyes.

Kui was delighted with the achievements of her grandson, for she who had hitherto been called Kui-the-Blind, was now Kui-the-Seeing. Tane asked her, "Have you any daughters?" "Yes," said Kui, "I have four. Take whichever you please as your wife." Now all these daughters were at some distance at work. After a short time the eldest, named Ina, came and was not a little surprised to see a stranger and to find her mother's sight restored. Tane was not pleased with Ina, who subsequently married the moon (Marama Nui).

Tane now inquired after the other daughters of Kui. The second soon made her appearance; it was Ina-who-disappears-with-the-day. Though fair, she did not please Tane. Kui called her third daughter Ina-who-disappears-at-midnight. She was very lovely, yet did not captivate the fastidious Tane. "I have but one daughter more," remarked Kui. "I will summon her." She came: it was Ina-who-rivals-the-dawn. She was, as her name implied, surpassingly beautiful. She became the wife of Tane, who considered himself to be well recompensed for restoring sight to Kui, once called The-blind.

But, after a time, Ina became jealous of her husband. They quarrelled, and Tane resolved to return to his own land. With this view he climbed up the famous cocoa-nut tree, the glory of The-land-of-red-feathers, and brought down a frond, which he wove into a basket of the sort known as the "clam-shaped," *i.e.* without an opening. He now procured a second frond, and therewith wove a second basket of a similar shape. Fastening one to each arm, he used these long baskets as wings, and with their friendly aid took his final flight to his own land Avaiki, from which he had so long been absent, and thus escaped from the tongue of the lovely but jealous Ina-who-rivals-the-dawn.

The scene of this story is laid in nether-land. This myth unquestionably points to Samoa, the group from which these people originally came. "Ukupolu" is evidently Upolu, and "Avaiki" is only another form of Savai'i.

Stories like this constituted the esoteric teaching of the priests of Motoro and Tane. The Polynesian idea of a god is mere *power*, without any reference to goodness. Their gods had all the faults of heathen men and women in an exaggerated degree.

The centipede, lizard, etc., were sacred; hence their appearance in the myth as minor divinities.

ECHO; OR, THE CAVE FAIRY.

Rangi was the first man; for Vātea was half man and half fish, and lived in the invisible world. When Rangi complacently surveyed the land which he had succeeded in dragging up from the shades, he resolved to explore every nook and corner, to ascertain whether there were any other inhabitants in his territory.

After travelling some distance along the northern division of the island without discovering the slightest trace of any living creature, he approached a romantic pile of rocks overhanging a tremendous gorge, by which the waters of the neighbouring valleys discharge themselves into the ocean. A number of caves converge at this point, the pathway to which is obstructed by vast boulders.

Here Rangi shouted, as was his wont, "Ōō" ("Hallo, there!"). To his surprise a voice from the rocks distinctly replied, "Ōō." Rangi asked, "What is your name?" Instead of a satisfactory reply, came the defiant query, "What is *your* name?" Rangi, bursting with indignation, now demanded of this unseen fellow-resident, "Whence do you come?" Still the invisible speaker declined to reveal herself; and the ears of Rangi were assailed with the irritating words, "Whence do *you* come?" Unable to endure this any longer, he cursed the hidden inhabitant of the cave, nicknaming her "Aitu-mamaoa," *i.e. the-ever-distant*, or *the-hide-and-seek-spirit;* but forthwith heard himself cursed in exactly the same tone and words. Evidently this satirical, unseen being was no respecter of persons. Rangi fell immeasurably in his own estimation at being thus unceremoniously addressed, and felt sure that it was intended as a reflection upon his illegitimate origin.

The first sovereign of Mangaia now resolved, at any cost, to get a sight of the insolent creature pertinaciously hiding in the rocks. Cautiously leaping from boulder to boulder, he entered the gorge, inquiring as he proceeded, for the hitherto invisible inhabitant; but receiving for his pains only sarcastic replies. The chasm grew darker and narrower, but Rangi bravely kept on his way. Upon suddenly looking up, to his astonishment, he found that the semi-circular roof was everywhere covered with transparent glittering pendants (stalactites), white, like a row of formidable teeth, almost touching his person, drops of cold water meanwhile falling like rain upon the stone flooring. Underneath

was a row of stumps (stalagmites), rising from the basement of the
the cave. Awe-stricken at the sight of these vast open jaws,
apparently about to swallow him up, he instinctively retreated a
few steps, and, looking up once more, for the first time caught
a glimpse of the face of a female fairy, heartily laughing at his terror.

As soon as Rangi recovered his equanimity, he inquired the
proper name of this formidable apparition. Her reply was, "I
am *Tumuteanaoa*," or Echo (literally, "the-cave-speaking-sprite").
"I am the being that everywhere inhabited the rocks of Mangaia
ere you set feet on the soil." Rangi now asked whether she had
any children. Echo replied, "I have a very numerous offspring,
named *Tumu-te-crue ma*, or Earth-diggers." "Where are they?"
demanded the inquisitive king. "They are on the mountains,
roaming about in the fern," replied the complaisant spirit of the
cave.

Rangi now left Echo, and went in search of her children. He
had not advanced far up the side of the nearest mountain, tramp-
ling down the fern and tall reeds, when he came upon a troop of
these "earth-diggers," or *rats!* Rangi wondered that the progeny
were so unlike their mother, who could on no account be per-
suaded to leave her favourite haunts in the rocks.

The cave where Rangi first made the acquaintance of Tumuteanaoa, or Echo, was thenceforth named Aitu-mamaoa,[1] or the
home of the ever-distant, or hide-and-seek spirit.

---

[1] The writer, in company with the Rev. J. Chalmers, once explored
Aitu-mamaoa for half a mile, until the torches were nearly burnt out and
the roof necessitated a creeping posture. About midway a running stream
crossed our path. We sung a number of hymns, and were delighted to hear,
at a great height above our heads in utter darkness, a most perfect echo—
as if an unseen choir were singing in perfect unison with our torch-lit
company.

In the course of his subsequent explorations, Rangi often met with this notable nymph Echo, who seemed to be ubiquitous, and learnt that besides the "earth-diggers" in the dry grass and fern of the mountains, she had another numerous offspring inhabiting the valleys and the dark waters of the little lake in Veitatei, viz., shrimps, eels, and other fresh-water fish abounding there and in the interior gorges and chasms of the adjacent rocks—her own constant resort.

Rangi thus found that his little world was already teeming with inhabitants, all descended from the great Tumu-te-ana-oa. No disturbance or difficulty ever arose therefrom, as Echo was a nymph of a gentle and harmless disposition; her only fault being that she was a little satirical when addressed by strangers.

It was often contested by the sages of former times, whether Rangi, after all, was rightly designated the first inhabitant of Mangaia, seeing that he found Echo already in possession of the rocks and caves. They came at last to the conclusion, that whilst Rangi was the first *man* and king, Echo was the first and parent *fairy*—the numerous sprites inhabiting rocks, valleys, hills, and streams constituting the prolific progeny of "the cave speaking sprite."

At the Marquesas, to this day, divine honours are paid to Echo, who is supposed to give them food, and who "speaks to the worshippers out of the rocks."

THE PRINCE OF REED-THROWERS.

Upon one occasion Tangaroa chanced to see the lovely Ina-ani-vai, *i.e. Ina-solicited-at-the-fountain*, bathing at a stream named Kapuue-rangi, and at once became enamoured of her charms. The god unfastened his girdle, which mortals call the rainbow, and by this dazzling pathway descended to earth. The fair but frail Ina could not resist the advances of the great Tangaroa; and in the course of time she gave birth to Tarauri and Turi-the-Bald. She chose to live apart from her friends, so that the divine origin of her offspring was long unsuspected. Both Tarauri and Turi were flaxen-haired.

There was at the same time a man named Pinga, whose seven sons were alike noted for their shortness of stature and for their proficiency in the art of reed-throwing.[1] The clever dwarf sons of Pinga induced Turi-the-Bald to try his luck in this game. Again and again was Turi beaten by the clever sons of Pinga, so that he wept with vexation and shame.

Now the elder brother had taken no part in these games. But he was distinguished for his skill in wrestling with lads of his own age, and for catching a small fresh-water fish, called kokopu, abounding in the tiny streams which thread the valleys. The mode of angling said to have been invented by Tarauri, and still in use amongst enterprising lads, was curious. The leaves of the pandanus, or thatch, tree are furnished with somewhat formidable thorns. The serrated edges of a stout leaf are pared off; the

---

[1] On Mangaia this popular game was practised by men, the women being spectators; or by women, the men being spectators: *never* by men and women together, as in some islands.

narrow pieces are then carefully tied together with a bit of hibiscus bark, care being taken that there be at least two thorns or tiny fish-hooks on either side, and that these little hooks point upwards. The slit midrib of a long cocoa-nut frond furnishes the fishing rod—the thorny hooks being secured to the tapering end. The sport is enjoyed wherever the stream is dammed up for the purpose of irrigating the little taro-patches of the valleys, or to enable women and children the more easily to fill their empty calabashes with water. The voracious little kokopu leaps to catch the bait—its favourite morsel, the shrimp—when it finds itself a prisoner on one of the thorns of this quaint fish-hook.

The " seven dwarf sons of Pinga " were delighted with the adroitness of Tarauri, although as yet his name and that of his brother were unknown. Pinga desired his sons to ask the lads their names,—a most unpleasant task to a South Sea Islander. The boys good-naturedly told their names, but did not reveal the secret of their divine origin. As soon as Pinga heard their names, he astonished his " seven dwarf sons " by exclaiming, " Why, these are my grand-children ! Bring them here."

Very willingly did the lads take up their abode with their newly-found grandfather for a while. One day " the seven dwarf sons of Pinga " made preparations for their favourite amusement of reed-throwing, purposing this time to measure their skill with Tarauri himself. They started off to the deepest recesses of the valleys, where the longest reeds grow. Tarauri, with affected modesty, declined to accompany his seven dwarf uncles, saying to them, " Your broken reeds will be good enough for a clumsy fellow like me." After a while they returned, each with a bundle of fine reeds, and sat down to get them ready. First of all it was necessary to secure with a piece of strong bark the *thick* end of the reed, which might strike against a stone and be broken. Then the *smaller* end was nicely rounded, so as not to injure the finger of the player; finally, the reeds were slightly singed over a fire, in order to render them perfectly straight.

The game commenced; but still Tarauri was without a single reed (tao). "The seven dwarf sons of Pinga," having each thrown his reed, called upon Tarauri to come forward and try *his* luck. They were all on the tiptoe of expectation to see what he would do in this emergency. Tarauri rose from the ground, and advancing towards the appointed place for throwing, thus invoked the aid of his father Tangaroa :—

Kauō iake, kauō iake,
Uō iake te mārama, te mārama,
Ia Ruanuku e, Ruanuku ma Tangaroa,

Omai taku tao, ei teka nāku,
Ei teka ki te taua ē !

Oh, be propitious, oh, be propitious,
Grant me light and success.
Great Ruanuku, associated with Tangaroa,
Send me a reed for this game,
That the victory may be mine !

At these last words there fell from the skies at the feet of Tarauri a noble reed, perfectly straight, and gaily adorned with red-parrot feathers, the first ever seen on the island. Thus the divine parentage of Tarauri was discovered. Confidently advancing to the place for throwing the reeds, Tarauri swung his arms jauntily in preparation, and again invoked divine aid :—

Apai na, apai na rava ïa, e Tarauri, i te tai karongata,
Taki na uri e kai ai, e rere ai ē, tu arangaranga,
Apai na, e Tangaroa, to manga !

Bear it away, oh, bear it far away, for Tarauri's sake, to the treacherous ocean.
Guide the flight of my reed, that it may rise to a dizzy height.
Great Tangaroa, here goes thine own !

At this, "the seven dwarf sons of Pinga," dreading a disgrace to themselves, rushed to encircle Tarauri, so as to render it apparently impossible for him to exhibit his divinely acquired superiority in the art of reed-throwing over these well-practised but mere human players. A second time the invocation was repeated to Tangaroa, but again the jealousy of his newly-found relatives prevented him from throwing his gaily ornamented reed. A pause ensued, when Tarauri observing that the legs of one of the seven were a little open, in an instant drove the heaven-sent reed through the gap of the living enclosure. Wonderful, indeed, was the flight of the reed : it rose and rose in the air until lost in the azure skies, where it remained *eight whole days !* At last the slender shaft fell at Areuna,[1] the original marae of the Mautara, or priestly tribe. Thus did Tangaroa redeem the disgrace of his younger son Turi-the-Bald. And great, indeed, was the chagrin of " the seven dwarf sons of Pinga " to be thus beaten by young Tarauri, who thus at his first trial, aided by his divine parent, proved himself to be the true patron and chief of all reed-players.

By some this myth is placed in " the land of Ukupolu," *i.e.* Upolu. The very archaic form of the invocations attests the antiquity of this story.

Of the many songs for reed-matches, none would be complete without a reference to Tarauri the chief patron of the game.

---

[1] Areuna is on the south of the island, and is regarded as the ancient home of the priests of Motoro, who swayed Mangaia—as priests first, and afterwards as chiefs—down to the establishment of Christianity.

The early part of this myth may serve to explain why in heathenism all illegitimate children were designated " tamariki na te Atua," *i.e. children of the gods.*

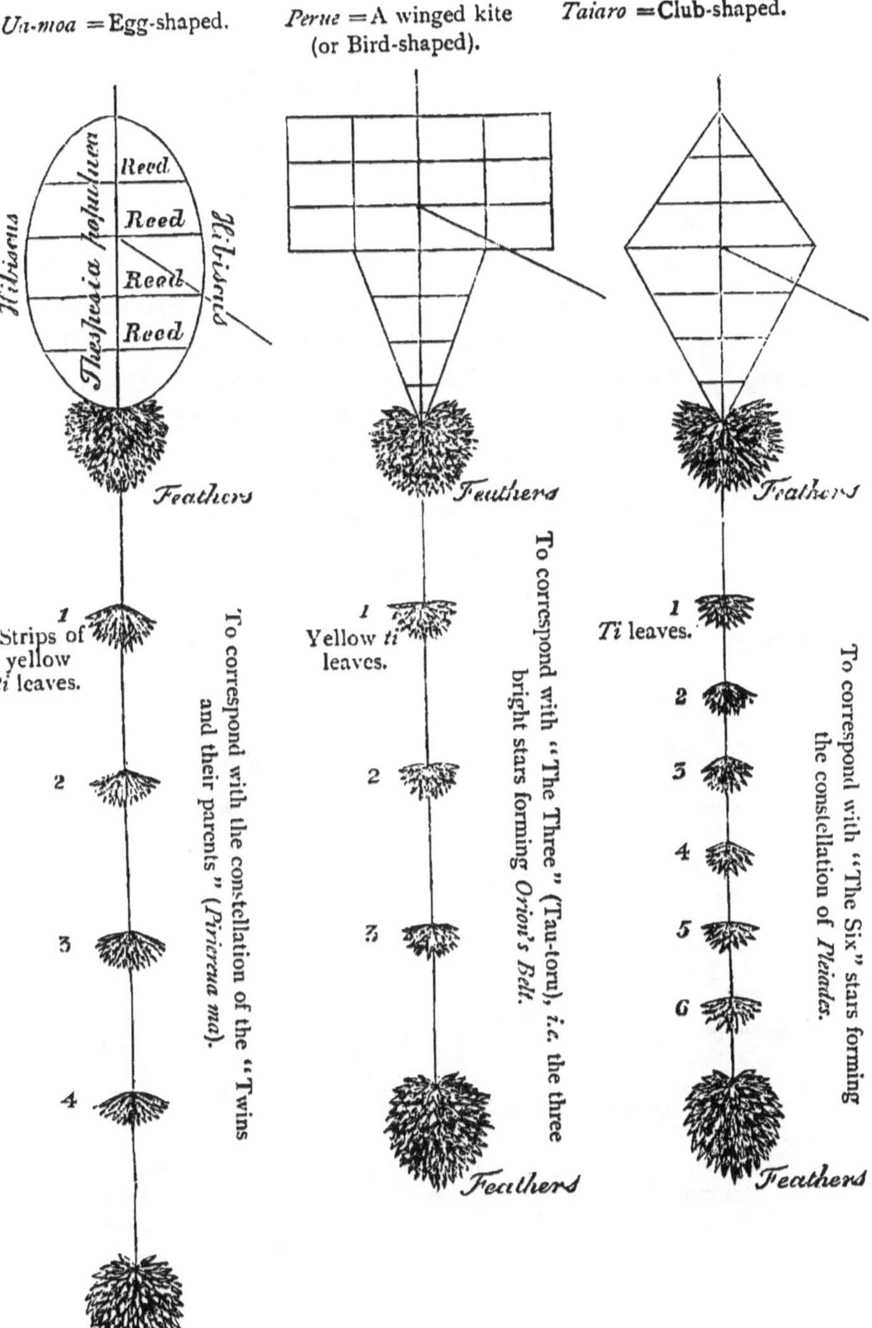

Ua-moa = Egg-shaped.
Perue = A winged kite (or Bird-shaped).
Taiaro = Club-shaped.
Hibiscus
Thespesia populnea
Hibiscus
Reed
Reed
Reed
Reed
Feathers
Feathers
Feathers
Strips of yellow ti leaves.
1
2
3
4
Feathers
To correspond with the constellation of the "Twins and their parents" (Pirierua ma).
Yellow ti leaves.
1
2
3
Feathers
To correspond with "The Three" (Tau-toru), i.e. the three bright stars forming Orion's Belt.
Ti leaves.
1
2
3
4
5
6
Feathers
To correspond with "The Six" stars forming the constellation of Pleiades.

THE ORIGIN OF KITE-FLYING.

Tane in the shades once challenged Rongo to a game of kite-flying. But the issue of this trial of skill was the utter discomfiture of Tane by his elder brother Rongo, who had secretly provided himself with an enormous quantity of string. From this first kite-flying mortals have acquired the agreeable pastime, the condition of each game being that the first kite that mounts the sky should be sacred to, and should bear the name of, Rongo, the great patron of the art. The names of all *subsequent* kites were indifferent. To this contest reference is made in—

A KITE SONG FOR TENIO'S FÊTE.

BY KOROA, CIRCA 1814.

Call for the dance to lead off.

Ua kapi te puku i Atiu !

The hill-top[1] Atiu is covered with kites,

Na tere manu a Raka ē !

Pets of Raka who rules o'er the winds.

Ka aka ē !

Dance away !

Solo.

Taipo ē !

Go on !

Chorus.

Ua kapi te puku i Atiu !

See, yon hill-top Atiu covered with kites—

Na tere manu a Raka ē !

Pets of Raka, god of winds.

Solo.

Aē !

Aye.

Chorus.

E manu pēru au ē !

I am a bird[2] (*i.e.* kite) of beautiful plumage.

---

[1] A hill on the east of Mangaia is so named, in memory of Akē's visit to the island.

[2] Kites were either *egg*-shaped, *club*-shaped, or *bird*-shaped. As the latter were more difficult to make, they were scarce, and greatly admired by the childish old men who delighted to fly them on the hill-tops of Mangaia.

	Solo.
Tomo i te rangi koukou ē!	Cleave, then, the dark clouds.
	Chorus.
Moaia ea koe e Tautiti,	Take care lest Tautiti gain the day.
	Solo.
Taumoamoa e Tane e na Rongo oki,	Once Tane and Rongo tried their skill.
Tere manu aitu ki Iva ē!	With divine kites in spirit-land.
	Solo.
Naai te ao i poto ē	Who was beaten ?
	Chorus.
Na Tane, tei raro io na kumu ē	Tane ; for his string fell short.
	Solo.
E mano o te ao !	Two thousand fathoms of string !
	Chorus.
Na Rongo ;	Yes ; 'twas Rongo's,
Te vai ra i te aka i te rangi ē!	Whose kite touched the edge of the sky.

UTI'S TORCH; OR, WILL-A-WISP.

Riding across the island alone one dark rainy night, I was delighted to see just ahead what seemed to be a man carrying a lighted torch. I shouted to my supposed companion to wait a little until I could get up to him. Receiving no reply, I spurred my horse ; but as the creature made its way with difficulty through the deep mire, I was not a little annoyed to see the light dancing on and on. But as it kept to the path I suspected nothing. A clump of trees now hid the windings of the road : this mocking companion seemed to dart through its gloomiest recesses in a most inexplicable manner. After a long and weary chase the light forsook the beaten track, and hovered over the deep waters of the little lake in that neighbourhood. I had been chasing an *ignis fatuus!* Upon reaching home that night, and relating my adventure, the natives jestingly remarked, "Uti has been lighting up your path with her torch."

In the very depths of nether-land is a district named Manomano, or *Countless*, swayed by a female fairy called Uti. Her delight is to climb up at night to this world of ours, provided with a torch, in search of food. Sometimes Uti's torch may be seen slowly moving along the reef; now on the rocky shore; occasionally she threads the damp valleys, where prawns abound, and thence will glide up mountain ridges. But Uti's chief resort is the neighbourhood of the lake already referred to. Sometimes the fairy moves alone; at other times attended by one or more of her daughters, each taking a different route. It was Uti who first taught the women of this upper world the pastime of catching the sleeping fish by torch-light,[1] or waylaying crabs ashore, or shrimping in her favourite lake on the south of the island. Hence the old song:—

Tungia te ai, e Uti,	Light thy torch, O Uti,
Ei turama ia Manomano.	That illuminates spirit-world (literally, Manomano).
Kua pou Rurapu	Our taro has been robbed;
Ma raua o Tevakaroa.	Our lands are all bare.
E tu te anau a Vātea :	Wake up, ye children of Vātea :
E ara te po,	Keep watch through the night—
Aore e karo i te rangi.	The gloomiest, wettest night—
O Iro ua tātāi mai raro mai	When Iro creeps up to play his pranks
Nai te papa ia Tu.[2]	From the depths inhabited by Tu.

[1] There can be no doubt that most kinds of fish do sleep, or remain in a sort of torpor, during the night. Not so predatory fish, sharks, etc., etc.

[2] "Tu" is a shortened form of "Tu-metua" = *Stick-by-the-parent*, who lives in the lowest department of Avaiki with the great mother *Vari*, in *silence*, but with intelligence. Here it merely expresses the great depth from which the fairy clambers up.

The first night of the native calendar was sacred to Iro (in Tahitian, Hiro ; in New Zealand, Whiro), the patron of thieves, as being his natal night ; or, as sceptical moderns think, a moonless night is naturally favourable to a thieving expedition. It is hoped that the great divinities, *i.e.* "the children of Vātea," will not allow Iro's tricks to pass with impunity. Uti is invoked to come to the aid of the sufferers, by lighting her torch over the taro patches to be robbed : for the boldest thief would be terrified by the sight, and would precipitately retire.

Vaangaru, lamenting (circa 1815) for his dead mother-in-law, Anau, sings :—

Taumata ra i te tai :	She glances at the sea
Kua eke i Kopuaterea.	And plies her torch-fishing.
Tunu mai i te ai ramarama.	Then resting awhile at Araoa,
Tunu maira i te rama	Cooks part of the spoil.
I nunga i Araoa i te takanga	Ere leaving that pleasant spot
I tangi e moimoi aroa,	She carefully relights her torch—
Tungia rava te rama na Uti !	As taught by the fairy Uti.

MOSQUITOES.

These most annoying insects are said to have been unknown in Mangaia, until a woman named Vēvē landed with her children from Aitutaki. In those days ear-ornaments of a prodigious size were worn by men and women. To admit these clumsy adornments, the ears were slit in childhood and enlarged by constant pressure, until at last a small cocoa-nut [1] (vāō) could be inserted. Fragrant leaves and even flowers were put inside, and the opening carefully plugged up.

Now Vēvē, on leaving her native island, filled up the hollow of

[1] This is a literal truth.

her enormous ear-ornaments *with mosquitoes, so as to have the pleasure of hearing their continual hum !* But shortly after landing on the eastern part of the island, she went to a pleasant retired little stream, to enjoy the luxury of a bath, and left her singular ear-ornaments on the grassy bank. That same night she went torch-fishing on the reef, and there recollected her missing ear-plugs. Upon returning home, she found two of her children stung to death by the mosquitoes, *which had by their loud humming contrived to burst their prison-house !* Her other two children had escaped with their lives by entirely immersing their bodies in the neighbouring stream, their mouth and nostrils only being above water.

Vĕvĕ set fire to her dwelling, hoping to exterminate the noxious insects she had thoughtlessly introduced to her future home. The majority, indeed, perished; but a few escaped to the neighbouring rocks. From that remnant the present disagreeable race of mosquitoes are descended. To this old belief Tenio refers in his fête song :—

Kua topa te poe i te taringa :	Thy ear-ornaments were lost;
Kua vare paa i Vaikaute.	When bathing at Vaikaute.
Na tangi namu i vāvai.	The loud humming burst them open.
Kua kai te namu ka pou raua.	Alas! they stung both children to death.

It is the custom of the natives to keep burning outside each house a log of dry iron-wood, which if left alone will, like touch-wood, smoulder on until the whole is consumed. Of course the smoke readily penetrates the reed sides of a native hut, and drives away the mosquitoes. But as the smoke does not invariably suffice to expel these irritating foes, it is the custom to sleep with the head and face well wrapped up.

In the hot, damp season, if a native cannot sleep on account of mosquitoes, he lights a torch and waits until all his pertinacious little foes are delightedly buzzing round it. He then slowly carries the light outside, of course conducting the insect-army with it. Suddenly quenching the torch, he now rushes back inside the house and closes the sliding door.

"THE-LONG-LIVED."

The formation of Mangaia is remarkably hilly. In the middle of the island is a hill, half a mile long and 250 feet wide, named Rangimotia, or *Centre-of-the-heavens*, from which the lesser hills branch out on every side.

This central hill was considered very sacred in the olden time, for there the kings of past generations adjusted the sacred girdle on warriors bound on secret murdering expeditions in the name of Rongo. The condition of wearing this girdle was, "succeed or die." About a century ago a rash chief, named Uarau, resolved to celebrate his accession to supreme temporal power by holding a grand feast on this sacred spot. The leading men of the day were sure that such an act of daring impiety would draw down the anger of the gods, and therefore deprived Uarau of his chieftain-ship. The reason alleged for the sacredness of the hill is this :—

A god, Te-manava-roa,[1] or *The-long-lived*, lies buried, face downwards, at Rangimotia. His proportions are wonderful: the length of the level hill—half a mile—being the measurement of his *back !* His *head* is at Butoa, towards the sun-rising. The marked depression between, is the *neck* of The-long-lived. His *right arm* is the line of hills stretching away to the S.E., a distance of two miles, and touching the mission premises at Tamarua. His

---

[1] One of the three primary stationary *spirits* bears this name, but must be distinguished from this buried giant.

left arm is represented by a hill-range, of equal length, on the opposite side of the island. The *right leg* of The-long-lived is the line of somewhat irregular hills extending about three miles on the S.W. of the island. The *left leg* is a chain of equal length on the N.W.

These "arms" and "legs" serve one important purpose—to mark off the different districts into which the island is naturally divided.

It is in allusion to this myth that the southern half of Mangaia is invariably called "the *right* side," and the northern half "the *left* side." The eastern part of Mangaia is always termed the "pauru" or *head.*

Whenever, in the olden time, a large stranded fish was obtained, this fancy guided the cutting up and presentation of the different parts of the fish. The *head,* as a matter-of-course, went to the two chiefs at "the sun-rising," *where the head of The-long-lived was supposed to lie.* The central part of the fish would go to the two chiefs of the central portion of Mangaia—the fish being divided along the back-bone, in order that the shares might be equal.

The tail was divided between the two remaining chiefs, whose homes are at "the sun-setting."

The larger portions were subdivided, until each individual had a minute share. But these subdivisions were not made until the name of the chief of the entire district had first been proclaimed.

To this day, in all great feasts, the etiquette is, after calling out the name of the king, to announce in a prescribed order the names of the six chiefs of Mangaia, beginning with one of the chiefs on the east, and then going round in regular order until the second chief on the east had been called out, and the circuit of the island completed. This is done now partly as a matter of custom, and partly as a matter of real convenience—jealousy being thus prevented. Few of the younger people understand the ancient reason for the practice.

HUMAN ARTS AND INVENTIONS.

The employments of mortals are mere transcripts of what was supposed to be going on in Avaiki, their knowledge and skill being derived from the invisible world. The first *axe* ever seen on earth (*i.e.* Mangaia) was, handle and all, of stone from the shades. The grand secret of *fire* was introduced by Māui from nether-world. The female employment of *cloth-beating* was derived from the she-demon Mueu, who in the shades is ever beating the flail of death. The art of *torch-light fishing* was gained from the goddess Uti, who on damp nights loves to come up from Avaiki with a lighted torch (*ignis-fatuus*) to wander over the island. The art of *stealing* would infallibly come to grief, did not Iro himself come up on moonless nights from spirit-land, for the express purpose of assisting mortals in playing their thievish tricks. The *ovens* in daily use, especially the enormous ovens for cooking *ti* (*dracoenae terminalis*) roots, are derived from Miru's awful oven ever blazing in Hades. The *art of war* was learnt from Tukaitaua and Tutavake, denizens of nether-land. The *intoxicating draught* was copied from that which the hateful mistress of the invisible world presents to her victims. The pleasant and harmless *game of ball-throwing* was first taught to Ngaru by fairy-women; and introduced by him to this world. Veêtini came from the dead to instruct mankind how *to mourn for their deceased relatives.*

An obvious explanation of this style of thought is the universal tendency of the heathen mind to trace to a supernatural source everything in earth, air, or sea. Another suggestion I would make ;—their ancestors undoubtedly brought with them the knowledge of necessary and useful arts from Savai'i, the " Avaiki " and original home of these islanders. In the eastern islands they speak of having come from Hawai'i (= Savai'i), or the " Po," *i.e. Night.* By " Night " is intended the far-west, where the sun sets, leaving these eastern islands in darkness. Po, Hawai'i, Avaiki, and Savai'i are convertible terms.

·The heathen of these islands were everywhere *Realists* in philosophy, without knowing it. This is the fundamental error of unenlightened nations.

PERILS OF BEAUTY.

Ngaroariki,[1] wife of Ngata, king of Rarotonga, was famed for her beauty. She was the envy of gods and men. On one occasion she was thrown into a thicket of thorns by four men, who thought she could never get out alive. (The thorns of this formidable creeper resemble fish-hooks. Woe betide the unfortunate man that gets entangled amongst them.) Tangaroa, tutelar god of Rarotonga, took pity on the hapless beauty, and sent Oroio and Roaki with long, heavy sticks to beat down the thicket, and thus afford deliverance. Another time, when rambling near the sea, she heard a siren voice calling to her, " O loveliest of women, come hither !" She felt impelled to follow the voice. The pathway led over a *bua* (*beslaria laurifolia*) which overspread a rock. Tangaroa whispered to her to tread only the *green* branches, as

---

[1] Ngaroariki = *the lost queen.* Ngata = *difficult.*

whoever treads upon the *dead* branches is necessarily bound to spirit-land. She did so. But as she passed on to the sea whence the voice proceeded, she was suddenly caught in a net by two demons, and was utterly helpless in their hands. As she was being borne away to destruction, Tangaroa again interposed on her behalf, and tore the net to pieces and delivered the fair captive. On a third occasion, Ngaroariki told her husband that she was going to bathe in a retired spot. He attempted to dissuade her from her purpose, saying that she might be attacked by the cruel hag Moto (= *the striker*), who was known to be jealous of her charms. Ngaroariki loved to have her own way, and went off gaily to the fountain, and there greatly diverted herself by beating the water with her hands.

It happened that the envious woman was preparing cloth in her own dwelling, which was not far away from the bathing-place. As soon as she heard the splashing of the water, she knew that it was Ngaroariki, and immediately left off work and sought how she might wreak her vengeance upon the defenceless queen.

Tangaroa noticed that Moto's flail ceased to beat, and concluded that she was planning some evil against Ngaroariki. Wishing to save the ill-fated beauty, he despatched his bird-messenger, the kuriri, who chirped thus :—

Teuteuae,[1] ruerueae, e tu ra, e oro ra,   Haste, haste, arise, flee for thy life !
     aere ra.

The warning was repeated two or three times ; but Ngaroariki paid no heed. While she was yet splashing about in the fountain, Moto violently assaulted the unprepared bather. She then, with a keen shark's tooth, shaved off the whole of her hair, which was so profuse that it made eight large handfuls. Her face was next so

---

[1] The alliteration is beautiful : the sense of both words is the same.

disfigured that it was impossible for any one to recognize the once beautiful queen. Her pretty yellow ear-ornament of stained fish-bone, and her fine pearl-shell daintily suspended from her neck, were snatched away. Her gay clothes were all taken from her, and she was wrapped round in a single piece of old black *tapa*. When at length the hag Moto retreated with the spoil, poor Ngaroariki, utterly forlorn and changed in appearance, hid herself in the forest.

Her husband Ngata, astonished that his queen did not return home, searched everywhere for her ; but in vain. After some time a grand reed-throwing match in honour of the king came off. The party who throws the farthest wins the day. The chief people of the island were present, and in succession threw their long reeds with various degrees of success. When Ngata and his retinue came forward to exhibit their skill, it happened that their reeds passed near where the lost queen was hiding her deformity and misery. She was wasted to a skeleton through grief and want of food. She knew well to whom the reeds belonged. One after another, as they swept past, they were caught by her and broken in pieces. It was reported to the king that his reeds had actually been destroyed by some ugly, wretched-looking woman. Ngata, greatly incensed, hastened to punish her insolence. Again and again he kicked her, reviling her for her ugliness and impudence. As soon as the king was gone, Ngaroariki wailed thus :—

Takatakaiia, takatakaiia te mea vaine Ngata ariki,
I Vaitakaiara te nekuere.

O royal Ngata, tramplest thou thus—

Tramplest thou thus on thine own perishing wife?

The king was told what she had said. Was it possible that this ugly creature was indeed his lost wife? He immediately

returned and looked attentively at her face, but could see no like-
ness to his beloved Ngaroariki.   Yet there could be no mistaking
the meaning of her words.   At last he bethought himself to open
her mouth ; and, on doing so, immediately recognized the pearly
teeth of his lost one.   He asked what had happened to her.   She
told him all.   Off started Ngata, followed by his wife, in search of
the sorceress.   She was employed as usual in beating out cloth.
The king demanded whether she had touched Ngaroariki and had
stolen her queenly ornaments.   The hag admitted that these
charges were true, but begged the king not to kill her, as she
would give back the stolen treasures, and restore her to her
pristine beauty.   The ornaments and clothing were produced.   The
sorceress then collected the viscid fluid of the hibiscus and the
orongā (*urtica argentea*), and prepared a sort of gum which she
plastered all over the bald head of Ngaroariki.   The hair was
thus made by the sorceress to adhere as formerly.   The eyebrows
were restored in the same way.   The hag having, with infinite
labour, repaired the damage she had done to the person of the
queen, hoped to be forgiven.   But Ngata thirsted for revenge.
Besides, the jealous Moto might invent some new method of
injuring his beloved one.   Without heeding her entreaties for
mercy, the king stoned the sorceress to death, as he believed.
Accompanied by Ngaroariki, he was proceeding home, when, to
his utter astonishment, he heard Moto again at her old employment, beating out native cloth.   He returned to the hag, who
appeared to be uninjured by what had occurred.   A second time
Ngata stoned the sorceress ; but again she revived and returned
to her old work.   Driven to his wits' end, he at last hit upon a
plan which proved successful ; it was to stone her until, as
previously, life seemed extinct, and then to sever the limbs and

bury them in different parts of the island. Thus, at length, an end was put to the malicious tricks of the envious Moto, and the lovely Ngaroariki lived in peace with her royal husband.

ORIGIN OF PIGS AT RAROTONGA.

Of the seven islands constituting the Hervey Group, Mangaia and Aitutaki are the only ones without a native breed of pigs. The first were landed in 1823 by the martyr Williams. On occasion of the annual May festivities in 1852, a thousand pigs were killed and eaten! Of late years the number of these useful animals has greatly fallen off, owing to the desolation occasioned by successive hurricanes.

The only quadruped previously known on Mangaia was the *rat*, which was considered to be delicious eating. To this day a rat-hunt is rare sport for boys, who afterwards divide the spoil. Their seniors have relinquished the practice of rat-eating. " As sweet as a rat " is a common proverb ; and the Rarotongans revile Manga-ians as " rat-eaters."

The following is the legend given to account for the origin of pigs at Rarotonga :—

Some two miles from the settlement of Avarua is a place named Kupolu, where there once lived the aged blind Maaru, and his son Kationgia. They lived by themselves in a pleasant spot, not far from the base of mountains whose summits are nearly always robed in clouds.

In consequence of the continual fighting of those days, there was a most severe famine. Maaru became too feeble to stir from the house ; so that the boy had to provide, as best he could, for the wants of the old man and himself. Kationgia could find nothing better to eat than the stump of the banana, which ordinarily no one would condescend to taste.   Very diligently did he grate these stumps on a lump of madrepore coral, strain off the farina into a tub hollowed out of a solid tree, and mixing a little of the refuse (ota), in order to give it substance, cooked the whole in the oven.   Kationgia would now go on the reef to fish, in order to get something to render this wretched diet palatable. The fish, when obtained, was grilled over a fire, on an extempore gridiron of green cocoa-nut branches.

The dutiful son invariably gave to his aged parent the banana-root pudding and the larger fish, whilst he satisfied the cravings of his own appetite on sea-slugs and shell-fish.   Maaru, wearied of this diet, and suspected Kationgia of playing him a trick.   Possibly the secret of his boy's uncomplaining cheerfulness was that he reserved all the good things for his own eating, knowing that his old father was stone blind.   Resolved to find out the truth, he waited till his son had gone on the reef to fish.   Maaru now felt about for the calabash of salt water, and spilled its contents.   In due time the son returned with some fish, and prepared their meal. But to his surprise, the salt water was gone.   Without a word of complaint the lad started back to the beach to refill the empty calabash with this indispensable condiment.

This was just the opportunity the old blind father desired. Everything was spread for his own dinner and for his son's : he resolved to ascertain what his boy was living on from day to day, seeing that his own fare was so indifferent.   To his grief he found that Kationgia had been really starving himself, whilst the father had constantly eaten the only tolerable food obtainable.   Maaru wept at the thought of what his poor boy had endured for his sake : hearing, at length, the footsteps of the lad, he restrained his tears.

The meal was finished in silence. The old man then requested Kationgia to come to him. The boy obeyed, wondering at this novel proceeding. The blind Maaru then felt all over his person, and found him to be a living skeleton. Father and son now wept together.

Kationgia was told to prepare an oven. " What have we to cook ? " naturally asked the son. The father repeated his command. When the oven was nearly ready, Maaru directed his son to dig about the posts of the house, where he had, with a wise forethought, during a previous season of plenty, concealed a quantity of food against the time of scarcity.

Near the first post was a large quantity of " mâi," or sour bread-fruit, carefully packed up in leaves.[1] About the second post was a lot of excellent chestnuts (*tuscarpus edulis*). To crown the whole, a bunch of four cocoa-nuts was discovered close to the third principal support of their dwelling. Said the old father, " Cook all this food ; for we will have a feast to-night. When I am gone, dig about all the minor posts of this house, and you will find plenty of food expressly reserved for this time of sore need."

That evening father and son enjoyed the luxury of a second meal. Maaru then solemnly said, " I have eaten my last food. I am about to die. As soon as the breath is out of my body, take me to Nikao (a good fishing-place about a mile distant). On no account carry me ; but drag me there. Conceal my body in the bush ; cover it well with leaves and grass. At the expiration of four days, come and look at my body. Should you see worms crawling about, cover me over again with fresh leaves and grass. At the expiration of another four days come back—*and something*

[1] Thus packed and buried in the.earth, it will keep good two or three years.

will follow you. Peace will be restored to this island, and you will be king!"

That same night the old man died. Kationgia faithfully carried out the last wish of his parent. The bruised corpse was deposited in the dense ironwood forest, not far from the beautiful white sandy beach of Nikao. At the end of four days the lad revisited the sequestered grave, and saw worms crawling about. According to the instructions of Maaru, he gathered abundance of fresh leaves and grass, and piled them over the corpse to a great height. But when, after the expiration of another four days, he paid a second visit to the grave, he was surprised to see the entire mass strangely heaving;—it was all commotion! Alarmed at this, he rushed away home in horror. His ears, however, were assailed and his steps arrested with *the novel grunts of the first brood of pigs on Rarotonga.* In that first brood were all the varieties of white, black, and speckled, which have since prevailed. These young pigs, of their own accord, followed Kationgia to his home at the foot of the mountain. They increased at a wonderful rate, and made their owner famous all over the island.

Being now a man of consideration, Kationgia married to advantage. Peace prevailed, and eventually, on account of his owning these wonderful animals, he was elected king! Such was the reward of his filial piety.

To the present day pigs at Rarotonga are, in allusion to this story, called "e iro no Maaru" = *worms of Maaru.*

Kationgia = *bite and smell,* as if the model child of their heathen antiquity *only bit and smelt* his own share of food.

A spot at Rarotonga is to this day called Kupolu.

SEEKING FOR LIGHT.

AN AITUTAKIAN MYTH.

Te-erui, son of Te-tareva = *the expanse*, lived long in utter darkness in the shades (Avaiki). He had heard that there was somewhere a land of light; very earnestly he desired to visit it. He ruminated as to the best way of attaining his purpose, and finally resolved to make a canoe, in which he might paddle away to "the land of light."

Te-erui divulged his secret purpose to his brother Matareka = *smiling face.* Being of one mind, they at once set off in search of suitable wood for their purpose. As they felled the trees, they chanted these words :—

> Nga Te-erui, nga Matareka e amo i te toki i te tumu o te rakau.
> E aumapu ma taku toki, e aumapu.

> Te-erui and Matareka have brought their axes to the root of this tree.
> Merrily rings the axe ! merrily O !

The trees fell. The top and branches were speedily lopped off, the outer bark was peeled off, and the trunks hollowed out into two fine canoes. The outriggers were secured. The first canoe was named, " Weary of Darkness ;" the second, "Sleepless Nights." These enterprising brothers dragged their canoes to the ocean's edge, set up a mast and sail in each, and started for the much-wished-for " land of light." When the winds grew light, they diligently plied their paddles. On and on they went, and, to their great joy, reached a region called " Glimmering of Light." Here they met with a great misfortune—their canoes upset. They, however, swam back for their lives, and succeeded in reaching their homes again. In no degree discouraged by the result of this, their first experiment, the brothers cut down two trees, chanting as before :—

> Te-erui and Matareka have brought their axes to the root of this tree.
> Merrily rings the axe ! merrily O !

The trees fell ; and in due time the canoes were completed. One was named, " Unalterable Purpose ;" the other, "Sidle Along " (because unable to go direct). These new canoes were launched, and a second time the brothers started off in search of " the land of light." All went on well until they arrived at the comparatively pleasant region of " Glimmering of Light," where their fragile barks were sunk by the violence of the waves. The adventurous voyagers happily succeeded in swimming back to shore a second time. But Te-erui and Matareka did not despair. Again they felled timber for two new canoes in the place of those they had lost, singing as before :—

> Te-erui and Matareka have brought, etc.

When these canoes were completed, they were respectively called " Tack In," and " Tack Out." Once more the brothers, each in a separate canoe, started off in search of "the land of light," but were again doomed to disappointment ; for, on reaching the region of " Glimmering of Light," the rough waves again broke up their canoes. Te-erui and Matareka, however, got back to shore a third time.

The brothers now doubted whether they would ever succeed in getting to the wished-for land. They resolved to try once more. Again they selected the best trees for their purpose ; and, whilst cutting them down, sang as formerly, "Te-erui and Matareka," etc. When these canoes were completed, they held a consultation as to the probable cause of their previous failures.

The carpenter, or priest, inquired the name of the masts of the former canoes. The brothers replied, "Te-tira-o-Rongo," *i.e. The mast of Rongo.* The carpenter remarked, "It is on this account that you have hitherto failed. Change the name, and you will yet succeed." "What name do you propose?" asked the brothers. "Call it," said the priest-carpenter, "O-tu-i-te-rangi-mārama"[1] = *Erect in the Light of Heaven.* This was gladly agreed to. Everything was at length completed for the fourth expedition in search of "the land of light." What with paddling and sailing, they reached the dangerous region of "Glimmering of Light," and saw the mad billows seemingly resolved again to swallow up the frail barks. But "Erect in the Light of Heaven" kept on through storm and calm until they reached "the land of light"—a region where they could clearly see each other; where the sun shone brightly, and all was pleasant.

No more caring to return to the dark land from which they had originally set out, they looked about for a resting-place, and at last espied a half-sunken island ahead. But the ocean waves were threatening, and the surf rolled heavily against the coral reef. The brothers fought against these billows, and lo! the sea became smooth. Nearing the partially submerged island, they could find no dry place on which to set their feet. The brothers again contended with the ocean; the shallow waters vanished, leaving the island elevated far above the surrounding ocean. Te-erui and Mata-reka took possession of their new-found home in "the region of light," and thenceforth appropriately called it "Aitu-taki" = *God-led.*

Such is the legendary history of the "Adam" of Aitutaki. It is, of course, a highly exaggerated account of the voyage of the

---

[1] A possible meaning of this name is "Tu-(bathed)-in-the-Light-of-Heaven." I prefer that given in the text.

first settlers from Avaiki = Savai'i, the sun-setting, to "the land of light," *i.e.* the sun-rising. Said the heathen priests to Papehia, one of their first teachers, "Te-erui was the first man; we know nothing about your Adam."

RATA'S CANOE.

A LEGEND FROM AITUTAKI.

In the fairy land of Kupolu lived the renowned chief Rata, who resolved to build a great double canoe, with a view of exploring other lands. Shouldering his axe, he started off to a distant valley where the finest timber grew. Close to the mountain stream stood a fragrant pandanus tree, where a deadly combat was going on between a beautiful white heron (ruru), and a spotted sea-serpent (aa). The origin of the quarrel was as follows :—

The heron was accustomed, when wearied with its search after fish, to rest itself on a stone rising just above the waters of the coral reef, and chanced to defile the eyes of a monstrous sea-serpent, whose hole was just beneath. The serpent, greatly enraged at this insult, resolved to be revenged. Raising its head as far as possible out of the water, it carefully observed the flight of the white heron and followed in pursuit. Leaving the salt water of the reef, it entered the mountain torrent, and eventually reached the foot of the fragrant pandanus, where the unconscious victim was sleeping. The sea-serpent easily climbed the pandanus by means of one of its extraordinary aerial supports or roots ; and now, holding on firmly with its twisted tail, began the attack by biting the lovely bird.

They fought hard all through that night. At dawn, the white heron seeing Rata passing that way, plaintively called out, "O Rata, put an end to this fight." But the sea-serpent said deceitfully, "Nay, Rata; leave us alone. It is but a trial of strength between a heron and a serpent. Let us fight it out." Again the white heron begged Rata to interfere; and again the crafty sea-serpent bade Rata go on his way—which he did, being in a great hurry to fell timber for his canoe. But as he walked heedlessly along, he heard the bird say reproachfully, "Ah! your canoe will not be finished without my aid." Still Rata heeded not the white heron's cry for help, but entered the recesses of the forest. Selecting the finest timber he could find, he cut down enough for his purpose, and at sunset returned home.

Early on the following morning the chief returned to the valley, intending to hollow out the trees he had felled on the previous day. Strangely enough, the logs were missing: not a lopped branch, or even a chip or a leaf could be seen! No stump could be discovered, so that it was evident that the felled trees had, in the course of the night, been mysteriously restored to their former state. But Rata was not to be deterred from his purpose, so having again fixed upon suitable trees, a second time he levelled them to the ground.

On the third morning, as he went back to the forest to his work, he noticed that the heron and the serpent were still fighting. They had been thus engaged for two days and nights without intermission. Rata pursued his way, intending to hollow out his canoe, when to his astonishment, as on the previous day, the fallen trees had resumed their original places, and were in every respect as perfect as before the axe had touched them. Rata guessed by their position and size, which were the trees that had twice served him this trick. He now for the first time understood the meaning of what the suffering white heron had said to him on the first day, "Your canoe will not be finished without my aid."

Rata now left the forest and went to see whether the white heron was alive. The beautiful bird was indeed living, but very much exhausted. Its unrelenting foe, sure of victory, was preparing for a final attack when Rata chopped it in pieces with his axe, and thus saved the life of the white heron. He then went back to his work, and for the third time felled the timber for his canoe. As it was by this time growing dark, he returned home to rest.

From the branch of a distant tree the somewhat revived white heron watched the labours of Rata through the livelong day. As soon as the chief had disappeared in the evening, the grateful bird started off to collect all the birds of Kupolu to hollow out Rata's canoe. They gladly obeyed the summons of their sovereign, and pecked away with their beaks until the huge logs were speedily hollowed out. Next came the more difficult task of joining together the separate pieces. The holes were bored with the long bills of the sea birds, and the cinet was well secured with the claws of the stronger land birds. It was almost dawn ere the work was completed. Finally, they resolved to convey the canoe to the beach close to Rata's dwelling. To accomplish this, each bird—the small as well as the large—took its place on either side of the canoe, completely surrounding it. At a given signal they all extended their wings, one to bear up the canoe, the other for flight. As they bore the canoe through the air they sang, each with a different note, as follows :—

E ara rakau ē ! E ara rakau ē !	A pathway for the canoe ! A pathway for the canoe !
E ara inano ē !	A path of sweet-scented flowers !
E kopukopu te tini o Kupolu	The entire family of birds of Kupolu
E matakitaki, ka re koe ! Oō !	Honour thee (Rata) above all mortals ! Oō !

On reaching the sandy beach in front of Rata's dwelling the canoe was carefully deposited by the birds, who now quickly disappeared in the depths of the forest.

Awakened by this unwonted song of the birds, Rata hastily collected his tools, intending to return to his arduous employment in the valley. At this moment he caught sight of the famous canoe, beautifully finished off, lying close to his door. He at once guessed this to be the gratitude of the king of birds, and named the canoe " Taraipo " = *Built-in-a-night* (or *Built-in-the-invisible-world*).

Rata speedily provided his bird-built canoe with a mast and a sail, and then summoned his friends, and laid in food and water for his projected voyage. Everything being now ready, he went on board, and was just starting when Nganaoa asked permission to go in this wonderful vessel. But Rata would not consent. The crafty Nganaoa seeing the canoe start without him ran to fetch an empty calabash, knocked off the top, and squeezing himself in as best he could, floated himself off on the surface of the ocean, until he got a little ahead of the canoe. The people in Rata's canoe were surprised to see an apparently empty calabash floating steadily just before their vessel. Rata desired one of his men to stoop down to pick up the calabash, as it might prove useful. The man did so, but to his astonishment found it very heavy— actually containing a man compressed into the smallest possible compass.

A voice now issued from the calabash, O Rata, take me on board your canoe." " Whither away ? " inquired the chief. " I go," said the poor fellow inside the calabash, " warned by an oracle, to the land of Moonlight, to seek my parents Tairitokerau and Vāiaroa." Rata now asked, " What will you do for me if

I take you in ? "   The imprisoned Nganaoa replied, " I will look after your mat sail."   " I do not want your help," said Rata. " Here are men enough to attend to the great mat sail."

After a pause, Nganaoa, still unreleased from his awkward position, again earnestly addressed Rata : " Let me go in your canoe."   " Whither away ? " again demanded the chief.   " I go," said Nganaoa, " warned by an oracle, to the land of Moonlight, to seek my parents Tairitokerau and Vāiaroa."   Rata again asked " What *now* will you do for me if I take you in ? "   The reply issued from the calabash, " I will unweariedly bale out the water from the bottom of your canoe."   Again Rata said, " I do not want your help.   I have plenty of men to bale out the water from the bottom of the canoe."

A third time, in similar terms, Nganaoa entreated permission to go in the canoe—to paddle it whenever the wind should grow light or adverse.   But Rata would not accept his services.

At last, upon the fourth application, the desponding Nganaoa was successful, on the promise to destroy all the monsters of the ocean which might infest their path.   Rata wisely reflected that he had entirely forgotten to provide against this emergency ; and who so fertile in expedients as Nganaoa, who was now permitted to emerge from his calabash, and to take his place armed at head of the canoe to be on the look-out for monsters.

Swiftly and pleasantly, with a fair wind, they sped over the ocean in quest of new lands.   One day Nganaoa shouted, " O Rata, here is a terrible foe starting up from the main."   It was an open *clam* of fearful proportions.   One shell was ahead, the other astern—the canoe and all on board lying between !   In another moment this horrid clam might crush them all by suddenly closing its mouth !   But Nganaoa was ready for the emergency.   He seized his long spear and quickly drove it down into the fish. so that the bivalve instead of suddenly snapping them all up sank immediately to the bottom of the ocean.

This danger escaped, they again sped pleasantly on their way. But after a while the voice of the ever vigilant Nganaoa was heard : "O Rata, yonder is a terrible enemy starting up from ocean depths." It proved to be an octopus of extraordinary dimensions. Its huge tentacula encircled the vessel in their embrace, threatening to destroy them. At this critical juncture Nganaoa seized his spear and fearlessly drove it through the head of the octopus. The tentacula now slowly relaxed, and the dead monster floated off on the surface of the ocean.

Again they pursued their voyage in safety. But one more great peril awaited them. One day the brave Nganaoa shouted, "O Rata, here is a great *whale !*" Its enormous mouth was wide open ; one jaw beneath the canoe, and the other above it ! The whale was evidently bent on swallowing them up alive. Nganaoa, the slayer of monsters, now broke his long spear in two, and at the critical moment when the whale was about to crush them all, he cleverly inserted both stakes inside the mouth of their foe, so that it became impossible for it to close its jaws. Nganaoa nimbly jumped inside the mouth of this great whale and looked down into the stomach, and lo ! there sat his long lost father Tairitokerau and his mother Vāiaroa, who had been swallowed alive when fishing by this monster of the deep. The oracle was fulfilled ; his voyage was prosperous.

The parents of Nganaoa were busily engaged in platting cinet. Great was their joy at seeing their son, being assured that deliverance was at hand. Nganaoa resolved, whilst extricating his parents, to be fully revenged upon the whale. He therefore extracted one of the two stakes—the remaining one sufficing to prevent the monster from enclosing him as well as his parents in this living tomb. Breaking this prop into two pieces, he converted them into fire-sticks. He desired his father to hold firmly the lower one, whilst he worked assiduously with the upper stick, until at length the fire smouldered. Blowing it to a flame, Nganaoa set fire to the fatty portion of the stomach. The monster, writhing in agony, sought relief in swimming to the nearest land, where, on reaching the sandy beach, father, mother, and son quietly walked out through the open mouth of the stranded and dying whale.

The island proved to be Iti-te-mărama, or Moonlight. Here the canoe of Rata was drawn up on the beach, and for a time they all lived pleasantly. They daily refreshed themselves with its fruits and fish, adorning their persons with fragrant flowers. At length they longed for the land of their birth in Avaiki, and they resolved to return. The canoe was repaired and launched; food and water were laid in; the great mat sail was set up, and at length the brave navigator Rata, with the scarcely saved parents of Nganaoa, and the entire party, started once more. After many days, but without further peril, they eventually reached their original homes in the lands of the sunsetting.

This myth materially differs from the Rarotongan one, to which Mr. Williams refers in the " Enterprises " (chap. xiii.), which relates how Tangiia first came to Rarotonga. In the latter part, one is strongly reminded of the story of Jonah: the natives look upon it as a distorted version of the Bible narrative. The myth says " a whale " (toora) swallowed the parents of Nganaoa;

whereas the native Bible merely states that "a great fish" (ika maata) swallowed Jonah.

This myth, which may be regarded as one of the primitive stories of the race, points to Samoa. At Pangaroa, in the island of Upolu (in Rarotongan and Aitutakian story *K*upolu; but in Mangaian traditions *Uk*upolu), amid some rocks near the sea, is a block of *stone*, about twenty-seven feet in length, very much resembling a canoe, and called "the canoe of Rata !"

The story of Rata was unknown at Mangaia. Yet a reference to this hero occurs in a canoe-making song—

Tāpāia e Una ē !	Slash away, O Una,
E toki purepure o tai enua.	With the wonderful axe from another land.
A tua te vao ia Rata	E'en with that which enabled Rata
Kua inga te rakau !	To fell the forest.

"The Song of the Birds" ("A Pathway for the canoe," etc.) has always been in use at Aitutaki and Rarotonga as one of those chanted in hauling heavy timber.

The bird intended by the native word "ruru" is a matter of dispute amongst the islanders; some asserting it to be the albatros, others say it is the white heron. The objection to the former is, that is is purely a roamer over the ocean. The fish intended is the "vaaroa," or spotted sea-serpent, which attains the length of eight feet, and is very vindictive. It may seem incredible that a species of eel should climb trees, but such nevertheless is said (by the natives) to be the fact. On low coral islands, where the pandanus grows close to the lagoon, it is common for this fish to make its way over the sand and broken coral until, reaching the shafts which support the trunk, it climbs with great ease in search of lizards which sleep on the branches. The octopus climbs the same tree for the sake of the sweet-scented flowers and fruit.　Like the octopus, this sea-serpent is an expert rat-catcher—feigning death until the unwary rat comes within its reach.　The sight of a human being causes it to return to the water with the utmost expedition.

PRAYER OR CHARM FOR A THIEF OR A MURDERER.

USED BY THE CHIEF RAOA AND HIS CLAN.

Tena rava te tira :	Here is our sure helper.
Ka tu i nunga,	Arise on our behalf :
Ka tu i mua i te are :	Stand at the door of this house,
E tira Omataianuku :	O thou divine Omataianuku !
E tira Outuuturoroa ;	O thou divine Outuutu-the-Tall,
Oavaavaroroa.	And Avaava-the-Tall !
Tei iti au era tangata kekeia,	We are on a *thieving*[1] expedition—
O ua rere i maui ia kiritia ;	Be close to our left side to give aid.
I taviria ia turua.	Let all be wrapped in sleep.
Ia turua a nu koe e te atua i te are :	Be as a lofty cocoa-nut tree to support us.
Ka mate koe i te atua i te are.	O house, thou art doomed by our god !
Tamoe i te au mea katoa	Cause all things to sleep.
Tena rava te moenga, maora atu na.	Let profound sleep overspread this dwelling.
E moe, e te tangata noou te are.	Owner of the house, sleep on !
E moe, e te tirango noou te are.	Threshold of this house, sleep on !
E moe, e te portipoti noou te are.	Ye tiny insects inhabiting this house sleep on !
E moe, e te ueue noou te are.	Ye beetles inhabiting this house, sleep on !

---

[1] "Keia," applies equally to *thieving* and *murdering*.

E moe, e te kakaraunga noou te are. — Ye earwigs inhabiting this house, sleep on !

E moe, e te ro noou te are. — Ye ants inhabiting this house, sleep on !

E moe, e te mātā noou te are. — Dry grass spread over the house, sleep on !

E moe, e te pou noou te are. — Thou central post of the house, sleep on !

E moe, e te tauu noou te are. — Thou ridge-pole of the house, sleep on !

E moe, e te oka noou te are. — Ye main rafters of the house, sleep on !

E moe, e te tarava noou te are. — Ye cross beams of the house, sleep on !

E moe, e te kao noou te are. — Ye little rafters of the house, sleep on !

E moe, e te tiritiritama noou te are. — Ye minor posts of the house, sleep on !

E moe, e te au noou te are. — Thou covering of the ridge-pole, sleep on !

E moe, e te kakao noou te are. — Ye reed-sides of the house, sleep on !

E moe, e te rau noou te are. — Thatch of the house, sleep on !

O te mata i mua o te tangata — The first of its inmates unluckily awaking

E ara mai nei,—vareaio ! — Put soundly to sleep again.

Mea po te atua oi te io tangata. — If the divinity so please, man's spirit must yield.

Aere katoa, tukua i te rangi, e Rongo. — O Rongo, grant thou complete success !

This prayer was uttered as near as possible to the dwelling to be robbed.   The users of it were famous for their success.

CHAPTER VIII.

HADES; OR, THE DOCTRINE OF SPIRIT-WORLD.

THE proper name for Hades is Avaiki; in Tahitian, Hawai'i; in New Zealand, Hawaiki.   Many other expressions occur in their ancient songs and myths, but they are to be regarded as designations for places or territories in Avaiki, the vast hollow over which the island is supposed to be placed.   As the dead were usually thrown down the deepest chasms, it was not unnatural for their friends to imagine the earth to be hollow, and the entrance to this vast nether-world to be down one of these pits.   No one can wonder at this who knows that the outer portion of Mangaia is a honeycomb, the rock being pierced in every direction with winding caves and frightful chasms.   It is asserted that the Mission premises at Oneroa are built over one of these great caverns, which extends so far towards the sea that the beating of the surf can be distinctly heard, whilst the water, purified from its saline particles, continually drips from the stony roof.   The

inland opening to this subterranean territory was the grand
repository of the dead, and is known by the significant name of

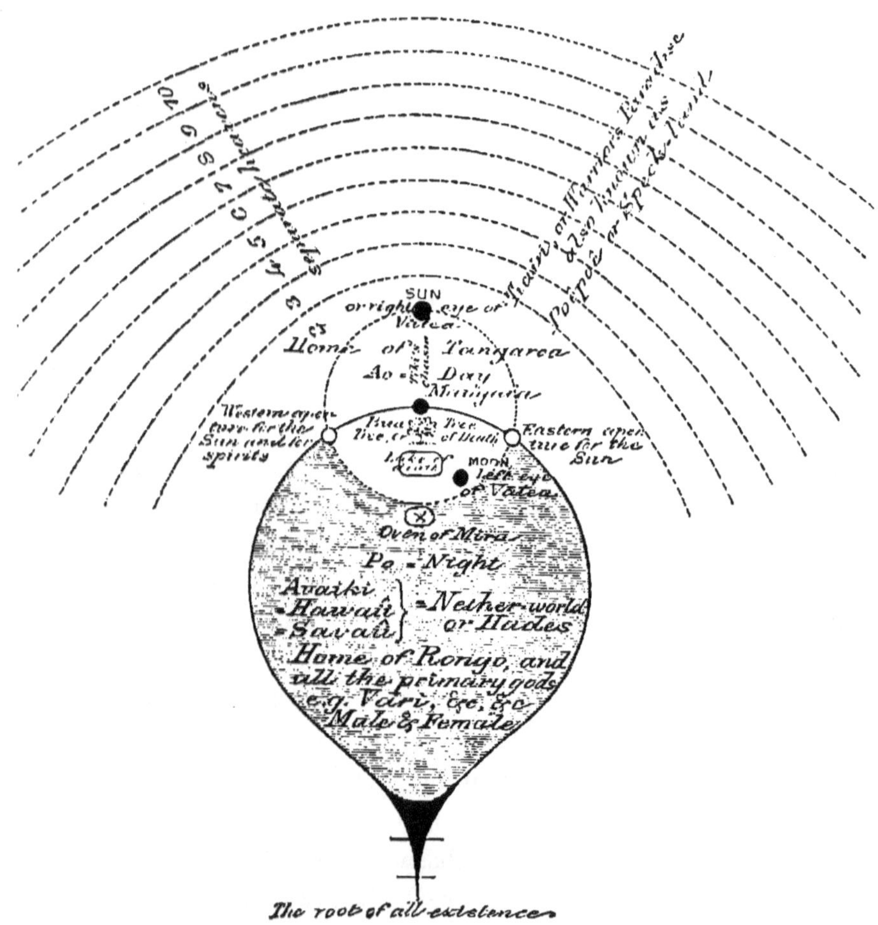

THE UNIVERSE, ACCORDING TO THE IDEAS OF THE NATIVES OF
MANGAIA.

Auraka = *don't.* Doubtless this is the true origin of their idea of the whereabouts of spirit-world.

The proper denizens of Avaiki are the major and lesser divinities, with their dependants. These marry, multiply, and quarrel like mortals. They wear clothing, plant, cook, fish, build, and inhabit dwellings of exactly the same sort as exist on earth. The food of immortals is no better than that eaten by mankind. The story of Kura's marvellous escape from Hades represents some districts of spirit-land as inhabited by cannibals, whose delight is to entrap unwary mortals to their destruction—it is to be presumed without the knowledge of dread Miru. Birds, fish, and rats; the mantis, beetle, and centipede; the cocoa-nut tree, the pandanus, the myrtle, the *morindo citrifolia*, and the yam, —all abound in Hades, either for the support or adornment of immortals. Murder, adultery, drunkenness, theft, and lying are practised by them. The arts of this world are fac-similes of what primarily belonged to nether-land, and were taught to mankind by the gods. The visible world itself is but a gross copy of what exists in spirit-land. If fire burns, it is because latent flame was hidden in the wood by Mauike in Hades. If the axe cleaves, it is because the fairy of the axe is invisibly present. If the iron-wood club kills its victim, it is because a fierce demon from Tonga is enshrined in it.

At a spot named Aremauku, about half a mile from the principal village, on a cliff overhanging the western ocean, it was pretended that the direct road to spirit-land existed. Through it continual communication was anciently kept up with Hades. By this route Māui descended to the home of Mauike, and wrested the secret of fire. In one district lived a race possessed of only *one* eye apiece! At evening the Sun-god Rā drops down through the opening made for his convenience at the edge of the horizon, and thus lights up the inhabitants of the nether-world. One myth asserts that he descends thus frequently to Avaiki to visit his wife *Tu*, who lives with the Great Mother Vari, at the very bottom of the vast cocoa-nut hollow—knees and chin meeting !

Hence the ancient proverb, "*Day here; night in Avaiki,*" and *vice versa.* As the priest Teka sang (1794):—

| Ua po Avaiki | 'Tis night now in spirit-land; |
| Ua ao nunga nei. | For 'tis light in this upper world. |

At the appointed interval, the Sun-god Rā climbs up, not without great difficulty, out of nether-world through a hole at the edge of the eastern horizon, and lights up Mangaia. That his movements are so reasonable and regular is due to the exertions of Māui.

The high-road to Avaiki is for ever closed. This was not the fault of mankind, but the penalty of the excesses of the denizens of spirit-land. They became very troublesome to mankind—continually afflicting them with disease and death. They occasioned great dearth by stealing all kinds of food, and even ravished the women of this world. The brave and beautiful Tiki, the sister of Veêtini, determined to put an end to these annoyances. For this purpose she rolled herself *alive* down into the gloomy opening, which immediately closed upon her. From that memorable day the spirits of mortals have been compelled to descend to Avaiki by a different route. Happily, however, the natives of Avaiki no longer dare molest mankind. The closed chasm is known by the name " te rua ia Tiki " = *Tiki's hole.*

The spirits of the dead were often spoken of as wandering along the margin of the sea most disconsolately; not a little annoyed at the extreme sharpness of the rocks, and the entanglement of their feet in the bindweed and thick vines. They were arrayed in ghostly net-work, and a fantastic mourning of weeds picked upon the way, relieved, however, by the fragrant heliotrope which grows freely on the barren rocks. A red creeper, resembling dyed twine, wound round and round the head like a turban, completed their ghostly toilet.

Rather inconsistently with this, a smooth, shelving piece of coral rock on the western coast is known as "te renanga a te atua," *i.e.* the place where ghosts blanch their new-made garments; *as if* during the weary months of their wanderings over the rough rocks they were driven, like the living, to prepare new clothing from time to time, and thus replace the garments torn by the bushes and thorny creepers. Was it to assist in the manufacture of such garments that females were invariably buried with one or more cloth mallets used in life?

The great delight of these weeping, melancholy spirits, was to follow the sun.[1] At the summer solstice, January, he apparently rises out of the ocean opposite to *Anā-kura* (the "red-cave," so called as receiving the red rays of the morning); at the winter solstice, June, rising at *Karanga-iti* ("the little welcome," winter being but half welcome). These points became, therefore, grand rendezvous of disembodied spirits: those belonging to the northern half of the island assembling at the last-named rendezvous, Karanga-iti; those, by far the greater number, belonging to the southern half of the island meeting at the former, Anā-kura.

Many months might elapse ere the projected departure of the ghosts took place. This weary interval was spent in dances and

---

[1] The dead, if buried at all, were buried with the feet towards the setting sun, on account of this ancient solar worship.

in revisiting their former homes, where the living dwell affection-
ately remembered by the dead. At night-fall they would wander
amongst the trees and plantations nearest to these dwellings,
sometimes venturing to peep inside. As a rule, these ghosts were
well-disposed to their own living relatives ; but often became
vindictive if a pet child was ill-treated by a step-mother or other
relatives, etc.

Sometimes wearied with these wanderings, the ghosts huddled
together in the Red-cave, the stony base of which is constantly
laved by the waves of the Pacific, rolling in with terrific violence
from the east. Or, if it so pleased their fancy, they clambered up
the open, lawn-like place above the cave, out of reach of the
billows and foam of the ocean (now a favourite resting-place for
fishermen, where they cook and eat part of their finny spoil).
This open grassy space, so renowned in their songs and myths
concerning the dead, is known as " One-ma-kenu-kenu " = THE
smooth spot, or *the well-weeded spot*. A coarse species of grass
covers the sandy soil, pleasingly contrasting with the utter barren-
ness beyond, where Desolation seems to be enthroned.

The precise period for final departure was fixed by the leader
of the band. But if no distinguished person was amongst them,
they must of course wait on until such a leader was obtained.
Thus in the beautiful classic laments for Vera, *he* is represented
as the chosen captain of the dead, as his uncle Nagarā ruled over
the living about 125 years ago.

The chief of this disconsolate throng resolves to depart.
Messages are sent to collect those stray ghosts who may yet be
lingering near their ancient haunts. With many tears and last
lingering looks they assemble at the Red-cave, or on the grassy
lawn above it, intently watching the rising of the sun. At the

first streak of dawn the entire band take their departure to meet
the rising sun.　This done, they follow in his train as nearly as
may be : *he* in the heavens above, *they* at first on the ocean
beneath, but afterwards over the rocks and stones (always avoid-
ing the interior of the island),[1] until late in the afternoon of the
appointed day they are all assembled at Vairorongo, facing the
setting sun.

" Vairorongo " means " Rongo's sacred stream."　It is a little
rivulet rushing out of the stones at the marae of Rongo, where in
the olden time only the priests and kings might bathe.

At last the congregated throng, whose eyes are fixed upon the
setting sun, feel that the moment has come when they must for
ever depart from the cherished scenes of earth—despite the tears
and solicitations of relatives, who are frequently represented as
chasing their loved ones over rocks and across fearful precipices,
round half the island.　The sun now sinks in the ocean, leaving
a golden track ; the entire band of ghosts take a last farewell, and
following their earthly leader, flit over the ocean in the train of
the Sun-god Rā, but not like him destined to reappear on the
morrow.　The ghostly train enter Avaiki through the very
aperture by which the Sun-god descends in order to lighten up
for a time those dark subterranean regions.

This view is expressed in the beautiful myth of Veêtini.

After the crowd of spirits had taken their departure, a
solitary laggard might sometimes be left behind—arriving at the
appointed rendezvous only in time to see the long annual train
disappear with the glowing sun.　The unhappy ghost must wait

---

[1] The rocks encircling the island and near the sea were the home of the
vanquished in battle, too often hunted or starved to death ; also the temporary
home of these *exile spirits.*

till a new troop be formed for the following winter, its only amusement being "to dance the dance of the *tiitii*, or starved !" or to "toss pebbles in the air" through the weary months that intervene.

The point of departure for spirit-land is called a "reinga vaerua." There are three on Mangaia, all facing the *setting sun*. The boundary of the Mission premises at Oneroa is marked on one side by a bluff rock standing out by itself like a giant facing the west. It was believed that the spirits of those buried in that grand repository of the dead " Auraka," at the proper season left its gloomy, winding subterranean passages and divided themselves into two bands : the majority starting from " Araia " and lodging on the fatal *bua* tree ; some—those issuing from "Kauava"— going in mournful procession to the projecting rock alluded to, thence leapt one by one to a second and much smaller block of stone resting on the inner edge of the reef, and thence again to the outer and extreme edge of the reef on which the surf ceaselessly beats. From this point they take their final departure to the shades in the track of the sun.

At Atua-koro, on the north-west coast of the island, are two great stones very similarly placed by the hand of nature. This was considered to be an arrangement for the convenience of ghosts on that part of the island. Like the former these stones are known as " Reinga vaerua," *i.e. Leaping-place-of-souls !*

These are but trifling modifications of the highly poetical representation of disembodied spirits, NOT *the slain*, being impelled to follow in the train of the setting sun to spirit-land.

At Rarotonga the great " reinga " or " rereanga vaerua " was at Tuoro ; on the *west* of the island, as at Mangaia. So, too, in all the other islands of the group.   At Samoa, a spirit leaving the dead body at the most easterly island of that group would be compelled to traverse the entire series of islands, passing the channels between at given points, ere it could descend to the subterranean spirit-world at the most *westerly* point of Savai'i.

However, the standard and esoteric [1] teaching of the priests was that the souls of the dying leave the body ere breath is quite extinct, and travel to the edge of the cliff at Araia (= *hindered*, or *sent back*) near the marae of Rongo, and facing the west.   If a friendly spirit should meet the solitary wanderer at any point of the sad but inevitable journey from the place where the seemingly dead body lies, and should say, " Go back and live," the now joyful ghost at once returns to its old home and re-inhabits the once forsaken body.   This is the native theory of *fainting*.

But if *no* friendly spirit interfere, the departing soul pursues its mournful travels and eventually reaches the extreme edge of the cliff.   Instantly a large wave (the sea is about 100 yards distant) approaches to the base, and at the same moment a gigantic *bua* tree (*beslaria laurifolia*), covered with fragrant blossom springss, up from Avaiki to receive on its far-reaching branches unhappy human spirits.   Even at this last moment, with feet almost touching the fatal tree, a friendly voice may send the spirit-traveller back to life and health.   Otherwise, he is mysteriously impelled to climb the particular branch reserved for his own tribe and conveniently brought nearest to him.   The worshippers of

---

[1] The difference is merely as to the *mode of access* to the shades,—whether by following the setting sun, or by climbing on a branch of the mysterious *bua* tree.   *In either case the* END *of all who die a natural death is to be cooked and eaten by Miru, her children and followers.*

Motoro have a branch to themselves, the worshippers of Tane have another—the tree in question having just as many branches as there are principal gods in Mangaia. The whole batch of lesser Tanes congregate on one great branch, etc., etc.

Immediately the human soul is safely lodged upon this gigantic tree, the *bua* goes down with its living burden to nether-world. While yet on the tree the wretched spirit looks down to the root, and to his horror sees a great net spread out beneath to catch it.[1] This net, from the strong meshes of which there is no escape, is firmly held by Akaanga and his assistants. The doomed spirit at last falls into this fatal net, and is at once submerged in a lake of fresh water which lies near the foot of the gigantic *bua* tree and bears the name of Vai-roto-ariki = *the-royal-fresh-water-lake.* In these treacherous waters captive ghosts exhaust themselves by wriggling like fishes in the vain hope of escape. The great net is eventually pulled up, and the half-drowned spirits tremblingly enter the presence of the inexpressibly ugly Miru, generally called " the ruddy " (Miru Kura), because her face reflects the glowing heat of her ever-burning oven. The hag feeds her unwilling visitors with red earth-worms, black beetles, crabs, and small blackbirds.

The grand secret of Miru's power over her intended victims is the " kava " root (*piper mythisticum*). It consists of one vast root, and is named by her " Tevoo," being her own peculiar property. The three sorts of " kava " known in the upper world were originally branches off this enormous root ever-growing in

---

[1] Hence the proverb in regard to the dying, " Ka ei i roto i te kupenga tini mata varu " = " *Will be caught in the net of innumerable meshes,*" *i.e.* the net of Akaanga. It is curious that the proverb should outlive the faith on which it was founded.

Avaiki.   Miru's four lovely daughters are directed to prepare bowls of this strong kava for her unwilling visitors.   Utterly stupefied with the draught, the unresisting victims are borne off to the oven and cooked.   Miru, with her son and peerless daughters, subsist on these human spirits.   The refuse is thrown to her servants, Akaanga and others.   Such is the inevitable fate of those who die a natural death, *i.e.* of women, cowards, and children.   They are *annihilated.*[1]

Not so warriors slain on the field of battle.   The spirits of these lucky fellows for a while wander about amongst the rocks and trees in the neighbourhood of which their bodies were thrown, the ghastly wounds by which they met their fate being still visible. A species of cricket, rarely seen, but whose voice is continually heard at night plaintively chirping "kere-kerere-tao-tao," was believed to be the voice of these warrior spirits sorrowfully calling to their friends.   Hence the proverb, "The spirit cricket is chirping" (Kua tangi te vava).   At length the first slain on each battle-field would collect his brother ghosts at a place a short distance beyond Araia (the point of departure for those who perish by sickness), still on the edge of the cliff, and facing the setting sun.   It overlooks the marae of Rongo, the god of battles. Indeed, one extraordinary myth represents Rongo as coming up from nether-world at certain periods in order to feast himself upon the spirits of those slain in battle assembled for their last journey.   With bits of ripe banana Rongo tempts them to his side, and then treacherously swallows them whole !   But these ghosts have the consolation of escaping the *fire* of Miru : besides, they are eventually disengaged *alive* from the intestines of the

[1] Some " wise men " will have it that these spirits live again after passing through the intestines of Miru and her followers.

grim war-god. They at last rise to the upper sky and join their warrior brethren there.

But the more pleasing version represents these ghosts as lingering awhile on the cliff. Suddenly a mountain springs up at their feet. The road by which they ascend this mountain is over the spears and clubs by which they were slain. Arrived at the summit, they leap into the blue expanse, thus becoming the peculiar clouds of the winter (or dry) season. These clouds are to be distinguished from the ordinary rain clouds.

The warrior spirits of past ages, as well as those recently slain, together constitute the dark clouds of morning which for a while intercept the bright rays of the sun throughout the year.

During the rainy season they cannot ascend to the warrior's Paradise. In June, the first month of winter, the atmosphere is pervaded by these ghosts, to whom the chilliness of death still clings. Their great number hides the sun for days together, occasioning the dull heavy sky, chillness and oppression of spirits usual at that season of the year. This lasts till the beginning of August, when the coral tree opens its blood-red blossoms, and the sky becomes mottled, and light fleecy clouds pass over the heavens. It it the spirits of the brave dead preparing for their flight. The heavens soon become cloudless; the weather bright and warm. It is because they have taken their departure. The living now resume their ordinary avocations in comfort.

The spirits of those who die a natural death are excessively feeble and weak, as their bodies were at dissolution; whereas the spirits of those who are slain in battle are strong and vigorous, their bodies not having been reduced by disease.

These ghosts were said to have "*leaped into the expanse*" (kua rere ki te neneva). This cheerful home of the brave is sometimes called Tiairi, from the name of the place where Matoctoeā, the first man ever slain at Mangaia, is said to have fallen : the idea being " the land which Matoetoeā first inhabited," *i.e.* the expanse of heaven.　At other times it was termed Poêpoê, or *Speck-land;* because in the distance of the upper sky these warrior spirits appear as the veriest specks.

The spirits of the slain are immortal.　They are clothed with garlands of all sorts of sweet-scented flowers used in mundane dances.　The white gardenia, the yellow *bua*, the golden fruit of the pandanus, and the dark crimson, bell-like blossom of the native laurel are gracefully interwoven with myrtle for this purpose.

The employment of these fortunate spirits is to laugh and dance over and over again their old war-dances in remembrance of their achievements in life.　In every possible way they enjoy themselves; but look down with ineffable disgust upon those wretches in Avaiki who are compelled to endure the indignity of being covered with dung falling from their more lucky friends above.　A well-known and ludicrous proverb refers to the vain flapping of the wings of the unhappy spirits in Avaiki who, besmeared with filth, are endeavouring, though to no purpose, to escape out of Akaanga's net.

The natural result of this belief was to breed an utter contempt of violent death.　Many anecdotes are related of aged warriors, scarcely able to hold the spear, insisting on being led to the battle-field, ·in hope of gaining a soldier's paradise.　One may well exclaim, "Light and immortality were brought to light by the Gospel."

A song lying before me represents the ghosts of certain warriors belonging to the tribe of Tane as "wandering about at Maungaroa and Maputū," the most famous maraes belonging to that family, there to await the period appointed for them to ascend, like the rest, to " Speck-land."

In allusion to the myth of the *bua* tree, a person who has been very ill and yet has recovered will even now playfully say, " Yes, I have set foot upon a branch of the *bua* tree, and *yet* have been sent back (by God) to life ! "

Those who die a natural death were said " to go to *night*, or *darkness* (aere ki te po), implying that they are doomed to be cooked and eaten by Miru, *i.e.* annihilated. The happier lot of warrior-spirits was " to go to *day*, or *light*" (aere ki te ao). Of course, as Christian missionaries, we have not failed to make use of phrases so well adapted to our purpose. The standard expression for " heaven" is "*the day, or light of God ;* " the converse is simply " night, or darkness."

On the northern part of this island is a deep indentation in the reef. The rush of waters from the reef meeting the ocean occasions a miniature whirlpool. To account for this simple fact, it was said that a piece of sacred sandstone was once thrown down there : and *hence* the never ceasing turmoil of waters. In the time of Ngauta, a party of fishermen—Karaunu and others— dreamt that they were swept away at this ill-omened place. An attacking party overheard the relation of the dream, and made it come true by slaying them all and throwing their bodies into the seething eddy.

This unpromising place was regarded as *one* entrance to the shades, chiefly for the worshippers of Motoro. The destined traveller *in his sleep* sees a house built on long poles rising above the restless waters, with a ladder to ascend to it. The sides of this house are of closely-fitting yellow reeds, adorned with black cinet. Outside this snug, tempting little dwelling are hung new calabashes, etc., etc., to decoy the passer by. Should the spirit-traveller pause to admire this illusive hut, he will in all probability feel impelled to climb the ladder and take possession of some of the good things hung all round. The moment his hand is on the exquisitely braided yellow cinet, by which the calabashes are suspended, to his horror, house, ladder, visitor, and calabashes are all swept away into the depths of the ocean, and the doomed spirit finds himself in the unwelcome spirit-world, and in the power of Miru.

There are said to be three such "houses of Motoro," or invisible soul-traps to catch unwary spirits. This is but a variation of the doctrine of the *bua* tree, to meet the circumstances of those who have the ill-luck to be sucked down by the three miniature whirlpools existing here.

Since the introduction of Christianity the belief has sprung up that "Avaiki," from which the first inhabitants of this island came, is "Savai'i," the largest island in the Samoan Group. In the Hervey dialect the *S* is dropped, and the break between the two *i*'s filled up with *k*. At the Penrhyns the natives speak of "going to *Savaiki*," when referring to death. Dropping the *S*, we have the usual form "Avaiki." In the Tahitian islands the *H* takes the place of *S*, and the word becomes "Hawai'i," there being no *K* in the Tahitian dialect. Thus Avaiki, Hawai'i, and Savai'i are slightly varying forms of the same word. Savai'i lying *west*, or as these islanders say, "*down*," it would be strictly correct to assert that their ancestors "*came up*" from Savai'i.

This view of the origin of all these eastern islanders is confirmed by the continual recurrence of the names of western islands in the ancient songs and traditions of the natives. In addition to the names of all the near islands of the Hervey and Tahitian Groups, we have "Manu*k*a," *i.e.* Manu'a, "Tutuila," "*Uk*upolu," for "Upolu," of the Samoan Group. "The distant land of Vavau" is referred to in song ; also Rewa. Tonga continually recurs. A double canoe of "Tongans-sailing-through-the-skies" landing on the south of Mangaia, founded the warlike Tongan tribe, now almost extinct. It is well known that that adventurous race once held possession of Savai'i and conquered Niuē.

Places on Mangaia are called Niuē, Rotuma, and Papua. These are ancient appellations indicating, as it seems to me, the course of the original settlers. The reader will recall the names of Savage Island, Rotumah, and the vast island of New Guinea.

It has been suggested that the northern Avaiki (Hawai'i) was the original home of the islanders. A careful study of their mythology produces an irresistible conviction that Savai'i, the original Avaiki, is the true centre from which this race emigrated, willingly or unwillingly, some five or six centuries ago. How their ancestors got to Samoa remains to be discovered ; but the ordinary trade winds north of the equator would make that easy, even if they did not step from island to island, starting from the Malayan peninsula, ever pursued by the savage Negrito races.

The son of the elder of three brothers from Avaiki was named "Pāpā-rangi"—literally, *the sky-beater*. This is the very name by which all foreigners are designated at Samoa at this day. It was evidently in commemoration of the first settlers having "burst through the sky," in order to get to Mangaia.

Mokiro's son was named " Vaerua-rangi " = *Spirit-of-the-sky.*

"Te-akataaira," the name of the third brother from Avaiki, signifies *arrived.* Thus' the very names of the three royal brothers from Avaiki signify voyagers from the sun-setting. It suited the purpose of the priests of the dominant tribe in after times, to assert that Avaiki is the hollow of the vast cocoa-nut shell, over the aperture of which Mangaia is placed. In later times it came to be believed that all these distant islands were situate in nether-land. Their ancestors came from " Avaiki ; " and the spirits of those who died a natural death went to "Avaiki," *i.e. to the homes of their ancestors.*

That "Avaiki" and " Po " are interchangeable is clear from the name of a gloomy rent in the rocks at Ivirua, known as " Avaiki-te-po," that is, *Avaiki, or night.*

The old proverb " Na Avaiki e ranga "=*Avaiki will revenge it,* means "the gods whose home is in Avaiki, particularly Rongo, will revenge it." Sometimes it is said of depth, "deep as Avaiki;" and figuratively of craft or knowledge, "so and so is Avaiki," *i.e.* rivals the depth of Hades in wisdom, etc. In every instance *unknown depth* is implied. " Araara i Avaiki"=*think of Avaiki,* as being about to die.

The Samoan [1] heaven was designated *Pulotu* or *Purotu,* and was supposed to be under the sea. In these eastern islands the same word means " the perfection of beauty." May not this be an adaptation from the former?

At Samoa only *pigs die,* men by a euphemism " finish." The spirits of the dead are said " to go on a journey." Of great men it is asserted that " they have gone to a meeting of chiefs," *i.e.*

[1] Compare Dr. Turner's Nineteen Years in Polynesia, pp. 235-7.

in the invisible world. In relation to the death of such, " the heavens are said to be opened," " the clouds have rolled away," *i.e.* to admit the spirits of these grandees.

At Rarotonga the grand rendezvous of ghosts was at Tuoro, facing the setting sun. Those from *Avarua* travelled the ordinary road towards this rocky point of departure for the invisible world. Until very recently, near the sandy beach of Nikao, in sight of the inevitable Tuoro, stood a stately tree known as " the weeping laurel" (te puka aueanga), where disembodied spirits halted awhile to bewail their hard fate. If unpitied and not sent back to life, the enfeebled and disconsolate traveller passed on to the rendezvous and climbed on a branch of an ancient *bua* still flourishing. Underneath is a natural circular hollow in the rock where *Muru* spreads his net. Should the branch of this *bua* break off through the weight of the ghost, the victim is instantly caught in the net. Occasionally, however, a lively ghost would tear the meshes and escape for a while, passing on by a resistless inward impulse towards the outer edge of the reef, in the hope of traversing the ocean. But in a straight line from the shore is a second round hollow, where *Akaanga's* net is concealed. In this the very few who escape out of the hands of Muru are caught without fail. Escape is impossible. The delighted demons (taae) take the captive ghosts out of their nets, dash their brains out upon the sharp coral, and carry off in triumph their victims to the shades to *eat*.

Ghosts from *Ngatangiia* ascended the noble mountain range which extends across the island from east to west, dipping into the sea at Tuoro. Inexpressibly weary and sad was this journey over a road inaccessible to mortals. For this tribe at the rendezvous of ghosts was appointed a large iron-wood tree, some of whose branches were green, some dead. The spirits that trod on the *green* branches came back to life ; whilst those who had the misfortune to crawl on the *dead* branches were at once caught in the net of either Muru or Akaanga.

Warrior spirits were more fortunate, and were said to " aere kia Tiki," that is to join Tiki, the first who *so* died. At Mangaia Tiki is a *woman*, sister to Veêtini, the first who died a natural death.

Tiki sits at the threshold of a very long house with reed sides, in Avaiki, *i.e.* the shades. All around are planted shrubs and flowers of undying fragrance and beauty. This guardian of the Rarotongan Paradise is ever patiently awaiting new arrivals from the upper world. It was customary at Rarotonga to bury with the dead the head and kidneys of a hog, a split cocoa-nut, and a root of " kava" (*piper mythisticum*), to enable the spirit-traveller to make an acceptable offering to Tiki, who thus propitiated, admits the giver inside his dwelling. Here, sitting at their ease, eating, drinking, dancing, or sleeping, are assembled the brave of past ages, ready to welcome the new comer, and to relate over again the story of their sanguinary achievements performed in life.

The luckless ghost who had no present for Tiki was compelled to stay outside in rain and darkness for ever, shivering of cold and hunger.

At Titikaveka, near the sea, is a mass of blood-red stone. It was believed that there is *in the sky* an oven for cooking human spirits ; the blood of these victims dropping down on the rock gives it a deep red colour !

At Aitutaki it was usual to place at the pit of the stomach of the corpse the kernel of a cocoa-nut and a piece of sugar-cane. At Mangaia the extremity of a cocoa-nut frond served the same purpose, as a charm or safe-conduct on entering the invisible world.

The sacred men of Pukapuka, or Danger Island, gave me in 1862 two " ere vaerua, " *i.e. snares for catching souls*, made of stout cinet. One snare is 28 feet long, the other about half that length. The loops are arranged on either side, and are of different sizes to suit the dimensions of ghosts ; some being thin, others stout. When a person was very sick, or had given offence to the sacred men, the priests hung up some of these " soul-traps " in the upper branches of trees near the dwelling, and pretended to watch the flight of the spirit. If the spirit of the sick man, in the shape of an insect or a small bird, did *not* enter the snare, the patient recovered ; but if, as the sacred men averred, the wretched ghost became entangled in one of the meshes, there was no hope. The demon " Vaerua," or " Spirit " presiding over spirit-world, hurried off the unlucky ghost to the shades to feast upon, for ceremonial offences.

The spirits of those who escape the anger of Vaerua follow the track of the setting sun, and find themselves in a spacious house owned by Reva. Inside are a number of mats, on each of which a divinity keeps watch over the souls belonging to him. These disembodied spirits amuse themselves with beating gongs, dances, and devouring the *essence* of offerings of food hung up in the marae by relatives in the upper world. A fierce sea-god keeps ceaseless watch all round this house, in case any of the land-gods inside should pity one of these forlorn ghosts and allow it to escape back to its old earthly tenement.

At Uea, one of the Loyalty Islands, it was the custom formerly when a person was very ill to send for a man whose employment it was "*to restore souls to forsaken bodies.*" The soul-doctor would at once collect his friends and assistants, to the number of twenty men and as many women, and start off to the place where the family of the sick man was accustomed to bury their dead. Upon arriving there, the soul-doctor and his male companions commenced playing the *nasal* flutes with which they had come provided, in order to entice back the spirit to its old tenement. The women assisted by a low whistling, supposed to be irresistibly attractive to exile spirits. After a time the entire procession proceeded towards the dwelling of the sick person, flutes playing and the women whistling all the time, *leading back the truant spirit!* To prevent its possible escape, with their palms open, they seemingly drove it along with gentle violence and coaxing. On approaching the village they danced and shouted, " We have brought back the spirit of so and so !" Then would succeed loud laughter and vociferations of delight at the cleverness of their leader, the spirit-doctor.

On entering the dwelling of the patient the vagrant spirit was ordered in loud tones at once to enter the body of the sick man, who, as might be supposed, would not be a little moved by the entire procedure. A good feasting would be provided by the relatives of the invalid. Sometimes the poor fellow died : the cause assigned by the soul-doctor would be that the spirit had refused to re-inhabit its former dwelling on account of the smallness of the feast.

AITUTAKIAN HELL.

The priests asserted that at death human spirits descend to the domains of the goddess Miru, whose body is frightfully deformed and her countenance terrible. For unknown ages she had feasted on the spirits of the dead, but at length was checkmated by a brave man named Tekauae, [1] or *the-chin.* Being apparently near death, he directed his friends, as soon as the breath was out of his body, to get a cocoa-nut, and cautiously cracking it to disengage the round kernel from the shell. This kernel was wrapped up in a piece of cloth and placed next to the stomach of the dead, being completely concealed by the grave coverings.

In due time Tekauae descended to spirit-world, and was greatly shocked at the dreadful aspect of the mistress of those regions. Miru had but *one breast*—the other had somehow been cut off. Only *one leg* was perfect—the other had been amputated at the knee. But *one arm* was complete—the other had been cut off at the elbow.

The deformed hag commanded Tekauae to draw near. The trembling human spirit obeyed, and sat down before Miru. According to her unvarying practice she set for her intended victim a bowl of food, and bade him eat it quite up. Miru with evident anxiety waited to see him swallow it.

As Tekauae took up the bowl, to his horror he found it to consist of *living centipedes.* The quick-witted mortal now recollected the cocoa-nut kernel at the pit of his stomach, and hidden from Miru's view by his clothes. With one hand he held the bowl to his lips, as if about to swallow its contents ; with the other he secretly held the cocoa-nut kernel, and ate it—the bowl concealing the nut from Miru. It was evident to the goddess that Tekauae was actually swallowing *something:* what else could it be but the contents of the fatal bowl ? Tekauae craftily contrived whilst eating the nourishing cocoa-nut to allow the live centipedes to fall on the ground one or two at a time. As the intended

---

[1] Mangaian " te kauvae " = chin.

victim was all the time sitting on the ground, it was no difficult achievement in this way to empty the bowl completely by the time he had finished the cocoa-nut.

Miru waited in vain to see her intended victim writhing in agony and raging with thirst.   Her practice on such occasions was to direct the tortured victim-spirit to dive in a lake close by, to seek relief.   None that dived in that water ever came up alive ; excessive anguish and quenchless thirst so distracting their thoughts that they were invariably drowned.   Miru would afterwards cook and eat her victims at leisure.

Here was a new event in her history : the bowl of living centipedes had been disposed of, and yet Tekauae manifested no sign of pain, no intention to leap into the cooling but fatal waters.   Long did Miru wait; but in vain.   At last she said to her visitor, "Return to the upper world" (*i.e.* to life).   "Only remember this—do not speak against me to mortals.   Reveal not my ugly form and my mode of treating my visitors.   Should you be so foolish as to do so, you will certainly at some future time come back to my domains, and I will see to it that you do not escape my vengeance a second time."

Tekauae accordingly left the shades, and came back to life. His friends, delighted at his recovery, inquired where his spirit had been, and how it had fared.   He heeded not the anger of Miru and the promise of secrecy made to her, but informed the inhabitants of this upper world what they might expect should they unfortunately fall into the clutches of this foe to mankind.

AITUTAKIAN HEAVEN.

There is, also, a good land, Iva, under the guardianship of
Tukaitaua,[1] a being of pleasing and benevolent aspect, as well
as of a gentle disposition. In Iva there is abundance of good
food : the finest sugar-cane grows there. The fortunate spirits
who get to this pleasant land spend their time in the society of
Tukaitaua, chewing with unalloyed appetite this sweet sugar-cane.

Tekauae warned the people of this world to be on their guard
against Miru. The way to avoid her is to have a cocoa-nut kernel
and a piece of sugar-cane placed close to the stomach at death—in
order to deceive Miru. Departing spirits thus provided go to the
pleasant land of Iva, and lying at their ease, evermore feast on the
richest food and chew sugar-cane.

DRAMATIC SONG OF MIRU, MISTRESS OF SPIRIT-WORLD.

FOR TEREAVAI'S FÊTE.   COMPOSED BY KAPUA, 1824.

Chorus.

Na Miru te umu i Avaiki,
Ei rangi tae ia Tane ē !

Miru has an oven[2] in spirit-land,
Like that which devoured (the tribe
   of) Tane.[3]

Solo.

Aē !

Aye !

[1] At Mangaia "Tukaitaua" was of a malevolent disposition, the first
violent death being due to his prowess. Tukaitaua taught the world the art of
war.

[2] The oven in daily use in each household, and particularly the monster
ovens in which it was the office of the tribe of Tane to cook *ti* roots (*dracoena
terminalis*), were said to have been derived from Miru's original oven in Hades.

[3] The reference is to the tribe of Tane, twice treacherously destroyed by
their foes in the fires of their own ovens.

Chorus.

Ei rangi tae ia Tautiti,	An end was put to the dance, Tautiti,
E kai karii na Rongo ē !	By the warlike behest of Rongo.
O Tane mata reirua !	Alas, Tane ! author of all our amuse- ments,

Solo.

Nai mata reirua ē,	Those pleasures all came to an end ;
Na Miru oki te umu ka roa	For Miru's dread oven for ever burns
I raro ē !	In the shades !
E nunumi atu e i te aerenga āē !	She devours all who go down.

Chorus.

E nunumi atu,	She devours
Ka aere paa i te umu tao	All who approach the blazing oven
I te umu kai na Miru ē !	Where Miru's food is to be cooked.
Noea Miru ?	Whence came Miru ?
No Avaiki, i te po anga noa ē !	From Avaiki (spirit-land), out of horrid darkness.

Tao na i te ekī !	Prepare thy intoxicating draught.[1]
E ti rakoa ē !	Cook the graceful *ti*—
E ti uaua ē !	Spare not the prolific *ti ;*
E ti tara are ē !	Nor even that grown at thy doorway,
E ti nongonongo ia Avaiki ē !	And that which is the pride of Hades.
Ae, Miru, naau tena !	Ah, Miru ! such are thy tricks !

An ancient farewell in prospect of dissolution was, " Ei ko na ra, tau taeake, *ka aere au i te tava ia Miru,*" *i.e.* " Farewell, brother, *I go to the domains of Miru !*" How inexpressibly affecting ! " Having no hope, and without God in the world."

The mistress of the invisible world, so cruel to visitors, was very tenderly attached to her only son Tautiti. She would permit no one to carry his drinking water but herself. On dark nights, or

---

[1] Miru is charged by the chorus to prepare the intoxicating cup in order to stupefy her intended victims. She is represented as building up a vast oven of *ti* roots of all kinds for a feast ; but Miru's *ti* roots are human souls ! (The song is not quite complete.)

when deep sleep had locked up the senses of mortals, Miru would make her way to the well-known fairy streams Auparu and Vaikaute, carrying the empty calabashes to be filled. To this there is an allusion in Tereavai's Fête Song :—

E taa vai no Tautiti.	A calabash of water for Tautiti.
Na Miru rai e kāve,	Miru herself will provide it,
Kia inu Tane i te vai kea ra ē !	So that Tane may drink this living water.

Her " peerless " daughters were often seen and admired ; but the mother was most solicitous to conceal her ugly form.

SNEEZING.

The philosophy of sneezing is, that the spirit having gone travelling about—perchance on a visit to the homes or burying-places of its ancestors—its return to the body is naturally attended with some difficulty and excitement, occasioning a tingling and enlivening sensation all over the body. Hence the various customary remarks addressed to the returned spirit in different islands. At Rarotonga, when a person sneezes, the bystanders exclaim, as though addressing a spirit, " A, kua oki mai koe " = " Ha ! you have come back." At Manihiki and Rakaanga (colonised from Rarotonga) they say to the spirit, " Aere koe ki Rarotonga " = " Go to Rarotonga." At Mangaia the customary address is, " Ua nanave koe " = " Thou art delighted."

The following well-known lines refer to Poêpoê, or *Speck-land.* (For Umuakaui, circa 1823.)

Puputa motu taua ē !	Alas, we part for ever !
Ka aere au tei *Poêpoê !*	I go alone to *Speck-land.*
E enua akarere Mangaia e taea mai ai !	My home, Mangaia, for ever fades from sight.

Here is a reference to *Tiairi*, by Koroa, in his "Lament for Tãẽ," who was slain circa 1815.

Vaerua aere i tai	Spirits wandering towards the sea ;
I Rangikapua te nuku o te Atua	At Rangtkapua is assembled a divine host—
Ia tu roèroê.	A feeble, tottering throng !
Tākina koe iia ?	Whither goest thou, friend ?
I Puara-moamoa i aka i *Tiairi*,	From the leaping-place I go to dance at *Tiairi*,
I pare i te kiato.	Clothed in fragrant flowers.

Another reference to *Tiairi* occurs in a lament for the sons of Rori, 1790 (circa).

Na tokotoru a Rori	Three brave sons of Rori
Ei tupeke pare kura e !	Wearing noble head-dresses !
Tera roa te anau te aka mai i te ngaere	Yonder are they dancing the war-dance
I te kapa toa i *Tiairi.*	Of brave spirits in *Tiairi.*

When Ikoke heard of the murder of his beloved younger brother Takurua, he feelingly said, "We will meet in the warriors' resting-place,"[1] *i.e.* "I, too, will die a violent death, so that we may meet in the warriors' heaven." Not long after, this wish was granted ; for he fell in the battle of Tuopapa by those who had slain his brother. Ikoke could, according to his faith, only meet his favourite brother by a violent death, as all who die a natural death are devoured by Miru.

Another saying of theirs in reference to the unseen world is : "Ka aere i nunga i te puokia ei aka i Tiairi :" "We will go to yon place of safety, Tiairi, to dance the warriors' dance."

------

[1] "I nunga i te puokia maua e araveitu ei."

Subjoined is a mention of the famous *bua* tree from the shades (Arakauvae's funeral games for his father, circa 1817).

E metua tane ra ē, Vara, kua topa ra i te io,	My father Vara, thou art forsaken by thy god.
Kua veevee te po, ka eke atu ai ē !	Night is at hand, whither thou must descend.
E rua metua i raro ē !	Alas, to be deprived of both parents !
E metua tane ia Kovi, kua pa te rakau ē !	Thy father Kovirua watches thy wasting frame,
Ei toko ake i te maki ra e !	And vainly seeks to re-invigorate it.
Mitikia mai Koviruā, taraia mai, taraia ra ē !	Day by day thy once-rounded limbs are *adzed* away —
Taraia ra e te io tupu na Motoro.	Pitilessly adzed away by thy god Motoro ;
Kua vai te ata ivi e ! Toou anga rakau oi ra e !	So that only a living skeleton is left.
Tu maira tei runga koe i te *pua* i mareva.	Take thy place on the *bua* tree in the shades.
Kua mǎreva te metua i oro i Avaiki.	Lost for ever is the parent gone to Avaiki.

A FAREWELL (VEÊ) CHANTED AT A REED-THROWING MATCH FOR WOMEN.

COMPOSED IN MEMORY OF VAIANA, BY HER HUSBAND NAUPATA, IN 1824.

Solo.

Teiia'ua ngaro ē ?	Whither has she gone ?

Chorus.

Tei Avaiki e oro atu,	She has sped to Avaiki,
Kore e ariu tei te nii moana :	She disappeared at the edge of the horizon,
Tei te opunga i te rā.	Where the sun drops through.
Ka tangi i reira !	We weep for thee !

Solo.

Ka tangi ana 'i,
Oki ra a kimi ra aē!

Yes, I will for ever weep,
And ever seek for thee!

Chorus.

Tangi au ka tangi e,
Tangi ki te vaine ua ngaro rā,
Aore koe e tu e angairi.

Bitter tears I shed for thee ;
I weep for the lost wife of my bosom.
Alas! thou wilt not return.

Solo.

Mai tu e angairi!

Oh, that thou *wouldst* return!

Chorus.

Ariu mai i te ao ē!
Oki maira iaku nei.
Akia koe, ua motu ïa tarereia au!

Stay ; come back to this world!
Return to my embrace.
Thou art as a bough wrenched off by the blast!

Solo.

Mai tārērē au ē tei Avaiki—
Te enua mamao i oro atu na ē!

Wrenched off, and now in Avaiki—
That distant land to which thou art fled.

The author of this " farewell " became a devoted servant of the Lord Jesus Christ. These words are exceedingly popular with the natives. Part is omitted.

Rakoia, chanting (in 1815) the praises of his first-born, Enuataurere, who was accidentally drowned at Tamarua, says :—

O Enuataurere i te tai kura i te moana.
Te nunga koe i te uru o te kare i tai ē!

Enuataurere now trips o'er the ruddy ocean.
Thy path is the foaming crest of the billow.

Aue ē! Enuataurere ē!
Enuataurere ē!

Weep for Enuataurere,—
For Enuataurere.

CHAPTER IX.

VEÊTINI;[1] *OR, THE IMMORTALITY OF THE SOUL.*

THE first who ever died a *natural* death in Mangaia was Veêtini. He was the only and much beloved son of Tueva and his wife Manga. But Veêtini, when in the prime of early manhood, sickened and died. The parents, in their grief, instituted those signs of mourning and funeral games which were ever afterwards observed amongst these islanders. The chief mourners were Tueva, Manga, and the lovely Tiki—the attached sister of Veêtini. All these, with the more distant relatives, blackened their faces, cut off their hair, slashed their bodies with shark's teeth, and wore only " pakoko," or native cloth, dyed red in the sap of the candle-nut tree, and then dipped in the black mud of a taro-patch. The very offensive smell of this mourning garment is symbolical of the putrescent state of the dead. Their heads were encircled with common fern, singed with fire to give it a red

---

[1] The allegorical character of this interesting myth is evident from the names. Veêtini means *all-separating;* Tueva, *mourner;* Manga, *food,* in allusion to the custom of offering food to the dead. Tiki signifies *fetched:* if a person dies, his spirit is said to be " fetched."

appearance.[1] It was on account of Veêtini that the *eva*, or dirge, in its four varieties, and the mourning dance, were invented and performed by the sorrowing relatives day by day.

These melancholy ceremonies occupied from ten to fifteen days, according to the rank and age of the party deceased. During the entire period of mourning no beating of bark for native cloth was permitted in the district where the death occurred. A woman wishing to beat out her bark must go to another part of the island. The object in view was to avoid giving offence to the female demon Mueu, who introduced cloth-beating to this world; but who herself beats out cloth of a very different texture. *Her* cloth-flail is the stroke of death. So long as the mourning and funeral games were going on, Mueu was supposed to be present; when all was over she returned to her home in Avaiki, or the shades. Hence the proverb when a person dies, " Era, kua tangi te tutunga a Mueu," *i.e.* "Ah ! Mueu's flail is once more at work !"

The last resting-place of Veêtini is at Rangikapua, a green spot about half a mile from the sea. The rays of the setting sun fall upon the hill, about 100 feet above the level of the ocean, thus distinguished. On the evening he was buried the dirges and dances that had been invented in his honour were performed. The parents and the sister looked wistfully towards the *north*, hoping for his return to their midst—but in vain !

The day following they walked in sad procession, slowly chanting dirges expressive of passionate desire again to embrace the departed, along the *western* shore of the island. At night,

---

[1] Since the establishment of Christianity this extravagant mode of mourning for the dead, with the single exception of the bad-smelling "pakoko," has been discontinued.

exhausted with grief and weariness, they slept in one of the rugged caves near the sea, having in vain strained their eyes over the ocean path where the spirit of Veêtini had so lately disappeared.

The mourning band next sought the lost one on the *southern* and almost inaccessible shore of Mangaia; still there was no response to the loud cries and entreaties of the disconsolate parents and the lovely Tiki.

At last they arrived at the *eastern* coast, and gazed over the vast expanse swept by the life-giving trade-winds. Once more the lamentations and funeral dances were duly performed. At night they occupied the Ruddy Cave (Ana-kura). The entrance to this spacious cave is washed by the surf. Ere dawn Tueva rose from his stony couch to watch the rising of the sun. The shadows of night were fast passing away. In a few minutes more the sun rose in all its wonted glory. Tueva now noticed a tiny dark speck beneath on the ocean, which, as the sun advanced on its course, grew larger and drew nearer, passing over the ocean in the bright trail of the sun. On arriving nearer still, this wonderful object, lightly skimming over the crest of the waves, proved to be no other than their own lost Veêtini !

The now rejoicing parents rushed forwards to kiss their son, who was indeed Vcêtini, yet not altogether like his former self. He said to the joyful throng that he had been permitted to revisit this upper world in consequence of the passionate lamentations of his parents, and to comfort their sorrowing hearts. He also came to show mortals how to make offerings of food to please the dead. For himself, he had come and must depart in the bright track of the sun, being now a denizen of spirit-land. However, to gratify his parents and friends, Veêtini asked great Tangaroa to detain

the sun for a short time in its course, in order that he might rest
and converse awhile with his relatives. The prayer was granted,
and the sun was detained while Veêtini and his friends pleasantly
rested in a sort of extempore house, or booth, erected for him on
the spot known as Karanga-iti.

At length Veêtini rose, and led the half-glad and half-sorrowful
procession along the beach towards the west, the sun now moving
on as usual in the heavens. At last they reached Vairorongo, or
Rongo's sacred stream, directly facing the setting sun. Here they
rested a few minutes only, as day was fast fading away. Not far
distant on the hill lay the body of Veêtini. As the sun disappeared beneath the horizon, and the ocean was covered with its
golden light, Veêtini said he must go. The weeping parents
begged him to stay with them. The son replied, " I cannot ;
I do not belong to this world now ; " and then shouted im-
patiently :—

Takai ïa te rā	Thrust down the sun,
Ei eke i Tekurutukia.	That I may descend to nether-land !

The parents now endeavoured to detain him by force ; but,
lo ! they grasped at a shadow. They watched him gliding swiftly
over the western ocean in the ruddy track of the sun, and, with its
last rays, Veêtini, now a tiny distant speck in the train of the king
of day, for ever disappeared.

VAIPO'S DIRGE FOR VEÊTINI.

FOUNDED ON THE PRECEDING MYTH.

(FIRST PERFORMED CIRCA 1794 : FOR THE SECOND TIME IN 1819.)

Call for the music and dance to begin.

Kua pa te rongo i Avaiki
Kua inga paā Veêtini
Aue ka mate ē !

The news has sped to Avaiki
Of Veêtini about to die.
Sad day of death !

Solo.

Taipo ē !

Go on !

Chorus.

Akatu are i Karanga-iti,

A house is built for him at Karanga-
iti

I te rua paa i te rā ē !

To face the rising sun.

Solo.

Aē !

'Tis done !

Chorus.

Kua tau paā Vêetini i te rangi ;

Veêtini has gained the sky [*i.e.* the
place where the sun drops down] ;

Ka oro !
O na mavae ia Avaiki ē !

Has fled !
Oh, all-dividing Spirit-world !

Solo.

Kakea mai e i te tautua aē !

Whence came he ?

Chorus.

Kakea mai i te tautua ia Avaiki
Ka rekireki mai e,
I nunga i te moana.
Kua titotito aere Veêtini.

He came up out of Spirit-world,
Stepping lightly on his path
O'er the treacherous waves.
Veêtini is again trembling on the
wing.

E kāū, kāū mai e !

He skims, he skims the sea !

Solo.

E aru atu i to miringa aē !

Alas, he follows thy track, [O Sun !]

Chorus.

E aru atu i to miringa,	Yes, he follows thy dazzling light,
O te rā paa e opuopu atu na ē !	As thou gently settest in the ocean.
Takai ïa te rā,	Thrust down the sun,
Ei eke i Tekurutukia !	That he may descend to nether-land.

THE CLOSING OR DAY-SONG FOR TENIO'S FÊTE.

BY KOROA. CIRCA 1814.

Call for the dance to lead off.

Iti pakakina o te rā e !	Day is breaking ;
Ka roi te tere o Tautiti	The visit of Tautiti [1] is drawing to a close—
Ka aka ē !	Dance away !

Solo.

Taipo ē !	Go on !

Chorus.

Kua aati te nio o Veêtini	Alas, the teeth of Veetini [2] are all broken,
Kua akama i te ao ē !	He is ashamed to linger in the light.

Solo.

Ao mata ngaa ē !	The eye of day is unclosing.

Chorus.

E aru mai ia Tautiti	Come, obey the behests of Tautiti.
Kai a mata tuitui kakā ra o Vātea e !	As a burning torch is the opening eye of Vātea.
Ungaunga te rā e tu e ara!	Awake from thy slumbers, O Sun arise.

It is in reference to this myth of the sad journeyings of the beautiful Tiki with her parents in search of Veêtini, that at the

----

[1] Tautiti was supposed to be present at the particular dance of which he was the originator. As soon as it was over, he returned to the shades.

[2] Broken by death, *i.e.* no longer *eats.*

breaking up of a funeral party it is commonly said, " Ka ruru i te tere ia Tiki ka aere ei," *i.e.* "The weary travels of Tiki are over : we part."

A principal reason why Veêtini's spirit was permitted to revisit this world, was to institute the practice of propitiating the good-will of the dead by offerings of food.   This is alluded to in a ancient song about Veêtini, by Kirikovi, circa 1760.

VEÊTINI MEETING HIS FATHER.

Tueva aka-itu i te eva i te metua,	Tueva, who seven times lamented for his boy,
Ae ; eaa toou ara i te ao nei ?	Asked, "Why didst thou return to this world ?"
I ana mai au i te kave	" I came," (said Veêtini,) "to instruct you
I te pākuranga ma te meringa,	In making food-offerings to the dead,
Meringa mai Avaiki e,	Offerings to those in spirit-world ;
Meringa mai io tatou metua	Gifts from their relatives,
E noo i te ao nei. Ei aa ?	Who yet linger in this upper world."

Such was the belief and practice of heathenism.   As soon as the corpse was committed to its last resting-place, the mourners selected five old cocoa-nuts, which were successively opened, and the water poured out upon the ground.   These nuts were then wrapped up in leaves and native cloth, and thrown towards the grave ; or, if the corpse were let down with cords into the deep chasm of " Auraka," the nuts and other food would be successively thrown down upon it.   Calling loudly each time the name of the departed, they said, "Here is thy food ; eat it."   When the fifth nut and the accompanying " raroi," or pudding, were thrown down, the mourners said, "Farewell ! we come back no more to thee !"

Seventeen years ago, Arikikaka, the last heathen of Mangaia, lost his only son—a consistent church member. The old man was inconsolable at his loss. How could it be otherwise with a heathen parent? The corpse was buried with his mother's deceased relatives, on the west of the island. The friends had dispersed to their respective homes. A day or two after, Arikikaka and his wife walked with difficulty across the island, arriving at dusk at the grave of their beloved son, with a basket of cooked food and some unopened cocoa-nuts. With many tears and affectionate words they called upon their boy to eat the food and drink the nuts (carefully opened for the convenience of the ghost at the grave, and the contents poured out upon the earth), which they had carried six miles. The aged couple slept under a tree, close to the last resting-place of their son ; and at dawn on the following morning departed. How sad that, whilst their son died in the faith and hope of the Gospel, the parents should cling to the effete superstitions of a bygone age ! It is, however, pleasing to add that in May, 1865, Arikikaka and his wife were baptized. In this case "at eventime there was light."

A few years previous to the discovery of the island by Captain Cook in 1777, Ngarā, priest of Motoro, was paramount chief of Mangaia. His nephew Vera died, it was believed, in consequence of having incurred the anger of that divinity by setting fire to a forest of thatch trees growing on the eastern part of the island. Not that the pandanus trees were sacred, but the oronga (*urtica argentea*), growing between them, was considered to be " the hair of Motoro."

Very imposing funeral rites were performed for this lad, on account of his relationship to Ngarā. As in the case of Veêtini, the relatives are said to have paraded the island in the vain hope of Vera's return. The body was conveyed to Tamarua and thrown down Raupa, a fearful chasm, 150 feet deep, and having communication with the sea. The entrance to this gloomy place is in the Mission premises at that village. The sorrowful parents slept in a cave hard by, in the hope that Vera would return for a day, in answer to their passionate laments. Next day the disappointed parents, followed by a long procession of mourners, returned to their dwellings.

DIRGE FOR VERA : A DEATH-TALK.

COMPOSED BY UANUKU. A "TIAU," OR PARTIAL WEEPING. CIRCA 1770.

TUMU.	INTRODUCTION.
	Solo.
Turokia i Vairorongo ;	At Vairorongo,[1] towards the setting sun—
Noo mai koe i te aiai	Tarry with us this evening.
Ka aere au, e Manga e,	I go far away, mother,
	Chorus.
I te ara taurere ki Iva ē !	By a perilous path to spirit-land.

PAPA.	FOUNDATION.
	Solo.
Pare mai Vera i te kau ara,	Halt, Vera, on thy journey :
Ariua te mata i Mangaia.	Turn thine eyes towards Mangaia.
Te karo nei i o metua,	Look again at thy parents,
Te roè nei i te ao ō !	Whose days are spent in tears,

---

[1] Wherever the body might be buried, the spirits of the dead assembled at Vairorongo, facing the setting sun, to await the proper period for their departure. "Iva " (= Nukuhiva) I have rendered "spirit-land "—its true meaning here.

                              Chorus.

E niaki i te tere i Anakura e aere ei   Resting in the Red-Cave by the way.

         UNUUNU TAI.   FIRST OFFSHOOT.

                              Solo.

Turokia ē   Towards the setting sun

                              Chorus.

         i tona are ē!   is his home!

I tona are, e manga kai nā Vera.   A home and food in plenty for Vera.

Tu a rau kura Tueva akatapu.   Tueva, encircled with red leaves, is mourning.

                              Solo.

Tu a rau kura Tueva akatapu.   Tueva, encircled with red leaves, is mourning.

Kua tangi te ike a Mueu   Alas! the death-flail of Mueu is beating.

Kua taroê ua miringa, e Vera ē!   Weeping, we follow thee, beloved Vera.

    Ka aere au, e Manga ē,   I go far away, mother,

                              Chorus.

I te ara taurere ki Iva ē!   By a perilous path to spirit-land.

           PAPA.   FOUNDATION.

                              Solo.

Pare mai Vera i te kau ara,   Halt, Vera, on thy journey.

    Etc.   etc.   etc.   Etc.   etc.   etc.

         UNUUNU RUA.   SECOND OFFSHOOT.

                              Solo.

Vāia   Rush forth,

                              Chorus.

    te rua e, i te tokerau ē!   O north-west wind![1]

I te tokerau, e ngaa mai ki tai.   Bear him gently on his way.

Iki ki te iku parapu—   Awake, O south-west—

---

[1] The north-west and south-west are known as "spirit-winds." It is fabled that the latter restored Veêtini to his friends. Perchance it will restore Vera to his sorrowing parents. Mautara, the grandfather of Vera, was dead at the period (more than a century ago) when this song was composed. The name of the illustrious chief is put for Ngarā, his youngest son, then "lord of Mangaia."

Solo.

ki te iku parapu

          O south-west.

Tei te turuki mai Vera ē !

Perchance Vera will return.

Te tangi nei a Mautara ē !

Even Mautara weeps for thee,

Te tirae tangata i pou rai.

How desolate is our home !

Ka aere au, e Manga ē,

I go far away, mother,

Chorus.

I te ara taurere ki Iva ē !

By a perilous path to spirit-land.

PAPA.

FOUNDATION.

Solo.

Pare mai Vera i te kau ara,

Halt, Vera, on thy journey,

Etc. etc. etc.

Etc. etc. etc.

UNUUNU TORU.

THIRD OFFSHOOT.

Solo.

Kaukau,

Skim,

Chorus.

Vera e, i tuāanga ē !

Vera, the surface of the ocean,

I te tuāanga to nga mata i te tai o

The ocean-path once traversed by

Ngakē.

Ngakē.[1]

Solo.

Porutu te ua i te moana,

Torrents of rain obstruct thy journey,

Te toa ranga nuka te atua

Yet by the aid of a mighty god

E tau ai te tere o Vera e

The band led by Vera shall safely reach

Tei Tikura moana !

Their home beneath the glowing ocean.

Ka aere au, e Manga ē,

I go far away, mother,

Chorus.

I te ara taurere ki Iva ē !

By a perilous path to spirit-land.

PAPA.

FOUNDATION.

Pare mai Vera i te kau ara

Halt, Vera, on thy journey :

Etc. etc. etc.

Etc. etc. etc.

---

[1] Ngakē was one of the three first slain, inconsistently represented as traversing the ocean.

UNUUNU Ā.	FOURTH OFFSHOOT.

Pokai

Solo.

        Slowly

Chorus.

    te tere e ia tau ai ē !　　　traverse these rugged shores,
Kia tau Vera i rangi maanga　　　Ere Vera gain the western skies.
No Maautaramea te tere i oki mai.　　Veêtini [1] once returned to earth.

Solo.

Te tere i oki mai Vera ē !　　　O that Vera might but revisit earth,
Tei tipurei moana i !　　　Gliding over the shimmering sea.
   Ka aere au, e Manga ē,　　　I go far away, mother,

Chorus.

I te ara tiroa ki Iva ē !　　　By a perilous path to spirit-land.

     PAPA.　　　FOUNDATION.

Pare mai Vera i te kau ara,　　　Halt, Vera, on thy journey,
  Etc.   etc.   etc.　　　Etc. etc. etc.

    UNUUNU RIMA.　　　FIFTH OFFSHOOT.

Solo.

E kiato　　　Lash firmly

Chorus.

   te vaka e kia mau ai ē !　　the outrigger of thy bark,[2]
Kia mau ai i Koatu-taii-roa.　　Ere starting on thy long voyage.
Noo mai Vera i te tapaa i muā !　　Linger awhile, Vera, on the sea-
               shore—

Solo.

I te tapaa i mua 'i o te tangi tai　　On the beach where the waves beat ;
I ara mania : kua taatonga 'i　　Near this rough path.　Must thou go
Ki raro i tei Tuatua-pipiki,　　To the regions of the sun-setting ?
   Ka aere au, e Manga e,　　　I go far away, mother,

---

[1] In the original a second name [Maautaramea] is substitued for Veêtini, which I have dropped.

[2] Vera's spirit is actually starting.　The canoe is on the outer edge of the reef ready to cleave the billows.　See that the outrigger is well secured, or the voyager will certainly be drowned.　*What the outrigger is to the canoe, the god is to the soul.*　Without this necessary aid, tread not this treacherous ocean-path.

Chorus.

I te ara taurere ki Iva ē !   By a perilous path to spirit-land.

PAPA AKAOTI.   LAST FOUNDATION.

Solo.

Pare mai Vera i te kau ara, Halt, Vera, on thy journey:
Ariua te mata i Mangaia.   Turn thine eyes to Mangaia.
Te kare nei i o metua,   Look again at thy parents,
Te roe nei i te ao ē !   Whose days are spent in tears,

Chorus.

E niaki te tere i Anakura e aere ē !   Resting in the Red-Cave by the way.

AKAREINGA.   FINALE.

Ai e ruaoo ē ! E rangai ē ! Ai e ruaoo ē ! E rangai ē !

The beauty of this dirge is much enhanced by covert allusions throughout to the myth of Veêtini. At the conclusion of each stanza, in the native, the name "Manga," *i.e.* the mother of Veêtini, occurs, instead of the name of Vera's own mother. To prevent confusion of ideas, I have throughout rendered it "mother."

To this day it is said of the dying at Rarotonga, "So-and-so *is passing over the sea.*"

The foregoing dirge has been presented exactly as recited at their "death-talks." On account of the numerous repetitions, those succeeding will be given in an abbreviated form.

THE GHOSTS LED BY VERA PREPARING FOR THEIR FINAL DEPARTURE.

A "TIAU," OR PARTIAL WEEPING. BY UANUKU, CIRCA 1770.

TUMU.	INTRODUCTION.
	Solo.
Akarongo, Vera, i te tangi tai.	List, Vera, to the music of the sea.
Reki atu koe i te ara pepe ;	Beyond yon dwarfed pandanus trees
Tangi mai paa i Maunuroa.	The billows are dashing o'er the rocks.
Tutu atu ka aere ;	'Tis time, friends, to depart ;
	Chorus.
O te uru matie kura ra e te nau.	Our garments are mourning weeds and flowers.

PAPA.	FOUNDATION.
	Solo.
Reki atu koe i te ngau rua ;	Advance to yonder level rock ;
E tatari koe i te parapu,	There to await the favouring wind
Năku mai paa i tua moana.	That will bear thee o'er the sea.
Te karo nei Mitimiti e,	(Thy father) Mitimiti looks sorrowfully on
	Chorus.
I te vivi matangi, e taku tere ē !	The departing band led by thee.

INUINU TAI.	FIRST OFFSHOOT.
	Solo.
Akarongo Vera ē,	List, dear Vera,
	Chorus.
i te tangi tai ē ?	to the music of the sea.
Kua pātai tau ara,	Thou art a wretched wanderer,
Na te uru o Iva—	Almost arrived at Iva—

Solo.

na te uru o Iva 'i.	yes, at Iva ;
Mai Iti au, mai Tonga e,	Once from Tahiti, then from Tonga ;
Mai Onemakenukenu ;	*Now* bound to the land of ghosts,
O te rua mato ngaa ei.	Entered though the gaping grave.
Tutu atu ka aere ;	'Tis time, friends, to depart ;

Chorus.

O te uru matie kura ra e te nau ē !	Our garments are mourning weeds and flowers.

INUINU RUA.   SECOND OFFSHOOT.

Solo.

Ariunga atu ē	I turn my eyes

Chorus.

I tai enua ē ;	to another land.
I tai enua patiki atu tau vaerua.	In some other region may my spirit rest !
Tei koatu tauri, tei te ngutu i te rua,	On this trembling stone, at the edge of the chasm (I stand)—

Solo.

Tei te ngutu	At the entrance

Chorus.

i te rua 'i.	Of this dark chasm.
O puaka ngunguru, tei te veenga i te papa.	My path is over yon black rocks near the sea.
Na rotopu i Vaenga, tei o Tamakoti,	Over the roughest and sharpest stones
E takina aereia e te ui rauono.	I lead this feeble troop of ghosts.
Noea ra ? ikonei, na nunga atu	Whence come we ? We are awaiting
Ki te miri,	The long-hoped-for

Solo.

nanu atu	south-eastern

Chorus.

ki te miri	breeze
Tei kopua-reia ; a tai ra tomokia.	To waft us over the far-reaching ocean.
Tei are toka, tu ra i te rae,	We have wandered hither and thither,

Tei Teunu i te kea, ka eke na tai e,
Stepping lightly on the sea-washed sandstone.

Na koatu putuputu, tei kaiti-te-rā.
Over thickly studded rocks we have come.

Kua kapitia e te po, akaroimata i reira,
Overtaken by darkness we sit down to weep,

Solo.

Vaka roimata no Vera e !
A tearful band, under the guidance of Vera.

Angiangi te ua i te aiai ;
At one time a drizzling shower

Tairo atu i te tau are no Moke,
Hides from view the heights of the interior ;

Kua parea e te au tai.
At another we are besprinkled with ocean spray.

Tutu atu ka aere;
'Tis time, friends, to depart ;

Chorus.

O te uru matie kura ra e te nau ē !
Our garments are mourning weeds and flowers.

INUINU TORU.

THIRD OFFSHOOT.

Solo.

Aere tu ē
Press forwards

Chorus.

i Raumatangi ē.
on our journey;

Kia ripoia na Tautuaorau.
Take care that we miss not the way.

Solo.

E kake i Auveo,
Yonder is the landing-place,

Chorus.

o te mata o Katoanu,
Auveo,

O te ui ava e ngaro, o Taumatatai.
The entrance of which is so difficult to find.

Tera to metua,
There, too, is my father,

Solo.

tei runga i Pepeura.
watching our course.

Taueue o te rā, tukuroi ki Teone.
The sun is low ; rest we awhile.

Chorus.

E mania ra tau vaevae i te takai,

Our feet are worn out over these stones ;

Kua avanga Raupa.

Yonder is the gloomy cave Raupa.

Anuenue i Omoana, e tangata matiroe-roe.

Let us move slowly on our way.

Tei Tuatuakare, i raro i Auneke :

We friendless ghosts have reached Auneke.

Eanga ki runga; eanga ki raro;
E anga ki te rā e ana atu.

Look eastward ; look westward ;
Gaze at the setting sun.

Solo.

Ana atu paa Mitimiti, e amoremore

Ah! Mitimiti is following hard behind,

I to miringa; takiri koe kia oki mai.
Noo mai paa i Tepukatia.
Tutu atu ka aere ;

Beckoning me to return.
Here let us halt awhile.
'Tis time, friends, to depart ;

Chorus.

O te uru matie kura ra e te nau ē !

Our garments are mourning weeds and flowers.

INUINU Ā.

FOURTH OFFSHOOT.

Solo.

Ka iia Vera ra ē,

Thy feet, Vera,

Chorus.

e te rau kovi ē,

are entangled with wild vines.

Mataratara i Vavau, te nooanga tan-gata.

Art thou bound for Vavau, the home of ghosts ?

I Rangioroia,

Over

Solo.

mai Rangi

the foaming billows

Chorus.

panakonui :

wilt thou voyage ?

Tei Omaoma-atu-na, o te ara tai rau,

Thread now thy way through groves of pandanus,

O te enua tuarangi, te Omangatiti ;

The favourite haunt of disembodied spirits ;

Ariki Utakea i Takanga-a-tuturi.

Near where the royal Utakea landed,

Solo.

Na Ooki aitu ki te papa o Aumea.	A level beach laved by the sea.
Tikiriri e atua, ei ara paa noku e,	The cricket-god is chirping to direct thy path,
I angamakoitia, ki tuki naupata,	Through the thickets to the shore
I te pou o Atuturi, turi ai	Where the spirits of the dead wander.
Koukou rouru, e Vera e,	Bathe thy streaming locks, Vera.
Omai tai noku ora e, o Te-ata-i-maiore.	Grant me a new life, O Light of the morning !
Tutu atu ka aere;	'Tis time, friends, to depart;

Chorus.

O te nau matie kura ra e te nau ē !	Our garments are mourning weeds and flowers.

INUINU RIMA.   FIFTH OFFSHOOT.

Solo.

Buapua-ariki	Descendant of the kings

Chorus.

i Mauke-tau,	of Mauke;
Kua ikiikitia e, e te matangi au ra	Favoured one, led by a prosperous wind
No te tumu i te rangi, tei Kopuakanae,	From the root of the skies to these shores,
Tei Nukuterarire, e angaanga ikonei,	Ere taking a long farewell, turn back !
Na Mokoaeiau Vaio ra ikonei,	Idol of my dwelling, remain awhile,

Solo.

Vaio ake ia turina kapara ; o te pua	Decked with the buds of sweet-scented flowers
Taurarea e, raumiremire no Tutuila.	And fragrant leaves brought from Tutuila.
Tutu atu ka aere ;	'Tis time, friends, to depart ;

Chorus.

O te uru matie kura ra, e te nau ē !	Our garments are mourning weeds and flowers.

AKAREINGA.   FINALE.

Ai e ruaoo e ! E rangi e !	Ai e ruaoo e ! E rangai e

In this "lament" it is supposed that the spirits of the dead have been marshalled by Vera on the eastern shore of Mangaia, and then weariedly led by him over the rocks and through the thickets of the southern half of the island, until reaching the point due west, where the entire troop take their final departure for the shades. "Auneke" is a point on the shore about midway between the rising and setting sun. The poet evidently places Vavau, Tonga, and Tahiti in the invisible world!

Very beautifully is the father, Mitimiti, represented as chasing the spirit of his beloved Vera in this mournful journey of ghosts round half the island. The ghosts stop occasionally to refresh themselves, their feet lacerated with the sharp stones over which the living can pass only when sandalled. They weep continually at the thought of leaving earth for ever. Many days are occupied in this sad journey. Mitimiti, taking advantage of these delays, hurries forward, and *almost* clutches the ever visible but airy form of his boy, which somehow eludes the detaining hand of the sorrowing parent.

PUVAI LEADING A BAND OF GHOSTS TO THE SHADES.

A "TIAU," OR PARTIAL WEEPING. COMPOSED BY IIKURA, CIRCA 1795.

TUMU.	INTRODUCTION.
Solo.	
E matangi tu i te nguare i Anākura,	A favouring breeze sweeps the entrance of the ghost-cave;
No Puvai, kua roiroi ka tere,	'Tis for Puvai, about to depart.
Chorus.	
Kua kake atu ki te uru kare ē !	Lightly he skims o'er the crest of the billows.

<table>
<tr><td>

PAPA.

Solo.

Ei kona ra, e au metua !
Eva ake ai iaku nei
I te naupata i Taamatangi.
Te tangi nei i te tama angai ra,

Chorus.

Ka uaki mai te matangi ki Iva ē !

</td><td>

FOUNDATION.

Solo.

Farewell, beloved parents !
Let a mourning procession follow [1]
Over the rugged shore of the south.
Weep for the son so tenderly natured,

Chorus.

Ere a fair wind bear me to spirit-
land ! (literally to Iva).

</td></tr>
</table>

<table>
<tr><td>

INUINU TAI.

Solo.

E matangi tu ē

Chorus.

   i te nguare ē!
I te nguare i Anākura.
Kua vā te tuarangi :

Solo.

Kua vā te tuarangi tei Kokirinui ē !

Kua niu aere i Tengaatanga i Ana
  orua.
  Kua roiroi ka tere,

Chorus.

Kua kake atu ki te uru kare ē !

</td><td>

FIRST OFFSHOOT.

Solo.

A favouring breeze

Chorus.

   sweeps the entrance
Of the ghost-cave Anākura.
List to the hum of the ghosts !

Solo.

'Tis the hum of spirits passing o'er
  the rocks ;
That crowd along the beach by Double
  Cave.
  He is about to depart.

Chorus.

Lightly he skims o'er the crest of the
  billows.

</td></tr>
</table>

<table>
<tr><td>

INUINU RUA.

Solo.

Te vaka i te vaka

Chorus.

   o Puvai ē !
Kua tipoki i te riu i te oa.

</td><td>

SECOND OFFSHOOT.

Solo.

Yonder is the bark—

Chorus.

   the canoe—of Puvai
Sorrowfully he bends over it !

</td></tr>
</table>

---

[1] That is of living friends and relatives, *not* ghosts.

Solo.

Kua tipoki i te riu i te oa'i.

Aye, very sorrowfully does he bend over it!

Noo mai koe i te ta ia mua,
Kua kakau i te kirikiriti
Riu atu te aro ki tera enua.
Kua roiroi ka tere

Take thy seat, son, in front.
Clothed in ghostly network; [1]
And turn thy face to yonder land.
He is about to depart.

Chorus.

Kua kake atu ki te uru kare ē !

Lightly he skims o'er the crest of the billows.

INUINU TORU.

THIRD OFFSHOOT.

Solo.

Parepare i tai ē

Let a south-west wind

Chorus.

i te parapu ē !
I te parapu, vāia mai i te tokerau
Na Tiki e oe atu ; na Tiki e oe atu.

ruffle the sea.
Awake thou north-west.
Tiki, sister of Veêtini, leads the way.

Solo.

Motuanga enua Mangaia no Puvai.

Mangaia fades from the sight of Puvai,

Kua peke ke i nga taoa.

Driven away by the violence of the winds.

Kua roiroi ka tere

He is about to depart.

Chorus.

Kua kake atu ki te uru kare ē !

Lightly he skims o'er the crest of the billows.

INUINU Ā.

FOURTH OFFSHOOT.

Solo.

Tama aroa ē

Beloved child

Chorus.

na Motuone ē !
Na Motuone, tangi mai ē
I te uru o te maunga,

of Motuone—
Of Motuone, thy weeping mother,
Glance fondly back on the hills

---

[1] Network was said to be part of the clothing of departed spirits.

Solo.

I te uru o te maunga 'i.	And mountains of the interior.
Ka ano ki Tamarua'i,	Come back to the fair vale of Tamarua,
Kia tae ki Angāuru.	The place where thou wast born.
Kua roiroi ka tere	He is about to depart.

Chorus.

Kua kake atu ki te uru kare ē !	Lightly he skims o'er the crest of the billows !

AKAREINGA.	FINALE.
Ai e ruaoo e ! E rangai e !	Ai e ruaoo e ! E rangai e !

This song is precisely parallel with those relating to Vera. Nephew to Potiki, supreme temporal chief of Mangaia, Puvai by his early death is qualified to lead off a band of ghosts to the shades. Great honours were paid to him as the near relative of the living ruler òf the island.

———

From a Christian point of view the following " lament " is very affecting :—

KOROA'S LAMENT FOR HIS SON KOURAPAPA [1]

(*Endearingly shortened into " Ura "*). *Circa* 1796.

FOR THE "DEATH-TALK OF KOURAPAPA."

TUMU.	INTRODUCTION.
	Solo.
Karangaia e Koroa e,	Koroa gave the command—
E pa akari na Tueva,	A feast of cocoa-nuts, like Tueva's [2] of old,
Na Ura oki i te rua ē !	For dear Ura in his grave ;—

---

[1] Koura-papa = *small shrimp.*

[2] " Like Tueva's of old."   " Like Tiki's."   The former was the father, the latter the lovely sister, of the mythical Veĉtini.

The feast was " all dry," because it was ill prepared, and lay exposed for an entire day at the entrance to the gloomy cave " Auraka."   At nightfall the food was wrapped up in native cloth and thrown down to the corpse.

Chorus.

Butungākai na Tiki oki i rarā e !   A feast for ghosts, all dry, like Tiki's.

PAPA.   #### FOUNDATION.

Solo.

Nai kume au i te ngutupa,——   At the entrance to thy sad home I
                                                      shout—
Teia to pākuranga !   " Here is the feast
Tei raro Ura i te taeva   For Ura who lies at the bottom

Chorus.

te enua ïa, e vae !   of the deep cave."

INUINU TAI.   #### FIRST OFFSHOOT.

Solo.

Karangaia ra e   'Twas Koroa

Chorus.

Koroa nei ē !   that gave the command.
E Koroa nei, Kua rongo e,   Alas ! Koroa heard (his boy) lament-
                                                      ing—
Kua kai ongutungutu,   " The ghosts fought over my food ;—

Solo.

Kua kai ongutungutu, aore au e tongi   Fought so fiercely that I did not get a
  ana.   taste.
Kua kirikiritia e te ueuera kakā   Evil spirits [1] stole it all away.   (Their
                                                      chief)
O Naukino, na pakoti i te ara nei.   Nau-the-Bad would not let me get
                                                      near it."
Na Ura oki i te rua e !   'Twas for Ura in his grave

Chorus.

Putungākai na Tiki oki i rarā e !   We bore a feast, all dry, like Tiki's.

---

[1] " Evil spirits," more literally, " *bright* evil spirits ;" but brightness is in
our ideas associated with goodness. These " Dii inferi " at night became
luminous ; *not so* the unfortunate *human* spirits that go down to their abode.
Yet these spirits are supposed to linger a while about the cave where their dead
bodies had been thrown ; the period for their final departure to the shades not
having come.

| | *Solo.* |
| Putungākai ē, | That feast for the dead, |

	Chorus.
na Tiki oki ē,	like Tiki's—long ago,
Na Tiki oki na Ura.	Was designed for our beloved Ura,
Te porea mai i te toketoke kura,—	Who is condemned to feed on *red worms;*

	Solo.
I te toketoke kura 'i, i te viivii taae.	Yes, on earth-worms and other vile creatures.
Akaatua atu ana oki te tangata, e tau potiki.	Pet child, thou hast taken thy place amongst the gods.
Na Ura oki i te rua ē!	'Twas for Ura in his grave

| | *Chorus.* |
| Putungākai na Tiki oki i rarā e! | We bore a feast, all dry, like Tiki's. |

| INUINU TORU. | THIRD OFFSHOOT. |

| | *Solo.* |
| Nai kume au ra | At the entrance |

	Chorus.
i te ngutupa ē!	to thy sad home I shout,
I te ngutupa pakia io i te umauma.	And despairingly beat my breast.
Voa atu to metua, voa atu to metua 'i e Koroa 'i.	Thy father Koroa is sadly seeking for thee.

	Solo.
Kua o koe i te tupu i te tākanga o te ueue ;—	Thou art now compelled to feed on *black beetles,*
Na manga a te tangata mate.	The food of disembodied spirits.
Na Ura oki i te rua e!	'Twas for Ura in his grave

| | *Chorus.* |
| Putungākai na Tiki oki i rarā ē! | We bore a feast, all dry, like Tiki's. |

E tatau atu ē

ia po rima ē !

Ia po rima e tau ai na umu manga

E kave tere : kua oti na ropānga ;—

Wait patiently

five days

And we will prepare yet another feast.

Again and again will we do this.

Solo.

Kua oti na ropānga 'i, e Koroa 'i.
Pururu tau nagarau, e tama akaaroa.

One atu au i te kainga.

Na Ura oki i te rua e !

Koroa will not quickly weary.
Then, beloved son, our mourning will be over,

And finally we'll return to our dwell-ings.

'Twas for Ura in his grave

Chorus.

Putungākai na Tiki oki i rarā ē !

We bore a feast, all dry, like Tiki's.

INUINU RIMA.

FIFTH OFFSHOOT.

Solo.

Kua rarā oki ra ;

All dry is thy food

Chorus.

kua roia e !

Kua roia i te karaii ma te momo'o.

Ei ko na ra, kai ai.

and bad ;

The relish with it is *crabs* and *black-birds.*[1]

Farewell ; eat.

---

[1] The reference is to the " Momoô," a beautiful but small species of the blackbird, which has a pleasing note. It was then regarded as the incarnation of the god " *Moô*," who delights to secrete men and things. " Momoô " is strictly " the Moô-bird." This bird is caught with extreme difficulty, being very expert in hiding itself in rat holes, tufts of grass, etc. Its eyes are fiery red. When the Pakoko tribe went on a murdering expedition, this blackbird was supposed, if propitious, to lead the way by a ball of fire lighting up the path of warriors. These pretty birds were regarded as suitable food for the dead, *i.e.* for dwellers in the " po " = *darkness*, on account of their *blackness.* Hence the appropriateness of *crabs* and *black* beetles as diet for the ghosts ; besides, crabs, beetles, and worms bore into the soil, or crawl about in caves where the dead lie.

Solo.

Ei ko na ra, kai ai, e Ura, i to me- ringa 'i.	Farewell. Enjoy thy feast, my Ura.
Kua akaui maua i to enua.	We return no more to thee.
Pāi ïa mai to putungākai i te kainga.	We go back to our desolate home.
Na Ura oki i te rua ē !	'Twas for Ura in his grave

Chorus.

Putungākai na Tiki oki i rarā ē	We bore a feast, all dry, like Tiki's.

AKAREINGA.	FINALE.
Ai e ruroo e ! E rangai e !	Ai e ruaoo e ! E rangai e !

Kourapapa died at the age of four or five years, and was uncle to my worthy native co-pastor Sadaraka.   This was all the consolation heathenism could give the afflicted parent Koroa, who was associated at that time with his father Potiki in the government of the island.

It was believed that the ghosts ate the "essence" (ata) of these food offerings.   The living friends never (like the Chinese) ate the solid residuum.   To do so would be sacrilege.

ANOTHER LAMENT FOR KOURAPAPA.[1]

BY KOROA, CIRCA A.D. 1796.

TUMU.	INTRODUCTION.
Ua roiroi ka aere ē !	The little voyager is ready to start.
Mirimiri Koroa ia rurou	Koroa is distracted for his boy.
Naoeoe te aue a Koi	(The rocks) re-echo the cries,
Roimata i te anau.	Of Koi the heart-broken mother.

---

[1] This and the subsequent "laments" are given without the solos and choruses being marked off.   With the aid of the preceding specimens, the reader will easily see how they were actually chanted.

PAPA.

Kapitia ra e te matangi i pae ake ē !
Pae ake Ura i ruruta ē !

A roi te roi o te ngarie,
Oro atu na kimi motu ke
No taua, ia kite e oki mai ?
E tere akaonga e Ruru ē

FOUNDATION.

Should an ill wind o'ertake thee,
Seek shelter, O Ura, my spirit-child.
Go on thy way, fated voyager !
Go seek some other land ;——
Then return to fetch *me.*
'Tis a spirit pilgrimage, O mother.

UNUUNU MUA.

Ka roi te roi ē i tai enua ē

I tai enua tumiri te ua o te kakara.

Na te uanga kuru koe,
E vae, e tau ai i te kainga.
Na te uanga kuru koe,
E vae, e tau ai i te kainga.
Mirimiri Koroa ia rurou.
Naoeoe te aue a Koi
      Roimata i te anau.

FIRST OFFSHOOT.

Speed, then, on thy voyage to spirit-land,
Where a profusion of garlands awaits thee.
There the bread-fruit tree,
Pet son, is ever laded with fruit.
Yes ; *there* the bread-fruit
Is for ever in season, my child.
Koroa is distracted for his boy.
(The rocks) re-echo the cries
Of Koi the heart-broken mother.

UNUUNU RUA.

Tuoro atu ō i te tokerau ē !
I te tokerau te taka nei i te aanga.
E kauaka ïa—e kauaka tai—
E kauaka ïa—e kauaka tai—
No te Kaura, e tuamotu no Mangaia,

Ua puia e te aua mei te moana.
Mirimiri Koroa ia rurou.
Naoeoe te aue a Koi
      Roimata i te anau.

SECOND OFFSHOOT.

Awake, thou spirit-bearing winds !
Gently waft him o'er the ocean.
Yonder is a frail bark—
Yes ; yonder is a frail bark.
'Tis a canoe full of spirits from Mangaia,
Hurried o'er the sea by fierce currents.
Koroa is distracted for his boy.
(The rocks) re-echo the cries
Of Koi the heart-broken mother.

UNUUNU TORIU.

Pae ake Ura ra, i ruruta nei ē !
I ruruta nei tei paenga o Kurarau,
Tei paenga o Kurarau,—
Pangitia te vaine reua,
Ua tae koe! Ua tae Metua
I te maora nui i Onemakenu kenu !

THIRD OFFSHOOT.

Oh for a shelter from the tempest
On some well-sheltered shore !
Yes ; on some well-sheltered shore !
The mother mourns the dead :—
But thou and thy sister have reached
The gathering-place of spirits,

Ua iri te pa kura o Tueva.
Mirimiri Koroa ia rurou.
Naoeoe te aue a Koi
      Roimata nui i te anau.

Whilst we lament, like Tueva of old.
Koroa is distracted for his boy.
(The rocks) re-echo the cries
Of Koi the heart-broken mother.

UNUUNU Ā.

E tere ïa, e tere akaonga ē !
O ngai te akarua, aore e tae tika,
Aore e tae tikai : kua topa
I te tere o Kovi ia Angatoro.
Ua puia e te auā mei te moana.

Mirimiri Koroa ia rurou,
Naoeoe te aue a Koi
      Roimata nui i te anau.

FOURTH OFFSHOOT.

Prosperous be thy perilous pilgrimage
May soft zephyrs waft thee on !
Maybe thou hast miscarried,
Too late to accompany the ghosts
Which are hurried o'er the sea by
      fierce currents.
Koroa is distracted for his boy.
(The rocks) re-echo the cries
Of Koi the heart-broken mother.

AKAREINGA.
Ai e ruaoo ē !　E rangai ē !

FINALE.
Ai e ruaoo ē !　E rangai ē !

DEATH-LAMENT FOR VARENGA, DAUGHTER OF AROKAPITI.

COMPOSED BY KOROA, CIRCA 1817.

TUMU.

Tei Iti au, e Varenga e,

Kua kite Aro kua noo tane i Avaiki,
Te ānia mai e te ata e !
Te Vivitaunoa ra tau moe ē !

INTRODUCTION.

Varenga, who came from the "sun-rising,"[1]
In spirit-land is now wed.
She was wooed by a Shadow !
Such was my dream on the mountain.

PAPA.

Tau moe ra tei Iti, e Arokapiti ē !

Uira e rapa ia maine ē !

FOUNDATION.

My dream was of thee at the sun-rising—
Thy form dazzling as lightning.

---

[1] Referring to the ancient home of the tribe of Tane at "Iti" (= Tahiti), or "the sun-rising." The "ancestral marae" where her remains were laid was expressly selected (being due east) with an eye to this circumstance.

Kimi koe i te kavainga
O mata ngaae, tau itirere i te ao ē !
Tei te enua taparere maunga·c̄ !

Thou wert watching for the dawn
When I awoke from my sleep
On the steep mountain side.

UNUUNU TAI.

Tei Iti oki ra o Varenga nei ē !

O Varenga nei !
Na Miru e akarito kia tupu a vaine,

Kia tupu a vaine 'i.
Kua tioria e te are tangata i Pan-
goauri
Tei Vaekura, tei Vaikaute nei.
Te ānia mai e te ata e !
Te Vivitaunoa ra tau moe c̄ !

FIRST OFFSHOOT.

Varenga, who came from "the sun
rising :"
Yes, my Varenga !
Miru[1] will cherish thee in thy
maidenhood—
Thy lovely maidenhood !
In life thou wert the admiration of
all,
Wherever thy light steps wandered.
Now thou art wooed by a Shadow !
Such was my dream on the moun-
tain.

UNUUNU RUA.

Enua i enua ē, taparere c̄ !

Taparere i Maungaroa,
Tei nunga i te tuarongā ;
Tei nunga i te tuarongā 'i,
Tei Tuarangi, tei Araturakina e !

Tei Rinui aina 'i ?
Te ānia mai e te ata e !
Te Vivitaunoa ra tau moe c̄ !

SECOND OFFSHOOT.

Thou wast buried in the ancestral
marae
On the side of steep Maungaroa,
Hidden by the tall fern —
Aye, hidden by the tall fern.
Perchance thy spirit is revisiting the
spot,
Hovering amongst the wild rocks.
Now thou art wooed by a Shadow !
Such was my dream on the moun-
tain.

UNUUNU TORU.

Kua veru te are i Kauava ē !

THIRD OFFSHOOT.

Thy house[2] in the west is decayed.

---

[1] It is hoped that the great beauty of this damsel will induce the dread
Miru to forego her horrid repast, and in its stead adopt her as her daughter-in-
law.

[2] Near the sea, on the western part of this island, is a cave called
"Kauava," where some families of ghosts loved to congregate. In this
neighbourhood a house had been set up for the special accommodation of this
distinguished spirit. But it is now hopelessly decayed, *i.e.* she is about to

Tei Kauava, kua oti i te akatu,	At the gathering-place of ghosts is this home,
E nga tupuna kia kioro ua ra :	Built by thine ancestors, where spirits
Kia kioro ua ra'i ia aiai,	Rest awhile and chatter in the evening ;
E kaunuku atu ai io Tumaronga,	Or wander about at the edge of the cliffs ;
E niaki mai i te uru mato.	Or sit on the stones gazing at the interior.
Te ānia mai e te ata ē !	Now thou art wooed by a Shadow !
Te Vivitaunoa ra tau moe ē !	Such waš my dream on the mountain.

AKAREINGA.	FINALE.
Ai e ruaoo ē ! E rangai ē !	Ai e ruaoo ū ! E rangai ū !

LAMENT FOR MOURUA ·

(THE FRIEND OF CAPTAIN COOK).

BY UANUKU, CIRCA 1780.

TUMU.	INTRODUCTION.
Kua tu te are i Imogo ;	There is a spirit-dwelling at Imogo :
E enua koe no Kavoro,	'Tis the burial-place of Kavoro,
Kua tupuria e te rakau.	In a shady grove.
O te ukenga i nunga 'i !	There we dug his grave ;
O te one kuru i crue !	There the red soil was thrown up.
O taua nei te aroa 'i tangi ē !	How bitter the widow's grief !

PAPA.	FOUNDATION.
Ukea mai Kavoro ē !	But Kavoro was disinterred ;
I te rua ē i tanu ai.	Was taken out of the grave where he had lain.

descend finally to nether-world. Ghosts from this cave, when the coral tree blossomed, took their departure by leaping from a rock in the Mission premises to a smaller one on the *inner* part of the reef ; thence to the *outer* edge of the reef ; and then tripping over the ocean, like Veêtini, disappeared with the sun in nether-world. Although these disembodied spirits avoid the fragrant but fatal *bua* tree, they cannot escape Miru, mistress of the shades.

Kua eteia te ara nio
Kua vai te ivi i te mokotua ;
  Kakaro io au e
Kua ngaro iaaku te angaanga ē !

The teeth all exposed—
His form, oh, how wasted,
As we gazed on him
Now so mournfully changed !

UNUUNU TAI.

Kua tu te are ē tei Imogo ē !
Tei Imogo, e enua koe no Kavoro.
Kua otinga atu na,
Kua otinga atu na 'i.
Kua tanu kere i uri ra ki te rua ē !

    O te ukenga i nunga 'i !
    O te one kura i erue !

    O taua nei te aroa tangi ē !

FIRST OFFSHOOT.

There is a spirit-dwelling at Imogo,
For there our Kavoro was buried.
    There we parted ;
    Aye, parted for ever !
Shallow was the grave where we
      buried him,
    There we dug his grave ;
    There the red soil was thrown
      up.
How bitter the widow's grief !

UNUUNU RUA.

Uri mai te aro ē i to vaine ē !
  I to vaine ia Turuare,

SECOND OFFSHOOT.

Look once more at thy wife—
  At thy beloved Turuare ; [1]

---

[1] The night Mourua (Kavoro) was slain, Turuare, the most beloved of his three wives, and her little son Taingarue, were with him in the fishing hut on the beach which they temporarily occupied. The father feared lest his little boy should be struck, but he escaped unhurt. Not so the mother of Taingarue, who bravely stripped off her own clothing in order to break the force of the blows aimed at her husband. For a time she was successful ; but, despite the efforts of this heroic woman, Mourua fell, the wife's arm being broken in the fray.

Upon the retirement of the exultant party of Potai, the elder son of Mourua came to Turuare's help. The body of the slain warrior was laboriously carried by a very circuitous route, so as to escape observation, to a gorge called Imogo, half a mile from the scene of murder. In performing this last office of love, the son had at first only the aid of Turuare, who was herself suffering from the anguish of a broken arm ; but afterwards friends arrived from the interior. A grave was speedily dug with their iron-wood spades, and the body of Mourua, wrapped in several folds of native cloth, was laid in the grave. Instead of filling it with earth, it was merely covered with a large stone, so as to elude the notice of his foes.

It happened that the women of that part of the island, when employed in collecting candle-nuts, availed themselves of this large stone for shelling them.

Kua peka te rima ka akauta,	She whom thou once clasped in thy arms,
Kua peka te rima ka akauta 'i.	Intwining her in thy fond embrace.
Angi nga rua, taura rima te mou.	We who lived so happily together, now part,
Kua rikarika te tama i te toa akarĕrĕ,	The cruel spear slew thee, to the horror of thy son.
Tamaki tutai ē, tamaki a ta ē!	Thou wast attacked by stealth in the night,
Oi atu koe i vao, kua pa ra, kiritia,	(Entreating thy wife), "Escape, leave me, for I am struck,
Tukua o au no te mate ē!	I am doomed to die!"
O te mate ïa i tangi no Kavoro i tai.	Thus perished beloved Kavoro by the sea.
Tei Nukutaipăria, te vai rai i reira.	His bleeding corpse lay on the sandy beach.
Naai e takitaki? Taua ka apai	Who shall bear it? Wife and son will carry it away,
Ka uuna kia ngaro ē!	And hide it where foes shall find it never!
Tupeke atu na ē, tupeke atu na, kia mamao,	Bear him, aye, bear him far away;
O te kimi te mataku, o te kimi te mataku,	So that if carefully sought by his foes,
Ka kitea i te ngara anga.	His body shall ne'er be found.

The family felt so sure that Mourua must be dreadfully annoyed by the incessant noises over his head, that they disinterred the body; which, although in an advanced state of decay, was re-anointed with fragrant oil and re-invested with fine white cloth. In a few days it was borne across the island to Tamarua, and finally thrown down the deep and gloomy chasm—Raupā. A night or two after, one of the sons had a dream, in which Mourua reproached his relatives for the bad treatment he had received at their hands, for no sooner had his body reached the bottom of Raupā, *where so many of his own victims had been so unceremoniously hurled at different times*, than the slain rose up, and most vigorously pummelled his bones until they became intolerably sore!

However, it was too late to remove him again. The motive for letting the corpse down Raupā was to prevent its falling into the hands of his numerous *living* enemies.

Kua aite te po, kua popongi i tai,

Night is wearing away.   On the beach

Kua aenga te ata i te ngongoro a te vaine.

The first streak of morning reveals the widow's tears.

I raro i te roroutu ; kua teitei te ruru

Concealed amongst the trees, tremblingly

I te kakenga i Katoe ki runga i te tokoraa

They climb the rocks.   On yon level top

Ki te utu a Terimu, taukapua tatou :

They repose beneath the shade of the *utu* tree,[1]

Tei Tapataparangi.   Apai tu na uta,

Near the brow of the hill.   Again they take the corpse.

Tei Atupa te ara ; te kimi nei i te rua.

Yonder is the narrow path : select a grave.

Eiia ra tanu ai ?   Ei Imogo,

Where shall it be?   Let it be at Imogo,

Kia tae mai au i te veivei aere ē !

Where I can often come to weep.

Tuku io, e Teau !   Koia te rua kia akaaka.

Lay him gently down, O Teau, in the lowly grave.

Taaturia te koatu.   Akaruke atu ia Kavoro.

Pile up the stones.   Farewell, Kavoro !

O te ukenga i nunga 'i
O te one kura i erue.

There we dug his grave,
There the red soil was thrown up.

O taua nei te aroa 'i tangi ē !

How bitter thy widow's grief !

UNUUNU TORU.

THIRD OFFSHOOT.

Taingarue ē ! rave ake koe.

O Taingarue, mayst thou be protected !

E rave ake koe, e taua ariki !
Kia karo ake Nekaia !

Mayst thou live, pet son !
Be loving to thy brother, O Nekaia ![2]

---

[1] The noble Barringtonia tree.

[2] "Nekaia" was the eldest daughter of Mourua, whose husband, Uanuku, composed this death-lament for his warlike father-in-law.   Their son "Patiatoa," or "Tiki," is adjured to take under his protection his young relative Taingarue.   Patiatoa (= *pierced-with-a-spear*) died of measles in 1854, at an advanced age.   Not long before his death, he was admitted to the Church upon a profession of his attachment to Christ.   I well recollect his bent and venerable figure the day he came to be a candidate.   He was a priest, and a special depository of all the lore of idol-worship.   He was a "koroma-

Kia karo ake Nekaia 'i !
Na Patiatoa e uuna 'i !
Etai rā no vaevae, e taua ariki,
    E maru aina iaau ?
    O te ukenga i nunga 'i
    O te one kura i erue.

    O taua nei te aroa 'i tangi ē !

Ah ! Nekaia, be gentle to him.
Patiatoa, too, will shield thee,
For many a day to come, dear child.
Will he be safe in thy hands ?
    There we dug his grave.
    There the red soil was thrown up.
How bitter thy widow's grief !

UNUUNU Ā.

Okitumurua ē i te tanumanga ē !
    I te tanumanga 'e !
Apai au teiia ? Tei te rua taeva.

    Tei te rua taeva 'i.
Apairia atu Kavoro nei.
Kua pe te papa e vai ai, atikauria.
    O te ukenga i nunga 'i,
    O te one kura i erue.

    O taua nei te aroa 'i tangi ē !

FOURTH OFFSHOOT.

A second time thou wast buried,—
    Committed to the earth !
Whither shall we bear thee ? To some deep chasm :
    To some fathomless fissure.
Come, let us carry Kavoro there, for
His body is fast crumbling to dust.
    There we dug his grave.
    There the red soil was thrown up.
How bitter thy widow's grief !

AKAREINGA.

Ai e ruaoo ē   E rangai ē !

FINALE.

Ai e ruaoo ē ! E rangai ē !

---

tua," or instructor of kings—a peculiarly sacred office. It was a striking homage to Christianity to see this aged man give the lie to all that had given him rank and fame amongst his countrymen during a long life, and when past the ordinary term of human life, come and sit humbly at the feet of Jesus. But when the Sabbath came for Patiatoa to partake of the tokens of His Saviour's dying love for the first time, he was too weak to walk so far. His sons extemporized a platform of a number of green branches, and carried the aged disciple to the foot of the pulpit, where he received the ordinance of the Lord's Supper for the first and last time in his long eventful life.

The "second offshoot" is called "*a surprise*" (unuunu *rako*), on account of its great length, and because the weeping is continuous. The fact is, the song evinces blank, hopeless sorrow and tears from the beginning to the end. One of Vera's laments also contains a verse or two of "surprise."

A SPIRIT-JOURNEY.

A DIRGE FOR PUKUKARE AND KOURAPAPA, BY THEIR FATHER KOROA, CIRCA 1796.

TUMU.

Te io kikino o tau potiki,
  Kua pa te rakau
Ki te miro ia vero i mate ua !

Ki, rave atu na koe, kare ē !

INTRODUCTION.

Thy god, pet child, is a bad one ;
For thy body is attenuated.
This wasting sickness must end thy
  days.
Thy form once so plump, now how
  changed !

PAPA.

Moe araara Pukukare ē reirē !
Ua tauria e te maremare
Ua tupo ua ngongā ua rai.
" Teia au, e Ruru e, ka eke, atu !
Taka e, tei Avaiki te moenga."

FOUNDATION.

The nights of Pukukare are sleepless—
Are spent in coughing and pain.
Panting for breath, he gasps out—
" Mother, I am going to leave you.
My rest will be in spirit-world."

UNUUNU TAI.

Te io ! i te io ra e kikino e !
Kikino ra, e vae !
Kai akakorekore Turanga ē !

  Ta ta keke mai ē !
Ua taka te eka i te atua o Rurungapu.

  E tika paa tai rangi ē !
Tai manuiri ei akarongo
Ki te miro ia vero i mate ua !

Ki, rave atu na koe, kare ē !

FIRST OFFSHOOT.

Ah, that god—that bad god !
Inexpressibly bad, my child !
The god " Turanga " is devouring
  thee,
Although only partially his own.
I am disgusted with the god of thy
  mother.
Oh, for some other Helper !
Some new divinity, to listen
To the sad story of thy wasting
  disease !
Thy form once so plump, now how
  changed !

UNUUNU RUA.

Akaete te maki ē, ua toira ē !
Ua toira i to kaki e tuarangi

SECOND OFFSHOOT.

Thy disease went on increasing.
Like a demon squatting on thy
  shoulders,

Ko te uā o Taa !
Mei te uā o Taa, me tairia mai,
Kia mārekaeka, ua toko auau !
　Mei toko auau ra !
Ua kakau i te vai o Ruanuku,
No Rongo paa, no Tangaroa,
Ka puaki e mamā ki nunga
I to kiri, mei nunga ra i to kiri.
Rikarika te mate ia vero.
O te rua tapu o te rua noa—
Na tuataka i te motu anga ia Puku-
　kare.
Ua rakaraka te io Ngariki.

I moria e ao ia matengatenga,
Norea-norea, norea te kiko.
Reia-reia, reia e manā !
E vae, kua tae koe i te orcore
Ia Ikurangi e enua kai marama,

E enua kai marama no Tonga-iti,
Na Tonga ra, na veravera o Iti ngaru-
　erue.
Ka mimiti ki te aro o Vātea !

Ka oki au ! A oti te ariki o Tonga

Ua kake atu na i katoa i te taurere,
Ua taparere i Enuakura na Oarangi

Ei ingoa manuiri tei Tatangakovi au !
Te kai maira i te au tai,
I te pia paa i te vai i Vaikapuarangi,

Ua tunoko i te matoroa,
Ua akarongo i te tangi tai tei Aarua ē !
Te aiai ua ra oa te vaerua mato
I te naupata, ua takangaia.
E Kourapapa, tei Opapa te ngai i
　turukia'i !

Was the swelling on thy neck.
Thou wast fain to be fanned,
To gain relief from burning fever—
A fever sure to return.
Thou wast loved in the sacred streams
Of Ruanuku, Rongo, and Tangaroa.
Sometimes hopes of thy recovery
Vainly flattered thy friends.
Again thy body wasted away,
And the mouths of ancestral caves
Seemed to gape for our Pukukare.

The god (Motoro) of Ngariki is en-
　raged.
Wherefore this pining death,
And thy flesh ever wasting away.
At length thou takest a long flight.
Dear child, ere now thou hast reached
The loftiest heights of Mount Iku-
　rangi,
Where the moon itself is devoured
By the gods from Tonga and Tahiti.

Thou shalt enter the presence of great
　Vātea.

I go home now.　So, too, will the
　king from Tonga.
Thou hast entered the expanse ;
And wilt visit "the-land-of-red-par-
　rot-feathers,"
Where Oārangi was once a guest.
Thou feedest now on ocean spray,
And sippest fresh water out of the
　rocks,
Travelling over rugged cliffs,
To the music of murmuring billows.
Thy exile spirit is overtaken
By darkness at the ocean's edge.
Kourapapa there sleeps.　All three [1]

Tei Opapa te ngai i turuki ai
Nga tokotoru.   Ua kakaro i te ata ata
   rā.

Stood awhile to gaze wistfully
At the glories of the setting sun.

I te opunga 'tu e Tireo ma te Oiro.
Ua iterere nga po o te atua ra ē !
Ua tau ua 'i ē te enua kino i raro.
I pa te umere, uaua, oaoa.
Oai te akatu ?   Oai te akatu ?
Koouou aere i Tuatuakare

Moonless nights shall pass, ere
The fatal one shall arrive
To conduct you to the dismal shades.
The denizens will be astonished
At the arrival of you, pet children.
The ghosts sorrowfully crowd round
   the spot,

I te uiui matangi, tauoaoaia ra

Whence the wings of the wind shall
   bear

E te Iva tureture i te umu kavakava
Tei Ovave aina e ariki tua rirē,
   Karekare au ē !

Them to great spirit-land, where
A dreadful oven awaits all who
   Pass o'er the ocean.

AKAREINGA.
Ai e ruaoo ē !   E rangai ē !

FINALE.
Ai e ruaoo ē !   E rangai ē !

INTRODUCTION TO THE FÊTE OF RIUVAKA.

COMPOSED BY KIRIKOVI, CIRCA 1760.

Solo.

O Tane metua i Avaiki ē !
   Tu mai i to akari !

Great parent Tane of the shades,[2]
   Rise, eat this feast !

---

[1] " Pukukare " was older than the "pet Kourapapa."   A deceased young sister is " the third " referred to in this song, which pertains to the "death-talk of Kourapapa."

[2] Riuvaka was a worshipper of Tane.   Hence the praises of his deity are celebrated throughout this " Introductory Song."   Kirikovi was supreme temporal chief of Mangaia at the date of the discovery of the island by Captain Cook, in 1777.

The " parent Tane," was " Tane-papa-kai," *i.e. Tane-piler-up-of-food*, son of Papa.

Chorus.

Eiaa te rua ia Tiki	Wherefore the chasm of Tiki ?
Ei poani ia Avaiki.	To shut down the natives of Avaiki (nether-world).
Tueva aka-itu te eva i te metua.	Tueva, who seven times lamented for his boy,
Ae; eaa toou ara i te ao nei	Asked, Why didst thou return to this world ?
I ana mai au i te kave	I came (said he) to instruct you
I te pākuranga ma te meringa,	In making food-offerings to the dead,
Meringa mai Avaiki e,	Offerings to those in spirit-world ;
Meringa mai i o tatou metua	Gifts from their relatives
E noo i te ao nei. Ei aa ?	Who yet linger in this upper world.

Solo.

Oai te roa i te eiva, e Tane ?	Wherefore this delay in thy dance, O Tane ?

Chorus.

Oi te rangi Orovaru ? E vãia	Is it a fiat of the gods ? Break through it.
Oi te rangi mataotao ? E vãia.	Is it the lowering clouds of war ? Dissipate them.
Ei ! ei ! e Papa, taku metua !	Ha ! Ha ! Great Papa is my (Tane's) mother.
Ae, e Papa, oro atu koe,	But why, Papa, didst thou descend
E Avaiki o, akaatua mai !	To Avaiki, to obtain the honours of a goddess ?
Ae, ua puapau ai koe i to upoko,	Ah ! thou hast shaved thy head ![1]
Ie uiia o ē, oai te atua	Should it be asked, Which of the gods
I keinga 'i o tatou metua ?	Devoured our parents ?
Ae, ua ara iaku.	The fault is all my own.
E ariki taotaoaia e te tuarangi,	I (Tane) am a sovereign possessed of an evil spirit.

---

[1] Shaving the head was one way of mourning for the dead. Tane glories in having occasioned this mourning. This is a reference to Tane-Ngakiau, or *Tane-striving-for-power*, from Iti (Tahiti), who was believed to kill people prematurely, *by devouring their souls*. Of course, their bodies, however strong and healthy formerly, quickly faded and died after this !

Aitoa, e Rongo, kia unuia te tumu
I o tatou metua ! Aue ! Aitoa !

Yes, Rongo, I will drink up the souls
Of our ancestors. *I will, without fail.*

Aue tou e !   E Papa, taku metua !

I fear naught ; for great Papa is my mother.

Call for music and dance.

Tataia i te tanga o Tane :
O te vaa ia i tuku ai te kaara.

Beat the drum [1] of Tane—
Those lips which so sweetly speak.

Solo.

Taipo ē !

Go on.

Chorus.

Kua tangi reka te vaa o Tane.

How pleasant is] the voice of Tane (*i.e.* the drum).

Rutu ake i te rangi.

The very heavens re-echo.

Solo.

Ka rutu au, e Tan !

Tane, I will beat thy drum !

Chorus.

Oai tuā roi au ē ?
E Papa, taku metua !

But who shall take the lead ?—
I (Tane), for Great Papa is my mother.

Second call for music and dance.

E kakara tuputupu,

Let there be abundance of fragrant leaves,

E kakara koritonga
E maire titatoe e a kake.

Magnificent, sweet-scented flowers,
With garlands of myrtle for the advent (of Tane).

Solo.

Taipo ē !

Go on !

Chorus.

Uru are te kakara i tau ai.

Cull all sorts of fragrant flowers.

Solo.

Aē !

Aye !

---

[1] The dance was specially under the patronage of Tane. Hence the big drum used on the occasion is called " the voice of Tane."

Chorus.

E maire e kakara tuputupu.	Abundance, too, of sweet-scented myrtle.
O Aratea te ei.	And white pandanus blossoms.

Solo.

Porutu te vai e tei te moana aē!	But what if torrents of rain should fall?

Chorus.

Porutu te vai i te moana ē!	Though torrents of rain should fall,
Auenei, apopo Tautiti ē!	To-night and to-morrow we will be merry.
Ua kokoti Avaiki i te rau o te pua	Fairies [1] from the shades are preparing;
Tapokipoki rauru e i te maire,	Are entwining myrtle leaves with their hair,
E rau maire tapu e no te ariki	Robbing the sacred myrtle of the king of its sprigs.
Tei nunga te kapa i te Rongo Nui no Tane.	The fête comes off on the nights [2] dedicated to Rongo and Tane.

[1] The peerless daughters never failed to honour the fêtes of Tane with their presence. Like mortals, they will come attired with sweet-scented flowers and myrtle sprigs. It is pretended that the fairy toilet is nearly complete; the dance must for very shame lead off without delay.

[2] The night of the 26th of each month was sacred to Tane; the night following to Rongo.

CHAPTER X.

ADVENTURES IN SPIRIT-WORLD.

AN ESCAPE FROM SPIRIT-LAND.

In the Sacred Islet lived Enecne, his wife Kura, and his sister
Umuei. These women were young and fair, and loved to roam
the woods in quest of sweet-scented flowers, which they weaved
into wreaths and necklaces. On one occasion they fortunately
discovered a noble *bua* (*beslaria laurifolia*), whose far-spreading
branches were covered with fragrant yellow blossoms. The
sisters-in-law sat awhile at the foot of the tree discussing the
division of the spoil. It was clear that Kura should collect on
one side of the tree, and Umuei on the other. But the great
central branch seemed the richest prize of all. It was eventually
agreed that Kura should have this treasure.

The young women set to work in good earnest; but, after a
time, it became evident that Kura was gathering more than fell to
her share. To punish her, Umuei took possession of the coveted
central branch. The wife of Eneene was speedily chastised for
her covetousness without the intervention of Umuei; for the
branch on which she was leaning heavily in order to steal some of

her sister-in-law's, suddenly broke. Kura, basket and all, fell with the branch of the sacred tree, cleaving the earth, and continued to fall until she reached Avaiki, or spirit-world. The ghosts, happening to be on the look-out, caught her in their arms, so that she was not killed by the fall. The captive Kura was hurried off to a considerable distance, and at once firmly tied up to the central post of a house. It was settled by these infernals—called "the army of Marama"—that to-morrow Kura should be cooked and eaten. A special guard was set over her, both blind and aged, named Tiarauau. At regular intervals the old fellow would shout, "E Kura e!" (O Kura), to which the unvarying reply of the victim was, "E Tiarauau e!" (O Tiarauau). Thus was the blind wakeful guardian assured of the safety of his prisoner.

Now Umuei, witnessing the sudden fall and entire disappearance of Kura into the very bosom of the earth, ran weeping to inform Eneene. Anxious, if possible, to recover his wife, he bethought himself of his god Tumatarauua, himself manufactured out of the *bua*. Invoking the aid of the god, and carrying it in his arms, he went to the very spot where his wife had lately disappeared; and, pronouncing the invocation to the divinity of the sacred *bua* tree, the earth opened and he descended to spirit-land. Eneene at once began his search for his beloved young wife, so suddenly removed from his sight. Now the name of that particular part of nether-world was Marama. As, fortunately for Eneene, it was night at the period of his entrance, his presence in the shades was unnoticed. Anxiously wandering about from place to place, he heard the loud interrogations of the old blind keeper and the replies of Kura herself. His lost wife was found; but the puzzle was how to get her away without exciting the suspicions of Tiarauau and other hungry denizens of the shades,

Cautiously peering in all directions through the darkness, he discovered a cocoa-nut tree with *eight* cocoa-nuts on it. Eneene climbed the tree, carefully plucked a single nut : holding the stem between his teeth, he silently descended to the ground. This process was repeated again and again, until the tree was cleared, without attracting the notice of the ever-watchful Tiarauau. With extreme care during that long night Eneene succeeded in husking the nuts and scraping out their contents, too, without noise.

There were *eight* paths leading to the house where Kura was kept prisoner. Eneene was careful liberally to scatter the finely grated cocoa-nut over all these pathways, and close to the house itself. The rats, scenting the rich food, now came by hundreds to feast themselves. They even fought and quarrelled over the delicious morsels, not only on the ground but on the low-thatched roof, enough to drive a man out of his senses. Certainly it seemed strange to Tiarauau that the rats should be so unusually noisy. Amidst this turmoil, Eneene climbed the roof and cautiously removed part of the thatch to discover in what part of the house his wife was tied up. At this moment the old blind guardian called out, " O Kura !" Listening intently to the reply, he discovered that his poor trembling young wife was in the middle of the dwelling. Advancing to where the voice seemed to come from, Eneene carefully removed part of the thatch, put down his hand and touched his imprisoned wife. The astonished Kura asked in an undertone, " Who that was ? " and received the joyful answer, " Your own husband Eneene." The roof of the house was sufficiently low to permit the husband to untie the cords by which his wife was tied up to the post. He then drew her up on the roof to himself. Eneene now directed her to descend to the ground, and run off as fast as she could to the foot of the closed chasm by which she had so summarily entered Avaiki, and there to await his arrival.

Eneene now let himself down through the low roof, and occupied the place of the released prisoner, so as to give her time to escape. The old guard called out as usual, " O Kura ! " to which Eneene replied, closely imitating the voice of his wife, " O Tiarauau ! " The trick was not discovered, either by Tiarauau or the drowsy inmates of the prison-house. Eneene now thought it to be high time to provide for his own safety. Crawling up through the hole in the thatch, he cautiously let himself on the ground and ran as nimbly as he could to the appointed rendezvous, where he found his trembling wife waiting for him.

There was no time to be lost, for he could hear the echo of Tiarauau's stentorian voice giving the alarm. Clasping his wife in his arms, he offered the following prayer to his god :—

Pūpū-kākāoa,	United in one fate,
Pureke-pureke,	We ascend, we rise,
E ao, e ao !	To light, to light,
Kua avatea !	To clear mid-day.

At these potent words the gloomy rent again opened, and both were borne through the chasm up to this world of ours, where it was still daylight. A moment later, and the enraged "army of Marama" would have caught Eneene and Kura, so close were those infernal hosts upon their heels.

The *bua* was in some islands used in the manufacture of idols, on account of its fine grain and being almost imperishable. The purport of the myth is to indicate the standard faith of the past— that the souls of the dead congregate on this tree, and on its branches are borne by a merciless fate to Hades.

THE ADVENTURES OF NGARU.

In Shady-Land[1] (Marua) there lived the brave Ngaru, his mother Vaiare, and the grandfather of the lad, who was no other than Moko, or Great Lizard, the king of all lizards. Tongatea, the youthful wife of Ngaru, was the envy of all Shady-Land on account of her fairness. Thirsting for distinction, Ngaru resolved to try his strength against some of the numerous monsters and evil spirits of his time. He learned from his grandfather that two fierce enemies of mankind had their appropriate home in the ocean, viz. Tikokura, or *the-storm-wave*, and Tumuitearetoka, or *a vast shark*, which fed exclusively upon human flesh. These evil spirits always went in each other's company; but Ngaru determined to meet both. The enterprise seemed hopeless; for who had ever escaped their anger? Ngaru's first care was to provide himself with a surf-board of the lightest description, which he named Orua = *the-two*, in allusion to the two sea-gods he was about to encounter. He now appeared on the inner edge of the reef, carrying his surf-board; but the wide coral surface was perfectly dry. Moko sat on a projecting crag of rock to watch over the safety of his grandson, who now advanced to the outer edge of the reef, where the surf ceaselessly beats, and loudly cursed these sea-monsters by name. Tikokura and Tumuitearetoka smarted under this unprovoked insult, and resolved to be revenged on Ngaru without delay. All of a sudden the dead calm which had made the reef dry changed into a furious tempest. Long breakers rushed inland far beyond the accustomed bounds of the sea, and spent themselves against the gnarled roots of the utu trees. Moko still kept his place on his rocky eminence,

[1] That is, the shades.

whilst his grandson floated daringly out to sea on the crest of the retreating billow. The shark-god, perceiving his opportunity, crept stealthily behind his intended victim, and was preparing for the final leap which would seal the fate of the impious Ngaru, when the quick eye of Moko caught sight of his dark outline, and shouted lustily to the boy, " The shark is under you." Ngaru, hearing this, instantly leapt high in the air, so that this first attempt failed. The foe now leapt in the air after Ngaru ; but he dived under the water and again escaped. The disappointed god was excessively enraged ; so that it was needful for Ngaru to put forth all his skill and strength to avoid the open jaws of the monster. Tumuitearetoka became crafty ; but Ngaru was still craftier : Moko often giving his pet grandson timely warning of the insidious approach of the adversary. For eight weary days and nights this terrible contest went on, until the exhausted Ngaru put an end to it by throwing his surf-board to the sea-monsters, who gladly retired to their ancient haunts in the deep blue ocean.

Great was the delight of the old grandfather and of his countrymen at the exploit of Ngaru, the first who had dared the sea-gods in their own domain, and yet had escaped with life. But the hero himself was sadly battered, and his skin excoriated with the sharp coral. He made his way home ; but on the road fell in with his fair wife Tongatea. Arrived at a fountain, they determined to bathe ; but a friendly dispute took place who should have the first dip. It was finally arranged that the husband should take the precedence. Once in, Ngaru was in no hurry to get out. At sunset he got out, and the wife was horrified to find that his skin had become almost black through long exposure to salt-water, during the mighty contest with the monsters of the deep. Reviling Ngaru for his blackness, she ran off to her friends.

When at length Ngaru reached home, Moko inquired what had become of his fair spouse, and learnt that, disgusted with her husband's appearance, she had fled to Teautapu. Said Moko, " Nothing blackens the skin so soon as the sea and the sun." The grandson inquired how his skin could be blanched. Moko said, " The only way to blanch your skin is to treat you as green bananas are treated when they are to be ripened.[1] Ngaru agreed to this proposal. Accordingly they dug a deep hole in the ground, and lined it with layers of sweet-scented fern-leaves. Ngaru descended into this hole, and was duly covered with leaves ; a thin layer of earth crowned the whole. On the eighth day flashes of lightning proceeded from the spot where Ngaru had so long been buried, increasing in intensity until it smote away earth and leaves, permitting him to emerge from his strange abode. It then became evident that these flashes of light proceeded from the face and person of Ngaru, being in reality the dazzling fairness of his skin. But there was one drawback : the steam of the blanching oven had rendered Ngaru perfectly bald. Moko sent his mother Vaiare to great Tangaroa, to ask for some new hair. It was given ; but when Moko examined it, it proved to be *frizzly*. Moko resolved not to spoil the head of his fair grandson with such a wretched mop. Vaiare took it back to the god, and asked for some better hair. Tangaroa put the suppliant off with some *light yellow*.[2] " This will never do," said Moko ; " I must have *the best*." Once more Vaiare trudged back to the god to beg him to exchange the hair. Finding that there was no escape from the importunity of the grandfather,

---

[1] In the native language " ta-para," or *blanched :* Europeans would say " ripened."

[2] A detestable colour in the eyes of a Hervey Islander. Tangaroa's *own hair* was of the objectionable light yellow.

Tangaroa gave a profusion of wavy, smooth raven locks. Moko was delighted, and gladly secured it to the bald pate of his fair grandson.

The lightning, or dazzling flashes of light, from the face and person of Ngaru reached even to the distant abode of Tongatea (= *the fair Tongan*), so that everybody said, " Behold the dazzling fairness of Ngaru !" Said the runaway wife, " This Ngaru you praise must be a different individual from the Ngaru I know." The bystanders asserted that it was her despised husband ; but Tongatea remained incredulous.

Now, Tongatea had got up a reed-throwing match for women ; but men were invited from all parts to decide upon the merits of the game, and to applaud the successful throwers. At the time appointed all the fair ones, gaily attired and covered with fragrant garlands, stood ready to begin the amusement of the day, each with a long reed in her right hand. Tongatea, as mistress of the day, was about to make the first throw, when Ngaru made his appearance, and was at once recognized by the fair runaway. Her arm fell powerless by her side. She struggled to conceal her emotion, and to proceed with the game, but could not. Such a violent tremor seized Tongatea, that it was with difficulty that she retained her garments about her person. All was confusion : the intended sport of the day was lost. As the visitors disappeared, the weeping, repentant, love-smitten wife followed Ngaru, entreating him to return to her. Ngaru, in whose heart still rankled the bitter insult in reference to his former dusky colour, in this moment of triumph said to the penitent, " *Never* will I return to thee." The despairing Tongatea hearing this, set off in search of some poisonous kokii kura, chewed it, and died.

There lived in Avaiki, or nether world, a fierce she-demon,

named Miru, who, envious of the great fame of Ngaru, resolved to destroy him in her fearful, ever-blazing oven. But before enjoying this horrid banquet, it was needful to decoy him into her domains. Nor did this seem difficult. She at once directed two Tapairu, or *peerless ones*—her daughters—to ascend to this upper world to induce the brave Ngaru to marry them both. Kumutonga-i-te-po = *Kumutonga-of-the-night*, and Karaia-i-te-ata = *Karaia-the-shadowy*, were to induce him to pay a visit to the shades in their agreeable society: once there, his fate was sealed in Miru's estimation. On their entering the dwelling of Moko, Ngaru feigned to be asleep, whilst his grandfather tried to discover their real intent. They averred that their mother, Miru, had sent them to escort Ngaru to Avaiki; that as soon as they arrived, Ngaru was to be united to both these " peerless women," with whom the daughters of mortals could not for a moment be compared.

Moko, suspecting the real nature of their visit, sought to gain time by exercising the utmost hospitality to his unwonted guests. Whilst these fairy women were enjoying themselves, the king of lizards (Moko) sent his servants, *i.e.* all the little lizards,[1] on a secret mission to Miru's domains in the under world to ascertain what dangerous weapons were at her disposal, and what were her usual avocations. Off scampered the little lizards in all possible haste; and on arriving at Avaiki, unperceived by Miru, they noticed that the old, deformed, and inexpressibly ugly hag had a house full of kava (*piper mythisticum*), kept exclusively for the purpose of stupefying her intended victims, who were

---

[1] The black and yellow lizards hide during the day in the caves supposed to be the high-road to spirit-land ; whereas the common green variety suns itself all the day on the leaves and grass.

eventually cooked in her mighty oven, and eaten by herself, her fair children, and her servants.　These little keen-sighted lizards safely returned to this upper world, and reported to their sovereign what they had discovered.　Moko privately told this to his son, and admonished him to be careful, or he would infallibly perish, as multitudes had done before him.　As evening drew on, all three started off on their journey to the land of Miru in the shades.　The mode of transit was peculiar.　These "peerless ones" had with them rolls of finest tapa, in which they insisted upon wrapping up their future husband ; they then secured the bundle well with cords, and slung to a long pole, carried off Ngaru in triumph.　After some time Kumutonga-of-the-night and Karaia-the-shadowy began to ascend a mountain named " The-heavenly," when the imprisoned husband became conscious of a steep and sudden movement, and prayed thus :—

Oi au tiria, tiria	Put me down, put me down.
Oi au tārā, tārā	Set me free, set me free.
Tārāia akera	Oh that I had liberty
Kia kite au i teia maunga	To gaze on this mountain !
O te maunga poro oa teia	'Tis surely the mountain spoken of
A tau tupuna a Moko Roa,	By my grandfather, " The long-Lizard ; "
Tau metua a Vaiare,	And by my mother Vaiare (*stay-at-home*).[1]
Tau vaine a Tongatea.	And by my wife, " The fair Tongan."

To this Kumutonga and Karaia responded (temporarily releasing Ngaru) :—

Kiritia kai e kinana !	Thou shalt be forthwith devoured !
To koivi, vaio i Erangi maunga !	Thy *body* shall rot on this " Heavenly mountain,"

---

[1] Evidently in allusion to sickness.　The sick "stay at home."

<table>
<tr><td>To vaerua, e kave i te po</td><td>Thy *spirit* shall be borne to the shades,</td></tr>
<tr><td>Na to maua metua na Miru !</td><td>To furnish a repast for our mother Miru.</td></tr>
</table>

To this Ngaru replied, "'Tis thus you treat your intended husband !"

Again wrapping up and cording their intended victim, they bore him to another spur of the same mountain range. Conscious of this, the imprisoned victim again prayed to be released :—

<table>
<tr><td>Oi au tiria, tiria, etc., etc.</td><td>Put me down, put me down, etc., etc.</td></tr>
</table>

To this entreaty the same ominous reply was given as before :—

<table>
<tr><td>Kiritia kai e kinana ! etc.</td><td>Thou shalt be forthwith devoured, etc.</td></tr>
</table>

To this Ngaru replied, "'Tis thus you treat your intended husband !" At this the "peerless ones" again seized upon Ngaru, wrapped him again in numerous folds of tapa, and well securing their victim with cords, bore him along until, reaching a shady grove of chestnut trees, they set him down and unfastened the cords. These fairy women now hastened to fetch some kava, [1] named "Miru's own," and gave it to him to chew. Ngaru chewed the whole, and still, to their amazement, remained wakeful and active : on him alone of the children of men the powerful narcotic failed to produce its usual effects. The ever-blazing oven of Miru was ready for its victim. The voice of the pitiless Miru was now heard : "Kumutonga-of-the-night and Karaia-the-shadowy, bring along your husband ; the oven of Miru is waiting for him." At these words Ngaru put on the girdle his grandfather

---

[1] The three sorts of "kava" known in *this* world are but *offshoots* from the original root.

had wisely provided for his use. Thus equipped, the dauntless visitor from the upper world proceeded in search of the hag Miru and her dread oven. At this juncture the voice of the anxious Moko was heard in the shades : " Return, Ngaru—yonder is the oven in which she means to cook you." Heedless of this warning, the brave visitor went on his way, and finding the red-hot stones of the oven raked ready for the victim, he asked the horrid mistress of the invisible world what she meant to do with this burning oven. Miru promptly replied, " *To cook you !*" Ngaru reproached her thus : " Ah, Miru ! my grandfather Moko did not prepare an oven for *your* daughters ; but gave them food to eat, cocoa-nut water to drink, and sent them away in peace ! *You* cook and devour *your* visitors ! "

At these words the heavens became intensely black. Ngaru walked to the edge of the flaming oven, and placed one foot on the red-hot stones. At this critical moment the clouds, which had been gathering ever since he had entered Avaiki, burst suddenly. A fearful deluge [1] of waters extinguished the blazing oven, and swept away Miru herself, her younger fairy daughters, and all her servants and accomplices. Ngaru was saved by clutching hold of the stem of the nono,[2] the beautiful Tapairu girls, who allured him to the domains of Miru, held each by one of his legs, and so escaped the fate of their mother and sisters. These fairies taught Ngaru the art of ball-throwing.

After a time the waters entirely abated. Ngaru, wearied of the society of these attractive but dangerous fairy women, succeeded in finding a dark, winding passage to a land called

---

[1] A deluge-myth is inserted in a forthcoming popular volume, entitled " Life in the Southern Seas."

[2] *Morindo citrifolia.* Its root is wonderfully tenacious.

Taumareva (= *expanse*), where fruits and flowers grow profusely, and the inhabitants of which excelled in flute-playing.[1]   Here he married a girl kept by her parents inside a house in order to whiten her skin.   Time passed pleasantly in this new residence. But one day two pretty little birds, known as " Karakerake," perched upon the ledge of a pile of rocks.   Ngaru immediately recognized them as belonging to Moko, and asked them whether they came at his grandfather's bidding.   The birds nodded assent, whilst Ngaru wept for joy, and prayed thus :—

Karakerake ē, tukua iora te taura !	Ye little birds, pray drop a cord :
O te taura oa tena i tukuia 'i o maua ariki	Aye, the cord used for the imperious
O Rākā maumau ē. Tukua, tukua ra ikona !	Orākā,[2] the all-devouring. Drop, drop it at once !

At these words two cords fell, one from the feet of each bird. Securing himself by means of this double rope, Ngaru gave the signal to the birds, and without a word of farewell to his late spouse and her musical countrymen, was borne aloft to this upper world, and was safely deposited in the presence of Moko, who had long been ill, pining for the presence of his brave Ngaru, so long a prisoner in the shades.

Ngaru had conquered the monsters of the deep ; had conquered the aversion of the proud Tongatea ; had been buried in the earth ; had descended to the shades, where he had proved victor over the hitherto unconquered Miru and her satellites. One more trial was reserved for Ngaru, ere he should be permitted to live in peace.   The last foe was a heavenly one.

---

[1] A piece of bamboo pierced with *three* holes, and blown through the nose.

[2] Orākā, *i.e.* " Auraka," the dreadful chasm down which the dead were thrown: here, " *the gates of Hades.*"

One day the people of this world were astonished at the sight of a large basket (some say " a vast fish-hook ") let down from the sky. Two or three anxious to see the wonders of the upper world, hitherto unexplored, entered the basket and were speedily drawn up out of sight. Not many days after, this process was repeated; but it came to be noticed, after a time, that none ever came down again to report what they had seen. This looked decidedly suspicious. The fact was, a sky-demon named Amai-te-rangi, or *Carry-up-to-heaven*, had taken a fancy to feed on human flesh, and had invented the basket and ropes as a means of satisfying hunger. Hearing from his victims of the prowess of Ngaru, he resolved to entrap and devour him. Now the basket itself was a very attractive object, and on the day of Ngaru's return from his visits to the invisible world it was let down close to the dwelling of Moko. Ngaru, regarding this as a challenge, determined to ascend and have a fight with its owner. The more wily Moko detained his heroic grandson until his faithful little lizard subjects should go up and find out what was going on in the sky. The word having been given by The-king-of-lizards, a number of his sharp-eyed attendants entered the basket, which was speedily pulled up by Amai-te-rangi. On discovering that he had only caught a number of miserable little reptiles, he was greatly chagrined. Meanwhile the nimble subjects of Moko overran the place. When next the basket was let down, they were permitted to go down in it. They reported to Moko what they had seen : the gigantic size of " Carry-up-to-heaven ; " beautiful women engaged in ball throwing ; a huge chisel and mallet in the hands of the sky demon ; and piles of human bones.

Ngaru fearlessly got into the beautiful basket, and was at once drawn up by the delighted Amai-te-rangi, who anticipated a good feast, as the intended victim was uncommonly heavy. Upon touching the magnificent paving of blue stone, Ngaru found the demon drawn out to his full size, chisel and mallet in hand ready to deal the fatal blow. At this moment the human hero gave it a sudden jerk, that precipitated himself and the basket down to earth again. The disappointed demon hastily drew up Ngaru again, resolving not to permit him to escape a second time. But the grandson of Moko was not to be outwitted; for as soon as the basket again touched the solid vault of heaven, he once more jerked it back to earth. Amai-te-rangi eight times pulled his ropes, until his strength was nearly exhausted; but at last, to his satisfaction, saw Ngaru coolly walk out of the basket and confront his giant foe, who again prepared to deal the fatal blow with that chisel from which no mortal had hitherto escaped.

Now Moko had foreseen all this, and to provide for the safety of Ngaru, each time the basket touched the ground had sent into it a number of lizards, which leaped out on the sky as soon as the basket touched the blue paving, unregarded by the demon, whose whole thoughts were concentrated on the destruction of this fearless human enemy. At the moment his huge arms were uplifted to effect the murder of Ngaru, all these faithful guardians rushed up the legs of Amai-te-rangi, covering his face, neck, arms, and body. Particularly clustering about the armpits, they tickled the giant to such a degree that it was impossible for him to strike with precision. Again and again the monster endeavoured to brush off these little fellows from his naked body, so that he might accomplish his purpose; but the lizards pertinaciously returned to their appointed task of distracting Amai-te-rangi's thoughts and movements, until at length this cruel enemy of mankind, utterly unable to slay Ngaru, and tickled almost to madness, dropped chisel and mallet. Ngaru, seizing these weapons, succeeded in killing Amai-te-rangi, and then let himself down to earth again, accompanied by his four-footed protectors, and carrying with him the chisel and mallet of his slain foe. Ere leaving, he tried *ball-throwing* with Ina and Matonga, who kept eight balls going at a time, and succeeded in beating them too.

Such were the exploits of this Polynesian Hercules.

In the original, when describing the repentance of Tongatea at the reed-throwing match, the question is asked, " Whose place in *Manono* is vacant?" The reply is, "Tongatea's." " Why, then, does she not begin?" There is a spot on Mangaia so named ; but every one believes that the reference is to the island of " Manono," in the Samoan Group. The wife's name, " Tongatea," means The-fair-Tongan. I believe this story to have been one brought by the original settlers when they came originally from Avaiki, or Savai'i. It is no objection to this view that the myth, as *now* told, is localized here, as a long residence would be sure to produce this. The proper depositories of such lore invariably assert that they were introduced here from other lands.

The story of Miru is merely a vivid representation of their old belief as to the state of those who die a natural death. Fairy women come to fetch Ngaru : he is like any other corpse, wrapped up in tapa, and well corded, and borne by two individuals to the deep cavernous domain of Miru. " Orākā " is but a disguise for " Auraka," the great repository of their dead, from which two cords pull up the victor upon his return to life.

In this story Miru and all her servants and two of her " peerless " daughters perish. The ever-burning oven, too, is extinguished. But the standard belief of the past represents Miru as immortal, and the oven as still blazing and consuming the spirits of all who die a natural death. Does not this myth express a deep-seated hope and intense yearning after that real victory over death and hell which Christianity alone can satisfy?

Apai-te-rangi is in heaven the exact counterpart of Miru in the shades; but still a man of divine descent—Ngaru—comes off victor!

It is a curious fact that one family on Mangaia claims descent from this sky-demon Apai-te-rangi. But this heavenly descent did not prevent the "Āmai" tribe from being devoted to furnish sacrifices to Rongo from generation to generation. (The name is indifferently spelt Amai and Apai.)

As Miru in the shades is the parent of Tapairu, or "peerless" fairy women, so in the sky Apai-i-te-rangi has about him a set of Tapairu women, whose sole employment is ball-throwing—some keeping seven, others eight, balls going at a time. One of these heavenly fairies is Ina, another is named Matonga. Ngaru introduced the art to this world.

The basket of the heavenly monster is the counterpart of the stupefying kava, of Miru, his chisel and mallet answering to the fiery oven of the shades.

THE DRAMA OF NGARU.

A REED-THROWING MATCH FOR WOMEN, IN HONOUR OF PATIKIPORO. COMPOSED BY TUKA, CIRCA 1815.

Two women.

Akiakia tute te manava ia Tevoo 'i
> Strip the branches[1] off Miru's "kava" tree

Ei mana paa no Ngaru Avaiki,
Koia i pau taae !
> To stupefy wonder-working Ngaru,
> Victorious over all monsters,

Tepoi arire na Moko ra,
Na Vari-ma-te-takere ē !
> Pet grandson of Moko,
> Descended from Vari-originator-of-all-things.

Chorus.

Te taa o te rangi
A tuku te ata apai Ngaru ē,
I te kakenga atu rava.
> The natives of the sky
> Let down a trap to catch Ngaru,
> Who ascended on high.

Two women.

Kake atu Ngaru i te tautua,
I te tau aro o te Moko kura i tau ē,
Ka pare nei kia Apai-te-rangi ē !
> To save Ngaru the golden lizards
> Climbed up the front and back,
> Baffling cruel Apai-te-rangi.

Kua kino Ngaru ei te tacke aē !
> T'was Ngaru blackened by diving,

Chorus.

Kua kino Ngaru i te taeke,
E anga turoko ka oro ai Tongatea ē !
Tei Itikau te roki
> Ngaru blackened in the billows,
> The sight disgusted the fair Tongan,
> Whose loved resort is at Itikau.

Two women.

Tei Itikau te roki ē !
> Yes ; her loved resort is at Itikau.

---

[1] The *root* only of the *piper-mythisticum* is chewed to make the stupefying drink. But *Miru's* own original plant, of enormous size, in the shades is narcotic even to its *branches.* The inebriate spirits are helplessly carried to the fatal oven, and are cooked. Ngaru alone defeats her cruel arts.

Chorus.

Pāpā paka, a inu ra i te vai o Mărua,

Refresh yourselves, fair ones, in Shady-Land,

E rua enua e pēi ai te pēi.

Like celestials proficient in ball throwing.

<table>
<tr><td>INUINU TAI.</td><td>FIRST OFFSHOOT.</td></tr>
</table>

Two women.

Pēi ikiiki na Ngaru ē !

Oh ! the wondrous skill of Ngaru.

Chorus.

Tera rava te karanga,
E karanga ia Ngaru.
Iti mai rapa te uira,
E uira tu akarere,
Na mana o Ngaru-tai.

List to yonder voice !
'Tis addressed to Ngaru.
Lightning is emitted from his person,
And flashes all around.
Great is the might of Ocean-loving Ngaru.[1]

Noea toou mana?
No raro i Avaiki,—
Na Vari-ma-te-takere,
Na ooki atu na,

Whence this unheard of power ?
From the depths of spirit-land,
From Vari-originator-of-all-things,
Who sends him back again (to this world).

Tena ïa ia kava.

Ah! there comes the stupefying draught.

E tere aa ra, e Miru ?
E tere kai tangata !

What have you come for, Miru ?
I come to devour mankind.

Two women.

Takina ra Avaiki, e Miru ē !

Do thy worst, Miru !

Chorus.

Ei rapanga uira i tane.

Provoke not the flashing lightning of your betrothed—

---

[1] Ngaru = *wave* : a play on the name is intended, as well as a reference to his first exploit.

Two women.

Tane oro ki Iti![1]	The betrothed, whose loved resort is at Itikau—

Chorus.

Aē, Ngaru-tai.	Aye, Ocean-loving Ngaru.

Two women.

Akiakia tute te manava ia Tevoo 'i,	Strip the branches off Miru's kava tree,
Ei mana paa no Ngaru Avaiki, Koia i pau taae!	To stupefy wonder-working Ngaru, Victorious over all monsters.
Tepoi arire na Moko ra, Na Vari-ma-te-takere ē!	Pet grandson of Moko, Descended from Vari-originator-of-all-things.

Chorus.

Te taa o te rangi A tuku i te ata apai Ngaru ē, I te kakenga atu rava.	The natives of the sky Let down a trap to catch Ngaru, Who ascended on high.

Two women.

Kake atu Ngaru i te tautua I te tau aro o te moko kura i tau e, A pare nei kia Apai-te-rangi-ē!	To save Ngaru the golden lizards Climbed up the front and back, Baffling cruel Apai-te-rangi.
Kua kino Ngaru e i te taeke aē!	'Twas Ngaru blackened by diving,

Chorus.

Kua kino Ngaru i te taeke, E anga turoko ka oro ai Tongatea ē, Tei Itikau te roki.	Ngaru blackened in the billows: The sight disgusted the fair Tongan, Whose loved resort is at Itikau.

Two women.

Tei Itikau te roki ē!	Yes; her loved resort is at Itikau.

---

[1] " Iti," an abbreviation for " Itikau," the name of a famous resort for lovers on the west of the island.

Chorus.

Pāpā paka, a inu ra i te vai o Mărua. — Refresh yourselves, fair ones, in Shady-Land,

E rua enua i pēi i te pēi. — Like celestials proficient in ball-throwing.

INUINU RUA. — SECOND OFFSHOOT.

Two women.

O Mărua tai o are ē! — In Shady-Land is thy true home.

Chorus.

Takina o Ngaru-tai — Lift up Ocean-loving Ngaru ;
Na Kumutonga i apai, — Kumutonga shall bear thee on
E apai ki Avaiki, — Until thou reach spirit-land
Ei kai na Miru-Kura, — As food for the ever-ruddy Miru—
Ei tane Ngaru tai — Our betrothed Ocean-loving Ngaru.
Akiakia tute, akiakia kava, — Strip the branches off the "kava" tree,

Te manava ia Tevoo. — To stupefy thy senses.
Tātāia e Iva, porotua te rangi ra. — The heavens are black—torrents descend.

Kakea ra e Ngaru te enua — But Ngaru passes on to Taumareva—
Taumāreva, te enua iri kura e, — The land of scarlet garments,
Na te taa o te rangi. — At the edge of the skies.
E tere aa ra, e Miru ? — What have you come for, Miru ?
E tere kai tangata. — I come to devour mankind.

Two women.

Takina ra Avaiki, e Miru ē! — Do thy worst, Miru !

Chorus.

E rapanga uira i tane — Provoke not the flashing lightning of your betrothed—

Two women.

Tane oro ki Iti! — The betrothed, whose loved resort is at Itikau.

Chorus.

Ae, Ngaru-tai. — Aye, Ocean-loving Ngaru.

R

Two women.

Akiakia tute te manava ia Tevoo 'i,	Strip the branches off Miru's "kava" tree,
Ei mana paa no Ngaru Avaiki,	To stupefy wonder-working Ngaru,
Koia i pau taae !	Victorious over all monsters.

Chorus.

Oi au tiria, tiria.	Put me down, put me down.
Oi au tarā, tarā,	Set me free, set me free.
Tarāia akera,	Oh, that I had liberty
Kia kite au i teia maunga.	To gaze at this mountain !
O te maunga poro oa teia	'Tis surely the mountain spoken of
A tau tupuna a Moko-Roa,	By my grandfather "The-long-Lizard,"
Tau metua a Vaiare,	And by my mother Vaiare,
Tau vaine a Tongatea.	And by my wife, "The-fair-Tongan."

Kiritia kai e kinana !	Thou shalt be forthwith devoured !
To koivi, vaio i Erangi maunga !	Thy *body* shall rot on this "Heavenly Mountain"
To vaerua, e kave i te po	Thy *spirit* shall be borne to the shades,
Na to maua metua na Miru !	To furnish a repast for our mother Miru.

Kumutonga, Karaia-i-te-ata ōi,	Hist, Kumutonga ! Hist, Karaia-the-Shadowy,
Tukua maira ta korua tane,	Bring me your intended husband,
Kua roa oa te umu a Miru !	For the oven of Miru is waiting !

Aore a e pau atu i tau moko ;	I will not part with my grandson.
E tapu te tikinga vaine a Ngaru	'Tis thus ye fairies treat Ngaru.

Tuku atu te taura i Enua-Kura.	Pray drop down some cords to Spirit-Land ;
E taura viriviri, e taura varavara,	Ropes of many strands and of great strength,

Ruia e tematangi, kakea e Ngaru,

Swaying to and fro in the breeze, yet able

Kakea e te rangi tautua,
Kakea e te rangi tuamano.

To bear Ngaru, the heaven-climber,
Resolved to explore all nature.

E tuku te taura i Enua-Kura ē !

Pray, drop down some cords to Spirit-Land.

Mauria !

Hold fast. (*Great emphasis.*)

Mauria, e Ruateātonga,
Te pitonga i te taura
I tukua 'i i maua ariki.
O Rākā maumau ē !
Tukua, tukua ra ikōna !

Spirit of the shades ! hold fast
To the end of these ropes,
Intended to rescue our favourite
From all-devouring " Auraka,"
Drop, drop them down at once !

Oki mai, e Ngaru !
Tera 'tu te umu e tao iaau !

Hasten back, Ngaru !
Yonder is the oven intended to consume you.

This curious drama was performed at Tamarua by daylight, at the base of the hill Vivitaunoa. Several women still living took part in the performance. One was named Miru for the occasion ; a second Moko ; a third Ngaru. Two others represented the daughters of Miru—Kumutonga and Karaia-i-te-ata. These fairies, at the proper time, carried over the crest of the hill a large bundle like a seeming corpse, ready to be thrown down " Auraka," the last resting-place of the dead. An oven was made, but no fire lighted. Two cords were fastened to the woman who sustained the part of Ngaru, and who was dragged to the edge of the supposed oven.

The husband of Patikiporo is still living. He has for many years sustained a good Christian profession.

The part commencing "Put me down," etc., down to "a

repast for our mother Miru," is taken from the myth, which is known to be of great antiquity.

Sadaraka well recollects the performance, at which, as a male, he could only be a spectator.

THE BALL-THROWER'S SONG; OR, THE FAIRIES BEATEN BY NGARU.

FOR THE FÊTE OF POTIKI, CIRCA 1790.

Call for the dance to lead off.

Pei ikiiki tei to rima, e rua toe,

Keep the balls all going; two are left,

Tei Iva e; a tai ra koē.

In all spirit-land thou hast no equal.

Solo.

Taipo ē!

Go on!

Chorus.

Pei aea nga Tapairu no Avaiki;

Here are fairy players from nether-land,

No nunga paa i te rangi ē!

As well as natives of the sky.

Solo.

Ae ē!

Aye!

Chorus.

Pei aea i te pei itu, i te pei varu, e Ina e!

Ina alone keeps seven, yea, eight balls in motion.

Ka rē koia o Matonga-iti kau rērē.

Little Matonga is beaten—utterly beaten.

Solo.

Ka re oki, e Matonga e, i te pei—
Ka topa i to rima ; a tai ō!

Ah! Matonga, thou art beaten—
At the outset a ball has fallen to the ground.

INUINU TAI.

FIRST OFFSHOOT.

Solo.

Tiria mai taku pei.

Give me the balls.

Chorus.

E pei ka topa i te rima o nga tupuna
     'tu,
  Na Teiiri na Teraranga.
Taku rima, taku ei kapara turina,
  Ua toro, pati kura konikoni,
  No nunga no te akinga pei
O nga Tapairu, tu tai e, kiri rua e,

Paiereiere ikitia i raro o Kaputai.

A tai nei vaine i nginingini ai,

  I toro pa titi, toro pa tata,

O te pua mata reka, o te akatu nga
  are
I ikitia i Marama Nui ē. Era koe,
  e Ina !

This art was taught me by the gods,

  By Teiiri and Teraranga.[1]
Encircled with chaplets of laurel,
  I select round scarlet fruits
  To serve as balls for our game,
For fairy women who once and again
Have come up from spirit-world to dance at Kaputai.[2]
Of these fairies the most strangely fascinating
  And proficient at our game is Ina.
Lovely blossom, whose home is in the sky,
Beloved wife of Full-Moon, I have beaten thee !

Solo.

Taipo ē !

Go on !

Chorus.

Pei aea nga Tapairu no Avaiki ;

No nunga paa i te rangi ē !

Here are fairy players from nether land,
As well as natives of the sky.

Solo.

Ae ē !

Aye !

Chorus.

Pei aea i te pei itu, i te pei varu, e
  Ina e !
Ka rē koia o Matonga-iti kau rērē :

Ina alone keeps seven, yea, eight balls in motion.
Little Matonga is beaten—utterly beaten.

---

[1] Gods presiding over the game of ball-throwing.
[2] The shore-king's residence, close by the altar of Rongo.

Solo.

Ka re oki e Matonga e i te pei—
Ka topa i to rima ; a tai ō !

Ah ! Matonga thou art beaten—
At the outset a ball has fallen to the ground.

INUINU RUA.　　SECOND OFFSHOOT.

Solo.

Tei nūnga !

How high !

Chorus.

I nunga o pei tini, i raro o taaonga.

All the balls in the air ; how dexterous the hand !

To kura pei kura, maautara,

The balls are all red and greatly admired.

Mea Auraka te metua, e nui ana,

Thanks to the divinities who taught thee,

E mau ana, peiia, tuia te toa i Rangi riri.
　　Anga mai te vai ia mata.
　　E vai tuaine, e vai tungane,
　　Riu atu to tau, anga mai to oro,
Teia taku pei, e pei ikiiki Marama rua ē !
　　Era koe, e Matonga !

Catch them, throw them in succession.
　　All eyes are fixed on thee.
　　Women and men in wonder
　　Gaze at thy face and form.
With these balls again I challenge you fairies.
　　I have beaten thee, too, Matonga !

Call the second.

Pei ikiiki tei to rima, e rua toe,

Keep the balls all going ; two are left.

Tei Iva e, a tai ra koe ē !

In all spirit-land thou hast no equal.

Solo.

Taipo ē !

Go on !

Chorus.

Pei aea nga Tapairu no Avaiki ;

Here are fairy players from nether-land,

No nunga paa i te rangi ē !

As well as natives of the sky.

Solo.

Ae !

Aye !

Chorus.

Pei aea i te pei itu, i te pei varu, e
  Ina e !
Ka rē koia o Matonga-iti kau rērē !

Ina alone keeps seven, yea, eight balls
  in motion.
Little Matonga is beaten—utterly
  beaten.

Solo.

Ka re oki, e Matonga e, i te pei,
Ka topa i to rima ; ā tai ō !

Ah ! Matonga, thou art beaten.
At the outset a ball has fallen to the
  ground.

INUINU TORU.

THIRD OFFSHOOT.

Solo.

A tāi !

Again !

Chorus.

Tai, rua, toru, ā, rima, ono, itu, varu.

One, two, three, four, five, six,
  even, eight balls !

Tu akarongo no Pai, no Manoinoi ariki
  E tangi te vai i Aratatia.
Akairi i nunga i Aramaunga i te
  kopuku.
  Aakina i te măro Akaina,
Na tumaanga nginingini i te rearea,
  E tangata e tu i Tōrea,
E mania i te kura, e mania i te rearea !

Pai and the royal Manoinoi admire.
  The crowd is astonished.
Akaina, though skilled in all arts,

  Surpassing the men of his day,
The bravest and wisest of men,
  Ne'er could equal thee.
Let perfect silence now be pre-
  served.

  Era koe, e Ina !

  Again I have beaten thee, Ina !

Solo.

Taipo ē !

Go on !

Chorus.

Pei aea nga Tapairu no Avaiki ;

Here are fairy players from nether-
  land,

No nunga paa i te rangi ē !

As well as natives of the sky.

Solo.

Ae ē !

Aye !

Chorus.

Pei aea i te pei itu, i te pei varu, e
    Ina e !

Ina alone keeps seven, yea, eight balls
    in motion.

Ka rē koia o Matonga-iti kau rērē.

Little Matonga is beaten—utterly
    beaten.

Solo.

Ka rē oki, e Matonga e, i te pei,

Ah ! Matonga, thou art beaten.

Ka topa i to rima ; ā tai ō !

At the outset a ball has fallen to the
    ground.

INUINU Ā.   FOURTH OFFSHOOT.

Solo.

E retia !

Avaunt !

E retia, e retia O Tua-niinii

Avaunt, avaunt, thou of a scraggy
    back !

Chorus.

E retia, e retia O Tua-ara-roa !

Avaunt, avaunt, thou of the long
    spine—

Ara-roa i te iki-tanga i te akamatenga.

Tall to deformity and ready to die.

Na kura pei kura, na tama reionga,

Give me my grand scarlet-balls,

Na kakara onu e rutu i te tua o Vātea.

Like young turtle in the palm of
    Vātea.

Re tai, re rua, re toru, re ā,

Beaten once, twice, thrice, yea, four
    times ;

Re rima, re ono, re itu, re varu,

Beaten again, again, and again ;

Re iva, re ngauru, tinitini, manomano,

Beaten times innumerable, all of you.

O Arauru, O Ara peipei, tei kai te
    reinga.

Pack up your traps, one and all—

Koi tangatangā iri, koi mata kerekere,

Ye sweet-scented ball-players from
    the skies

Koi nunga, koi raro, koi te patiu ē !
    Era koe, e Matonga !

And from nether-land—and be off !
    Again I have beaten thee,
    Matonga.

Third Call.

Pei ikiiki tei to rima, e rua toe.

Keep the balls all going ; two are
    left.

Tei Iva e, a tai ra koe ē !

In all spirit-land thou hast no equal.

Solo.

Taipo ē !	Go on !

Chorus.

Pei aea nga Tapairu no Avaiki ;
No nunga paa i te rangi ū !

Here are fairies from nether-land,
As well as natives of the sky.

Solo.

Ae ē !	Aye !

Chorus.

Pei aea i te pei itu, i te pei varu, e
    Ina e !
Ka re koia o Matonga-iti kau rērē !

Ina alone keeps seven, yea, eight balls
    in motion.
Little Matonga is beaten—utterly
    beaten.

Solo.

Ka re oki, e Matonga e, i te pei,
Ka topa i to rima ; ā tai ō !

Ah ! Matonga, thou art beaten.
At the outset a ball has fallen to the
    ground.

MAUTU.   CONCLUSION.

Fourth Call.

E ara pei na Kumutonga,

Na Karaia-i-te-ata e, a kake ē !

And now a game of ball-throwing
    with Kumutonga,
With Karaia - the - shadowy from
    nether-world.

Solo.

Taipo ū !	Go on !

Chorus.

Te pei maira te peinga i te ata.

Play as ye are wont in the shades.

Solo.

Ae ū !	Aye !

Chorus.

Te rere maira te manu pepe kura.

A bird of gay plumage is watching
    you.

Solo.

E ara pei oki ra na Karaia ae ō !	A game of ball-throwing with Karaia !

Chorus.

E ara pei na Kumutonga,	A game of ball-throwing with Kumutonga
Na Karaia-i-te-ata.	And her sister Karaia-the-shadowy.
Aore paa e kitea te ikōnga i te rima !	The quick movements of the fingers are invisible.

Of the sky-fairies, Ina and Matonga were the most clever at this game. Both, however, are vanquished by Ngaru : in the first and third stanzas Ina is beaten; in the second and fourth, Matonga. In the "conclusion" Ngaru is trying his fortune with the infernal sirens with equal success.

In the dance the performers imitated the movements of the ball-throwers, without balls, however.

The contemptuous language of the fourth stanza is in direct contradiction of the standard belief in their "peerless" beauty. It is a sly hit at certain ladies at the dance personifying the two sets of fairy women. Proud of their assumed name, "Tapairu," they are really the butt of the whole assembly.

A JOURNEY TO THE INVISIBLE WORLD.

A TAHITIAN MYTH.

Ouri bare *Oemā* two sons, of whom Arii was the elder, and Tavai the younger. On one occasion, for a trivial offence, some of the father's relatives severely beat little Tavai, who was his mother's pet. Ouri was so enraged at this, that her husband Oemā descended to Hawaii to hide his shame.   The now regretful wife waited many days in vain for his return.

Little Tavai, who was naturally a brave child, resolved to go in search of his father.   On mentioning his intention to his mother and older brother, the former strongly objected, whilst the latter volunteered to accompany him.   Said Tavai to Arii, "Stay to take care of our mother."   But Arii would on no account consent to be left behind by his younger brother.

The mother, finding it impossible to detain her beloved children, disclosed to them the secret road to spirit-land, and taught them the needful formula.

Using this charm, the earth clave asunder, and the lads descended.   They now found themselves in the land of Kui-the-Blind.   Arii was excessively alarmed at her appearance, and confessed his fears to his younger brother, who only remarked, "I told you not to come, but you *would* have your own way."

Now Kui was employed in cooking her daily oven when the brothers approached her and in silence watched her operations. Kui did not suspect the presence of these intruders.   The food in her oven consisted of :—

> 2 heads of taro.
>
> 2 plantains.
>
> 2 halves of bread-fruit.
>
> 2 packages of sour bread-fruit paste.

Laying on a goodly pile of leaves, she covered in her oven and pressed it down with large stones.   Kui now sat quietly inside her house till it was done, still ignorant of the presence of mortals.

When she judged the food to be sufficiently cooked, she opened her oven.   She took up a taro and placed it in her basket. On putting out her arm to take up the second—lo, it was gone !

Kui was greatly surprised, but did not speak.   She thought, "What daring fellow has invaded my land and come to steal my food?"

Kui next took up a plantain and put it into her basket.   But on seeking for the second—lo, it was gone!   And thus, too, of the bread-fruit and the packages of sour bread-fruit paste.

The old blind woman, now thoroughly enraged, exclaimed, "Whoever this is that has dared to come to my land, *I will devour him.*"   She then re-entered her house, carrying the diminished supply of food.   Tavai whispered to his elder brother, "Beware of her tricks: touch nothing belonging to her."   At this moment Kui-the-Blind came out, armed with a terrible fish-hook fastened to a long line.   This she swung backwards and forwards, all the while chanting a song, in order to catch the thief.   The lads contrived to keep clear of it, but threw a pandanus log at it.   The log was hooked.   Whilst Kui was pulling in her line with immense satisfaction, the boys chanted these words :—

> Carefully secure *thy* fish,
> Ere *thou* be o'ertaken by a shark.

To which Kui replied :—

> For him that is caught by my hook
> There is no hope.   Strong is my hook.
> Its name is ("Furnisher of) food for immortals."
> The line is called "The indivisible."

Kui seized her supposed victim, which proved to be a mere log of wood.   Angry at this, she again threw out her dreadful fish-hook.   This time she caught the elder boy Arii.   Both the brothers wept bitterly.   Kui again chanted the former ominous words, "For him," etc.   When the youthful victim had almost arrived at the doorway where the cruel blind woman sat, the brave Tavai ran forwards, and seizing the fatal string snapped it asunder by sheer force, thus rescuing Arii from her pitiless clutches. The brothers then entered the house of the now defenceless Kui, and discovering the stone axe with which she was accustomed to despatch her victims, slew her therewith. Her body was next chopped in pieces; the house pulled down and set on fire, thus consuming this foe of mankind.

Tavai now proposed that they should resume the search for their father, and that Arii, as the elder, should take the lead.

The brothers accordingly prepared to leave the land of Kui-the-Blind.

Arrived at the sea-shore, they walked over the ocean and saw a *red* streak ahead on the surface of the water. On drawing nearer to the red streak, they found a *red* shark swimming underneath. Arii trembled and entreated Tavai to go in front. As the younger brother sturdily refused, Arii had still to go on. The great red shark now rose to the surface, and said :—

O era taata e aere
Na raro i te moana ra ē !
Keinga korua e au !

Yon daring travellers
O'er the briny sea
Shall furnish my repast.

These words struck both lads with terror, but Tavai, recollecting himself, replied :—

> Art not thou our aged ancestor,
> Nutaravaivaria ? And are not we
> The offspring of Oemā and Ouri ?

The enormous fish now learning that these boys were his own grandchildren, allowed them to get on his back, and conveyed them safely to the shore of Rauai'a-Nui, where Tavai landed. The red shark now asked Tavai to give him Arii to eat. But the brave boy said, "You must *not* devour him, for I have but one brother." Three times did the red shark ask for Arii : three times was the request denied by Tavai.

Now there was a great abundance of cocoa-nuts in this new land. Tavai climbed the trees and gathered the nuts, so that the ground was everywhere covered with the fallen nuts. Tavai's next work was to tie these nuts together in fours and count them. In all there were a thousand nuts, which he with no little labour placed on the back of the great red shark. And not until the last four was given up did the shark give up his brother.

Arii and Tavai spent three days on that island. On the morning of the fourth day the red shark came back. The lads again mounted on his back and were borne over the ocean in search of their lost father. Now the boys had provided themselves with cocoa-nuts to eat by the way. All but one had been disposed of during their long voyage. At their wits' end to know how to open it, they broke it on the head of the shark. Pained by the smart blow, the red shark dived down to the bottom of the ocean, leaving the boys swimming on the surface. When at length the strength of Arii was exhausted, the red shark again rose to the surface, and generously forgiving the late offence, carried them to shore. This is the farthest limit of spirit-land.

The brothers now travelled about in search of the inhabitants. They fell in with a man who asked what they were in quest of. They told him that they were seeking for their father, and inquired whether he could give them any intelligence respecting him. The old man advised them to apply to the oracle. Tavai at once started off to the residence of the famous priest. Without ceremony they opened the door and entered. The priest sharply asked "What stranger is this that has dared to come to my land?" Tavai, annoyed at this brusque reception, struck the priest on his head, causing him to writhe in agony. Having thus humbled the priest, he asked him where Oemā was. The priest replied, "Yonder—he is dead. Go on until you meet an old woman—*she* has charge of the corpse."

At length they met an aged woman, and inquired where the dead body of Oemā was deposited. She promptly replied, "In the 'stercus' hole." The brothers said, "Go, then, and fetch it." They closely followed the old hag. On coming to the place, they found that he had long been dead, for only the skeleton remained. They tenderly took up the bones and wrapped them in a mat. They next killed the old woman, and burnt down her house. Not satisfied with this, they slew the priest and the first person they had met, and set fire to their dwellings.

Finally, these brave boys, Arii and Tavai, made their way back to this upper world, bringing to Ouri the bones of her long-lost husband. In doing this they traversed the old road, the chasm opening up again as the words taught by their wise-hearted mother were uttered by Tavai.

Compare this with the myths entitled, "A Bachelor God in Search of a Wife," and "The Wisdom of Manihiki." "Kui-the-Blind" figures in all three versions of their ancient faith.

CHAPTER XI.

FAIRY MEN AND WOMEN.

TAPAIRU; OR, FAIRY WOMEN AND MEN.

THE deformed and ugly Miru has her home in the nether-world, where she cooks human spirits in her oven. Her son Tautiti presides over the dance called by his name.[1] Besides Tautiti, the pitiless spirit-eater has four daughters, called Tapairu, or *peerless ones*, on account of their matchless beauty. They delight to make their appearance in this upper world whenever a dance is performed in honour of their brother. Thus, if a dance took place anywhere in the *northern* half of the island, they would be sure to make their appearance that evening at sunset, bathing at a little shady stream named Auparu (= *soft-dew*). These fairies would then climb the almost perpendicular hill overlooking the fountain, in order to dry themselves and to arrange their beautiful tresses in the moonbeams, ere proceeding to witness the

---

[1] The graceful " Tautiti " dance stands opposed to the " Crab," in which the side movements of that fish are most disagreeably imitated. Dances always took place by moonlight.

performances of mortals. But if the dance were to take place in the *southern* part of the island, these " peerless ones " would make their appearance at two little streams, named Vaipau and Vaikaute, and then perform their usual toilet on the crest of the neighbouring hill.

These fairies, always associated with the worship of Tane, would even deign to take part in the dance, provided that one end of the dancing ground were well covered with fresh cut banana leaves. But after merrily tripping it over these exquisitely fragile leaves through the livelong night, not one of them would be in any degree soiled or injured. As soon as the morning star rose they disappeared, and returned to their gloomy home in Avaiki.

Throughout the eastern Pacific islands " Tapairu," or " fairest of the fair," is a favourite name for girls.

The names of these fairies are :—

1. Kumutonga-i-te-po = Kumutonga-of-the-night.
2. Karaia-i-te-ata = Karaia-the-shadowy.
3. Té-rauara = Pandanus-leaf.
4. Te-poro = Point.

A SONG IN HONOUR OF MAUAPA.

BY PANGEMIRO, LORD OF MANGAIA, CIRCA 1816.

Turina eiā ra e te Aumania ra,
Kia turuki te vaine moe atu te tane o,
Na te ei pāpā kura.

Red necklaces for Mauapa,
To win the favour of the fair,
Mixed with leaves of purple hue.

Riro i Motuenga i te puku
Maunga ra i akamae te maire,
Taki rua o rau te tiare tapu.

On the mountains sit we down
To interweave beautiful flowers
With double rows of myrtle leaves.

s

Tangi atu au ra i te aunga tiere.	I love the fragrance of the flowers
Tei Auparu na vaine tau nongonongo	At Auparu, from fairy women
I te pa etu na Ina ē !	Arraying themselves by starlight,
Te aiai a Kura ! Eu ē ! Aē !	Whilst Ina in the moon looks on.
To are karioi ē Tekura-i-Tanoa.	Ah ! ye e'en surpass Tekura-of-Tanoa.

In each valley of this island are crevices in the soil, through which superfluous waters drain. The direct road to spirit-land, through Tiki's chasm, having long since been closed, fairies avail themselves of these narrow passages to climb up from time to time, in order to be present at the dances of mortals.

The fête of Terangai, ancestor of the present tribe of Tane, was specially honoured by fairy visitors. The fête came off at Butoa. Teporo and Terauara, fair daughters of Miru, availed themselves of the gorge just by, to come up out of nether-world to take part in the festivity. The sound of the great drum used on that occasion reached to the very depths of spirit-land, inducing four other fairies—usually said to be males, and, of course, connected with Miru—also to climb up to witness their favourite dance, Tautiti. Oroiti [1] and Teauotangaroa [2] came up at a gorge known as Tuaoruku, on the south. Marangaitaiti [3] got up through a disagreeable-looking hole on the west, Marangaitaao [4] through a gorge at the north of the island. Guided by the sound of the drum, these four male fairy visitors tripped along different mountain ridges, until they all met at the fête ground, conspicuous by their unearthly beauty. At dawn they disappeared in the depths of Avaiki through the various crevices.

To this myth the prologue to Potiki's fête-songs alludes. After years of anarchy and bloodshed, peace was proclaimed in the name

---

[1] Oroiti = *slow-footed.*　　[2] Teauotangaroa = *reign-of-Tangaroa.*
[3] Marangaitaiti = *gentle-east-wind.*　　[4] Marangaitaao = *fierce-east-wind.*

of the gods.   At this, the first fête inaugurating the era of peace, it is hoped the fairies will be present as at Terangai's.   The greater gods, whose jealousies occasion the wars of mortals, should be chained.

PROLOGUE TO THE DRAMATIC FÊTE OF POTIKI, ON HIS ASSUMPTION OF THE TEMPORAL SOVEREIGNTY, CIRCA 1790.

Solo.

Vāia te rua i Avaiki,
Kia kake mai Oroiti e Tane ōi!

Open the entrance to spirit-world,
That Oroiti and Tane may come up.

Chorus.

Tireia Tautiti,
Kia aka i Onemakenukenu.

Tane aō i te tua o Terangai.

On this merry night
The ghosts are dancing on the smooth sward ;
As at Terangai's famed fête of old.

Solo.

Te moko ia Tautiti ē!
Karēia!

Tane is the patron of dancing.
(War dance).

Tukua, tukua ē!
Tukua ki rāro.

Down with your burdens,[1]
Down with them and rest.

---

[1] Each fête has its distinctive symbolism.   In Captain Cook's song, "caulking" is appropriately introduced : in *this* the employments of peace, as contrasting with those of war.   The "burdens" were bundles of long bamboos, suitable for fishing-rods.   These furnished employment for men in time of peace.   "The cloth-beating mallet" was intended to illustrate the work of industrious wives.   This could not be pursued with safety in time of war, as the far-reaching sounds would only guide the murderer to his prey.   At this fête, however, men beat mimic cloth-boards.   These fairies were acted—one coming from either end, met in the middle.

Chorus.

E ngae pu Avaiki i te papa,	Spirit-land is stirred to its very depths
E tukia ma te kaara.	At the music of the great drum.
Kua maū mai nei Teporo ma Terauara.	The fairies Teporo and Terauara have come up.
Takaia te papa i maui ;	Lead off the dance, ye of the left ;
Rumakina te papa i katau.	And you, too, of the right.
E era te taua i Tuaoruku	At Tuaoruku is a fairy dancing-ground,
Na Oroiti, na Teauotangaroa,	For Oroiti and Teauotangaroa,
Kimi pou enua ke atu.	Who have dared to come up to this world.

Solo.

Ka tutu Rongo i te rangi ē !	Great Rongo shakes his club.

Chorus.

No te ike tangi reka e papa i tuā.	Softly sounds the cloth-beating mallet o'er the sea.
Tutua ! Tutua !	Beat away ! Beat away !

Solo.

Kāno korua kiea ?	Whither go ye, fairies ?

Chorus.

Kāno maua a kimi ia Tautiti,	We go in search of the pleasing dance,
Kua ngaro mai nei.	So long disused.
Teia.	Here it is.
Teia te akatu, ma te akarongorongo,	Here are the dancers, the torch-bearers,
Ma te matakitaki.	And the spectators.

Solo.

Kāno korua kiea ?	Whither go ye, fairies ?

Chorus.

Kāno maua a kimi i te mārua kapa	We follow the merry sounds of dancing ;
Kua ana mai nei.	Therefore have we come.

Teia.

Teia te akarongorongo ma te mataki-
  taki.
Apaina eretia te anau Ātea,

    Te papa i te itinga ē!
      Apaina! Apaina!
Tautiti ngarue i Teakaruru.

      Eia ĭā! Eia ĭā.
        Iā! Iā!

Solo.

Vāia, e Marangaitaao, te rua i Avaiki.

Chorus.

  Kikimi mai! Aere mai!

Solo.

Vāia, e Marangaitaiti, te rua i Tipitake!

Chorus.

  Kikimi mai! Aere mai!
Kāno korua i Temangarea.

      Pua! Pua!
Ereti ua viriviri, ua varavara,

Ruia e te matangi mairā, mairā,
Ruia e te matangi mairā, mairā,
Kua oro Tautiti i Avaiki Nui ma te
  kaara.
Teia Marangaitaao te kimi atu nei.

      Tutua! Tutua!
Ka apai te tere i mua o te kaarā.

E taki aere i te uto o Terangai,

      I rakoa! I rakoa!

Here it is.

Here are the torch-bearers and the
  spectators.
Chain up the gods, the offspring of
    Vātea,
    That our sport be not spoiled.
      Avaunt! Avaunt!
Ha! I hear shouts of dances at
  Butoa!
      (War dance,
      twice performed.)

Open up for Marangaitaao an en-
trance from spirit-land.

Search us out, join our throng!

Open up for Marangaitaiti the dark
  gorge.

  Search us out, join our throng!
To what distant spot are these fairies
    bound?
    Beat away! Beat away!
Give me a many-stranded, powerful
  rope,
Waving to and fro in the wind,
Waving to and fro in the wind,
To pull up Tautiti and his drum out
  of Great Spirit-Land.
Here is the fairy Marangaitaao in
    search of us.
    Beat away! Beat away!
Let the fairies pass in front of the
  drum;
The fairies who once honoured the
    fête of Terangai,
    How dazzling! How brave!

Solo.

E uru tupu ariki te apai o te pau ē !
Now for a war-dance as we bear on this drum.

Karēia !
(War dance.)

Apai nuku, apai rangi !
Let all take a part ; toss it aloft.

Chorus.

Tuia uta, tuia tai.
Those over yonder ; those near at hand ;

Tuia i te kapa o Tautiti e te aka nei.
Prepare to lead off our fairy dance.

Solo.

Uakina e Kaukau te papa i Teaka-ruru,
The dance-loving tribe assembled of yore

Te papa o Terangai.
On the lands of Terangai.

Chorus.

Tatakina te kaara, urikākā.
Up with the great drum ; toss it in the air.

Solo.

Rumakina e Rongoimua,[1]
The illustrious Mautara fought

Te papa i Pekekura, te papa i te ngaere.
And conquered the island for us, his children.

Chorus.

Vaoo ra ikona tena kaara,
Up with this great drum ; toss it in air,

Ei poani i te rua i Avaiki.
And close up the mouth of spirit-world.

Solo.

Te miro o te tātā koe ō !
Come forward, ye players of melodious flutes,

Chorus.

Tautiti te kapa i Ātea.   Iā.
In honour of this dance of the gods !
(Shouts.)

---

[1] Mautara's true name was Rongoimua, but it has been entirely dropped in later years in favour of the nickname "Mautara," because he took to the cannibal ways of that outcast.

Call for the dance to lead off.

Tanumia Tevoo i Avaiki rangi taca ē!   "Miru's own" kava grows in spirit-
    land.

Solo.

Taipo ē!   Go on!

Chorus.

Te kava ru au e rupepea.   The finest and most intoxicating
    drink.

Solo.

Ae ē!   Aye!

Chorus.

E atua nio-renga i Iti, e Tane!   Tane, god with yellow teeth, was
    once expelled Tahiti,

Eaa ïa manu kai tangata ra ē!   Yellow with devouring mankind!

Solo.

Nai kava kura te kava akiakia 'i   Let the red "kava" be carefully
    plucked,

Te tere o turina kake ē!   As a draught for dancers in the upper
    world.

Te rangia te kava e no te atua ae ē!   Let the drink be prepared for the
    priests.

Chorus.

Te rangia te kava o te atua.   The sacred bowl of the priests is
    ready.

Kia inumia ia pau e i te titara are.   To be quaffed only by yon sacred
    men.

Solo.

Kiekie toro e!   Is there not yet another sort?

Chorus.

E rāui tapu e taki na,   'Tis too sacred for mortal use.

Solo.

Takina te kava, e vaio te noko	The shoots only may we strip off; the parent stem
Ia Tevoo i akamae ana ē!	Is "Miru's own," reserved for the destruction of souls.

These "Tapairu," or "peerless ones," were sometimes represented as taking up their abode with the sea-side king, who was regarded as being specially under their protection :—

Te ui a te Tapairu	The questionings of the Tapairus
A vari koe ia Kaputai	Who came up at Kaputai
Te moea ra te enua mārama ē!	To sojourn in a land of light.

After all, these fairies formed one family, known as "fairies from *nether*-world." Ngaru climbed the sky, in his passion for exploring all nature, and discovered a different set of "Tapairus" —all fair women. Of these the most celebrated is Ina, wife of the moon, and Little-Matonga. They are known as "fairies of the sky." Like those of nether-world, the heavenly fairies are wondrously skilled in ball-throwing, Ina being able to keep eight balls going at one time. Ngaru learnt the art from the nether-fairies in his long residence in their home. So proficient did he become, that he actually beat the nether and the sky fairies at their own game, which he afterwards introduced to this world.

Tukia koe tei Apepe	Thou wast smitten down at Apepe.
Ka aere ra, e Ati, i te enua poiri.	Ah, Ati! thou art bound to the land of darkness.
Kua pou au nei, Riuvaka ra,	Alas, Riuvaka, I am devoured of the gods,
Tai kai e ou te atua,	Who have assembled to feast upon me!
Te ravea ra e te are Tapairu	I was saved by the friendly Taparius
Tei te ara veerua.	Who met me on the road.

THE FAIRY OF THE FOUNTAIN.

In Rarotonga, at the pretty village of Aorrangi, is the small fountain of Vaitipi. On the night after full moon, a woman and a man of dazzling white complexion rose up out of the crystal water. When the inhabitants of this world were supposed to be asleep, they came up from the shades to steal taro, plantains, bananas, and cocoa-nuts. All these good things they took back to nether-world to devour raw.

Little did the fairies think that they had been seen by mortals, and that a plan was being devised to catch them. A large scoop net of strong cinet was made for this purpose, and constant watch set at the fountain by night. On the first appearance of the new moon they again came up, and, as usual, went off to pillage the plantations. The great net was now carefully outspread at the bottom of the fountain, and then they gave chase to the fair beings from spirit-world. The fairy girl was the first to reach the fountain, and dived down. She was at once caught in the net, and carried off in triumph. But in replacing the net after the struggle, a small space remained uncovered ; through this tiny aperture the male fairy contrived to escape.

The lovely captive became the cherished wife of the chief Ati, who now carefully filled up the fountain with great stones, lest his fairy spouse should return to nether-world.

They lived very happily together. She was known all over Rarotonga as the " peerless one (Tapairu) of Ati." She got reconciled to the ways of mortals, and grew content with her novel position. In the course of time she became pregnant, and when the period for her delivery had come, she said to her husband, "Perform on me the Caesarean operation, and then bury my dead body. But cherish tenderly our child." Ati refused to accede to this proposition, but allowed Nature to take her course, so that the fairy became the *living* mother of a fair boy.

When at length the child had become strong, the mother one day wept bitterly in the presence of her husband. She told him that it was grief at the destruction of all mothers in the shades upon the birth of the first-born. Would he consent to her return thither in order that so cruel a custom should be put an end to? Ati should accompany her. This was agreed upon, and accordingly the great stones were dragged up from the bottom of the fountain. All kinds of vegetable gums were now collected, and the fairy carefully besmeared the entire person of Ati, so as to facilitate his descent to the lower world.

Holding firmly the hand of her human husband, the fairy dived to the bottom of the fountain, and nearly reached the entrance to the invisible world. But Ati was so dreadfully exhausted, that out of pity for him she returned. Five times was this process repeated—in vain! The fair one from spirit-land wept because her husband was not permitted to accompany her; for only the spirits of the dead and immortals can enter.

Sorrowfully embracing each other, the "peerless one" said, "I alone will go to spirit-world to teach what I have learnt from you." At this she again dived down into the clear waters, and was never again seen on earth. Ati went sorrowfully back to his old habitation; and thenceforth their boy was called "Ati-ve'e" = *Ati-the-forsaken*, in memory of his lost fairy mother. *He* was surpassingly fair, like his mother from spirit-land; but strangely enough, his descendants are dark, like ordinary mortals.

It is to this lovely fairy woman the old song of the Ati clan alludes :—

Kua ve'eia te pou enua,	She has descended again to spirit-world !
Ka paa 'i te rau atua o Ati e i Vaitipi ē !	Men praised the divine being first seen by Ati at the fountain.
Akana tu a kino te inangaro !	But his heart is now filled with grief.

Hence the origin of the common name " Tapairu " = *peerless one,* in memory of their fairy ancestress.

CHAPTER XII.

DEATH-TALKS AND DIRGES.

GHOST-KILLING (TA I TE MAURI).

Upon the decease of an individual, a messenger ("bird," so called from his swiftness) was sent round the island. Upon reaching the boundary line of each district, he paused to give the war-shout peculiar to these people, adding "So-and-so is dead." Near relatives would start off at once for the house of the deceased, each carrying a present of native cloth. Most of the athletic young men of the entire island on the day following united in a series of mimic battles designated "ta i te mauri," or slaying the ghosts.

The district where the corpse lay represented the "mauri," or ghosts. The young men belonging to it early in the morning arrayed themselves as if for battle, and well-armed, started off for the adjoining district, where the young men were drawn up in battle array under the name of "aka-oa," or friends. The war-dance performed, the two parties rush together, clashing their spears and wooden swords, as though in right earnest. The sufferers in this bloodless conflict were supposed to be malignant spirits, who would thus be deterred from doing further mischief to mortals.

The combatants now coalesce, and are collectively called " mauri," or ghosts, and pass on to the third district. Throughout the day their leader carries the sacred " iku kikau," or cocoanut leaf, at the pit of his stomach, like the dead. Arrived at this third village, they find the younger men ready for the friendly conflict, and bearing the name of " aka-oa." " The battle of the ghosts " is again fought, and now with swelling numbers they pass on to the fourth, fifth, and sixth districts. In every case it was supposed that the ghosts were well thrashed.

Returning with a really imposing force to the place where the corpse was laid out in state, a feast was given to the brave ghost-killers, and all save near relatives return to their various homes ere nightfall.

So similar was this to actual warfare, that it was appropriately named " e teina no te puruki," *i.e.* " a younger brother of war."

DEATH-TALKS.

The " ghost-fighting " took place immediately after the decease ; the " dirge-proper " months afterwards. The former was common to all ; the latter was reserved for persons of distinction. Sometimes the friends of the illustrious dead preferred a grand tribal gathering for the purpose of reciting songs in their honour. This was called " e tara kakai," or " talk about the *devouring*," *i.e.* a " death-talk." For when a person died, it was customary to say, " he was *eaten-up* by the gods."

A " death-talk," like the festive " kapa," *i.e.* dance, came off at night : but whilst the other was performed under long booths, the former took place in large houses built for the purpose, and of course well lighted with torches.

As many as thirty songs, called "tangi," were often prepared for a death-talk. These were the "weeping songs." Each "tangi" was supplemented with a song designated a "tiau," or "pe'e" proper. Thus, in all, as many as sixty separate songs would be mournfully chanted in honour of the dead. Of course the merit would greatly vary. Each adult male relative must recite a song. If unable to compose one himself, he must pay some one to furnish him with an appropriate song. The warrior chief and poet, Koroa, supplied to different parties ten different songs for one "death-talk."

A near relative of the deceased was appointed to start the first "tangi," or "crying-song." At the proper pauses the chorus catches up and carries forward the song. In the "tangi" the weeping is reserved for the close, when the *entire assembly* abandon themselves to passionate cries and tears. A song of this description invariably begins, "Sing we——" (Tiō ra).

The appropriate "tiau," or "pe'e" proper, follows. "Tiau" means "a slight shower;" and metaphorically, "a *partial* weeping." The songs relating to Vera and Puvai are, with one exception, "showery" songs. In these the chief mourner was the solo. Whenever, as indicated, the entire assembly took up the strain, the former solo wept loudly until it again became his duty to take up his part in a soft plaintive voice.

The accompaniments of this performance were the great wooden drum, called "*the awakener*" (kaara), and the harmonicon. Sometimes the "paû" was added. The musical instruments were called into use *between* each song; in the case of the "showery" songs the great drum accompanied the grand chorus. The true accompaniment of the "crying songs" was the passionate weeping of all present.

The most touching songs were the most admired and the longest remembered. Several months were requisite for the preparations needful for a " death-talk." Not only had the songs and dresses *and complexions* to be thought of, but a liberal provision of food for the guests.

If a person of consequence in the same clan died or was slain within a year or two, the old performance might be repeated with the addition of a few new songs. It was then termed "e veru," or " second-hand."

The songs relating to Vera are known as "te kakai ia Vera" = " the death-talk about Vera." So, too, the dirges for Mourua, the friend of Captain Cook, are known as appertaining to "the death-talk about Vaepae," his mother. These are ancient. Some of the best modern songs belong to " the death-talk of Arokapiti," whose eldest son was the first to embrace Christianity, which necessarily put an end to this high effort of heathen poetry.

EVA, OR DIRGE-PROPER.

Some months after the decease of a person of note, funeral games called " eva " were performed in honour of the departed. These entertainments invariably took place by day.

Ve'eteni was fabled to have been sent back to life for a day, in order to instruct mankind in the art of mourning, and to institute solemn " eva " in memory of the dead.

There are four varieties of the dirge-proper :—

1. The " eva *tapara*," or *funeral dirge, with blackened faces*, streaming with gore, shaved heads, and stinking garments. This was a most repulsive exhibition, and well expressed the hopelessness of heathen sorrow.

2. The " eva *puruki,*" or *war-dirge.* For this long spears were made, *as if for war;* only they were adzed out of orotea (a white, brittle sort of wood), *not* of fatal iron-wood (*casuarina equasitifolia*). The war-dirge for Tuopapa[1] is a famous specimen of this sort. Nearly all the natives of Mangaia were present on that occasion, arranged in two long columns facing each other, with a space of eighty yards between. The performance began with an animated conversation between the leaders of the two squadrons of supposed enemies, as to the grounds for war; to excite a lively interest in what followed. When this is concluded, the person most nearly related to the deceased begins the history of the heroic deeds of the clan by slowly chanting the introductory words. At the appointed pause both companies take up the strain and vigorously carry it forward. The mighty chorus is accompanied by a clashing of spears and all the evolutions of war. At the close of what in writing would be a paragraph a momentary pause takes place ; a new story is introduced by the soft musical voice of the chief mourner, caught up and recited in full chorus by both companies as before.

These war-dirges were most carefully elaborated, and embodied the only histories of the past known to these islanders.

3. The "eva *toki,*" or *axe-dirge.* In this *iron-wood* axes, *not stone,* were used ; that is, mimic axes, as the use of *stone* axes would infallibly end in bloodshed. In this scenic dirge the axes were used to cleave the cruel earth which had swallowed up the dead. Hades (Avaiki) was supposed to be under Mangaia. In cleaving the earth a vain wish was expressed that an opening might be made through which the spirit of the departed might return—tears streaming down the cheeks of the performers.

---

[1] Translated by the writer with a number of clan songs, but not yet published.

The axe-dirge was appropriate to artisans only, who enjoyed great consideration, seeing that such knowledge was the special gift of the gods.

4. The "eva *ta*," or *crashing-dirge*, in which each person belonging to the two supposed armies is furnished with a flat-spear or a wooden sword a fathom long. This differs from the war-dirge in the weapons used and in the style of composition. Reasons are assigned for the anger of the gods as shown in the death of their friends. A sort of comedy generally wound up these performances.

The "dirge-proper," dancing-fêtes, reed-matches, and "death-talks," were all comprehended under the general name of "eva," or "amusements" (called by Cook the "heeva").

KARAPONGA'S DIRGE-PROPER (EVA) IN HONOUR OF RURU (Circa a.d. 1816).

EVA-TOKI, OR AXE-DIRGE.

Solo.

Ia Rangi te toki ia Avaiki	Sing we of Rangi's axe [1] from the shades, —
E Rongo ōi !	Thou descendant of Rongo !

---

[1] The first house on Mangaia was built by Rauvaru at Tamarua, who slept in it as soon as it was finished, the long thatch ends hanging loosely down. A heavy shower of rain fell, causing the thatch to lie smoothly.

Now Rangi greatly admired this new invention of house-building ; but thought he could improve upon what Rauvaru had accomplished. He therefore descended to the shades (Avaiki), to pay a visit to his grandfather Rongo, who presented him with a wonderful axe, the handle and all being of stone in one piece, and withal very sharp. During the rain Rangi came up unobserved

Chorus.

Tera Tane-mata-ariki,	Here is Tane-of-royal-face,
Ei koti i te ua ma te rā,	Keen in rain and sunshine,
Ei tua i te pa rakau,	To lay low the loftiest trees.
E mae ai te toki ia Iti.	They are felled by the Tahitian axe.
Ie-kōkō-kōkō !	(War-dance.)

Era ei tiki i na tumangamanga	This axe is to slay the brave
E noo i te are !	When buried in sleep.
Taumaa Kaukare i te inapoiri,	E'en as Kaukare[2] perished in the night.
A motu oki ō !	The fiat went forth !
Kotia aea ia Ruateātonga.	The axe from spirit-land did the deed.

Kapitia oki te tiraa i Paataanga ō !	Prostrate they all lay on the ground.
E tama e ! E Uri e !	Alas for thee, eldest son !
Tena te tamaki.	They come rushing on.
Ka rua 'i ia Turanga ō !	Twice has the god Turanga[3] thus served our clan.
Taamaa te toki ia ake te upoko !	Their axes enter the skulls of the victims.
Ie-kōkō-kōkō !	(War-dance.)

from the shades, and trimmed the thatch of Rauvaru's house all round. Great was the astonishment of the owner in the morning to see what an improvement had been effected by an unseen friend during the peltering storm. The magic-axe of Rangi, named Ruateātonga, became the envy of men and the gods too. When Rangi died, it disappeared for ever.

[1] " Tane-of-royal-face " is the name of the axe-god, identified with the clever Mangaian method of securing ordinary stone axes to wooden handles. This valuable knowledge was introduced by Una from Tahiti (or Iti). These axes were equally valuable for felling trees *and men !* It is made to stand for the veritable axe which slew Kaukare and others.

[2] Ruru died a natural death ; but being on his mother's side descended from Kaukare, an animated description of that warrior's cruel end is introduced, with a natural cry for vengeance which was but too truly answered not long afterwards.

[3] The Tongan tribe introduced the iron-wood tree, and first made spears out of its timber. The god " Turanga " (now in the Missionary Museum) is put for the tribe.

Tena oa te toki pāekaeka a Tinirau.	This is the axe greatly coveted by the god Tinirau ;
Taraiia i te rangi te upoku o Kāe.	Now uplifted against the head of its victim :—
Ia totoia, ia tangi a pu te iku o te toora.	Irresistible as a blow from the tail of a whale.

Ia tangi kekina,   With a ringing sound

Ia tangi kekina,
Tuparua te kapu,
Ia motu a uka,
Ia eveeve ua,
Ia kite i te kata.
Taina ra!
Taki na te toki ia Iti,
Ei koti i te iku o te toora,
E puta i tokerau.
Taumaa o Te-ariki-takoto-i-vaenga-moana,
E tae a vai oki te pera o Tutavake ō!

With a ringing sound
Descend on the hapless skull.
As unresisting thatch
Is trimmed by this axe,
Let him feel its keen edge.
Slay him!
Lift the famed Tahitian axe,
To chop off the tail of the whale
Come from some northern sea.
Let the shark-god, supreme in the ocean, devour thee,
That avenging Tutavake may wade in human blood!

Puruki Tongaiti.
Ua ta Tongaiti.
E karongā na Rongo ;
E karongā tuturi.
Te vaka autu,
Te vaka aueke.
Kua pau Mangaia ōi !

The Tongans struck the blow.
The Tongans shed thy blood.
The war-god is delighted.
Shoulder to shoulder they come.
Will they prove victorious ?
Or are they destined to fail ?
The warriors of Mangaia have fallen !

Aue te tamaki e! ōi !
Aue, ka mate e !
Eaa te puruki ?
E toa te puruki—
Te vaa o Tongaiti—

Alas ! that fearful night.
How dreadful is death !
With what were they slain ?
With iron-wood spears—
The special teaching of the Tongans.

Te kai kākā,
Tumaeu kura e !
E ati mata tao,
Ei taki i te ara toko i te ngaere !

O poisonous wood,
Red like human blood,
That defies all other weapons,
That hurries the greatest chiefs to an untimely grave !

Iē-iē ! Iē-kōkō-kōkō.

(War-dance twice performed.)

The whole of this dirge, excepting the first two lines, was chorus.

This "eva" was performed by his father's clan, and takes precedence of Arokapiti's.

AROKAPITI'S DIRGE PROPER (EVA) IN HONOUR OF RURU. (Circa a.d. 1816.)

EVA TA, OR CRASHING-DIRGE.

Solo.

Ia Ruru te toko i te rā ōi !	Hail, Ruru, predestined chief!

Chorus.

Tera, e Ruru, te uira vananga ei unui i to manava !	O Ruru, the flashing lightning came to fetch thy spirit !
O Ruru atia vaie—	Cut down with a stroke—
Te kutu i te mangungu e karara i te rangi.	The crashing thunders of heaven salute thee.
Tie-koko koko.	(War-dance).
Vãvaia, e Rongo, te rua i te matangi,	Great Rongo, cleave an aperture in the horizon,
Ia katamutamu Avaiki.	Through which may be heard the whispers of spirit-land.
Koia aea i te kopuvaru.	Each (god) wields an octagonal club.
E maiti te pura o Tutavake e rere i erangi.	Sparks of fiery war fly up to heaven.
I aa to taumaa, e te rangi maoaoa ?	Why this curse, ye angry skies ?
To punanga, e te veri tautua ?	Art thou offended, O Centipede, everywhere present ?
Ka pura te ē i Ikurangi,	The enraged Mantis flits over mount Ikurangi.
Keia e te moko i Enua-kura.	The irate Lizard has arrived from the shades.
Ka moe koe, e te karaunga, i tona are.	Art thou, Earwig, in haste to occupy the dwelling (of the dead) ?

I akaaraia atu koe, e te tukununga.   The ever-watchful Spider is already weaving its web,

E tu ra koe, e te ueue :   And the drowsy Beetle is on the move.

To peau, e te manu ka rere.   Each insect is on the wing.

I narea koe e te potipoti—   Horrid vermin are devouring thee.

I narea koe e te vāvā—   The Cricket, too, is eating thee up,

E atare kai roro i te kikau.   (In league with) the despoiler of the cocoa-nut palm.

Taumaa to pauru, e te ro ;   A curse upon thy head, O Ant !

To komata toto, e te namunamuā,   And on thee, too, Mosquito, ever-thirsting for blood :

Na Tiereua koe e anau.   All children of the god Tiereua.

E manu tu ē mai koe, e te kereteki,   Ha ! there is a Grasshopper in the cruel throng,

Tokoa e te iva i vaenga moana.   Followed by a Dragon-fly from mid-ocean.

I turuanuku koe e Tutavake.   Oh that war-loving Tutavake would pity thee !

I turua mataotaoa te apai o te rangi.   Oh, that the fierce demon of the sky would save thee !

Eia e manu e pungaverevere.   Thou art doomed like a fly in a spider's web ;

Ei ei nuku na manu o te rangi,   Snared by the relentless fairies of the air ;

Pirake e piri te pāpāo !   Helpless as a fish in the meshes of a net.

Na tamaroa e tu i te taua,   Alas ! brave sons destined for fight,

Anaua te tamaroa e Tutavake ō !   Begotten of war-loving Tutavake,

O Miru te metua !   Dread Miru [1] awaits you.

E enua akarere Mangaia.   Mangaia will soon fade from your sight.

Puputa motu no Tirango,   Even great Tirango was slain,

E pa te rongo i Avarua.   He whose fame reached other lands.

---

[1] As Ruru did not die a warrior's death, his spirit necessarily enters the domains of cruel Miru.

Taevaia e Tane te manavaroa o te Keanui.	The clan of Tane was cut up by the shark-worshippers,
Oaia te ara puku i tu i Maungarua.	Who love to worship on steep Maungarua.
A puta koe i te rangi, e Rongo!	Favoured children of the god Rongo.
Oai te tiaki i te are o Tongaiti?	Who maintained the ancient fame of the Tongans?
O Teio, a tai. O Tevaki, a rua. Tirango, a toru.	Teio, Tevaki, and Tirango,
O Paia, ka ā. Teuira, ka rima. O Rarea, ka ono.	Paia, Teuira, and Rarea;—all six famous warriors.
E akaara i te moe o te koromātua i Mangonui—	They loved to waken the slumbers of the wise man at Mangonui,
E tu, e ara! E tu, e ara	(With the words) Get up! Get up!
E ara na tokorua te papakura.	Day would dawn upon these watchers,
Ka eva Tane i Tiairi.	Ah, Tiairi [1] is filled with the tribe of Tane.
Te tu ra oa Ruaika i Tikura, ua mau te rakei.	Brave Ruaika gaily equipped was speared.
Na Rerepuka i aae i te tua o Tuku-tuku,	Rerepuka attacked his foes from behind,
I rauka 'i tana taua.	And gained a decisive victory.
Na makona o Tutavake e tu i te taua;	Successful fishermen of the war-god
E akaara i te tiraa i te rau tamanu,	Avenged him who sleeps under the "tamanu" tree,
Tu iora ikona e Kotuku.	The fearless Kotuku.
Aore e taca teia paepae,—	This place is henceforth sacred.
E paepae tua-manomano.	None dare approach.
O tai i taeō, o Teiiri o Terarama.	Only the fairies may come, Teiiri and Terarama.
O tai i taeō, a tai paepae o Rongo.	Rongo himself has been here!

Solo.

E Ina ōi! E Ina ōi!	Hail,[2] Ina! Fair Ina!

---

[1] Tiairi is the warrior's paradise, in which the clan of Tane is supposed to have a large share, most of them having died a violent death. The reference is introduced to distract attention from the dismal fate of all who fall into the clutches of Miru.

[2] This is a sort of comedy. The performers now divide themselves into

Ua akia oa to puta vai na, e Ina! E Ina	Thy fruits are stolen. Alas! Ina, the moon-goddess.

Chorus.

A mau ; Tera rava te maoaoa.	Catch (the thieves.) The sky is threatening.

One half.

E kake ra koe, e te unga.	O Robber-crab, climb and catch them !

Other half.

Auā au e kake ; na te irave e kake.	I will not climb ; let the "Irave" catch them.

One half.

E kake ra koe, e te "Irave"—	O "Irave," climb and catch them !

Other half.

Auā au e kake ; na te "Papaka" e kake.	I will not climb ; let the "Papaka" catch them.

One half.

E kake ra koe, e te papaka.	O "Papaka," climb and catch them !

Other half.

Auā au e kake ; na te tupa e kake.	I will not climb ; let the "Tupa" catch them.

One half.

E kake ra koe, e te tupa.	O "Tupa," climb and catch them !

two bands, alternately addressing each other. At length two men, calling themselves mice, actually climb a pandanus tree well-laden with ripe fruit, and squeak ! Showers of nuts are scattered over the performers to their great amusement.

The "eva," or "dirge properly so called," was always performed by day; usually in the early morning.

The "irave," "papaka," and "tupa" are well-known varieties of the land-crab.

Other half.

Auā au e kake ; ne te karau e kake.   I will not climb ; let the tiny crab catch them.

One half.

E kake ra koe, e te karaii.   O tiny crab, climb and catch them !

Other half.

Auā au e kake ; na te kiore e kake.   I will not climb ; let the mouse catch them.

Two.

Noai teia ngai ?   Who is up there ?

Chorus.

Ake ! Ake ! Keka ! Keka ! ! Tutute ! Tutute ! !   What noises are these of nibbling and crunching—

Ngengene ! Ngengene ! ! Kaika ! Kaika ! !   Squeaking and fighting ?

Akaruke i te katu !   The hard shells are falling.

Pururu te katu a te kiore, te katu a te kiore.   They are scattered in all directions by the mice.

Tai naku, e Kio ! Tai naku, e Kio !   O mouse, give me some ! Pray give me some !

Tera ake oa te kuriri !   Hark to the song of the birds !

Tikaroa te iroiro.   Our amusement is concluded.

This dirge was performed by the mother's clan under the direction of Arokapiti. There happened to be thunder and lightning on the day Ruru died ; which was, of course, regarded as a celestial compliment to the dying chief.

All the minor gods (*i.e.* reptiles and insects) have resolved to kill the illustrious Ruru. None of the major gods pitying him, his ghost sorrowfully enters the shades.

"BLACKENED-FACE" DIRGE-PROPER FOR ATIROA.

BY HIS FATHER KORONÊU, CIRCA 1820.

Solo.

E Pange ōi! e rau raua ia tama.	Alas, Pangeivi! The case is hopeless.
Kua tomo te vaka!	The canoe [1] is lost ;

Chorus.

A, aore e tu, e taû atua.	Oh, my god (Tane) thou hast failed me !
I naau ai kua oki ō,	Thou didst promise life ;
E vaorakau rāui naau,	Thy worshippers were to be as a forest,
Aore tetai e tukua i te urungā piro.	To fall only by the axe in battle.
Ina tika oki Turanga,	Had it been the god Turanga—
E vaimangaro ra taana !	That liar! I would not have trusted *him.*
Parau aore, e kai oki taau.	Like him, *you* are a man-eater !
Taparu atura i te koi parara—	May thy mouth be covered with dung :
Kororo-kururu ua 'tu ra.	Slush it over and over !
E atua te tangata e oia !	This god is but a man after all !

Solo.

Tiria i mua, e Kori! Ei! Ei!	Plaster him well, friends. Ha! Ha!!
(*Women's* shouts).	

Chorus.

Tutae keinga e te tuarangi!	Dung is fit food for such gods !
Kua kau te metua i te ngarau !	We parents are in deep mourning,
E ngarau no Tiki.	Like that first used by Tiki.
Ei eva i te tama akaaroa ;	We mourn for our beloved first-born.
Ei tuveu i te are rangorango,	Oh, that one could stir up the gods,
Kia ara te tangata mate.	And cause the very dead to awake !
E takangā mate no Tutaemāro,	Yonder stands thy weeping mother.
Te taka ra i One-mākenukenu.	Thy spirit wanders about One-mākenukenu,

---

[1] " The canoe is lost " = " The child is dead."

E kimi i te ara,	Inquiring the reason
Kia kitea te ara i keinga 'i !	Why his poor body was devoured (by the gods).
Itia e Ruateātonga te ii	Fairy of the axe! cleave open
I te keremuta o Vātea	The secret road to spirit-land ; and
Ia amamā Avaiki !	Compel Vātea to give up the dead !

Solo.

Ūa, e Tiki, i te ū tuarangi !	Puff, [1] Tiki, a puff such as only ghosts can !

Chorus.

Aria !	Wait a moment.

Solo.

Ūa, uaia !	(Again I say) puff, puff away !
Kô !	(*Chorus* of pretended explosions !)

Chorus.

To taringa, e Pangeivi ;	A curse upon thee, priest Pangeivi.
I kai koe i taû tamaiti na !	Thou hast destroyed my boy.

As no one would undertake to compose an atheistic dirge for the angry mourner, Koronêu made his own. It was performed successfully amongst the other more regular dirges for Atiroa.

THE FIRST MURDER AND THE FIRST BATTLE.

The earlier part of the reign of Rangi was "the golden age" of these people. Children grew up to maturity; men became aged—their limbs tottering, their backs curved, and their teeth dropping out, so that they were fed again with the expressed juice of the cocoa-nut, poured into the mouth by means of the leaf of the tiere, or gardenia—still, Death had not made its appear-

---

[1] In Latin, *pedite.*

ance ; and of course war, famine, sickness, and pain were unknown.

But this happy state of things did not last. Even during the lifetime of the famous Rangi a mighty change took place.

There lived in those days a famous man named Matoetoeā. Many had tried to kill him ; but in vain. For as soon as the arms of an adversary were uplifted to strike him, a violent shivering and trembling would seize the limbs of the would-be murderer, so that the weapon would fall to the ground and Matoetoeā escape unharmed. Hence the saying in daily use, when any one shivers and his skin becomes rough in consequence, " he has been smitten by Matoetoeā " (te kiri o Matoetoeā).

There lived in spirit-land (Avaiki) a "brave," named Tukaitaua,[1] ever ready to perform the behests of Rongo. Hearing of the marvellous power possessed by Matoetoeā, he longed to measure his own strength with one of earth. With this view he came up to this upper world and searched over the island for his foe, until he found him. For the first time Matoetoeā's power of self-defence was at fault, and he easily fell under the blows of the redoubtable Tukaitaua. Ngakè and Akuru were also slain by this " brave ; " in all, three persons were murdered successively on one night by Tukaitaua—one from each of the three primitive tribes.

Thus death entered into the world (Mangaia). Matoetoeā was the first to die a *violent* death, as Veêtini afterwards was the first to die a *natural* one. Rangi was much grieved at this violent breach, now first made, in his hitherto peaceful domain. He sought everywhere for the unknown murderer ; but to no purpose. He therefore descended to (Avaiki) nether-land, to pay a visit to his grandfather Rongo, as the only possible way of discovering

---

[1] == " He whose delight it is to fight " (tu = *stand ;* kai = *eat ;* tau = *battle.*)

the murderer. Upon entering the presence of the great Rongo, he found Matoetoeā there, his head and face all covered with blood. Rongo asked Rangi what he had come for. Rangi replied, "To ascertain who murdered Matoetoeā." The war-god now inquired, "Have you not seen any new face in the upper world?" "I have," replied Rangi. "*He* is the murderer," rejoined Rongo.

Rangi, now thirsting for revenge, asked how he, a mortal, could kill Tukaitaua. Rongo said, "Go back to 'daylight;' *you* cannot conquer Tukaitaua. *I* will send some one to punish him." Upon this the king left the shades and returned to his old home in this upper world of light.

The war-god kept his word. There lived with him in spirit-land another "brave," Tutavake, cousin to the redoubtable Tukaitaua, who represented the elder branch of the family. The father of Tukaitaua was Tavarenga (Deceiving); the parent of Tutavake was Tuatakiri (Entirely-brave). Summoned to the presence of Rongo, Tutavake was ordered to go at once "to daylight" and slay Tukaitaua. "How can I manage it?" asked Tutavake. Rongo directed him to search through the six districts of Mangaia. "And if you cannot then discover him, climb the hills, and you will be sure to find his whereabouts. Only do not attack him early in the morning, for then he is in his full strength; nor in the evening, for as the shadow lengthens his strength increases. Recollect that as the shadow of morning shortens, Tukaitaua's strength wanes. At mid-day it is at the lowest point. Stand erect on a hill in the sun until its rays are vertical; then go and attack him."

Tutavake obeyed. Coming up to "daylight," he found the inhabitants of Auau (Mangaia) crowded together in the interior in terror of the unknown murderer of mankind. For some time he could get no clue to the exact whereabouts of Tukaitaua. He had indeed been seen occasionally performing his wonderful war-like evolutions hitherto unknown to mankind. Ascending a hill (which represents the left *heel* of the giant " Te-manava-roa ") he espied a small cloud of dust rising from a spot not far from "the-chasm-of-Tiki," by which constant communication was at that time kept up with nether-world. Tutavake cautiously approached the spot, and peered through the dense growth of trees and bush which surrounded the open space cleared by Tukaitaua for spear-exercise. There, indeed, was his unconscious foe vigorously fighting the air. Day after day, from dawn to sunset, this was Tutavake's sole delightful employment. On this occasion Tu-kaitaua was somewhat exhausted, for the sun was vertical. Ever and anon an "ugh" would escape the accomplished warrior, as he failed in some delicate movement. Encouraged by these heavy grunts of disappointment, Tutavake, spear in hand, suddenly darted from his hiding-place to the edge of the circle inside which his cousin was practising. The astonished Tukaitaua exclaimed:—

Ana mai ta Tauatakiri,	The son of " Entirely-brave " did not come
Kua pakua ta Tavarenga.	Until the son of " Deceiving " was exhausted.

Yet Tukaitaua did not for a moment cease his spear-practice. His antagonist followed him very adroitly, as he went round and round the great circular area, in order to avoid a hasty meeting. This was in accordance with the instructions of Rongo. Tu-kaitaua's obvious aim was to close in with his foe as quickly as possible, and to give the death blow. Seven times Tukaitaua wheeled round, but was skilfully avoided by Tutavake. The eighth time he made the circuit, it was evident that his strength was much impaired. At this Tutavake suddenly swung round in the opposite direction and dealt the hitherto invincible Tukaitaua a fatal blow on his head.

Rangi was delighted that the death of Matoetoeā and his friends was thus speedily avenged. Tutavake returned to the shades. But the former peaceful state of things could never be enjoyed again. Blood had been shed; first in sheer wantonness, next in just retribution. Ever since, mankind has been engaged in either aggressive or defensive warfare. Diseases of various kinds followed in the train, and lingering death; Veêtini being the first. Hurricanes and famines came, too, into existence.

Tukaitaua, when prowling round the island in search of Matoetoeā, etc., discovered in the exterior pile of rocks surrounding the fertile interior, a remarkable narrow gorge which runs right round,—not unlike a wide road, fenced on either side with imperishable walls of hardened sharp-pointed coral. Yet, strangely enough, in this coral large trees and beautiful creepers of different kinds grow luxuriantly. At various points in this natural road round Mangaia, Tukaitaua had cleared the bush and removed the rough loose stones in order to prosecute his favourite pastime : at one time with a long spear ; at another with a double-edged wooden sword; anon with a curved club ; occasionally with a sling.

The inhabitants of the world (Mangaia) contrived to get glimpses of the proceedings of this extraordinary fellow from behind trees or elevated blocks of rock ; without, however, being seen by him. For it was evidently a dangerous thing to go near a native of nether-world possessed of such fearful strength. It was in this furtive manner that mankind first learnt what sort of weapons to make and how to fight with them.

This knowledge was very seasonable. For not long afterwards there arrived at Tamarua, on the south of the island, a fleet of canoes of "Tongans-sailing-through-the-skies" (Tongaiti-akareva-moana). The leader of this formidable band was the first high-priest of the god Turanga. The secret of his successful navigation was *a vast ball of string which he held in his hand during his long voyage,* and which was quite exhausted upon their safe arrival on the southern coast of Mangaia.[1] Hence his name, Te-aò-roa, or *The-man-of-the-long-string.* In those days the now unruly ocean was smooth as the little lake in Veitatei; its surface occasionally disturbed with gentle ripples, so that it was the easiest thing possible to voyage over it at any time and in any direction. But in after ages, ceaseless wars and shedding of blood disturbed the course of the elements, and so gave rise to the fearful storms and cyclones we now suffer from.

A battle ensued between these driftaways from Tonga and the original possessors of the soil, who claimed to have come up out of nether-world. This was the *first* of the forty-two pitched battles which have been fought on Mangaia. This primary conflict took place at Te-rua-noni-anga," or *Valley-of-spoil.* Of this battle it is expressly asserted that as men fell in the ranks of Rangi, their places were immediately filled up by new warriors from the shades! Sceptical moderns think their places were filled up from a reserve force hidden behind the rocks. However, the result was that the warlike invaders, who had despised the small army of

---

[1] Until lately was shown the hole in the coral reef where "The-man-of-the-long-string" tied *this* end of the enormous ball of string! The bit of rock is now destroyed.

Rangi, and who were sure of securing the entire island to themselves, fled in utter disorder. The numerous names of different
points of road across the island to the cave of Tautua, where the
remnant took shelter, are but so many memorials of those slain in
the pursuit.

Of Rangi's victorious force three fell—one out of each of
the three original tribes. And thus was established the ancient
doctrine (ara taonga), that victory and chieftainship of all degrees
can only be secured by *first* shedding the blood of some of the
victorious party, so as to secure the favour of Rongo, the arbiter of
the destinies of war.

In the persons of Rangi and Tiaio, but in no other, the
secular and spiritual sovereignties were united.

Peace was secured by the offering up on the altar of Rongo a
human sacrifice, Vaioeve. Rangi now consented that the unfortunate Tongans should permanently occupy that part of the island
where they had so recently landed. The art of war would not,
however, have reached perfection but for these Tongan settlers,
who had the credit, or discredit, of introducing the iron-wood
tree, from the wood of which in after years *all* weapons of war
were manufactured.

The settlement of a Tongan colony on the south, and their
first conflict with the earlier inhabitants, are historical facts. Their
bravery is universally admitted.

The restless character of these Tongans is indicated in the
proverb, " *A stone-mouth* is needed to exhort the Tongans to keep
the peace," *i.e.* lips that never tire.

When dealing a death-blow it was sometimes said, " Go, eat
the stale food of Tukaitaua ; " the food in question being the club
and the spear which Tukaitaua loved so well.

CHAPTER XIII.

HUMAN SACRIFICES.

WHY HUMAN SACRIFICES WERE OFFERED.

RANGI'S first propitiatory offering to Rongo was a *rat* laid with great ceremony on the original marae of the god of war. But on descending to the shades to pay a visit to his divine grandfather, Rongo evinced his displeasure by averting his face from Rangi on account of his having been imposed upon with so unworthy a sacrifice. Rangi, who was naturally averse to blood-shedding, now learnt that *nothing less than a human sacrifice would give satisfaction.*

Upon his return to this upper world, Rangi successfully fought his first battle at a spot ever since called "Teruanoninga," or *Valley-of-spoil.* In this engagement the newly arrived colony from Tonga received a great check. A fugitive from the battle-field, Vaioeve, was overtaken and slain expressly for sacrifice to the god of War and of Night. Vaioeve was the *first human sacrifice ever offered on Mangaia.* The place where the victim fell still bears his name.

U

The practice once begun was continued until Christianity put a stop to it for ever. The second human sacrifice was Turuia, first priest of Tane on Mangaia, from Iti (Tahiti). Turuia was slain at the instigation of Tamatapu, during the lifetime of Rangi. The tribe of Tane arrived *after* the Tongans, and from being first regarded as guests, were devoted by the original lords of the soil —who claimed direct descent from the god Rongo—to furnish human sacrifices whenever required.

The successive priests of Tane, *viz.* Matariki, Tiroa, and Tepunga, were in after times slain and offered in sacrifice by the older tribe. The martial supremacy of Mautara alone saved Tevaki, the last of that devoted race, and from whom the present tribe of Tane is descended. As human sacrifices were indispensable, Mautara reverted to the original tribe of Tongans (in which Teipe was included), from which Rangi had selected the first human sacrifice. It is mournful to think that almost every member of these families was offered in sacrifice ; a few of their number being always reserved, and even cherished, for the express purpose of providing future sacrifices.

Later still, the Amai tribe was devoted on account of their complicity in a murder of a chief of the once all-powerful Mautara clan. Thus it became the custom to devote each new band of settlers (with one or two exceptions), on some pretence or other, to the altar. The only tribe never thus treated was the original one who worshipped Rongo and Motoro : the alleged reason being that Rongo would be angry if his own worshippers and so-called children were offered. With perfect consistency, then, it was proposed by the angry heathen, in 1824, to offer up Davida, the first Christian teacher, to the god Rongo. This was with the view of extinguishing Christianity. The plot almost succeeded.   Providentially, a convert named Mauapa [1] revealed it to Davida, and so set the Christian party on their guard.

————

The following ancient myth refers to the only instance related of stealing away the sacrifice from Rongo's altar ; for it is well known that fish were *not* offered to that god. *His fish were human victims.*

Three varieties of butterflies are indigenous on Mangaia : a large, velvety, purple beauty ; a somewhat smaller one, with red spots ; and a small, unattractive, yellow sort.

One day Rongo missed from his altar a fine sword-fish (aku) ; it had been stolen by the Lizard-god, Matarau, whose marae is at Aumoana,[2] at Tamarua.   Rongo ordered his swift messengers, the birds, to fly to that marae to see whether it was not hidden there. The birds obeyed, and found the stolen sword-fish in the sacred shade of the marae.   Hard by, in a gloomy little recess, the Lizard kept constant watch.   Now this Lizard had, as its name Matarau implies, two hundred eyes, besides eight heads and eight tails. So that all that the bird-messengers could do was to look on with awe at a distance, from the branches of the sacred trees. They returned to great Rongo, and told what they had seen. They were chided by Rongo, and bidden to return to the grove of the Lizard-god, and endeavour to bring away the " fish " stolen from his altar.   The birds returned, and in their zeal venturing too near the cave of the god possessed of two hundred eyes, were all summarily devoured.   Several other bird-messengers shared a similar fate.   Rongo now commissioned *rich velvety butterflies* to attempt the rescue ; but they, too, were all snapped up by the Lizard-god.   The *red* butterflies fared no better.   At last Rongo,

————

[1] A heathen song in honour of this man is given on p. 257.
[2] = Ocean current.

at his wits' end, hit upon a notable device to get back his stolen sacrifice : two little *yellow* butterflies were summoned to his presence, and were directed to a banyan tree growing out of the rocks just over the entrance to the cave where the ever-vigilant Lizard kept watch. Adhering to the *inside* of two *sere* yellow leaves, their presence would not be noticed. The trusty little messengers, so utterly insignificant in appearance, easily made their way unnoticed to the banyan tree. All the butterflies and moths of Mangaia hid themselves amongst the leaves in the immediate neighbourhood, in order to render assistance. Rongo now caused the " moio " (w. by n.) wind to blow violently across the island (in a straight line from the grove of Rongo to that of the Lizard-god). Down came a shower of *yellow leaves* with the two *yellow butterflies* upon the stolen " fish." Little did the Lizard suspect that two messengers of his rival Rongo were hidden underneath the multitude of leaves which caused his eyes to blink for a moment. The clever little butterflies inwardly chuckled, as success was now certain, for they had seized their prey. And now myriads of butterflies and moths of all sorts and colours came to the aid of their friends. The ears of the astonished Lizard-god were assailed by the defiant shouts of the war-dance, as the sword-fish was borne on the wings of the army of butterflies through the air across the island to the altar of Rongo. With infinite chagrin the Lizard-god helplessly watched the disappearance of his stolen " fish." As they fled they sang :—

E uru tupu ariki, e ika na Rongo !	Dance in triumph before this (fish) offering to Rongo.
E apai e takitaki aere.	Lift it on high ; bear it carefully on.

" Aumoana " is the ancient marae of the Tongan tribe, to

whom Vaioeve belonged. Unquestionably this is an allegorical account of the loss and recovery of Vaioeve, or some other very early victim; the object being to conceal the fact from the vulgar. That an ambush was formed, and two clever fellows dared the anger of the Lizard-god, in order to recover a stolen sacrifice (or "fish," as it was invariably termed) is very probable.

THE DRUM OF PEACE.

Upon gaining a decisive victory the leading warrior was proclaimed "temporal lord of Mangaia." The kingly authority was hereditary and distinct from that of the warrior chief: the former representing the spiritual, the other the temporal power. I believe Mangaia to be the only island in the Pacific where this distinction obtained. Kings were "te ara pia o Rongo," *i.e.* "the mouth-pieces, or priests, of Rongo." As Rongo was the tutelar divinity and the source of all authority, they were invested with tremendous power—the temporal lord having to obey, like the multitude, through fear of Rongo's anger. Peace could not be proclaimed or blood spilt lawfully without the consent of the king speaking in the name of the god Rongo. So sacred were their royal persons that no part of their bodies might be tattooed; they could not take part in dances or in actual warfare.

It sometimes happened that the temporal chief was at enmity with the king of his day. In this case the king would refuse to complete the ceremonies for his formal investiture; life would remain unsafe; the soil could not be cultivated, and famine soon followed. This state of misery might endure for years, until the obnoxious chief had in his turn been despatched, and a more agreeable successor fixed upon. All the multitudinous idolatrous ceremonies to secure peace would be now easily arranged by the king.

Seven distinct journeys would be made round the island by the victorious warriors, who with their women and children had hitherto huddled together in one encampment. Fully equipped, as if for battle, they would one day march round the island defiantly, to assert the absolute supremacy of the winning party. Man, woman, or child crossing their path that day was slain. Subsequent processions were of a more peaceful character, in order to perform idolatrous worship at each of the principal maraes. One of the more interesting of these was the ceremony of spear-breaking, in token of the cessation of war. After a renewed circuit of the island, the warrior chiefs would, with great formality, beat to pieces a number of second-rate spears of various shapes against a great chestnut tree (cut down a year or two since) growing opposite the principal interior marae. Another interesting symbol of peace was the setting up in *each* principal marae a forked stick, well notched, and called "*supports,*" intimating that the leading men who worshipped there should prove "supports" to the reign of peace now inaugurated. Miniature houses were erected on all these maraes ; each house being a fathom long and well thatched, with a little open door neatly screened with a strip of the best white cloth. These tiny houses were designated "conservators of peace" (are ei au). The idea was, that all the gods and all their worshippers should lay aside their animosities and unite in keeping the peace. In the language of those days, the entire assembly of gods form but "one house ;" the great point being that no divinity should feel himself neglected, and so take umbrage, and thus a *hole* be made through which wind and rain (war and bloodshed) might enter. If all the gods be propitious and united, they form a well-thatched house which no evil can invade.

The seventh and most important procession of all was to *beat the drum of peace all round the island.* But the indispensable preliminary to this was the securing an acceptable offering to Rongo, arbiter of war and peace. A man or woman must be slain, but not needlessly battered, for the express purpose, and laid upon the altar.

The victim was first exposed on a platform of pandanus-wood in the sacred district of Keia, and opposite to the idol-house; hence the name often applied to such, "pange-ara," or "laid-on-a-pandanus-tree." The entire body of victors now assemble in their gayest trappings, and well armed, in front of the victim, whilst "the praying-king" (te ariki karakia) slowly chanted twice the following—

PRAYER OVER A HUMAN SACRIFICE TO RONGO.[1]

E kaūra ! ura pīa !	Stately, noble priest !
Ura vanānga, ura turou,	Sweet peace, pleasant offering !
Turoua takaīa, takaia e māna,	Securely fastened and well-tied.
Rimarima tangata, angaanga tangata,	These human hands and human form,
Atīa a mana airi a tāpu :	Devoted to this fate by the gods :
Atia te īō, te io no Rongo.	Doomed to sacrifice by the god Rongo.
O Vātea te auranga moana,	Great Vātea is the guardian of the ocean.
Ie ruā rau'i au,	By him it is ruffled :
E ruā rua'i toro.	By him it is calmed.

[1] This prayer, and the "Prayer for Peace" on p. 299, are of unknown antiquity.

Ka tupu o te tōa,   Here is iron-wood of noble growth—
Ka rito o te tōa,   A most graceful tree,
Ka rārā o te tōa,   With numerous branches.
Ka kokoti o te tōa,   Fell this iron-wood tree ;
Ka era o te tōa,   Divide its trunk ;
Ka maikuku o te tōa,   Split it with wedges,
Ka ngaa o te tōa.   For the making of spears.

Tupu akera ïa uki e toa   In every age the iron-wood has yielded
    E maori no taua puruki ;   Death-dealing spears
    No taua te arutoa   For the use of warriors only—
    No tupuranga taua,   From time immemorial.
No taua kiea, no taua kiea !   And bravely have *we* wielded them !
E ti o te maunga o te matōni ;   The wild [1] *ti* root of the hills (was
                                           our food).
Teniteni te matakeinānga ;   But now we shall enjoy plenty.
Kōakōa te matakeinānga !   This day we heartily rejoice.

    Taua ra i te makitea,   Lately we hid in the rocks—
    I te punanga o te āo.   The refuge of the conquered.
Teniteni te matakeinānga ;   But now we shall enjoy plenty,
Kōakōa te matakeinānga !   This day we heartily rejoice.

The painfully interesting part of this incantation is lost ; the
stanzas relating to the division of the lands, when the nose and
ears of the victim were cut off and formally presented to the
expectant chiefs. The " prayer " only was chanted on this occasion.

After a few days the warriors would again deck themselves in
their gayest trappings, and well armed stood in front of the wooden
altar. The "praying king," assisted by his friends, now came
forward with a large coarse scoop-net of cocoa-nut fibre, used
only on such occasions ; and carried off the decayed sacrifice to
the pebbly beach at some distance. It was laid this time on a

---

[1] *Dracoena terminalis.*

smooth block of *sandstone* in front of the great national stone idol, Rongo. Hence the name frequently applied to human victims, " ikakaa," or *fish caught in the net* of Rongo. The incantation slowly chanted at the wooden altar in the interior near the marae of Matoro, god of day, was repeated at the natural stone altar on the shore at the marae of Rongo, god of night (atua po).

The " praying king," with a bamboo knife, now cut off the ears of the victim ; *the right ear* representing the *right, or southern,* half of the island ; *the left ear* representing the *left, or northern* half. Each ear was then subdivided into as many small portions as might serve to represent the various minor districts (tapere) of each half. The king now demanded, in a loud voice, " Who shall be lord, or warrior-chief, of Mangaia ? " According to a private agreement, the leading man amongst the winning tribes rose, and with dignity said, " Ei iaku Mangaia " = " Let me be lord of Mangaia." The entire assembly of warriors, by profound silence, confirmed the appointment. This chief now resumed his seat on the ground ; but to him, as supreme temporal lord, no part of the victim was given. In a prescribed order, the names of all the district-chiefs and landowners were proclaimed, each receiving from the hand of the king a portion of the ears of the victim wrapped up in a *ti* leaf. The great temporal chief invariably received the first portion, in the inferior capacity of district-chief. These bits of human ears were deposited in the different family maraes. They constituted an investiture to all offices and right to the possession of the soil. Without a human sacrifice there could be no formal possession of dignity or estate.

The *nose* of the victim was the portion of the kings and their recognized assistants. Thus the guardian of, and performer on, the sacred drum of peace had a share. The man who had the management of all great feasts, and was supposed to make the food grow, came in for *his* share of the nose. The " praying king," however, was the great spiritual dignity or pontiff, and as such came in for the best lands, in addition to the daily offerings of food of best quality.

And now the famous drum of peace, expressly made for this solemn occasion, would be beaten ; or, strictly speaking, would be heavily struck with the tips of the fingers. A feast occupied the attention of the warriors and chiefs between the presentation of the bits of human ears and the drumming. The performance first ook place on the marae of Rongo ; a procession was now formed of all the victorious tribes, headed by the king and the hereditary drum-beater, who carried the big drum. This object of mysterious reverence was simply part of a tree, dug out at one end with stone adzes ; the aperture being covered with a piece of shark's skin. Each relative of the hereditary drum-player carried a small drum, to increase the volume of sound, thus assuring fugitives hiding in the rocks and thickets that better days were dawning. The " praying king," at the head of the procession, chanted in a pleasing tone a prayer for peace to the gods. At a certain point all the males of the kingly families united their voices, and all the drums sent forth their agreeable, although monotonous, accompaniment.

I give the exact words from the lips of the aged king, who minutely related to me the whole of the ceremonies connected with the offering of human sacrifices and the drum of peace. For any but kingly voices to recite these " karakia," or " prayers," would have been to invoke the anger of the gods.

PRAYER FOR PEACE.

Akiakia Maruata ikitia taku atarau.	A bleeding victim has been chosen for our altar.
Iāia ia vaerea te tarutaru enua	By it are weeded out the evils of the land
O Avaiki mai raro ē !	Which spring up from nether-world.

All the drums and all the voices.

Teimāia rangi maia, rangi vaerea.	Let peace begin. May the sky be cloudless !
Teimāia rangi maia, rangi vaerea.	Let peace begin. May the sky be cloudless !
Vaerea tai taru ; vaerea.	Weed out all evils. Weed them out !
Vaerea ; vaerua i to makita, makita.	Weed, weed them out ; utterly and for ever !
Makitaria kitariā, kua rangi riri ē !	Aye, let each threatening cloud entirely disappear !

Upon entering each district the performance began anew. The circuit of the island was made in one day ;—the prayer being many times offered. At a certain spot, still marked by three stones, a spear was thrust into the big drum of peace, in token that the work was accomplished. Peace was secured. The great drum was hidden away in a.certain cave, kept an inviolable secret to this day. So that for each proclamation of peace a new drum (pau) must be dug out.

No music was ever half so sweet to the ears of the vanquished as the monotonous notes of the drum of peace. By it human life became sacred. Wretches, nearly dead from starvation and terror, hiding in the desolate " raei," now came forth boldly. Everywhere the fertile valleys became again dotted over with the dwellings of the victors and their vassals. These houses might be covered with substantial thatch ;—for had not the gods in each district been honoured with tiny ones of their own ? Thatched houses were not lawful until the drum had been beaten. A miserable shift was made with split cocoa-nut branches.

In the hope of winning the favour of the new lords of the soil, the survivors of the beaten tribes brought out from their hiding-places in the rocks fine braided hair ; white shells for the arms, used at dances ; fish-nets of the best quality ; wooden troughs and stone adzes. Some were fortunate in being protected by relatives, who usually allowed their unfortunate friends to retain *part* of their treasures. Some were avowedly protected to furnish human sacrifices at a future day. The birth of a child by such serfs was regarded with satisfaction by the unfeeling masters. As a rule, the wives of the conquered were the property of the victors. The serfs were expected to fish daily for the benefit of their lords, who generously permitted their dependants to eat the small, inferior fish themselves.

A feast was given by the victors to these serfs—a public recognition of their safety. This was called " taperu kai."

The coral-tree (*erythrina coralodendron*), which attracts every eye with its symbolical blood-red flowers, was now formally planted in the valleys in token of peace. This plant is almost imperishable. It was vainly hoped that the reign of peace might be equally enduring. Cocoa-nut trees were also planted all over the island to mark the duration of peace. The only warrior-chiefs under whom peace prevailed long enough for a cocoa-nut tree to bear, were Tuanui, Mautara, Ngarā, Potiki, and Pangemiro. Two only of these were long reigns—Mautara's, twenty-five years ; Potiki's, about twenty years. The other three certainly did not exceed seven years apiece. Sages praise these five great chieftains for causing peace to prevail *so long !*

Tradition tells of a period when war and bloodshed were unknown. That was in the days of Rangi, before Rarotongan chiefs had taught them to be cruel. Thanks be to God, that for more than forty years, under the benign influence of Christian truth, human life has been sacred.

After the drum of peace had been beaten, it became unlawful to carry weapons of any description. Aged men, however, were permitted to carry about a staff, five or six feet in length, to support their tottering limbs. Men daily carried about with them, in symbol of peace, an outrageously large fan, now obsolete. This fan was sufficiently large to protect the upper part of the body from sun or rain. It was found necessary to forbid its use in church, as the person of the owner was nearly hidden behind it. During the season of peace it was considered a most grave offence to cut down iron-wood on any pretence whatever; as under pretence of obtaining strong rafters for their houses, or the making of spades for husbandry, weapons of war might be manufactured.

When the martyr Williams touched at Mangaia in 1823, he learnt that a decisive battle had been fought two years previously; but the drum of peace had not been beaten. Hence their favourite saying, that the men of that generation were awaiting the arrival of the Gospel of the Prince of Peace, whose word and reign constitute the true drum of peace. Davida and Tiere first caused them to hear the sweet melody; they emerged out of their hiding-places into the peace, light, and freedom of Christianity. The Sacrifice laid on the divine altar was no longer an unwilling victim selected from the slave tribes, but the free-will offering of the Son of God.

The native words for " peace "[1] ("mangaia," "au "), also

---

[1] The Bible phrase, "*the peace of God,*" is rendered "*te au o te Atua*"= "*the rule and consequent peace of God.*"

denote "rule," or "reign;" *the rule* of the temporal lord lasting only so long as no blood was spilt. Once the charm broken, murders and reprisals might daily take place, provoking a pitched battle, sometimes a war of extermination. When the victors felt themselves secure, a human victim (sometimes more than one) must be secured, and all this burdensome ceremonial gone through again, ere peace and order could once more prevail. Hence the difficulty of native chronology; the "reigns," or "periods of peace," are most carefully enumerated; the years of war and anarchy are invariably omitted. The means for correcting their chronology is supplied by the lifetimes of their priests, which are well known. It is impossible that the errors should be serious, seeing the names of the three contemporaneous orders of priests (Motoro, Tane, and Tuaranga) are definitely ascertained.

The last time the peace-drum was played was about the year 1815. The victim selected was Teata. Of course the poor old bald-headed fellow was kept in ignorance of the intentions of the sacrificers. On a certain evening the victim-seekers assembled on the level top of the central hill, to receive at the hands of the king "the sacred girdle." Upon reaching, by an unfrequented mountain path, the hut of Teata, they found it empty. They were not a little perplexed; for should their presence in the village be known, their intended victim would effectually hide himself in the rocks. At last, under cover of darkness, some of them asked the assistance of Rakoia. But Teata was maternal uncle to Rakoia, who well knew that the old man was liable to sacrifice at any time, as his ancestors had been before him. Rakoia resolved to secure to himself the merit and profit of delivering Teata into the hands of his foes. A few minutes previously he had left his uncle in a lone house built on poles in the middle of the taro patches.   A short ladder led up to the hut.   With another relative (still living in 1875) and Teata, Rokoia had been rehearsing songs.   Then they chatted pleasantly about the dire famine then prevailing.   The old fellow patted his head, and remarked, " Could they get THIS (as an offering), the gods would send plenty again."   At length Teata Vainekavoro snored, and Rakoia quietly slipped down the ladder and went home.   As soon as the victim-seekers told him of their perplexity, Rakoia said, " Follow me, and you shall have your '*fish.*'"   A race now took place between two warriors as to the honour of giving the death-blow.   Rakoia led the way ; on arriving at the top of the ladder he carefully pointed out the sleeping form of his uncle Teata.   A single blow from the axe of Arokapiti ended the career of the old man, who an hour or two later in the same night was laid on the altar.   And thus it was that the drum of peace for Pangemiro's temporal sovereignty came to be beaten.   Hence the consideration ever paid amongst the chiefs to the word of Rakoia, who in 1846 succeeded his brother as chief, or governor, of Tamarua.   Rakoia was one of the first to embrace Christianity; and until his death, in 1865, I never saw anything inconsistent with his profession as a disciple of Jesus. He was a faithful friend to the missionaries, and his last intelligent words were addressed to me expressive of his hope.

At the period of his death he was about eighty years of age. He had fought in four pitched battles, besides several minor engagements.   He was accounted the best poet of his day.

After the death of Rakoia, a tract of taro-planting land in the possession of his nephews became a subject of discussion.   None of the younger men had a clue to the title by which it was held.

Some proposed to give it to another tribe, to whom it anciently belonged. The old men of the tribe then confessed that the land in question was Pangemiro's formerly, but was formally given to Rakoia as the price of Teata's blood! Shame had till then closed the lips of these old men; a shame which would never have been felt but for Christianity. According to the ancient dictum, "blood only can purchase what blood formerly secured." Of course Rakoia's family retain the land.

A month or two before the landing of Davida a sacrifice was sought for the public acknowledgment of Pangemiro's second election to the supreme temporal chieftainship. Reonatia was waylaid and slain (as was supposed) one night, upon his return from baracoota-fishing. A companion of his was uselessly slain at the same time. A long spear was driven through the body of the victim, and the body borne on a litter across the island to the altar. The coolness of the night revived Reonatia, after he had been laid on the altar, and the warriors had retired. He even descended to the ground, and despite the ghastly wound, unsteadily ran up the hillside a few yards. In a short time it was discovered, and this time a stone adze was employed to give the fatal blow, and the offering was replaced on the altar. But the dissensions which arose on account of this occurrence (that the gods were angry) prevented the completion of the ceremonies necessary to peace. Reonatia was the last human sacrifice ever laid on the altar of Rongo.

The betrayer of Reonatia was Rouvi, who took part afterwards in the destruction of the maraes and the pantheon, and became one of the brightest ornaments of our Church. At a very advanced age—say eighty-five—he passed away from our midst.

The heathen had prophesied that he would speedily die through the anger of the gods; but he outlived every vestige of the heathen party, and was universally respected for his consistent attachment to the Truth.

After the drum of peace had been sounded over the island, the king again employed his great net to remove the putrid carcass of the victim—now minus ears and nose—to a certain place in the bush within the limits of the marae. It was now designated an "ika aua na Papa," or *fish-refuse thrown to Papa*, mother of Rongo. She was supposed to come up at night to feed upon this ghastly banquet. The net itself was wrapped round and round the stone image of Great Rongo, and there allowed to decay. Inside this coarse net was the ordinary tiputa, or loose covering; on the head was a sort of hat made of folds of dark native cloth, giving to a spectator the impression that he was gazing at a living person.

Near the image of Rongo the Great stood a small stone figure bearing the name of " Rongo-i-te-arero-kute " = *Rongo-of-the-red-tongue.* This little unclothed, unworshipped divinity seems to have been placed at the back of his friend to give emphasis to the title Rongo Nui = *Rongo-the-Great.*

At Rimatara human sacrifices were continually being offered to Rono (= Rongo), but the " drum of peace " was unknown.

KIRIKOVI'S SACRIFICE.

CIRCA A.D. 1772.

After the battle at Teopu, the temporal lordship of Mangaia devolved upon Kirikovi. It was in his chieftainship, of some five or six years' duration, that Captain Cook touched at Mangaia. The first victim uselessly placed on the rude altar of Rongo, in order that the drum of peace might be beaten, was Arauru, who, with the rest of the Teipe clan, had been hiding with the ancient tribe of Ngariki inside a grand and almost inaccessible cave named Erue. For a consideration of some valuable lands, Toê, cousin to the doomed man, engaged to lure Arauru out of his secure hiding-place to his death. Nor was this a difficult task, as this treacherous relative himself lived inside the cave. Ere it was quite day, Toê proposed to his victim that they should go fishing. Arauru objected, on the ground of danger; but Toê, assured him that their foes had that day started off in a different direction. Accordingly they left Erue, and with some difficulty made their way through thickets towards the sea. When half-way (opposite to the present church), Arauru was startled by the loud chirp of a cricket in the air, and said to his deceitful companion, "Ara! tera rava te Atua karanga!" = "List to yon warning voice!" Twice did the unseen insect mysteriously address the infatuated Arauru, who kept on his way, and soon found himself encircled with armed men. That same day the unoffending victim was laid on the altar of Rongo. But Uanuku, the "wise man" (koromedua [1]) of his day, and the author of a well-remembered dirge for Vera, wept and protested against the prayers for peace being chanted over his relative. The body of Arauru was accord_ingly thrown down a neighbouring chasm.

A new and unobjectionable victim must be sought. Who so suitable as Maruata, who had no family ties to the winning tribes? Despite all pledges of safety for himself and his children, he was in the dusk of evening enticed out of the cave Erue to a short distance and despatched. The prayers were duly offered,

---

[1] Hence the native name for "Missionary," Orometua, meaning literally, "*a wise man, or instructor.*" "Orometua" is Tahitian for "Koromatua."

and all the other ceremonies performed. Thus Kirikovi was in-stalled paramount chief.

As there were several Maruatas, this one is known as "Maruata who fell at Ioapa," the place where the victim was clubbed being so named.

The wife of Maruata, who at an earlier period so narrowly escaped being eaten by Ngako, not only witnessed the cruel sacrifice of her husband, but also of some of her children in after years.

Toê was himself offered in sacrifice at the commencement of the next reign.

Arauru, Maruata, and Toê all worshipped the lizard-god Teipe.

A "CRYING" SONG FOR MARUATA

(PERTAINING TO THE "DEATH-TALK OF PUVAI").

BY KOROA, CIRCA 1795.

Used only by the Altar-tribe Teipe.

TUMU.	INTRODUCTION.
	Solo.
Tiō ra, tinaoia Maruata ē !	Sing we of Maruata, slain for the altar,

E kitea mai nga erepua tei iaau,
    E Mai ō !
	Though many were the promises
	    To thee, O Mai !

	Chorus.
Atuia mai taua ē ! Pae atiati Ngariki ō !	All, alas ! soon broken by Deceitful, lying Ngariki.

PAPA.

Solo.

Akamoe ana era, e Mai ē !

Chorus.

Akamoe koe i te ivi-roa :
E tamaki kiato i Erue, ua tanimo ē !

Solo.

Ua tanimo tai kopu.
Te raka nei tai aiai : ua ē ia Mai ē !

Chorus.

Maruata rā, tei o Ioapa ē !

UNUUNU TAI.

Solo.

Tinaoiā Maruata ra ē !

Chorus.

Tinaoiā Maruata nei :
Ua koā tei Ngariki.
Ua tapaia tai apaki,
Apāpatai ua tapariri.

Pikao rauti ra
I te taringa kotikoti
O Maruata ia ōtōia !

Na Rongo te take i tingeti
Ua kakina ē !

Solo.

Ua kakinā Maruata nei.
E kitea mai nga erepua tei iaau,
E Mai ē !

FOUNDATION.

Solo.

The clans were united, *yet* Mai[1]
fell !

Chorus.

Solemnly united to the ancient chiefs ;
Yet brother sold brother to death at
Erue.

Solo.

They cruelly sold thee.
Thou was deceived to thy death,
O Mai !

Chorus.

Yes, the Maruata who fell at Ioapa.

FIRST OFFSHOOT.

Solo.

Alas for Maruata, slain for the altar

Chorus.

Maruata was slain for the altar ;
(Ngariki only smiled thereat),
Like so many others of his tribe,
That but few now survive !

Wrapped in green *ti* leaves,
Slices of Maruata's ears
Announce all new possessions.

Thy head, sacred to Rongo,
Was hit and split in his name !

Solo.

Yes, Maruata, thy skull was split ;
Though many were the promises
To thee, O Mai !

---

[1] A second name for Maruata.

Chorus.

Atuia mai taua ē !	All, alas! soon broken by
Pae atiati Ngariki ē !	Deceitful, lying Nagriki.

UNUUNU RUA.

SECOND OFFSHOOT.

Solo.

Na Paeru te ivi i akamoea'i !

The chief Paeru made league with thee.

Chorus.

Na Paeru te ivi i akamoea'i.
Ua ū taua i te mate o Uarau,

Paeru himself made league with thee.
We too faithfully followed *their* fortunes,

Atuia mai e ua tapariri.

Who betrayed thee to thy death.

Pikao rauti ra
I te taringa kotikoti
O Maruata ia ōtōia.

Wrapped in green *ti* leaves,
Slices of Maruata's ears
Announce all new possessions.

Na Rongo te take i tingeti
Ua kakina ē !

Thy head, sacred to Rongo,
Was hit and split in his name.

Solo.

Ua kakinā Maruata nei.
E kakinā mai nga erepua tei iaau,
E Mai ē !

Yes, Maruata, thy skull was split;
Though many were the promises
To thee, O Mai !

Chorus.

Atuia mai taua ē !
Pae atiati Ngariki ē

All, alas ! soon broken by
Deceitful, lying Ngariki.

THE DEATH OF NGUTUKU (Circa 1810).

ARRANGED FOR THE NATIVE HARMONICON.

Voices only : as many as ten.

Ngutukū te tuku, e te matakeinanga ;

Ngutukū is doomed to perish, friends—

O taua teve, mangeo ua ra !

He who is as dangerous as the deadly "*teve.*"

Tena te tamaki, e tiki ia Kū tei roto i
    te rua.
    Kua motu i te rauaika.
      Nana ia ka ora.
    E tiki e ta i te rua o Tongaiti.

Vaarire te iki i te kapua e tangi ra.

Let us attack the guardian of the cave.	

Let us attack the guardian of the
    cave.
    His hour has come.
    He vainly dreams of safety.
Up, attack the stronghold of the
    Tongan clan.

Vaarire is the offering[1] for the altar
    —the price of peace.

Music and Voices.

Tēra! Ngutukū, Ngutukū, Ngutukū
    titiri !
    Ngutukū oki ka apai na
    I te kapua ei ika na Rongo.
Anatia kia mou, kia ketaketa.
Kotia Vaarire, kotia Vaarire, kotia
    Ngutukū.
    Ngutukū, Ngutukū titiri !

Look yonder ! Ngutukū, Ngutukū
    Ngutukū has fallen.
    Ngutukū is destined for the altar,
    As a peace-offering to Rongo.
Secure the victim well to the litter.
Vaarire is slain, Vaarire is slain,
    Ngutukū is slain !
    Yes, Ngutukū, Ngutukū is hurled
    down.

Voices only.

Kua maranga o Vaarire i te kapua !
E uru tupu ariki, e ika na Rongo !

    E apai e takitaki aere.

Ah, Vaarire is borne to the altar !
Dance in triumph before this offering
    to Rongo.[2]
    Lift it on high ; bear it carefully
    on.

Music and Voices.

Vaarire te ika i mua.

E Vaarire te ika i te kapua !
Tei runga au, na Tamarua,

Na Piti, e Piti, Piti,
I na Veitatei ra : tukuroi ra i Vaipia

Bear in front the sacrifice (fish),
    Vaarire.
Vaarire is destined for the altar.
We scaled the entrance to his cave at
    Tamarua.
We now bear him along the road
Until reaching Veitatei we rest at
    the stream.

---

[1] Vaarire was the original name of Ngutukū.   Wherever I have translated
"offering," the original is *fish*.

[2] The ancient song of the butterflies, on page 292, is incorporated into this
modern production.

A na! Iā iā!! tataki na!

And now for the war dance. Up with him.

Kua nauā. Oie puruki Rongo,

Oie puruki Rongo.

We have succeeded. Such is the fiat of Rongo!
So wills the god of war!

Romia mai, e te matakeinanga
Kia takitaki tatou : takaki na uriuri.

Ka apai ei kapua koe.

Onwards, onwards, brave friends.
Toss him aloft. Dance the war-dance.
Thou art on thy way to the altar.

Music and Voices.

Kua roiroi ka aere, a tau te vaapoiro,

Anatia te peru aō ;
Akairi ra i te ua,
Kia aere atu i te taatuatini, i te taatua-tini !

Once thou didst despatch[1] thy hurried meal ;
The well-secured basket of tackle
Slung to thy shoulder—
Thou madest thy way to the sea for sport.

E vaka no Ngutukū, e vaka taki koatu ;
E vaki taki aere.
Kua kakaro i te matangi.
Kua tu te rirei ; kua tu te rirei !

A canoe for Ngutukū. Put in some stones.
Launch thy frail bark.
Note well the wind.
The tokens are favourable ; 'twill be fair.

E maro tikoru e ! itikitiki rouru ē !

Itikitiki rouru ē !
Kotia ra e Kauare to metua, e Mua.

Kotia rā Ngutukū. Tena oa te tamaki !
Kotia rā Ngutukū ! Iā ē !
I koia koe i te rakau.
A puta koe i te puruki a Rongo ē !

Thy girdle is secured ; thy hair tied up,
Ready for the altar.
O Muare ! thy father was slain by Kauare.
Yes, Ngutukū was cut down by his hand.
Ngutukū fell ! (War-dance.)
The spear entered thy body !
Such is the resistless will of the god Rongo !

---

[1] Ngutukū was an expert fisherman ; hence the reference to his daily avocations in this and the following stanza.

Oi tatamaki koe ; oi tatamaki koe.	For thou art of a restless and doomed race.
O Taura tei mua ; Atiati te teina ;	Thy daughter [1] Taura leads the way : Atiati follows.
O Paraakere, o Veruara.	Then comes (the youngest) Paraakere with her mother.
Ka apai na to metua i te kapua !	*Your father is being borne to the altar!*

MAKITAKA'S LAMENT ON THE LOSS OF THE TEMPORAL SOVEREIGNTY.

COMPOSED BY TUKA, CIRCA A.D. 1815.

Recited at a Reed-throwing Match.

Solo.

Taku pua i tanu reka ē !	Fair tree planted by my hand !
Ua tanu ake koe i Tamarua—	Alas, for the tree of peace which
E tupu te au ē !	Once flourished at Tamarua !
Teipoi ārire riro akera Mangaia i te rave !	Alas, that Mangaia should be snatched from my grasp!

---

[1] By a refinement of cruelty only possible to heathenism, the bearers of the sacrifice address the weeping children in the words, " *Your* father is being borne to the altar." Muare, the only son of the victim, did not follow the corpse, as he would have been put to death. He survived to Christian times, and became a member of the Church. Years before the first teachers landed, he induced Reinga to compose this song in commemoration of his father's tragical fate. Muare found a melancholy pleasure in chanting this song to its proper accompaniment of the harmonicon : indeed, he quite excelled at this outrageous performance. A few years ago he died the death of a Christian. His sister Paraakere died recently.

Chorus.

Ia Makitaka te ua.	Makitaka, once supreme chief;
A motu te toa ia Ngaki te miro.	Now dispossessed by the fiat of Ngakiau.

Solo.

Ia Ngaki te miro ia Teata :	Ah! Ngaki[1] directed the sacrifice of Teata;
O te uri oki na Aemata :	Like all the descendants of Aemata,
Tei nunga ē i te kapua.	The victim was laid on the altar.
Kore rai ooku taeake !	Unpitied—unsaved !
Kore kore rai e taeake tangi ē !	Alas! unpitied—unsaved !

Chorus.

E tini na Tane i ka riro Mangaia.	Mangaia is now transferred.

Solo.

Ua riro rai Mangaia rai, e Teau.	Mangaia, friends, is lost.
Ua ō ia Maki,	The chiefs dealt treacherously
O te ivi koia i akamoea 'i ē !	After plighting their solemn troth.

UNUUNU TAI.   FIRST OFFSHOOT.

Solo.

Vaekura te pia i tara ē !	The priest of Tane planned it—

Chorus.

Vāia te Amama, Amama o Makitaka.	Split up the priestly tribe of Makitaka.
Vaekura te arataki.	So willed Vaekura.
Arataki aere atu	Do thy worst !
Eia tu eia toa ?	Why this bloodshed ?
Ei Mangaia, ei Ngariki ;	To win Mangaia for a new dynasty.
Ngariki o Makitaka.	The fame of Makitaka is gone.
E oa i te upoko ;	Strike the head (of the altar-victim).
R oa i to rae.	Strike the temples.
Ia tangi a pu ;	As if a conch-shell sounded
Ia tangi kekina ;	Is the falling of the axe.

---

[1] Ngaki is a shortened form of Tane Ngakiau.

Ia ara i te pa ;
   Ia ara i te mate.
   A tara nei e Tane.
Kare kaiti kau rere !

The wounded are shrieking :
Are awakened only to die !
Tane has gained the victory.
Alas ! Alas ! ! Alas ! ! Alas ! !

Solo.

Ua riro rai Mangaia rai, e Teau.
   Ua ē ia Maki,
O te ivi koia i akamoea 'i ē !

Mangaia, friends, is lost.
The chiefs dealt treacherously,
After plighting their solemn troth.

Teipoi ārire riro akera Mangaia e i te rave !

Alas, that Mangaia should be snatched from my grasp !

Chorus.

   Ia Makitaka te ua.
A motu te toa ia Ngaki te miro.

Makitaka, once supreme chief ;
Now dispossessed by the fiat of Ngakiau.

Solo.

Ia Ngaki te miro ia Teata :

Ah ! Ngaki directed the sacrifice of Teata ;

O te uri oki na Aemata.
Tei nunga ē i te kapua.
Kore rai ooku taeakē !

Like all the descendants of Aemata,
The victim was laid on the altar.
Unpitied—unsaved !

Kore kore rai e taeake tangi e !

Alas ! unpitied—unsaved !

Chorus.

E tini na Tane i ka riro Mangaia.

Mangaia is now transferred.

UNUUNU RUA.

SECOND OFFSHOOT.

Solo.

Tutukiria nga ivi e !

Let brother slay brother.

Chorus.

   Ka tu au ka aere,
   Ka aere taua ē !
   I nunga i te tuaronga.
   Taukarokaro i reira.
   Tena te vai maka.

I will arise and fight.
Join our band.
Away to yon plain
To fight our foes.
Stones are flying about,

E vai koatu ē !
E vai rakau ē !
Ka ui te vai.
A pa te vai.
A pa te toa ia 'Tauokura.
Ia katamutamu ia karearea.
Te vaa i koma 'i.
Te vaa i tara 'i.
Ka tara nei, e Tane.
Karē kaiti kau rere !

Out of the slings of the brave.
Spears are uplifted.
The chiefs pause a moment
To examine the omens.
Death-blows are being dealt.
Fearful are the shouts of the victors.
Alas, those lips that once spake !
Alas, the mouth once shouted !
Tane has gained the victory.
Alas ! Alas !! Alas !! Alas !!

Solo.

Ua riro rai Mangaia rai, e Teau.
Ua ē ia Maki,
O te ivi koia i akamoea 'i ō !

Mangaia, friends, is lost.
The chiefs dealt treacherously,
After plighting their solemn troth.

Teipoi ārire riro akera Mangaia i te ravē !

Alas, that Mangaia should be snatched from my grasp !

Chorus.

Ia Makitaka te ua.
A motu te toa ia Ngaki te miro.

Makitaka, once supreme chief ;
Now dispossessed by the fiat of Ngakiau.

Solo.

Ia Ngaki te miro ia Teata :

Ah ! Ngaki directed the sacrifice of Teata ;

O te uri oki na Aemata :
Tei nunga ē i te kapua,
Kore rai ooku taeakē !

Like all the descendants of Aemata,
The victim was laid on the altar.
Unpitied—unsaved !

Kore kore rai e taeake tangi e !

Alas ! unpitied—unsaved !

Chorus.

E tini na Tane i ka riro Mangaia.

Mangaia is now transferred.

CHAPTER XIV.

THE SEASONS, PHASES OF THE MOON, ETC., ETC.

THE SEASONS (NGA TINO MARAMA).

EREU, OR SUMMER.

(Rain, Heat, and Plenty.)

1. *Akaū.* Breadfruit appears ; chestnut and other trees *in blossom.* This month is also known as "the time of beautiful cocoa-nut leaves" (marama o te kikau). Akaū extends from the *middle of December to the middle of January.*

2. *Otunga.* Breadfruit and chestnut trees covered with *fruit*, but not ripe. Sprats[1] arrive. Hills covered with reeds in blossom.

PARŌRŌ, OR WINTER.

(Drought, Cold, and Scarcity.)

1. *Parōrō.* Cold south winds, withering up the wild vines everywhere.

2. *Manu.* *Incubation of birds.* The woodpecker bores the dead cocoa-nut for a nest. The *titi* bores the side of the mountain. . Coral-tree in blossom. Warrior-spirits take their departure from earth.

3. *Pipiri.* *Muffled up inside the house*, on account of the cold.

---

[1] The two months preceding the arrival of *sprats* are called " te karaii koā," or "time of exhausted crabs," they having made their way from the rocks to the sea to spawn. In like manner the interior of man is supposed to be empty and weak, until the arrival of sprats gives new life. During these hot and enfeebling months children are fractious and troublesome, *but should on no account be beaten !*

3. *Kautua,* or "kautua a kere-kere" = "*trail-of-the-eel.*" The soil is everywhere furrowed with water, as though traversed by eels. *Time of floods.*

4. *Akamākuru. Some breadfruit and chestnuts fall unripe, worm eaten.* So, too, some brave men are sure to die prematurely this moon. *Hurricane month* (end of March).

5. *Muriaa,* or "ruru anga kakao," *i.e.* the reed blossoms are shed upon the hills by *a late blow.*

6. *Uringa,* or "*dead.*" The leaves, etc., of the yam, arrow-root, etc., etc., fall.

7. *Miringa,* or "*finishing up*" (of the food of *ereu,* or summer season).

4. *K'aunuunu.* Papaka, or land-crab, comes out of its hiding-place to feed, and is easily caught. Also called "karaii," or "crab season."

5. *Mā'ū.*[1] *Spring up.* All tuberous roots in the soil spring into life. Also said—"kua tupu the anau kai" = "all plants in leaf."

6. *Vaetā.* Trees, stones, bush everywhere *covered with the vines* of the wild yam; the o'e, or *bitter* yam; mārarau, or *sweet* yam, etc., etc. Native arrow-root and "teve" roots are luxuriant. The year ends about the middle of December.

Thirteen moons in all.

The arrival of the new year was indicated by the appearance of *Matariki,* or Pleiades, on the eastern horizon just after sunset, *i.e.* about the middle of December. Hence the idolatrous worship paid to this beautiful cluster of stars in many of the South Sea Islands. The Pleiades were worshipped at Danger Island, and at the Penrhyns, down to the introduction of Christianity in 1857. In many islands extravagant joy is still manifested at the rising of this constellation out of the ocean.

The knowledge of the calendar belonged to the kings, as they alone fixed the feasts in honour of the gods, and all public spectacles. For others to dare to keep the calendar was a sin against the gods, to be punished with *hydrocele.*

---

[1] The same name for the Magellan clouds ; as if the *rising up of vapour,* or curling up of columns of smoke in the heavens.

CHANGES OF THE MOON (TE TAU AROPO).

IN THE WEST.

1 Iro. Sacred to Iro, patron of thieves. Favourable for thieving.
2 Oata = shadow, *i.e.* moon seen in shadow.
3 Amiama.
4 Amiama-akaoti, *i.e.* Last Amiama.
5 Tamatea.

{ Sprats arrive during these three days in Feb. Failing that, expect them the same days in March.

6 Tamatea-akaoti, *i.e.* Last Tamatea.
7 Korekore.
8 ☽ Korekore-akaoti, *i.e.* Last Korekore.
9 O Vari (*i.e.* Vari-ma-te-takere = the Originator-of-all-things.)
10 Una.
11 Maaru.
12 Ua.
13 E atua = A god.
14 O Tu, *i.e.* Tu-metua, the last made of the major gods.
15 ◯ Mārangi,[1] or Full-Moon.

IN THE EAST.

16 Oturu.
17 Rakau.
18 Rakau-roto, *i.e.* Second Rakau.
19 Rakau-akaoti, *i.e.* Last Rakau.
20 Korekore.
21 Korekore-roto, *i.e.* Second Korekore.
22 Korekore-akaoti, *i.e.* Last Korekore.
23 ☾ Tangaroa. Sacred to Tangaroa.
24 Tangaroa-roto. Second night sacred to Tangaroa.
25 Tangaroa-akaoti. Last night sacred to Tangaroa.
26 O Tane. Sacred to Tane.
27 Rongo-Nui, *i.e.* Rongo-the-Great. The 26th and 27th were *fête* nights—Rongo and Tane being patrons of their dances in time of peace.
28 Mauri = ghost.
29 Omūtu = ended.
30 ● Otire o Avaiki (abbreviated "Otireo") = *Lost in the depths of Avaiki.*

At Rarotonga the 13th is "Maitu," instead of "Atua" (sense similar). Otherwise this account of the changes of the moon is equally good for Rarotonga. Allowing for the difference of dialects, it is the same in the Tahitian islands.

[1] Cocoa-nuts were invariably planted at the full of the moon ; the size of the moon symbolizing the full roundness of the future fruit.

From the 17th to the 28th the nights were considered favourable for fishing ; also favourable for catching *the fish of the gods, i.e.* men. In other words, these were *murder nights.* Tangaroa (23rd) and O Tane (26th) and Rongo-Nui (27th) were the three " most lucky " for this cruel purpose.

The eastern Polynesians, like the New Zealanders, invariably reckon by *nights*—not, as we do, by days. For example, "*Po* ia koe i te aerenga ? " = " How many *nights* were you journeying ? " etc., etc.

THE MARINER'S COMPASS OF POLYNESIA.

To the Chinese belongs the honour of inventing the mariner's compass, long anterior to the Christian era. It was known to the Arabs in mediæval times, and from them, through the Crusaders, the knowledge spread over Europe.

There can be no reasonable doubt that Polynesia was peopled from Asia. Did the original settlers take with them the mariner's compass, or anything analogous thereto? May not the ancestors of the present South Sea Islanders have been far more civilized than their descendants? The absence of iron throughout Polynesia would easily account for the loss of the magnet. Subjoined is a plan of the winds for the Hervey Group from the lips of the ancient priests. With slight variations it will do for many other groups in the Pacific. The number of wind-holes in this plan exactly corresponds with the points of the mariner's compass. In the olden time, great stress was laid on this knowledge for the purpose of fishing, and especially for their long sea voyages from group to group. At the edge of the horizon are a series of holes, some large and some small, through which *Raka*, the god of winds,

and his children, love to blow.   Hence the phrase in daily use,
" *rua* matangi," or " wind-*hole*," where Europeans would simply
speak of " wind."   The " head " of the winds is supposed to be
in the east; by the time it has veered round to s.w. by w. it is

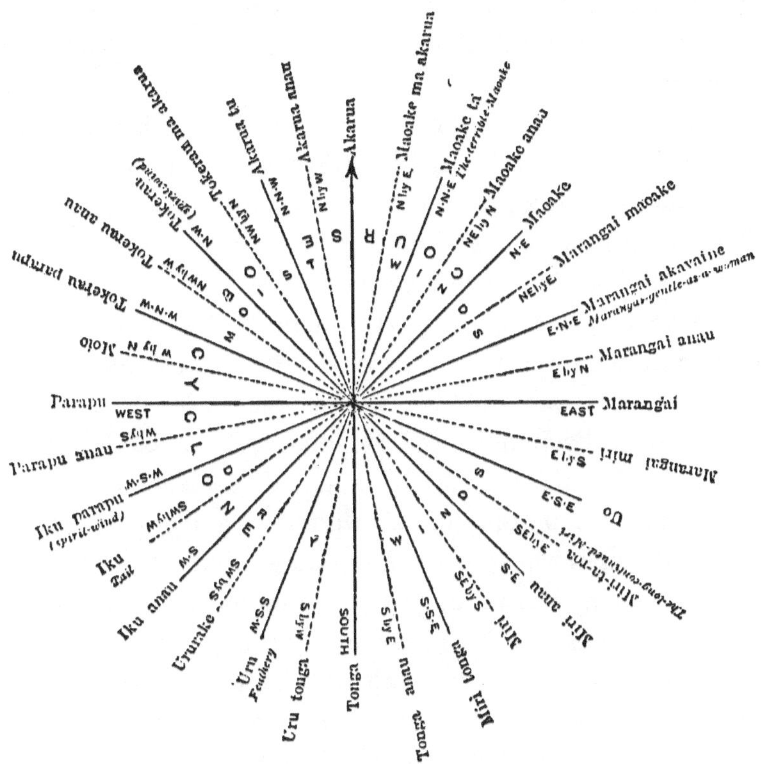

named the *iku*, or " tail ;" in fact, it is dying away until it becomes,
in the s.s.w., merely an *uru*, or " like the touch of a feather."
Cyclones, of course, begin in the N.E., and go on increasing in
violence until, on reaching the *iku*, or " tail," they moderate.
Passing on to the *uru*, or " feathery," there is a perfect calm,
mocking the desolations so lately wrought.

The whole of these names have, more or less, a figurative signification. The reader will observe the word *anau* (give birth) several times recurring. Taking, for example, *akarua* for N., the wind, in veering towards the W., becomes *akarua anau; i.e.* the north giving birth to a new wind (N. by W.). As the wind veers to the N.N.W, it is called *akarua tu;* that is, the *akarua* strong enough to stand.

Taking *maoake* for N.E., when the wind shifts a point it becomes *maoake anau;* that is, the N.E. giving birth (N.E. by N.). Advancing still towards the N., it is called *maoake ta*, or the killing or terrible *maoake* (N.N.E.), on account of the extreme violence of this wind when a cyclone blows.

The vast concave above was symbolised by the interior of a calabash, in the lower part of which a series of small apertures was made to correspond with the various wind-holes at the edge of the horizon. Each hole was stopped up with cloth. Should the wind be unfavourable for a grand expedition, the chief priest began his incantation by withdrawing the plug from the aperture through which the unpropitious wind was supposed to blow. Rebuking this wind, he stopped up the hole, and advanced through all the intermediate apertures, moving plug by plug, until the desired wind-hole was reached. This was left open, as a gentle hint to the children of Raka that the priest wished the wind to blow steadily from that quarter.

The operator having a good knowledge of the ordinary course of the winds, and the various indications of change, the peril of the experiment was not great.

Providence has supplied these islanders with an *unfailing* natural indication of an approaching cyclone. This is expressed in the phrase, " Kua taviriviri te kao o te meika "—*i.e.* the core of

the true native banana is strangely twisted and contorted some
weeks previous to a hurricane, as if to give warning of impending
danger.   This is usually associated with an extraordinary growth
of food.   Doubtless the excessive moisture and heat which occasion this rapid growth, and give rise to the strange twists of the
wondrously delicate leaves of this banana, are the real causes of
cyclones.

POLYNESIAN PLURALS.

Nearly all the plurals in use in the Hervey Group have a
definite signification as nouns.

1. A common plural is "*are,*" which literally means "*a house:*"
in its plural use it may be rendered "a-house-full-of," *i.e.* "many."
Thus—

 "e are atua" = "a *number of* gods;" literally, "a-house-
  full-of gods;"

 "e are apinga" = "a *number of* valuable things;" literally,
  "a-house-full-of valuable things."

2. A second plural is "*vaka*" = "*canoe;*" or, as it may be
rendered, "a-canoe-full-of."   Thus—

 "e vaka angela" = "a host of angels;" literally, "a-canoe-
  full-of angels;"

 "e vaka puruki" = "a host of warriors;" literally, "a-
  canoe-full-of warriors."

3. Another frequently used plural is "*pa*" = "*enclosure:* door."
Thus—

 "e pa puaka" = "a pig enclosure;" = a pig-sty;

 "e pa maunga" = "a range of mountains," *as enclosing a
  valley;*

" e pa enua " = " a group of islands," *as if* a portion of the ocean were thereby marked off or enclosed.

4. A commonly used plural is " *ata* " = " shelf to place all sorts of food on."   Thus—

" e ata pa " = " a number of doors ; "

" e ata kete " = " a number of food-baskets."

5. A still more interesting plural is " *rau* " = " *leaf.*"   Thus we may speak of " te *rau* tangata o te Atua," *i.e.* " a people *numerous as the leaves of a tree*, worshipping such and such a god." The figure is of a vast tree, the growth of ages.   The huge trunk represents the god, the branches the lesser divinities, the leaves the worshippers—ever dropping off by death, and ever being renewed by fresh births.   This is constantly applied to the servants of the true God : Jehovah being the trunk and branches, believers the leaves.

6. The last instance of plurals is " *maru* " = " *shadow,*" or " *shade.*"   Thus the natives daily speak of " te *maru* tangata o te Atua," *i.e.* " *the people who sit under the shadow of God.*"   The old idea was still of an ancient tree overshadowing the marae filled with worshippers.   The noblest trees affording the best shade were planted in their idol groves, not a twig of which might be plucked. As applied to Christian worshippers gathering Sabbath after Sabbath in the house of God to take refreshment under the shadow of the Almighty (Psalm xc. 1), the figure is extremely beautiful.

In the Tahitian dialect the " *r* " is dropped, "ma*r*u"[1] becoming

---

[1] The Aitutakians speak of " te taru ariki " = the chiefs, or kings Mangaians speak of " te *tau* ariki."   " Taru " on Mangaia is a verb, " to heap up," to " cover over with new soil."   It is easy to trace the connecting link of thought, *i.e.* the entire assembly of chiefs.

" *mau*," the ordinary plural of that group.   Doubtless our common plural "*au*" is the same as the "mau" of the Eastern islands.

The full form, "maru," is the dignified form to be used whenever the gods and chiefs are spoken of.

It is scarcely fair to regard "anau" = *family*, as a plural. Thus the natives speak of—

"te anau ika" = "the whole *family* of fish;"
"te anau kai" = "the whole *family* of plants."

A very polite mode of address in the Mangaian dialect is the use of the *third* person singular, dual, and plural, where in other languages the *second* person would be appropriate; reminding one of the use of the German *Sie*.

POLYNESIAN NUMERATION.

The mode of counting in use amongst the Papuan population of the Loyalty Islands, New Caledonia, and the New Hebrides, is worthy of notice.   They enumerate by fingers up to five, which makes "one hand;" ten is "two hands;" twenty is "an entire man," *i.e.* ten fingers and ten toes.   A hundred is "five men," and so on.

This plan is ingenious, but clumsy, being applicable only to small numbers.   Missionaries labouring in those islands have wisely discarded it.   I was much surprised when first I heard the school children at Aneiteum, Mare, and Lifu, repeating the *English* multiplication table with great facility and correctness, and on the Sabbath to hear the chapter and hymns announced in *English* figures—the natives turning to the right chapter or hymn in their own books. This innovation, however, has brought down upon the missionaries the ire of the French.

Throughout the Eastern Islands there has been no need for changing the original system of numeration. In the Hervey Group we have two distinct bases—four and ten. The former base is used in counting cocoa-nuts, which were from time immemorial tied up in *fours* (kaviri) :—

5 bunches (kaviri) of cocoa-nuts make one takau, *i.e.*				20
10 takau	„	„	rau, *i.e.*	200
10 rau	„	„	mano, *i.e.*	2,000
10 mano	„	„	kiu, *i.e.*	20,000
10 kiu	„	„	tini, *i.e.*	200,000

All beyond this is uncertain. To express more the natives simply heap up the highest figures, without any attempt at a definite signification; thus, "mano, mano; tini, tini," literally, "2,000 on 2,000; 200,000 on 200,000;" much as we say "myriads on myriads," or "millions on millions," *i.e.* innumerable.

In measures of length they were from time out of mind accustomed to the fathom (the outstretched arms of a tall man), half-fathom, span, and finger's length.

Ten fathoms (paru) make one "kume." In this way 100 would be called 10 "kume;" 200 would be 20 "kume," and so on.

Through the Eastern dialects there is a very close resemblance of the primary numerals. In the expression for *five, i.e.*

"e rima," or "*a* hand," we may trace a point of resemblance between the Papuan and Malay systems of numeration. Throughout the Ellice's Group *ten* is expressed by "katoa" = *all* (*i.e.* the fingers).

The "rau"[1] is a favourite number, continually occurring in their stories of the past. In a decisive battle fought circa eighty-nine years ago, Potai boasted a "rau" = 200 warriors; whilst the winner, Potiki, had only 120 (6 takau).

"Eternity" is often expressed by the phrase "e *rau* te tautau," *i.e.* "200 *ages.*" This is less poetical than the common "e *rimua* ua atu" = "until covered with the *moss* of unknown ages," as of a lofty cocoa-nut or other tree entirely moss-grown. Another mode of expressing the same idea is, "e tuatau ua atu," *i.e.* "time on on, still on."

---

[1] "Rau" also means "leaf," or "pandanus thatch." A native house requires about 200 reeds of thatch to complete one side: "rau," therefore, may mean indifferently a leaf, 200, or a "tua-rau," *i.e.* thatched side of a dwelling.

INDEX.

Caxton Printing Works, Beccles.

A LIST OF
C. KEGAN PAUL AND CO.'S
PUBLICATIONS.

ADAMS (F. O.), F.R.G.S.
The History of Japan. From the Earliest Period to the Present Time. New Edition, revised. 2 volumes. With Maps and Plans. Demy 8vo. Cloth, price 21*s.* each.

ADAMS (W. D.).
Lyrics of Love, from Shakespeare to Tennyson. Selected and arranged by. Fcap. 8vo. Cloth extra, gilt edges, price 3*s.* 6*d.*

Also, a Cheap Edition. Fcap. 8vo. Cloth, price 2*s.* 6*d.*

ADAMSON H. T.), B.D.
The Truth as it is in Jesus. Crown 8vo. Cloth, price 8*s.* 6*d.*

A. K. H. B.
From a Quiet Place. A New Volume of Sermons. Crown 8vo. Cloth, price 5*s.*

ALBERT (Mary).
Holland and her Heroes to the year 1585. An Adaptation from Motley's "Rise of the Dutch Republic." Small crown 8vo. Cloth, price, 4*s.* 6*d.*

ALLEN (Rev. R.), M.A.
Abraham; his Life, Times, and Travels, 3,800 years ago. Second Edition. With Map. Post 8vo. Cloth, price 6*s.*

ALLEN (Grant), B.A.
Physiological Æsthetics. Large post 8vo. 9*s.*

ALLIES (T. W.), M.A.
Per Crucem ad Lucem. The Result of a Life. 2 vols. Demy 8vo. Cloth, price 25*s.*

A Life's Decision. Crown 8vo. Cloth, price 7*s.* 6*d.*

AMATEUR.
A Few Lyrics. Small crown 8vo. Cloth, price 2*s.*

AMOS (Prof. Sheldon).
Science of Law. Fourth Edition. Crown 8vo. Cloth, price 5*s.*

Volume X. of The International Scientific Series.

ANDERSON (Col. R. P.).
Victories and Defeats. An Attempt to explain the Causes which have led to them. An Officer's Manual. Demy 8vo. Cloth, price 14*s.*

ANDERSON (R. C.), C.E.
Tables for Facilitating the Calculation of every Detail in connection with Earthen and Masonry Dams. Royal 8vo. Cloth, price £2 2*s.*

Antiope. A Tragedy. Large crown 8vo. Cloth, price 6*s.*

ARCHER (Thomas).
About my Father's Business. Work amidst the Sick, the Sad, and the Sorrowing. Crown 8vo. Cloth, price 2*s.* 6*d.*

Army of the North German Confederation.
A Brief Description of its Organization, of the Different Branches of the Service and their *rôle* in War, of its Mode of Fighting, &c. &c. Translated from the Corrected Edition, by permission of the Author, by Colonel Edward Newdigate. Demy 8vo. Cloth, price 5*s.*

ARNOLD (Arthur).
Social Politics. Demy 8vo. Cloth, price 14*s.*

Free Land. Crown 8vo. Cloth, price 6*s.*

AUBERTIN (J. J.).

Camoens' Lusiads. Portuguese Text, with Translation by. With Map and Portraits. 2 vols. Demy 8vo. Price 30s.

Aunt Mary's Bran Pie.

By the author of "St. Olave's." Illustrated. Cloth, price 3s. 6d.

AVIA.

The Odyssey of Homer Done into English Verse. Fcap. 4to. Cloth, price 15s.

BAGEHOT (Walter).

Physics and Politics; or, Thoughts on the Application of the Principles of "Natural Selection" and "Inheritance" to Political Society. Fifth Edition. Crown 8vo. Cloth, price 4s.

Volume II. of The International Scientific Series.

Some Articles on the Depreciation of Silver, and Topics connected with it. Demy 8vo. Price 5s.

The English Constitution. A New Edition, Revised and Corrected, with an Introductory Dissertation on Recent Changes and Events. Crown 8vo. Cloth, price 7s. 6d.

Lombard Street. A Description of the Money Market. Seventh Edition. Crown 8vo. Cloth, price 7s. 6d.

BAGOT (Alan).

Accidents in Mines: their Causes and Prevention. Crown 8vo. Cloth, price 6s.

BAIN (Alexander), LL.D.

Mind and Body: the Theories of their relation. Seventh Edition. Crown 8vo. Cloth, price 4s.

Volume IV. of The International Scientific Series.

Education as a Science. Crown 8vo. Third Edition. Cloth, price 5s.

Volume XXV. of The International Scientific Series.

BAKER (Sir Sherston, Bart.).

Halleck's International Law; or Rules Regulating the Intercourse of States in Peace and War. A New Edition, Revised, with Notes and Cases. 2 vols. Demy 8vo. Cloth, price 38s.

The Laws relating to Quarantine. Crown 8vo. Cloth, price 12s. 6d.

BALDWIN (Capt. J. H.), F.Z.S.

The Large and Small Game of Bengal and the North-Western Provinces of India. 4to. With numerous Illustrations. Second Edition. Cloth, price 21s.

BANKS (Mrs. G. L.).

God's Providence House. New Edition. Crown 8vo. Cloth, price 3s. 6d.

Ripples and Breakers. Poems. Square 8vo. Cloth, price 5s.

BARLEE (Ellen).

Locked Out: a Tale of the Strike. With a Frontispiece. Royal 16mo. Cloth, price 1s. 6d.

BARNES (William).

An Outline of English Speechcraft. Crown 8vo. Cloth, price 4s.

Poems of Rural Life, in the Dorset Dialect. New Edition, complete in 1 vol. Crown 8vo. Cloth, price 8s. 6d.

Outlines of Redecraft (Logic). With English Wording. Crown 8vo. Cloth, price 3s.

BARTLEY (George C. T.).

Domestic Economy: Thrift in Every Day Life. Taught in Dialogues suitable for Children of all ages. Small crown 8vo. Cloth, limp, 2s.

BASTIAN (H. Charlton), M.D.

The Brain as an Organ of Mind. With numerous Illustrations. Second Edition. Crown 8vo. Cloth, price 5s.

Volume XXIX. of the International Scientific Series.

BAUR (Ferdinand), Dr. Ph.
A Philological Introduction to Greek and Latin for Students. Translated and adapted from the German of. By C. KEGAN PAUL, M.A. Oxon., and the Rev. E. D. STONE, M.A., late Fellow of King's College, Cambridge, and Assistant Master at Eton. Second and revised edition. Crown 8vo. Cloth, price 6s.

BAYNES (Rev. Canon R. H.)
At the Communion Time. A Manual for Holy Communion. With a preface by the Right Rev. the Lord Bishop of Derry and Raphoe. Cloth, price 1s. 6d.

*** Can also be had bound in French morocco, price 2s. 6d.; Persian morocco, price 3s.; Calf, or Turkey morocco, price 3s. 6d.

Home Songs for Quiet Hours. Fourth and cheaper Edition. Fcap. 8vo. Cloth, price 2s. 6d.

This may also be had handsomely bound in morocco with gilt edges.

BELLINGHAM (Henry), Barrister-at-Law.
Social Aspects of Catholicism and Protestantism in their Civil Bearing upon Nations. Translated and adapted from the French of M. le Baron de Haulleville. With a Preface by His Eminence Cardinal Manning. Crown 8vo. Cloth, price 6s.

BENNETT (Dr. W. C.).
Narrative Poems & Ballads. Fcap. 8vo. Sewed in Coloured Wrapper, price 1s.

Songs for Sailors. Dedicated by Special Request to H. R. H. the Duke of Edinburgh. With Steel Portrait and Illustrations. Crown 8vo. Cloth, price 3s. 6d.

An Edition in Illustrated Paper Covers, price 1s.

Songs of a Song Writer. Crown 8vo. Cloth, price 6s.

BERNSTEIN (Prof.).
The Five Senses of Man. With 91 Illustrations. Second Edition. Crown 8vo. Cloth, price 5s.

Volume XXI. of The International Scientific Series.

BETHAM - EDWARDS (Miss M.).
Kitty. With a Frontispiece. Crown 8vo. Cloth, price 6s.

BEVINGTON (L. S.).
Key Notes. Small crown 8vo. Cloth, price 5s.

BLASERNA (Prof. Pietro).
The Theory of Sound in its Relation to Music. With numerous Illustrations. Second Edition. Crown 8vo. Cloth, price 5s.

Volume XXII. of The International Scientific Series.

Blue Roses ; or, Helen Mali- nofska's Marriage. By the Author of "Véra." 2 vols. Fifth Edition. Cloth, gilt tops, 12s.

*** Also a Cheaper Edition in 1 vol. With Frontispiece. Crown 8vo. Cloth, price 6s.

BLUME (Major W.).
The Operations of the German Armies in France, from Sedan to the end of the war of 1870-71. With Map. From the Journals of the Head-quarters Staff. Translated by the late E. M. Jones, Maj. 20th Foot, Prof. of Mil. Hist., Sandhurst. Demy 8vo. Cloth, price 9s.

BOGUSLAWSKI (Capt. A. von).
Tactical Deductions from the War of 1870-71. Translated by Colonel Sir Lumley Graham, Bart., late 18th (Royal Irish) Regiment. Third Edition, Revised and Corrected. Demy 8vo. Cloth, price 7s.

BONWICK (J.), F.R.G.S.
Egyptian Belief and Modern Thought. Large post 8vo. Cloth, price 10s. 6d.

Pyramid Facts and Fancies. Crown 8vo. Cloth, price 5s.

The Tasmanian Lily. With Frontispiece. Crown 8vo. Cloth, price 5s.

Mike Howe, the Bushranger of Van Diemen's Land. With Frontispiece. Crown 8vo. Cloth, price 5s.

BOWEN (H. C.), M. A.

English Grammar for Beginners. Fcap. 8vo. Cloth, price 1s.

Studies in English, for the use of Modern Schools. Small crown 8vo. Cloth, price 1s. 6d.

Simple English Poems. English Literature for Junior Classes. In Four Parts. Parts I. and II., price 6d. each, now ready.

BOWRING (Sir John).

Autobiographical Recollections. With Memoir by Lewin B. Bowring. Demy 8vo. Price 14s.

Brave Men's Footsteps.

By the Editor of "Men who have Risen." A Book of Example and Anecdote for Young People. With Four Illustrations by C. Doyle. Sixth Edition. Crown 8vo. Cloth, price 3s. 6d.

BRIALMONT (Col. A.).

Hasty Intrenchments. Translated by Lieut. Charles A. Empson, R. A. With Nine Plates. Demy 8vo. Cloth, price 6s.

BRODRICK (The Hon. G. C.).

Political Studies. Demy 8vo. Cloth, price 14s.

BROOKE (Rev. S. A.), M. A.

The Late Rev. F. W. Robertson, M.A., Life and Letters of. Edited by.

I. Uniform with the Sermons. 2 vols. With Steel Portrait. Price 7s. 6d.

II. Library Edition. 8vo. With Two Steel Portraits. Price 12s.

III. A Popular Edition, in 1 vol. 8vo. Price 6s.

Theology in the English Poets. — COWPER, COLERIDGE, WORDSWORTH, and BURNS. New and Cheaper Edition. Post 8vo. Cloth, price 5s.

Christ in Modern Life. Fourteenth and Cheaper Edition. Crown 8vo. Cloth, price 5s.

Sermons. First Series. Eleventh Edition. Crown 8vo. Cloth, price 6s.

BROOKE (Rev. S. A.), M.A.— *continued.*

Sermons. Second Series. Third Edition. Crown 8vo. Cloth, price 7s.

The Fight of Faith. Sermons preached on various occasions. Third Edition. Crown 8vo. Cloth, price 7s. 6d.

Frederick Denison Maurice: The Life and Work of. A Memorial Sermon. Crown 8vo. Sewed, price 1s.

BROOKE (W. G.), M. A.

The Public Worship Regulation Act. With a Classified Statement of its Provisions, Notes, and Index. Third Edition, Revised and Corrected. Crown 8vo. Cloth, price 3s. 6d.

Six Privy Council Judgments—1850-1872. Annotated by. Third Edition. Crown 8vo. Cloth, price 9s.

BROUN (J. A.).

Magnetic Observations at Trevandrum and Augustia Malley. Vol. I. 4to. Cloth, price 63s.

The Report from above, separately sewed, price 21s.

BROWN (Rev. J. Baldwin).

The Higher Life. Its Reality, Experience, and Destiny. Fifth and Cheaper Edition. Crown 8vo. Cloth, price 5s.

Doctrine of Annihilation in the Light of the Gospel of Love. Five Discourses. Third Edition. Crown 8vo. Cloth, price 2s. 6d.

The Christian Policy of Life. A Book for Young Men of Business. New and Cheaper Edition. Crown 8vo. Cloth, price 3s. 6d.

BROWN (J. Croumbie), LL.D.

Reboisement in France; or, Records of the Replanting of the Alps, the Cevennes, and the Pyrenees with Trees, Herbage, and Bush. Demy 8vo. Cloth, price 12s. 6d.

The Hydrology of Southern Africa. Demy 8vo. Cloth, price 10s. 6d.

BRYANT (W. C.)

Poems. Red-line Edition.
With 24 Illustrations and Portrait of
the Author. Crown 8vo. Cloth extra,
price 7*s*. 6*d*.

A Cheaper Edition, with Frontispiece. Small crown 8vo. Cloth, price
3*s*. 6*d*.

BURCKHARDT (Jacob).

The Civilization of the Period of the Renaissance in Italy.
Authorized translation, by S. G. C.
Middlemore. 2 vols. Demy 8vo.
Cloth, price 24*s*.

BURTON (Mrs. Richard).

The Inner Life of Syria,
Palestine, and the Holy Land.
With Maps, Photographs, and
Coloured Plates. 2 vols. Second
Edition. Demy 8vo. Cloth, price 24*s*.

*** Also a Cheaper Edition in
one volume. Large post 8vo. Cloth,
price 10*s*. 6*d*.

BURTON (Capt. Richard F.).

The Gold Mines of Midian
and the Ruined Midianite
Cities. A Fortnight's Tour in
North Western Arabia. With numerous Illustrations. Second Edition. Demy 8vo. Cloth, price 18*s*.

The Land of Midian Revisited. With numerous illustrations on wood and by Chromolithography. 2 vols. Demy 8vo.
Cloth, price 32*s*.

CALDERON.

Calderon's Dramas: The
Wonder-Working Magician—Life is
a Dream—The Purgatory of St.
Patrick. Translated by Denis
Florence MacCarthy. Post 8vo.
Cloth, price 10*s*.

CANDLER (H.).

The Groundwork of Belief.
Crown 8vo. Cloth, price 7*s*.

CARPENTER (W. B.), M.D.

The Principles of Mental
Physiology. With their Applications to the Training and Discipline
of the Mind, and the Study of its
Morbid Conditions. Illustrated.
Fifth Edition. 8vo. Cloth, price 12*s*.

CAVALRY OFFICER.

Notes on Cavalry Tactics,
Organization, &c. With Diagrams. Demy 8vo. Cloth, price 12*s*.

CHAPMAN (Hon. Mrs. E. W.).

A Constant Heart. A Story.
2 vols. Cloth, gilt tops, price 12*s*.

CHEYNE (Rev. T. K.).

The Prophecies of Isaiah.
Translated, with Critical Notes and
Dissertations by. Two vols., demy
8vo. Cloth. Vol. I., price 12*s*. 6*d*.

Children's Toys, and some
Elementary Lessons in General
Knowledge which they teach. Illustrated. Crown 8vo. Cloth, price 5*s*.

CHRISTOPHERSON (The late
Rev. Henry), M.A.

Sermons. With an Introduction by John Rae, LL.D., F.S.A.
Second Series. Crown 8vo. Cloth,
price 6*s*.

CLAYDEN (P. W.).

England under Lord Beaconsfield. The Political History of
the Last Six Years, from the end of
1873 to the beginning of 1880. Second Edition. With Index, and
Continuation to March, 1880. Demy
8vo. Cloth, price 16*s*.

CLERY (C.), Major.

Minor Tactics. With 26
Maps and Plans. Fourth and Revised
Edition. Demy 8vo. Cloth, price 16*s*.

CLODD (Edward), F.R.A.S.

The Childhood of the
World: a Simple Account of Man
in Early Times. Sixth Edition.
Crown 8vo. Cloth, price 3*s*.

A Special Edition for Schools.
Price 1*s*.

The Childhood of Religions. Including a Simple Account
of the Birth and Growth of Myths
and Legends. Third Thousand.
Crown 8vo. Cloth, price 5*s*.

A Special Edition for Schools.
Price 1*s*. 6*d*.

Jesus of Nazareth. With a
brief Sketch of Jewish History to
the Time of His Birth. Small
crown 8vo. Cloth, price 6*s*.

COLERIDGE (Sara).
Pretty Lessons in Verse for Good Children, with some Lessons in Latin, in Easy Rhyme. A New Edition. Illustrated. Fcap. 8vo. Cloth, price 3s. 6d.

Phantasmion. A Fairy Tale. With an Introductory Preface by the Right Hon. Lord Coleridge, of Ottery St. Mary. A New Edition. Illustrated. Crown 8vo. Cloth, price 7s. 6d.

Memoir and Letters of Sara Coleridge. Edited by her Daughter. Cheap Edition. With one Portrait. Cloth, price 7s. 6d.

COLLINS (Mortimer).
The Secret of Long Life. Small crown 8vo. Cloth, price 3s. 6d.

Inn of Strange Meetings, and other Poems. Crown 8vo. Cloth, price 5s.

CONWAY (Hugh).
A Life's Idylls. Small crown 8vo. Cloth, price 3s. 6d.

COOKE (M. C.), M.A., LL.D.
Fungi; their Nature, Influences, Uses, &c. Edited by the Rev. M. J. Berkeley, M.A., F.L.S. With Illustrations. Second Edition. Crown 8vo. Cloth, price 5s.
Volume XIV. of The International Scientific Series.

COOKE (Prof. J. P.)
The New Chemistry. With 31 Illustrations. Fifth Edition. Crown 8vo. Cloth, price 5s.
Volume IX. of The International Scientific Series.

Scientific Culture. Crown 8vo. Cloth, price 1s.

COOPER (H. J.).
The Art of Furnishing on Rational and Æsthetic Principles. New and Cheaper Edition. Fcap. 8vo. Cloth, price 1s. 6d.

COPPÉE (François).
L'Exilée. Done into English Verse with the sanction of the Author by I. O. L. Crown 8vo. Vellum, price 5s.

CORFIELD (Prof.), M.D.
Health. Crown 8vo. Cloth, price 6s.

CORY (William).
A Guide to Modern English History. Part I. MDCCCXV. —MDCCCXXX. Demy 8vo. Cloth, price 9s.

COURTNEY (W. L.).
The Metaphysics of John Stuart Mill. Crown 8vo. Cloth, price 5s. 6d.

COWAN (Rev. William).
Poems : Chiefly Sacred, including Translations from some Ancient Latin Hymns. Fcap. 8vo. Cloth, price 5s.

COX (Rev. Sir G. W.), Bart.
A History of Greece from the Earliest Period to the end of the Persian War. New Edition. 2 vols. Demy 8vo. Cloth, price 36s.

The Mythology of the Aryan Nations. New Edition. 2 vols. Demy 8vo. Cloth, price 28s.

A General History of Greece from the Earliest Period to the Death of Alexander the Great, with a sketch of the subsequent History to the present time. New Edition. Crown 8vo. Cloth, price 7s. 6d.

Tales of Ancient Greece. New Edition. Small crown 8vo. Cloth, price 6s.

School History of Greece. With Maps. New Edition. Fcap. 8vo. Cloth, price 3s. 6d.

The Great Persian War from the Histories of Herodotus. New Edition. Fcap. 8vo. Cloth, price 3s. 6d.

A Manual of Mythology in the form of Question and Answer. New Edition. Fcap. 8vo. Cloth, price 3s.

COX (Rev. Sir G. W.), Bart., M.A., and EUSTACE HINTON JONES.
Popular Romances of the Middle Ages. Second Edition in one volume. Crown 8vo. Cloth, price 6s.

COX (Rev. Samuel).
Salvator Mundi; or, Is Christ the Saviour of all Men? Sixth Edition. Crown 8vo. Cloth, price 5*s.*

The Genesis of Evil, and other Sermons, mainly Expository. Second Edition. Crown 8vo. Cloth, price 6*s.*

CRAUFURD (A. H.).
Seeking for Light : Sermons. Crown 8vo. Cloth, price 5*s.*

CRAWFURD (Oswald).
Portugal, Old and New. With Illustrations and Maps. Demy 8vo. Cloth, price 16*s.*

CRESSWELL (Mrs. G.).
The King's Banner. Drama in Four Acts. Five Illustrations. 4to. Cloth, price 10*s.* 6*d.*

CROMPTON (Henry).
Industrial Conciliation. Fcap. 8vo. Cloth, price 2*s.* 6*d.*

CROZIER (John Beattie), M.B.
The Religion of the Future. Crown 8vo. Cloth, price 6*s.*

D'ANVERS (N. R.).
Parted. A Tale of Clouds and Sunshine. With 4 Illustrations. Extra Fcap. 8vo. Cloth, price 3*s.* 6*d.*

Little Minnie's Troubles. An Every-day Chronicle. With Four Illustrations by W. H. Hughes. Fcap. Cloth, price 3*s.* 6*d.*

Pixie's Adventures ; or, the Tale of a Terrier. With 21 Illustrations. 16mo. Cloth, price 4*s.* 6*d.*

Nanny's Adventures ; or, the Tale of a Goat. With 12 Illustrations. 16mo. Cloth, price 4*s.* 6*d.*

DAVIDSON (Rev. Samuel), D.D., LL.D.
The New Testament, translated from the Latest Greek Text of Tischendorf. A New and thoroughly Revised Edition. Post 8vo. Cloth, price 10*s.* 6*d.*

DAVIDSON (Rev. Samuel), D.D., LL.D.—_continued._
Canon of the Bible : Its Formation, History, and Fluctuations. Third Edition, revised and enlarged. Small crown 8vo. Cloth, price 5*s.*

DAVIES (G. Christopher).
Rambles and Adventures of Our School Field Club. With Four Illustrations. Crown 8vo. Cloth, price 5*s.*

DAVIES (Rev. J. L.), M.A.
Theology and Morality. Essays on Questions of Belief and Practice. Crown 8vo. Cloth, price 7*s.* 6*d.*

DAVIES (T. Hart.).
Catullus. Translated into English Verse. Crown 8vo. Cloth, price 6*s.*

DAWSON (George), M.A.
Prayers, with a Discourse on Prayer. Edited by his Wife. Fifth Edition. Crown 8vo. Price 6*s.*

Sermons on Disputed Points and Special Occasions. Edited by his Wife. Third Edition. Crown 8vo. Cloth, price 6*s.*

Sermons on Daily Life and Duty. Edited by his Wife. Second Edition. Crown 8vo. Cloth, price 6*s.*

DE L'HOSTE (Col. E. P.).
The Desert Pastor, Jean Jarousseau. Translated from the French of Eugène Pelletan. With a Frontispiece. New Edition. Fcap. 8vo. Cloth, price 3*s.* 6*d.*

DENNIS (J.).
English Sonnets. Collected and Arranged. Elegantly bound. Fcap. 8vo. Cloth, price 3*s.* 6*d.*

DE REDCLIFFE (Viscount Stratford), P.C., K.G., G.C.B.
Why am I a Christian? Fifth Edition. Crown 8vo. Cloth, price 3*s.*

DESPREZ (Philip S.).
Daniel and John; or, the Apocalypse of the Old and that of the New Testament. Demy 8vo. Cloth, price 12*s.*

DE TOCQUEVILLE (A.).
Correspondence and Conversations of, with Nassau William Senior, from 1834 to 1859. Edited by M. C. M. Simpson. 2 vols. Post 8vo. Cloth, price 21s.

DE VERE (Aubrey).
Legends of the Saxon Saints. Small crown 8vo. Cloth, price 6s.

Alexander the Great. A Dramatic Poem. Small crown 8vo. Cloth, price 5s.

The Infant Bridal, and other Poems. A New and Enlarged Edition. Fcap. 8vo. Cloth, price 7s. 6d.

The Legends of St. Patrick, and other Poems. Small crown 8vo. Cloth, price 5s.

St. Thomas of Canterbury. A Dramatic Poem. Large fcap. 8vo. Cloth, price 5s.

Antar and Zara: an Eastern Romance. INISFAIL, and other Poems, Meditative and Lyrical. Fcap. 8vo. Price 6s.

The Fall of Rora, the Search after Proserpine, and other Poems, Meditative and Lyrical. Fcap. 8vo. Price 6s.

DOBSON (Austin).
Vignettes in Rhyme and Vers de Société. Third Edition. Fcap. 8vo. Cloth, price 5s.

Proverbs in Porcelain. By the Author of "Vignettes in Rhyme." Second Edition. Crown 8vo. 6s.

DOWDEN (Edward), LL.D.
Shakspere: a Critical Study of his Mind and Art. Fifth Edition. Large post 8vo. Cloth, price 12s.

Studies in Literature, 1789-1877. Large post 8vo. Cloth, price 12s.

Poems. Second Edition. Fcap. 8vo. Cloth, price 5s.

DOWNTON (Rev. H.), M.A.
Hymns and Verses. Original and Translated. Small crown 8vo. Cloth, price 3s. 6d.

DRAPER (J. W.), M.D., LL.D.
History of the Conflict between Religion and Science. Fourteenth Edition. Crown 8vo. Cloth, price 5s.
Volume XIII. of The International Scientific Series.

DREW (Rev. G. S.), M.A.
Scripture Lands in connection with their History. Second Edition. 8vo. Cloth, price 10s. 6d.

Nazareth: Its Life and Lessons. Third Edition. Crown 8vo. Cloth, price 5s.

The Divine Kingdom on Earth as it is in Heaven. 8vo. Cloth, price 10s. 6d.

The Son of Man: His Life and Ministry. Crown 8vo. Cloth price 7s. 6d.

DREWRY (G. O.), M.D.
The Common-Sense Management of the Stomach. Fifth Edition. Fcap. 8vo. Cloth, price 2s. 6d.

DREWRY (G. O.), M.D., and BARTLETT (H. C.), Ph.D., F.C.S.
Cup and Platter: or, Notes on Food and its Effects. New and cheaper Edition. Small 8vo. Cloth, price 1s. 6d.

DRUMMOND (Miss).
Tripps Buildings. A Study from Life, with Frontispiece. Small crown 8vo. Cloth, price 3s. 6d.

DU MONCEL (Count).
The Telephone, the Microphone, and the Phonograph. With 74 Illustrations. Small crown 8vo. Cloth, price 5s.

DU VERNOIS (Col. von Verdy).
Studies in leading Troops. An authorized and accurate Translation by Lieutenant H. J. T. Hildyard, 71st Foot. Parts I. and II. Demy 8vo. Cloth, price 7s.

EDEN (Frederick).
The Nile without a Dragoman. Second Edition. Crown 8vo. Cloth, price 7s. 6d.

EDMONDS (Herbert).

Well Spent Lives : a Series of Modern Biographies. Crown 8vo. Price 5*s*.

Educational Code of the Prussian Nation, in its Present Form. In accordance with the Decisions of the Common Provincial Law, and with those of Recent Legislation. Crown 8vo. Cloth, price 2*s*. 6*d*.

EDWARDS (Rev. Basil).

Minor Chords ; or, Songs for the Suffering : a Volume of Verse. Fcap. 8vo. Cloth, price 3*s*. 6*d*. ; paper, price 2*s*. 6*d*.

ELLIOT (Lady Charlotte).

Medusa and other Poems. Crown 8vo. Cloth, price 6*s*.

ELLIOTT (Ebenezer), The Corn-Law Rhymer.

Poems. Edited by his Son, the Rev. Edwin Elliott, of St. John's, Antigua. 2 vols. Crown 8vo. Cloth, price 18*s*.

ELSDALE (Henry).

Studies in Tennyson's Idylls. Crown 8vo. Cloth, price 5*s*.

Epic of Hades (The). By the author of "Songs of Two Worlds." Tenth and finally revised Edition. Fcap. 8vo. Cloth, price 7*s*. 6*d*. *** Also an Illustrated Edition with seventeen full-page designs in photo-mezzotint by GEORGE R. CHAPMAN. 4to. Cloth, extra gilt leaves, price 25*s*.

EVANS (Mark).

The Gospel of Home Life. Crown 8vo. Cloth, price 4*s*. 6*d*.

The Story of our Father's Love, told to Children. Fourth and Cheaper Edition. With Four Illustrations. Fcap. 8vo. Cloth, price 1*s*. 6*d*.

A Book of Common Prayer and Worship for Household Use, compiled exclusively from the Holy Scriptures. New and Cheaper Edition. Fcap. 8vo. Cloth, price 1*s*.

EVANS (Mark)—*continued*.

The King's Story Book. In three parts. Fcap. 8vo. Cloth, price 1*s*. 6*d*. each. *** Part I., with four illustrations and Picture Map, now ready.

EX-CIVILIAN.

Life in the Mofussil ; or, Civilian Life in Lower Bengal. 2 vols. Large post 8vo. Price 14*s*.

FARQUHARSON (M.).

I. Elsie Dinsmore. Crown 8vo. Cloth, price 3*s*. 6*d*.

II. Elsie's Girlhood. Crown 8vo. Cloth, price 3*s*. 6*d*.

III. Elsie's Holidays at Roselands. Crown 8vo. Cloth, price 3*s*. 6*d*.

FIELD (Horace), B.A. Lond.

The Ultimate Triumph of Christianity. Small crown 8vo. Cloth, price 3*s*. 6*d*.

FINN (the late James), M.R.A.S.

Stirring Times ; or, Records from Jerusalem Consular Chronicles of 1853 to 1856. Edited and Compiled by his Widow. With a Preface by the Viscountess STRANGFORD. 2 vols. Demy 8vo. Price 30*s*.

Folkestone Ritual Case (The). The Argument, Proceedings, Judgment, and Report, revised by the several Counsel engaged. Demy 8vo. Cloth, price 25*s*.

FORMBY (Rev. Henry).

Ancient Rome and its Con-nection with the Christian Religion : an Outline of the History of the City from its First Foundation down to the Erection of the Chair of St. Peter, A.D. 42-47. With numerous Illustrations of Ancient Monuments, Sculpture, and Coinage, and of the Antiquities of the Christian Catacombs. Royal 4to. Cloth extra, price 50*s*. Roxburgh, half-morocco, price 52*s*. 6*d*.

FOWLE (Rev. Edmund).

Latin Primer Rules made Easy. Crown 8vo. Cloth, price 3*s*.

FOWLE (Rev. T. W.), M.A.
The Reconciliation of Religion and Science. Being Essays on Immortality, Inspiration, Miracles, and the Being of Christ. Demy 8vo. Cloth, price 10s. 6d.

The Divine Legation of Christ. Crown 8vo. Cloth, price 7s.

FRASER (Donald).
Exchange Tables of Sterling and Indian Rupee Currency, upon a new and extended system, embracing Values from One Farthing to One Hundred Thousand Pounds, and at Rates progressing, in Sixteenths of a Penny, from 1s. 9d. to 2s. 3d. per Rupee. Royal 8vo. Cloth, price 10s. 6d.

FRISWELL (J. Hain).
The Better Self. Essays for Home Life. Crown 8vo. Cloth, price 6s.

One of Two; or, A Left-Handed Bride. With a Frontispiece. Crown 8vo. Cloth, price 3s. 6d.

GARDNER (J.), M.D.
Longevity: The Means of Prolonging Life after Middle Age. Fourth Edition, Revised and Enlarged. Small crown 8vo. Cloth, price 4s.

GARRETT (E.).
By Still Waters. A Story for Quiet Hours. With Seven Illustrations. Crown 8vo. Cloth, price 6s.

GEBLER (Karl Von).
Galileo Galilei and the Roman Curia, from Authentic Sources. Translated with the sanction of the Author, by Mrs. George Sturge. Demy 8vo. Cloth, price 12s.

GEDDES (James).
History of the Administration of John de Witt, Grand Pensionary of Holland. Vol. I. 1623—1654. Demy 8vo., with Portrait. Cloth, price 15s.

G. H. T.
Verses, mostly written in India. Crown 8vo. Cloth, price 6s.

GILBERT (Mrs.).
Autobiography and other Memorials. Edited by Josiah Gilbert. Third Edition. With Portrait and several Wood Engravings. Crown 8vo. Cloth, price 7s. 6d.

GILL (Rev. W. W.), B.A.
Myths and Songs from the South Pacific. With a Preface by F. Max Müller, M.A., Professor of Comparative Philology at Oxford. Post 8vo. Cloth, price 9s.

Ginevra and The Duke of Guise. Two Tragedies. Crown 8vo. Cloth, price 6s.

GLOVER (F.), M.A.
Exempla Latina. A First Construing Book with Short Notes, Lexicon, and an Introduction to the Analysis of Sentences. Fcap. 8vo. Cloth, price 2s.

GODWIN (William).
William Godwin: His Friends and Contemporaries. With Portraits and Facsimiles of the handwriting of Godwin and his Wife. By C. Kegan Paul. 2 vols. Demy 8vo. Cloth, price 28s.

The Genius of Christianity Unveiled. Being Essays never before published. Edited, with a Preface, by C. Kegan Paul. Crown 8vo. Cloth, price 7s. 6d.

GOETZE (Capt. A. von).
Operations of the German Engineers during the War of 1870-1871. Published by Authority, and in accordance with Official Documents. Translated from the German by Colonel G. Graham, V.C., C.B., R.E. With 6 large Maps. Demy 8vo. Cloth, price 21s.

GOLDSMID (Sir Francis Henry).
Memoir of. With Portrait. Crown 8vo. Cloth, price 5s.

GOODENOUGH (Commodore J. G.), R.N., C.B., C.M.G.
Memoir of, with Extracts from his Letters and Journals. Edited by his Widow. With Steel Engraved Portrait. Square 8vo. Cloth, 5s.

*** Also a Library Edition with Maps, Woodcuts, and Steel Engraved Portrait. Square post 8vo. Cloth, price 14s.

GOSSE (Edmund W.).
Studies in the Literature of Northern Europe. With a Frontispiece designed and etched by Alma Tadema. Large post 8vo. Cloth, price 12*s.*

New Poems. Crown 8vo. Cloth, price 7*s.* 6*d.*

GOULD (Rev. S. Baring), M.A.
Germany, Present and Past. 2 Vols. Demy 8vo. Cloth, price 21*s.*

The Vicar of Morwenstow: a Memoir of the Rev. R. S. Hawker. With Portrait. Third Edition, revised. Square post 8vo. Cloth, 10*s.* 6*d.*

GREY (John), of Dilston.
John Grey (of Dilston): Memoirs. By Josephine E. Butler. New and Revised Edition. Crown 8vo. Cloth, price 3*s.* 6*d.*

GRIMLEY (Rev. H. N.), M.A.
Tremadoc Sermons, chiefly on the Spiritual Body, the Unseen World, and the Divine Humanity. Second Edition. Crown 8vo. Cloth, price 6*s.*

GRÜNER (M. L.).
Studies of Blast Furnace Phenomena. Translated by L. D. B. Gordon, F.R.S.E., F.G.S. Demy 8vo. Cloth, price 7*s.* 6*d.*

GURNEY (Rev. Archer).
Words of Faith and Cheer. A Mission of Instruction and Suggestion. Crown 8vo. Cloth, price 6*s.*

Gwen : A Drama in Monologue. By the Author of the " Epic of Hades." Second Edition. Fcap. 8vo. Cloth, price 5*s.*

HAECKEL (Prof. Ernst).
The History of Creation. Translation revised by Professor E. Ray Lankester, M.A., F.R.S. With Coloured Plates and Genealogical Trees of the various groups of both plants and animals. 2 vols. Second Edition. Post 8vo. Cloth, price 32*s.*

The History of the Evolution of Man. With numerous Illustrations. 2 vols. Large post 8vo. Cloth, price 32*s.*

HAECKEL (Prof. Ernst.)—*continued.*
Freedom in Science and Teaching. From the German of Ernst Haeckel, with a Prefatory Note by T. H. Huxley, F.R.S. Crown 8vo. Cloth, price 5*s.*

HAKE (A. Egmont).
Paris Originals, with twenty etchings, by Léon Richeton. Large post 8vo. Cloth, price 14*s.*

Halleck's International Law; or, Rules Regulating the Intercourse of States in Peace and War. A New Edition, revised, with Notes and Cases. By Sir Sherston Baker, Bart. 2 vols. Demy 8vo. Cloth, price 38*s.*

HARDY (Thomas).
A Pair of Blue Eyes. New Edition. With Frontispiece. Crown 8vo. Cloth, price 6*s.*

The Return of the Native. New Edition. With Frontispiece. Crown 8vo. Cloth, price 6*s.*

HARRISON (Lieut.-Col. R.).
The Officer's Memorandum Book for Peace and War. Second Edition. Oblong 32mo. roan, elastic band and pencil, price 3*s.* 6*d.* ; russia, 5*s.*

HARTINGTON (The Right Hon. the Marquis of), M.P.
Election Speeches in 1879 and 1880. With Address to the Electors of North-East Lancashire. Crown 8vo. Cloth, price 3*s.* 6*d.*

HAWEIS (Rev. H. R.), M.A.
Arrows in the Air. Crown 8vo. Second Edition. Cloth, price 6*s.*

Current Coin. Materialism— The Devil—Crime—Drunkenness— Pauperism—Emotion—Recreation— The Sabbath. Third Edition. Crown 8vo. Cloth, price 6*s.*

Speech in Season. Fourth Edition. Crown 8vo. Cloth, price 9*s.*

Thoughts for the Times. Eleventh Edition. Crown 8vo. Cloth, price 7*s.* 6*d.*

Unsectarian Family Prayers. New and Cheaper Edition. Fcap. 8vo. Cloth, price 1*s.* 6*d.*

HAWKER (Robert Stephen).
The Poetical Works of.
Now first collected and arranged with a prefatory notice by J. G. Godwin. With Portrait. Crown 8vo. Cloth, price 12s.

HAWTREY (Edward M.).
Corydalis. A Story of the Sicilian Expedition. Small crown 8vo. Cloth, price 3s. 6d.

HEIDENHAIN (Rudolf), M.D.
Animal Magnetism. Physiological Observations. Translated from the Fourth German Edition, by L. C. Wooldridge. With a Preface by G. R. Romanes, F.R.S. Crown 8vo. Cloth, price 2s. 6d.

HELLWALD (Baron F. von).
The Russians in Central Asia. A Critical Examination, down to the present time, of the Geography and History of Central Asia. Translated by Lieut.-Col. Theodore Wirgman, LL.B. Large post 8vo. With Map. Cloth, price 12s.

HELVIG (Major H.).
The Operations of the Bavarian Army Corps. Translated by Captain G. S. Schwabe. With Five large Maps. In 2 vols. Demy 8vo. Cloth, price 24s.
Tactical Examples: Vol. I. The Battalion, price 15s. Vol. II. The Regiment and Brigade, price 10s. 6d. Translated from the German by Col. Sir Lumley Graham. With numerous Diagrams. Demy 8vo. Cloth.

HERFORD (Brooke).
The Story of Religion in England. A Book for Young Folk. Crown 8vo. Cloth, price 5s.

HINTON (James).
Life and Letters of. Edited by Ellice Hopkins, with an Introduction by Sir W. W. Gull, Bart., and Portrait engraved on Steel by C. H. Jeens. Second Edition. Crown 8vo. Cloth, 8s. 6d.
Chapters on the Art of Thinking, and other Essays. With an Introduction by Shadworth Hodgson. Edited by C. H. Hinton. Crown 8vo. Cloth, price 8s. 6d.

HINTON (James)—*continued.*
The Place of the Physician. To which is added ESSAYS ON THE LAW OF HUMAN LIFE, AND ON THE RELATION BETWEEN ORGANIC AND INORGANIC WORLDS. Second Edition. Crown 8vo. Cloth, price 3s. 6d.
Physiology for Practical Use. By various Writers. With 50 Illustrations. 2 vols. Second Edition. Crown 8vo. Cloth, price 12s. 6d.
An Atlas of Diseases of the Membrana Tympani. With Descriptive Text. Post 8vo. Price £6 6s.
The Questions of Aural Surgery. With Illustrations. 2 vols. Post 8vo. Cloth, price 12s. 6d.
The Mystery of Pain. New Edition. Fcap. 8vo. Cloth limp, 1s.

HOCKLEY (W. B.).
Tales of the Zenana; or, A Nuwab's Leisure Hours. By the Author of "Pandurang Hari." With a Preface by Lord Stanley of Alderley. 2 vols. Crown 8vo. Cloth, price 21s.
Pandurang Hari; or, Memoirs of a Hindoo. A Tale of Mahratta Life sixty years ago. With a Preface by Sir H. Bartle E. Frere, G.C.S.I., &c. New and Cheaper Edition. Crown 8vo. Cloth, price 6s.

HOFFBAUER (Capt.).
The German Artillery in the Battles near Metz. Based on the official reports of the German Artillery. Translated by Capt. E. O. Hollist. With Map and Plans. Demy 8vo. Cloth, price 21s.

HOLMES (E. G. A.).
Poems. First and Second Series. Fcap. 8vo. Cloth, price 5s. each.

HOLROYD (Major W. R. M.).
Tas-hil ul Kalām; or, Hindustani made Easy. Crown 8vo. Cloth, price 5s.

HOOPER (Mary).
Little Dinners: How to Serve them with Elegance and Economy. Thirteenth Edition. Crown 8vo. Cloth, price 5s.

HOOPER (Mary)—*continued.*

Cookery for Invalids, Persons of Delicate Digestion, and Children. Crown 8vo. Cloth, price 3s. 6d.

Every-Day Meals. Being Economical and Wholesome Recipes for Breakfast, Luncheon, and Supper. Second Edition. Crown 8vo. Cloth, price 5s.

HOOPER (Mrs. G.).

The House of Raby. With a Frontispiece. Crown 8vo. Cloth, price 3s. 6d.

HOPKINS (Ellice).

Life and Letters of James Hinton, with an Introduction by Sir W. W. Gull, Bart., and Portrait engraved on Steel by C. H. Jeens. Second Edition. Crown 8vo. Cloth price 8s. 6d.

HOPKINS (M.).

The Port of Refuge; or, Counsel and Aid to Shipmasters in Difficulty, Doubt, or Distress. Crown 8vo. Second and Revised Edition. Cloth, price 6s.

HORNER (The Misses).

Walks in Florence. A New and thoroughly Revised Edition. 2 vols. Crown 8vo. Cloth limp. With Illustrations.

Vol. 1.—Churches, Streets, and Palaces. 10s. 6d. Vol. II.—Public Galleries and Museums. 5s.

HULL (Edmund C. P.).

The European in India. With a MEDICAL GUIDE FOR ANGLO-INDIANS. By R. R. S. Mair, M.D., F.R.C.S.E. Third Edition, Revised and Corrected. Post 8vo. Cloth, price 6s.

HUTCHISON (Lieut.-Col. F. J.), and Capt. G. H. MACGREGOR.

Military Sketching and Reconnaissance. With Fifteen Plates. Small 8vo. Cloth, price 6s.

The first Volume of Military Handbooks for Regimental Officers. Edited by Lieut.-Col. C. B. BRACKENBURY, R.A., A.A.G.

HUTTON (Arthur), M.A.

The Anglican Ministry. Its Nature and Value in relation to the Catholic Priesthood. With a Preface by his Eminence Cardinal Newman. Demy 8vo. Cloth, price 14s.

HUXLEY (Prof.)

The Crayfish: An Intro- duction to the Study of Zoology. With Eighty-two Illustrations. Crown 8vo. Cloth, price 5s.

Volume XXVIII. of the International Scientific Scientific Series.

INCHBOLD (J. W.).

Annus Amoris. Sonnets. Fcap. 8vo. Cloth, price 4s. 6d.

INGELOW (Jean).

Off the Skelligs. A Novel. With Frontispiece. Second Edition. Crown 8vo. Cloth, price 6s.

The Little Wonder-horn. A Second Series of "Stories Told to a Child." With Fifteen Illustrations. Small 8vo. Cloth, price 2s. 6d.

Indian Bishoprics. By an Indian Churchman. Demy 8vo. 6d.

International Scientific Series (The).

I. **Forms of Water: A Familiar Exposition of the Origin and Phenomena of Glaciers.** By J. Tyndall, LL.D., F.R.S. With 25 Illustrations. Seventh Edition. Crown 8vo. Cloth, price 5s.

II. **Physics and Politics; or,** Thoughts on the Application of the Principles of "Natural Selection" and "Inheritance" to Political Society. By Walter Bagehot. Fifth Edition. Crown 8vo. Cloth, price 4s.

III. **Foods.** By Edward Smith, M.D., &c. With numerous Illustrations. Sixth Edition. Crown 8vo. Cloth, price 5s.

IV. **Mind and Body: The Theories of their Relation.** By Alexander Bain, LL.D. With Four Illustrations. Seventh Edition. Crown 8vo. Cloth, price 4s.

V. **The Study of Sociology.** By Herbert Spencer. Eighth Edition. Crown 8vo. Cloth, price 5s.

International Scientific Series (The)—*continued.*

VI. **On the Conservation of Energy.** By Balfour Stewart, LL.D., &c. With 14 Illustrations. Fifth Edition. Crown 8vo. Cloth, price 5*s.*

VII. **Animal Locomotion;** or, Walking, Swimming, and Flying. By J. B. Pettigrew, M.D., &c. With 130 Illustrations. Second Edition. Crown 8vo. Cloth, price 5*s.*

VIII. **Responsibility in Mental Disease.** By Henry Maudsley, M.D. Third Edition. Crown 8vo. Cloth, price 5*s.*

IX. **The New Chemistry.** By Professor J. P. Cooke. With 31 Illustrations. Fifth Edition. Crown 8vo. Cloth, price 5*s.*

X. **The Science of Law.** By Prof. Sheldon Amos. Fourth Edition. Crown 8vo. Cloth, price 5*s.*

XI. **Animal Mechanism.** A Treatise on Terrestrial and Aerial Locomotion. By Prof. E. J. Marey. With 117 Illustrations. Second Edition. Crown 8vo. Cloth, price 5*s.*

XII. **The Doctrine of Descent and Darwinism.** By Prof. Osca Schmidt. With 26 Illustrations. Third Edition. Crown 8vo. Cloth, price 5*s.*

XIII. **The History of the Conflict between Religion and Science.** By J. W. Draper, M.D., LL.D. Fourteenth Edition. Crown 8vo. Cloth, price 5*s.*

XIV. **Fungi;** their Nature, Influences, Uses, &c. By M. C. Cooke, LL.D. Edited by the Rev. M. J. Berkeley, F.L.S. With numerous Illustrations. Second Edition. Crown 8vo. Cloth, price 5*s.*

XV. **The Chemical Effects of Light and Photography.** By Dr. Hermann Vogel. With 100 Illustrations. Third and Revised Edition. Crown 8vo. Cloth, price 5*s.*

XVI. **The Life and Growth of Language.** By Prof. William Dwight Whitney. Second Edition. Crown 8vo. Cloth, price 5*s.*

XVII. **Money and the Mechanism of Exchange.** By W. Stanley Jevons, F.R.S. Fourth Edition. Crown 8vo. Cloth, price 5*s.*

International Scientific Series (The)—*continued.*

XVIII. **The Nature of Light:** With a General Account of Physical Optics. By Dr. Eugene Lommel. With 188 Illustrations and a table of Spectra in Chromo-lithography. Third Edition. Crown 8vo. Cloth, price 5*s.*

XIX. **Animal Parasites and Messmates.** By M. Van Beneden. With 83 Illustrations. Second Edition. Crown 8vo. Cloth, price 5*s.*

XX. **Fermentation.** By Prof. Schützenberger. With 28 Illustrations. Second Edition. Crown 8vo. Cloth, price 5*s.*

XXI. **The Five Senses of Man.** By Prof. Bernstein. With 91 Illustrations. Second Edition. Crown 8vo. Cloth, price 5*s.*

XXII. **The Theory of Sound in its Relation to Music.** By Prof. Pietro Blaserna. With numerous Illustrations. Second Edition. Crown 8vo. Cloth, price 5*s.*

XXIII. **Studies in Spectrum Analysis.** By J. Norman Lockyer, F.R.S. With six photographic Illustrations of Spectra, and numerous engravings on wood. Crown 8vo. Second Edition. Cloth, price 6*s.* 6*d.*

XXIV. **A History of the Growth of the Steam Engine.** By Prof. R. H. Thurston. With numerous Illustrations. Second Edition. Crown 8vo. Cloth, price 6*s.* 6*d.*

XXV. **Education as a Science.** By Alexander Bain, LL.D. Third Edition. Crown 8vo. Cloth, price 5*s.*

XXVI. **The Human Species.** By Prof. A. de Quatrefages. Second Edition. Crown 8vo. Cloth, price 5*s.*

XXVII. **Modern Chromatics.** With Applications to Art and Industry, by Ogden N. Rood. With 130 original Illustrations. Crown 8vo. Cloth, price 5*s.*

XXVIII. **The Crayfish:** an Introduction to the Study of Zoology. By Prof. T. H. Huxley. With eighty-two Illustrations. Crown 8vo. Cloth, price 5*s.*

XXIX. **The Brain as an Organ of Mind.** By H. Charlton Bastian, M.D. With numerous Illustrations. Second Edition. Crown 8vo. Cloth, price 5*s.*

International Scientific Series (The)—*continued.*

Forthcoming Volumes.

Prof. W. KINGDON CLIFFORD, M.A. The First Principles of the Exact Sciences explained to the Non-mathematical.

W. B. CARPENTER, LL.D., F.R.S. The Physical Geography of the Sea.

Sir JOHN LUBBOCK, Bart., F.R.S. On Ants and Bees.

Prof. W. T. THISELTON DYER, B.A., B.Sc. Form and Habit in Flowering Plants.

Prof. MICHAEL FOSTER, M.D. Protoplasm and the Cell Theory.

Prof. A. C. RAMSAY, LL.D., F.R.S. Earth Sculpture: Hills, Valleys, Mountains, Plains, Rivers, Lakes; how they were Produced, and how they have been Destroyed.

P. BERT (Professor of Physiology, Paris). Forms of Life and other Cosmical Conditions.

The Rev. A SECCHI, D.J., late Director of the Observatory at Rome. The Stars.

Prof. J. ROSENTHAL, of the University of Erlangen. General Physiology of Muscles and Nerves.

FRANCIS GALTON, F.R.S. Psychometry.

J. W. JUDD, F.R.S. The Laws of Volcanic Action.

Prof. F. N. BALFOUR. The Embryonic Phases of Animal Life.

J. LUYS, Physician to the Hospice de la Salpêtrière. The Brain and its Functions. With Illustrations.

Dr. CARL SEMPER. Animals and their Conditions of Existence.

Prof. WURTZ. Atoms and the Atomic Theory.

GEORGE J. ROMANES, F.L.S. Animal Intelligence.

ALFRED W. BENNETT. A Handbook of Cryptogamic Botany.

JENKINS (Rev. Canon).
   The Girdle Legend of Prato. Small crown 8vo. Cloth, price 2s.

JENKINS (E.) and RAYMOND (J.), Esqs.
   A Legal Handbook for Architects, Builders, and Building Owners. Second Edition Revised. Crown 8vo. Cloth, price 6s.

JENKINS (Rev. R. C.), M.A.
   The Privilege of Peter and the Claims of the Roman Church confronted with the Scriptures, the Councils, and the Testimony of the Popes themselves. Fcap. 8vo. Cloth, price 3s. 6d.

JENNINGS (Mrs. Vaughan).
   Rahel: Her Life and Letters. With a Portrait from the Painting by Daffinger. Square post 8vo. Cloth, price 7s. 6d.

Jeroveam's Wife and other Poems. Fcap. 8vo. Cloth, price 3s. 6d.

JEVONS (W. Stanley), M.A., F.R.S.
   Money and the Mechanism of Exchange. Fourth Edition. Crown 8vo. Cloth, price 5s.
   Volume XVII. of The International Scientific Series.

JOEL (L.).
   A Consul's Manual and Shipowner's and Shipmaster's Practical Guide in their Transactions Abroad. With Definitions of Nautical, Mercantile, and Legal Terms; a Glossary of Mercantile Terms in English, French, German, Italian, and Spanish. Tables of the Money, Weights, and Measures of the Principal Commercial Nations and their Equivalents in British Standards; and Forms of Consular and Notarial Acts. Demy 8vo. Cloth, price 12s.

JOHNSTONE (C. F.), M.A.
   Historical Abstracts. Being Outlines of the History of some of the less-known States of Europe. Crown 8vo. Cloth, price 7s. 6d.

JONES (Lucy).
   Puddings and Sweets. Being Three Hundred and Sixty-Five Receipts approved by Experience. Crown 8vo., price 2s. 6d.

JOYCE (P. W.), LL.D., &c.
Old Celtic Romances. Translated from the Gaelic by. Crown 8vo. Cloth, price 7s. 6d.

KAUFMANN (Rev. M.), B.A.
Utopias; or, Schemes of Social Improvement, from Sir Thomas More to Karl Marx. Crown 8vo. Cloth, price 5s.

Socialism: Its Nature, its Dangers, and its Remedies considered. Crown 8vo. Cloth, price 7s. 6d.

KAY (Joseph), M.A., Q.C.
Free Trade in Land. Edited by his Widow. With Preface by the Right Hon. John Bright, M. P. Third Edition. Crown 8vo. Cloth, price 5s.

KENT (Carolo).
Carona Catholica ad Petri successoris Pedes Oblata. De Summi Pontificis Leonis XIII. Assumptione Epiggramma. In Quinquaginta Linguis. Fcap. 4to. Cloth, price 15s.

KER (David).
The Boy Slave in Bokhara. A Tale of Central Asia. With Illustrations. Crown 8vo. Cloth, price 3s. 6d.

The Wild Horseman of the Pampas. Illustrated. Crown 8vo. Cloth, price 3s. 6d.

KERNER (Dr. A.), Professor of Botany in the University of Innsbruck.
Flowers and their Unbidden Guests. Translation edited by W. Ogle, M.A., M.D., and a prefatory letter by C. Darwin, F.R.S. With Illustrations. Sq. 8vo. Cloth, price 9s.

KIDD (Joseph), M.D.
The Laws of Therapeutics, or, the Science and Art of Medicine. Crown 8vo. Cloth, price 6s.

KINAHAN (G. Henry), M.R.I.A., &c., of her Majesty's Geological Survey.
Manual of the Geology of Ireland. With 8 Plates, 26 Woodcuts, and a Map of Ireland, geologically coloured. Square 8vo. Cloth, price 15s.

KING (Mrs. Hamilton).
The Disciples. A Poem. Third Edition, with some Notes. Crown 8vo. Cloth, price 7s. 6d.
Aspromonte, and other Poems. Second Edition. Fcap. 8vo. Cloth, price 4s. 6d.

KING (Edward).
Echoes from the Orient. With Miscellaneous Poems. Small crown 8vo. Cloth, price 3s. 6d.

KINGSLEY (Charles), M.A.
Letters and Memories of his Life. Edited by his Wife. With 2 Steel engraved Portraits and numerous Illustrations on Wood, and a Facsimile of his Handwriting. Thirteenth Edition. 2 vols. Demy 8vo. Cloth, price 36s.
  *** Also a Cabinet Edition in 2 vols. Crown 8vo. Cloth, price 12s.
All Saints' Day and other Sermons. Second Edition. Crown 8vo. Cloth, 7s. 6d.
True Words for Brave Men: a Book for Soldiers' and Sailors' Libraries. Fifth Edition. Crown 8vo. Cloth, price 2s. 6d.

KNIGHT (Professor W.).
Studies in Philosophy and Literature. Large post 8vo. Cloth, price 7s. 6d.

LACORDAIRE (Rev. Père).
Life: Conferences delivered at Toulouse. A New and Cheaper Edition. Crown 8vo. Cloth, price 3s. 6d.

LAIRD-CLOWES (W.).
Love's Rebellion: a Poem. Fcap. 8vo. Cloth, price 3s. 6d.

LAMONT (Martha MacDonald).
The Gladiator: A Life under the Roman Empire in the beginning of the Third Century. With four Illustrations by H. M. Paget. Extra fcap. 8vo. Cloth, price 3s. 6d.

LANG (A.).
XXII Ballades in Blue China. Elzevir. 8vo. Parchment, price 3s. 6d.

LAYMANN (Capt.).
The Frontal Attack of Infantry. Translated by Colonel Edward Newdigate. Crown 8vo. Cloth, price 2s. 6d.

LEANDER (Richard).
Fantastic Stories. Translated from the German by Paulina B. Granville. With Eight full-page Illustrations by M. E. Fraser-Tytler. Crown 8vo. Cloth, price 5s.

LEE (Rev. F. G.), D.C.L.
The Other World; or, Glimpses of the Supernatural. 2 vols. A New Edition. Crown 8vo. Cloth, price 15s.

LEE (Holme).
Her Title of Honour. A Book for Girls. New Edition. With a Frontispiece. Crown 8vo. Cloth, price 5s.

LEWIS (Edward Dillon).
A Draft Code of Criminal Law and Procedure. Demy 8vo. Cloth, price 21s.

LEWIS (Mary A.).
A Rat with Three Tales. With Four Illustrations by Catherine F. Frere. Crown 8vo. Cloth, price 5s.

LINDSAY(W. Lauder), M.D.,&c.
Mind in the Lower Animals in Health and Disease. 2 vols. Demy 8vo. Cloth, price 32s.

LLOYD (Francis) and Charles Tebbitt.
Extension of Empire Weakness? Deficits Ruin? With a Practical Scheme for the Reconstruction of Asiatic Turkey. Small crown 8vo. Cloth, price 3s. 6d.

LOCKER (F.).
London Lyrics. A New and Revised Edition, with Additions and a Portrait of the Author. Crown 8vo. Cloth, elegant, price 6s.
Also, a Cheaper Edition. Fcap 8vo. Cloth, price 2s. 6d.

LOCKYER (J. Norman), F.R.S.
Studies in Spectrum Ana-lysis; with six photographic illustrations of Spectra, and numerous engravings on wood. Second Edition. Crown 8vo. Cloth, price 6s. 6d.
Vol. XXIII. of The International Scientific Series.

LOMMEL (Dr. E.).
The Nature of Light: With a General Account of Physical Optics. Second Edition. With 188 Illustrations and a Table of Spectra in Chromo-lithography. Third Edition. Crown 8vo. Cloth, price 5s.
Volume XVIII. of The International Scientific Series.

LONSDALE (Margaret).
Sister Dora. A Biography, with Portrait engraved on steel by C. H. Jeens, and one illustration. Twelfth edition. Crown 8vo. Cloth, price 6s.

LORIMER (Peter), D.D.
John Knox and the Church of England: His Work in her Pulpit, and his Influence upon her Liturgy, Articles, and Parties. Demy 8vo. Cloth, price 12s.
John Wiclif and his English Precursors, by Gerhard Victor Lechler. Translated from the German, with additional Notes. 2 vols. Demy 8vo. Cloth, price 21s.

Love's Gamut and other Poems. Small crown 8vo. Cloth, price 3s. 6d.

LOWNDES (Henry).
Poems and Translations. Crown 8vo. Cloth, price 6s.

MAC CLINTOCK (L.).
Sir Spangle and the Dingy Hen. Illustrated. Square crown 8vo., price 2s. 6d.

MACDONALD (G.).
Malcolm. With Portrait of the Author engraved on Steel. Fourth Edition. Crown 8vo. Price 6s.
The Marquis of Lossie. Second Edition. Crown 8vo. Cloth, price 6s.
St. George and St. Michael. Second Edition. Crown 8vo. Cloth, 6s.

MACKENNA (S. J.).
Plucky Fellows. A Book for Boys. With Six Illustrations. Fourth Edition. Crown 8vo. Cloth, price 3s. 6d.
At School with an Old Dragoon. With Six Illustrations. Second Edition. Crown 8vo. Cloth, price 5s.

MACLACHLAN (Mrs.).
Notes and Extracts on Everlasting Punishment and Eternal Life, according to Literal Interpretation. Small crown 8vo. Cloth, price 3s. 6d.

MACNAUGHT (Rev. John).
Cœna Domini: An Essay on the Lord's Supper, its Primitive Institution, Apostolic Uses, and Subsequent History. Demy 8vo. Cloth, price 14s.

MAGNUSSON (Eirikr), M.A., and PALMER (E.H.), M.A.
Johan Ludvig Runeberg's Lyrical Songs, Idylls and Epigrams. Fcap. 8vo. Cloth, price 5s.

MAIR (R. S.), M.D., F.R.C.S.E.
The Medical Guide for Anglo-Indians. Being a Compendium of Advice to Europeans in India, relating to the Preservation and Regulation of Health. With a Supplement on the Management of Children in India. Second Edition. Crown 8vo. Limp cloth, price 3s. 6d.

MALDEN (H. E. and E. E.)
Princes and Princesses. Illustrated. Small crown 8vo. Cloth, price 2s. 6d.

MANNING (His Eminence Cardinal).
Essays on Religion and Literature. By various Writers. Third Series. Demy 8vo. Cloth, price 10s. 6d.

The Independence of the Holy See, with an Appendix containing the Papal Allocution and a translation. Cr. 8vo. Cloth, price 5s.

The True Story of the Vatican Council. Crown 8vo. Cloth, price 5s.

MAREY (E. J.).
Animal Mechanics. A Treatise on Terrestrial and Aerial Locomotion. With 117 Illustrations. Second Edition. Crown 8vo. Cloth, price 5s.

Volume XI. of The International Scientific Series.

MARKHAM (Capt. Albert Hastings), R.N.
The Great Frozen Sea. A Personal Narrative of the Voyage of the "Alert" during the Arctic Expedition of 1875-6. With six full-page Illustrations, two Maps, and twenty-seven Woodcuts. Fourth and cheaper edition. Crown 8vo. Cloth, price 6s.

Master Bobby: a Tale. By the Author of "Christina North." With Illustrations by E. H. BELL. Extra fcap. 8vo. Cloth, price 3s.6d.

MASTERMAN (J.).
Half-a-dozen Daughters. With a Frontispiece. Crown 8vo. Cloth, price 3s. 6d.

MAUDSLEY (Dr. H.).
Responsibility in Mental Disease. Third Edition. Crown 8vo. Cloth, price 5s.

Volume VIII. of The International Scientific Series.

MEREDITH (George).
The Egoist. A Comedy in Narrative. 3 vols. Crown 8vo. Cloth.

*** Also a Cheaper Edition, with Frontispiece. Crown 8vo. Cloth, price 6s.

The Ordeal of Richard Feverel. A History of Father and Son. In one vol. with Frontispiece. Crown 8vo. Cloth, price 6s.

MERRITT (Henry).
Art - Criticism and Romance. With Recollections, and Twenty-three Illustrations in *eau-forte*, by Anna Lea Merritt. Two vols. Large post 8vo. Cloth, 25s.

MIDDLETON (The Lady).
Ballads. Square 16mo. Cloth, price 3s. 6d.

MILLER (Edward).
The History and Doctrines of Irvingism; or, the so-called Catholic and Apostolic Church. 2 vols. Large post 8vo. Cloth, price 25s.

The Church in Relation to the State. Crown 8vo. Cloth, price 7s. 6d.

MILNE (James).
Tables of Exchange for the Conversion of Sterling Money into Indian and Ceylon Currency, at Rates from 1s. 8d. to 2s. 3d. per Rupee. Second Edition. Demy 8vo. Cloth, price £2 2s.

MINCHIN (J. G.).
Bulgaria since the War. Notes of a Tour in the Autumn of 1879. Small crown 8vo. Cloth, price 3s. 6d.

MIVART (St. George), F.R.S.
Contemporary Evolution : An Essay on some recent Social Changes. Post 8vo. Cloth, price 7s. 6d.

MOCKLER (E.).
A Grammar of the Baloo-chee Language, as it is spoken in Makran (Ancient Gedrosia), in the Persia-Arabic and Roman characters. Fcap. 8vo. Cloth, price 5s.

MOFFAT (Robert Scott).
The Economy of Consump-tion; an Omitted Chapter in Political Economy, with special reference to the Questions of Commercial Crises and the Policy of Trades Unions ; and with Reviews of the Theories of Adam Smith, Ricardo, J. S. Mill, Fawcett, &c. Demy 8vo. Cloth, price 18s.

The Principles of a Time Policy : being an Exposition of a Method of Settling Disputes between Employers and Employed in regard to Time and Wages, by a simple Pro-cess of Mercantile Barter, without recourse to Strikes or Locks-out. Reprinted from "The Economy of Consumption," with a Preface and Appendix containing Observations on some Reviews of that book, and a Re-criticism of the Theories of Ricardo and J. S. Mill on Rent, Value, and Cost of Production. Demy 8vo. Cloth, price 3s. 6d.

MOLTKE (Field-Marshal Von).
Letters from Russia. Translated by Robina Napier. Crown 8vo. Cloth, price 6s.

Notes of Travel. Being Ex-tracts from the Journals of. Crown 8vo. Cloth, price 6s.

Monmouth : A Drama, of which the Outline is Historical. Dedicated by permission to Mr. Henry Irving. Small crown 8vo. Cloth, price 5s.

MORELL (J. R.).
Euclid Simplified in Me-thod and Language. Being a Manual of Geometry. Compiled from the most important French Works, approved by the University of Paris and the Minister of Public Instruc-tion. Fcap. 8vo. Cloth, price 2s. 6d.

MORICE (Rev. F. D.), M.A.
The Olympian and Pythian Odes of Pindar. A New Transla-tion in English Verse. Crown 8vo. Cloth, price 7s. 6d.

MORSE (E. S.), Ph.D.
First Book of Zoology. With numerous Illustrations. Crown 8vo. Cloth, price 5s.

MORSHEAD (E. D. A.)
The Agamemnon of Æs-chylus. Translated into English verse. With an Introductory Essay. Crown 8vo. Cloth, price 5s.

MORTERRA (Felix).
The Legend of Allandale, and other Poems. Small crown 8vo. Cloth, price 6s.

NAAKE (J. T.).
Slavonic Fairy Tales. From Russian, Servian, Polish, and Bohemian Sources. With Four Illus-trations. Crown 8vo. Cloth, price 5s.

NEWMAN (J. H.), D.D.
Characteristics from the Writings of. Being Selections from his various Works. Arranged with the Author's personal approval. Third Edition. With Portrait. Crown 8vo. Cloth, price 6s.
**** A Portrait of the Rev. Dr. J. H. Newman, mounted for framing, can be had. price 2s. 6d.

NICHOLAS (Thomas), Ph.D., F.G.S.
The Pedigree of the English People : an Argument, Historical and Scientific, on the Formation and Growth of the Nation, tracing Race-admixture in Britain from the earliest times, with especial reference to the incorporation of the Celtic Abori-gines. Fifth Edition. Demy 8vo. Cloth, price 16s.

NICHOLSON (Edward Byron).

The Christ Child, and other Poems. Crown 8vo. Cloth, price 4s. 6d.

The Rights of an Animal. Crown 8vo. Cloth, price 3s. 6d.

The Gospel according to the Hebrews. Its Fragments translated and annotated, with a critical Analysis of the External and Internal Evidence relating to it. Demy 8vo. Cloth, price 9s. 6d.

NICOLS (Arthur), F.G.S., F.R.G.S.

Chapters from the Physical History of the Earth. An Introduction to Geology and Palæontology, with numerous illustrations. Crown 8vo. Cloth, price 5s.

NOAKE (Major R. Compton).

The Bivouac; or, Martial Lyrist, with an Appendix—Advice to the Soldier. Fcap. 8vo. Price 5s. 6d.

NORMAN PEOPLE (The).

The Norman People, and their Existing Descendants in the British Dominions and the United States of America. Demy 8vo. Cloth, price 21s.

NORRIS (Rev. Alfred).

The Inner and Outer Life Poems. Fcap. 8vo. Cloth, price 6s.

Notes on Cavalry Tactics, Organization, &c. By a Cavalry Officer. With Diagrams. Demy 8vo. Cloth, price 12s.

Nuces: Exercises on the Syntax of the Public School Latin Primer. New Edition in Three Parts. Crown 8vo. Each 1s.
*** The Three Parts can also be had bound together in cloth, price 3s.

O'BRIEN (Charlotte G.).

Light and Shade. 2 vols. Crown 8vo. Cloth, gilt tops, price 12s.

Ode of Life (The).

Third Edition. Fcap. 8vo. Cloth, price 5s.

O'HAGAN (John).

The Song of Roland. Translated into English Verse. Large post 8vo. Parchment antique, price 10s. 6d.

O'MEARA (Kathleen).

Frederic Ozanam, Professor of the Sorbonne; His Life and Works. Second Edition. Crown 8vo. Cloth, price 7s. 6d.

Oriental Sporting Magazine (The).

A Reprint of the first 5 Volumes, in 2 Volumes. Demy 8vo. Cloth, price 28s.

OWEN (F. M.).

John Keats. A Study. Crown 8vo. Cloth, price 6s.

OWEN (Rev. Robert), B.D.

Sanctorale Catholicum; or Book of Saints. With Notes, Critical, Exegetical, and Historical. Demy 8vo. Cloth, price 18s.

Palace and Prison and Fair Geraldine. Two Tragedies, by the Author of "Ginevra" and the "Duke of Guise." Crown 8vo. Cloth, 6s.

PALGRAVE (W. Gifford).

Hermann Agha; An Eastern Narrative. Third and Cheaper Edition. Crown 8vo. Cloth, price 6s.

PALMER (Charles Walter).

The Weed: a Poem. Small crown 8vo. Cloth, price 3s.

PANDURANG HARI;

Or, Memoirs of a Hindoo. With an Introductory Preface by Sir H. Bartle E. Frere, G.C.S.I., C.B. Crown 8vo. Price 6s.

PARKER (Joseph), D.D.

The Paraclete: An Essay on the Personality and Ministry of the Holy Ghost, with some reference to current discussions. Second Edition. Demy 8vo. Cloth, price 12s.

PARR (Capt. H. Hallam).

A Sketch of the Kafir and Zulu Wars: Guadana to Isandhlwana, with Maps. Small crown 8vo. Cloth, price 5s.

PARSLOE (Joseph).

Our Railways : Sketches, Historical and Descriptive. With Practical Information as to Fares, Rates, &c., and a Chapter on Railway Reform. Crown 8vo. Cloth, price 6s.

PATTISON (Mrs. Mark).

The Renaissance of Art in France. With Nineteen Steel Engravings. 2 vols. Demy 8vo. Cloth, price 32s.

PAUL (C. Kegan).

Mary Wollstonecraft. Letters to Imlay. With Prefatory Memoir by, and Two Portraits in *eau forte*, by Anna Lea Merritt. Crown 8vo. Cloth, price 6s.

Goethe's Faust. A New Translation in Rime. Crown 8vo. Cloth, price 6s.

William Godwin: His Friends and Contemporaries. With Portraits and Facsimiles of the Handwriting of Godwin and his Wife. 2 vols. Square post 8vo. Cloth, price 28s.

The Genius of Christianity Unveiled. Being Essays by William Godwin never before published. Edited, with a Preface, by C. Kegan Paul. Crown 8vo. Cloth, price 7s. 6d.

PAUL (Margaret Agnes).

Gentle and Simple : A Story. 2 vols. Crown 8vo. Cloth, gilt tops, price 12s.

*** Also a Cheaper Edition in one vol. with Frontispiece. Crown 8vo. Cloth, price 6s.

PAYNE (John).

Songs of Life and Death. Crown 8vo. Cloth, price 5s.

PAYNE (Prof. J. F.).

Lectures on Education. Price 6d.

II. Fröbel and the Kindergarten system. Second Edition.

PAYNE (Prof. J. F.)—*continued.*

A Visit to German Schools : Elementary Schools in Germany. Notes of a Professional Tour to inspect some of the Kindergartens, Primary Schools, Public Girls' Schools, and Schools for Technical Instruction in Hamburgh, Berlin, Dresden, Weimar, Gotha, Eisenach, in the autumn of 1874. With Critical Discussions of the General Principles and Practice of Kindergartens and other Schemes of Elementary Education. Crown 8vo. Cloth, price 4s. 6d.

PELLETAN (E.).

The Desert Pastor, Jean Jarousseau. Translated from the French. By Colonel E. P. De L'Hoste. With a Frontispiece. New Edition. Fcap. 8vo. Cloth, price 3s. 6d.

PENNELL (H. Cholmondeley).

Pegasus Resaddled. By the Author of "Puck on Pegasus," &c. &c. With Ten Full-page Illustrations by George Du Maurier. Second Edition. Fcap. 4to. Cloth elegant, price 12s. 6d.

PENRICE (Maj. J.), B.A.

A Dictionary and Glossary of the Ko-ran. With copious Grammatical References and Explanations of the Text. 4to. Cloth, price 21s.

PESCHEL (Dr. Oscar).

The Races of Man and their Geographical Distribution. Large crown 8vo. Cloth, price 9s.

PETTIGREW (J. Bell), M.D., F.R.S.

Animal Locomotion; or, Walking, Swimming, and Flying. With 130 Illustrations. Second Edition. Crown 8vo. Cloth, price 5s. Volume VII. of The International Scientific Series.

PFEIFFER (Emily).

Quarterman's Grace, and other Poems. Crown 8vo. Cloth, price 5s.

Glan Alarch : His Silence and Song. A Poem. Second Edition. Crown 8vo. price 6s.

PFEIFFER (Emily)—*continued*.
Gerard's Monument, and other Poems. Second Edition. Crown 8vo. Cloth, price 6s.

Poems. Second Edition. Crown 8vo. Cloth, price 6s.

Sonnets and Songs. New Edition. 15mo, handsomely printed and bound in cloth, gilt edges, price 5s.

PINCHES (Thomas), M.A.
Samuel Wilberforce: Faith —Service—Recompense. Three Sermons. With a Portrait of Bishop Wilberforce (after a Photograph by Charles Watkins). Crown 8vo. Cloth, price 4s. 6d.

PLAYFAIR (Lieut.-Col.), Her Britannic Majesty's Consul-General in Algiers.

Travels in the Footsteps of Bruce in Algeria and Tunis. Illustrated by facsimiles of Bruce's original Drawings, Photographs, Maps, &c. Royal 4to. Cloth, bevelled boards, gilt leaves, price £3 3s.

POLLOCK (W. H.).
Lectures on French Poets. Delivered at the Royal Institution. Small crown 8vo. Cloth, price 5s.

POUSHKIN (A. S.).
Russian Romance. Translated from the Tales of Belkin, &c. By Mrs. J. Buchan Telfer (*née* Mouravieff). Crown 8vo. Cloth, price 3s. 6d.

PRESBYTER.
Unfoldings of Christian Hope. An Essay showing that the Doctrine contained in the Damnatory Clauses of the Creed commonly called Athanasian is unscriptural. Small crown 8vo. Cloth, price 4s. 6d.

PRICE (Prof. Bonamy).
Currency and Banking. Crown 8vo. Cloth, price 6s.

Chapters on Practical Political Economy. Being the Substance of Lectures delivered before the University of Oxford. Large post 8vo. Cloth, price 12s.

Proteus and Amadeus. A Correspondence. Edited by Aubrey De Vere. Crown 8vo. Cloth, price 5s.

PUBLIC SCHOOLBOY.
The Volunteer, the Militiaman, and the Regular Soldier. Crown 8vo. Cloth, price 5s.

PULPIT COMMENTARY (The).
Edited by the Rev. J. S. EXELL and the Rev. Canon H. D. M. SPENCE.
Ezra, Nehemiah, and Esther. By Rev. Canon G. Rawlinson, M.A.; with Homilies by Rev. Prof. J. R. Thomson, M.A., Rev. Prof. R. A. Redford, LL.B., M.A., Rev. W. S. Lewis, M.A., Rev. J. A. Macdonald, Rev. A. Mackennal, B.A., Rev. W. Clarkson, B.A., Rev. F. Hastings, Rev. W. Dinwiddie, LL.B., Rev. Prof. Rowlands, B.A., Rev. G. Wood, B.A., Rev. Prof. P. C. Barker, LL.B., M.A., and Rev. J. S. Exell. Second Edition. One Vol., price 12s. 6d.

Punjaub (The) and North Western Frontier of India. By an old Punjaubee. Crown 8vo. Cloth, price 5s.

QUATREFAGES (Prof. A. de).
The Human Species. Second Edition. Crown 8vo. Cloth, price 5s.
Vol. XXVI. of The International Scientific Series.

RAVENSHAW (John Henry), B.C.S.
Gaur: Its Ruins and Inscriptions. Edited with considerable additions and alterations by his Widow. With forty-four photographic illustrations and twenty-five fac-similes of Inscriptions. Super royal 4to. Cloth, 3l. 13s. 6d.

READ (Carveth).
On the Theory of Logic: An Essay. Crown 8vo. Cloth, price 6s.

Realities of the Future Life. Small crown 8vo. Cloth, price 1s. 6d.

REANEY (Mrs. G. S.).
Blessing and Blessed; a
Sketch of Girl Life. With a frontis-
piece. Crown 8vo. Cloth, price 5s.

Waking and Working; or,
from Girlhood to Womanhood.
With a Frontispiece. Crown 8vo.
Cloth, price 5s.

English Girls: their Place
and Power. With a Preface by
R. W. Dale, M.A., of Birmingham.
Second Edition. Fcap. 8vo. Cloth,
price 2s. 6d.

Just Anyone, and other
Stories. Three Illustrations. Royal
16mo. Cloth, price 1s. 6d.

Sunshine Jenny and other
Stories. Three Illustrations. Royal
16mo. Cloth, price 1s. 6d.

Sunbeam Willie, and other
Stories. Three Illustrations. Royal
16mo. Cloth, price 1s. 6d.

REYNOLDS (Rev. J. W.).
The Supernatural in Na-
ture. A Verification by Free Use of
Science. Second Edition, revised
and enlarged. Demy 8vo. Cloth,
price 14s.

Mystery of Miracles, The.
By the Author of "The Supernatural
in Nature." Crown 8vo. Cloth,
price 6s.

RIBOT (Prof. Th.).
English Psychology. Se-
cond Edition. A Revised and Cor-
rected Translation from the latest
French Edition. Large post 8vo.
Cloth, price 9s.

Heredity: A Psychological
Study on its Phenomena, its Laws,
its Causes, and its Consequences.
Large crown 8vo. Cloth, price 9s.

RINK (Chevalier Dr. Henry).
Greenland: Its People and
its Products. By the Chevalier
Dr. Henry Rink, President of the
Greenland Board of Trade. With
sixteen Illustrations, drawn by the
Eskimo, and a Map. Edited by Dr.
Robert Brown. Crown 8vo. Price
10s. 6d.

ROBERTSON (The Late Rev.
F. W.), M.A., of Brighton.
Notes on Genesis. New
and cheaper Edition. Crown 8vo.,
price 3s. 6d.

Sermons. Four Series. Small
crown 8vo. Cloth, price 3s. 6d. each.

Expository Lectures on
St. Paul's Epistles to the Co-
rinthians. A New Edition. Small
crown 8vo. Cloth, price 5s.

Lectures and Addresses,
with other literary remains. A New
Edition. Crown 8vo. Cloth, price 5s.

An Analysis of Mr. Tenny-
son's "In Memoriam." (Dedicated by Permission to the Poet-
Laureate.) Fcap. 8vo. Cloth, price 2s.

The Education of the
Human Race. Translated from
the German of Gotthold Ephraim
Lessing. Fcap. 8vo. Cloth, price
2s. 6d.

Life and Letters. Edited by
the Rev. Stopford Brooke, M.A.,
Chaplain in Ordinary to the Queen.

I. 2 vols., uniform with the Sermons. With Steel Portrait. Crown
8vo. Cloth, price 7s. 6d.

II. Library Edition, in Demy 8vo.,
with Two Steel Portraits. Cloth,
price 12s.

III. A Popular Edition, in one vol.
Crown 8vo. Cloth, price 6s.

*The above Works can also be had
half-bound in morocco.*

*** A Portrait of the late Rev. F. W.
Robertson, mounted for framing, can
be had, price 2s. 6d.

ROBINSON (A. Mary F.).
A Handful of Honey-
suckle. Fcap. 8vo. Cloth, price
3s. 6d.

RODWELL (G. F.), F.R.A.S.,
F.C.S.
Etna: a History of the
Mountain and its Eruptions.
With Maps and Illustrations. Square
8vo. Cloth, price 9s.

ROOD (Ogden N.).
Modern Chromatics, with Applications to Art and Industry. With 130 Original Illustrations. Crown 8vo. Cloth, price 5s.
  Vol. XXVII. of The International Scientific Series.

ROSS (Mrs. E.), ("Nelsie Brook").
Daddy's Pet. A Sketch from Humble Life. With Six Illustrations. Royal 16mo. Cloth, price 1s.

ROSS (Alexander), D.D.
Memoir of Alexander Ewing, Bishop of Argyll and the Isles. Second and Cheaper Edition. Demy 8vo. Cloth, price 10s. 6d.

SADLER (S. W.), R.N.
The African Cruiser. A Midshipman's Adventures on the West Coast. With Three Illustrations. Second Edition. Crown 8vo. Cloth, price 3s. 6d.

SALTS (Rev. Alfred), LL.D.
Godparents at Confirma-tion. With a Preface by the Bishop of Manchester. Small crown 8vo. Cloth, limp, price 2s.

SAUNDERS (Katherine).
Gideon's Rock, and other Stories. Crown 8vo. Cloth, price 6s.
Joan Merryweather, and other Stories. Crown 8vo. Cloth, price 6s.
Margaret and Elizabeth. A Story of the Sea. Crown 8vo. Cloth, price 6s.

SAUNDERS (John).
Israel Mort, Overman : A Story of the Mine. Cr. 8vo. Price 6s.
Hirell. With Frontispiece. Crown 8vo. Cloth, price 3s. 6d.
Abel Drake's Wife. With Frontispiece. Crown 8vo. Cloth, price 3s. 6d.

SAYCE (Rev. Archibald Henry).
Introduction to the Science of Language. Two vols., large post 8vo. Cloth, price 25s.

SCHELL (Maj. von).
The Operations of the First Army under Gen. von Goeben. Translated by Col. C. H. von Wright. Four Maps. Demy 8vo. Cloth, price 9s.

SCHELL (Maj. von)—*continued.*
The Operations of the First Army under Gen. von Steinmetz. Translated by Captain E. O. Hollist. Demy 8vo. Cloth, price 10s. 6d.

SCHELLENDORF (Maj.-Gen. B. von).
The Duties of the General Staff. Translated from the German by Lieutenant Hare. Vol. I. Demy 8vo. Cloth, 10s. 6d.

SCHERFF (Maj. W. von).
Studies in the New In-fantry Tactics. Parts I. and II. Translated from the German by Colonel Lumley Graham. Demy 8vo. Cloth, price 7s. 6d.

SCHMIDT (Prof. Oscar).
The Doctrine of Descent and Darwinism. With 26 Illustrations. Third Edition. Crown 8vo. Cloth, price 5s.
  Volume XII. of The International Scientific Series.

SCHÜTZENBERGER (Prof. F.).
Fermentation. With Nu-merous Illustrations. Second Edition. Crown 8vo. Cloth, price 5s.
  Volume XX. of The International Scientific Series.

SCOONES (W. Baptiste).
Four Centuries of English Letters. A Selection of 350 Letters by 150 Writers from the period of the Paston Letters to the Present Time. Edited and arranged by. Large crown 8vo. Cloth, price 9s.

SCOTT (Leader).
A Nook in the Apennines: A Summer beneath the Chestnuts. With Frontispiece, and 27 Illustrations in the Text, chiefly from Original Sketches. Crown 8vo. Cloth, price 7s. 6d.

SCOTT (Robert H.).
Weather Charts and Storm Warnings. Illustrated. Second Edition. Crown 8vo. Cloth, price 3s. 6d.

Seeking his Fortune, and other Stories. With Four Illustrations. Crown 8vo. Cloth, price 3s. 6d.

SENIOR (N. W.).

Alexis De Tocqueville. Correspondence and Conversations with Nassau W. Senior, from 1833 to 1859. Edited by M. C. M. Simpson. 2 vols. Large post 8vo. Cloth, price 21s.

Sermons to Naval Cadets. Preached on board H.M.S. "Britannia." Small crown 8vo. Cloth, price 3s. 6d.

Seven Autumn Leaves from Fairyland. Illustrated with Nine Etchings. Square crown 8vo. Cloth, price 3s. 6d.

SHADWELL (Maj.-Gen.), C.B.

Mountain Warfare. Illustrated by the Campaign of 1799 in Switzerland. Being a Translation of the Swiss Narrative compiled from the Works of the Archduke Charles, Jomini, and others. Also of Notes by General H. Dufour on the Campaign of the Valtelline in 1635. With Appendix, Maps, and Introductory Remarks. Demy 8vo. Cloth, price 16s.

SHAKSPEARE (Charles).

Saint Paul at Athens: Spiritual Christianity in Relation to some Aspects of Modern Thought. Nine Sermons preached at St. Stephen's Church, Westbourne Park. With Preface by the Rev. Canon FARRAR. Crown 8vo. Cloth, price 5s.

SHAW (Major Wilkinson).

The Elements of Modern Tactics. Practically applied to English Formations. With Twenty-five Plates and Maps. Small crown 8vo. Cloth, price 12s.

*** The Second Volume of "Military Handbooks for Officers and Non-commissioned Officers." Edited by Lieut.-Col. C. B. Brackenbury, R.A., A.A.G.

SHAW (Flora L.).

Castle Blair: a Story of Youthful Lives. 2 vols. Crown 8vo. Cloth, gilt tops, price 12s. Also, an edition in one vol. Crown 8vo. 6s.

SHELLEY (Lady).

Shelley Memorials from Authentic Sources. With (now first printed) an Essay on Christianity by Percy Bysshe Shelley. With Portrait. Third Edition. Crown 8vo. Cloth, price 5s.

SHELLEY (Percy Bysshe).

Poems selected from. Dedicated to Lady Shelley. With Preface by Richard Garnett. Printed on hand-made paper. With miniature frontispiece. Elzevir. 8vo., limp parchment antique. Price 6s., vellum 7s. 6d.

SHERMAN (Gen. W. T.).

Memoirs of General W. T. Sherman, Commander of the Federal Forces in the American Civil War. By Himself. 2 vols. With Map. Demy 8vo. Cloth, price 24s. *Copyright English Edition.*

SHILLITO (Rev. Joseph).

Womanhood: its Duties, Temptations, and Privileges. A Book for Young Women. Second Edition. Crown 8vo. Price 3s. 6d.

SHIPLEY (Rev. Orby), M.A.

Principles of the Faith in Relation to Sin. Topics for Thought in Times of Retreat. Eleven Addresses. With an Introduction on the neglect of Dogmatic Theology in the Church of England, and a Postscript on his leaving the Church of England. Demy 8vo. Cloth, price 12s.

Church Tracts, or Studies in Modern Problems. By various Writers. 2 vols. Crown 8vo. Cloth, price 5s. each.

SMITH (Edward), M.D., LL.B., F.R.S.

Health and Disease, as Influenced by the Daily, Seasonal, and other Cyclical Changes in the Human System. A New Edition. Post 8vo. Cloth, price 7s. 6d.

Foods. Profusely Illustrated. Sixth Edition. Crown 8vo. Cloth, price 5s. Volume III. of The International Scientific Series.

SMITH (Edward), M.D., LL.B., F.R.S.—*continued.*

Practical Dietary for Families, Schools, and the Labouring Classes. A New Edition. Post 8vo. Cloth, price 3s. 6d.

Tubercular Consumption in its Early and Remediable Stages. Second Edition. Crown 8vo. Cloth, price 6s.

Songs of Two Worlds. By the Author of "The Epic of Hades." Fifth Edition. Complete in one Volume, with Portrait. Fcap. 8vo. Cloth, price 7s. 6d.

Songs for Music. By Four Friends. Square crown 8vo. Cloth, price 5s. Containing songs by Reginald A. Gatty, Stephen H. Gatty, Greville J. Chester, and Juliana Ewing.

SPEDDING (James). **Reviews and Discussions, Literary, Political, and Historical, not relating to Bacon.** Demy 8vo. Cloth, price 12s. 6d.

SPENCER (Herbert). **The Study of Sociology.** Eighth Edition. Crown 8vo. Cloth, price 5s.

Volume V. of The International Scientific Series.

STEDMAN (Edmund Clarence). **Lyrics and Idylls.** With other Poems. Crown 8vo. Cloth, price 7s. 6d.

STEPHENS (Archibald John), LL.D. **The Folkestone Ritual Case.** The Substance of the Argument delivered before the Judicial Committee of the Privy Council. On behalf of the Respondents. Demy 8vo. Cloth, price 6s.

STEVENS (William). **The Truce of God, and other** Poems. Small crown 8vo. Cloth, price 3s. 6d.

STEVENSON (Robert Louis). **An Inland Voyage.** With Frontispiece by Walter Crane. Crown 8vo. Cloth, price 7s. 6d.

STEVENSON (Robert Louis)—*continued.*

Travels with a Donkey in the Cevennes. With Frontispiece by Walter Crane. Crown 8vo. Cloth, price 7s. 6d.

STEVENSON (Rev. W. F.). **Hymns for the Church and Home.** Selected and Edited by the Rev. W. Fleming Stevenson.

The most complete Hymn Book published.

The Hymn Book consists of Three Parts :—I. For Public Worship.—II. For Family and Private Worship.—III. For Children.

*** *Published in various forms and prices, the latter ranging from 8d. to 6s. Lists and full particulars will be furnished on application to the Publishers.*

STEWART (Prof. Balfour), M.A., LL.D., F.R.S. **On the Conservation of Energy.** Fifth Edition. With Fourteen Engravings. Crown 8vo. Cloth, price 5s.

Volume VI. of The International Scientific Series.

STORR (Francis), and TURNER (Hawes). **Canterbury Chimes;** or, Chaucer Tales retold to Children. With Illustrations from the Ellesmere MS. Extra Fcap. 8vo. Cloth, price 3s. 6d.

STRETTON (Hesba). **David Lloyd's Last Will.** With Four Illustrations. Royal 16mo., price 2s. 6d.

The Wonderful Life. Thirteenth Thousand. Fcap. 8vo. Cloth, price 2s. 6d.

Through a Needle's Eye : a Story. 2 vols. Crown 8vo. Cloth, gilt top, price 12s.

*** Also a Cheaper Edition in one volume, with Frontispiece. Crown 8vo. Cloth, price 6s.

STUBBS (Lieut.-Colonel F. W.) **The Regiment of Bengal Artillery.** The History of its Organization, Equipment, and War Services. Compiled from Published Works, Official Records, and various Private Sources. With numerous Maps and Illustrations. 2 vols. Demy 8vo. Cloth, price 32s.

STUMM (Lieut. Hugo), German Military Attaché to the Khivan Expedition.

Russia's advance Eastward. Based on the Official Reports of. Translated by Capt. C. E. H. VINCENT. With Map. Crown 8vo. Cloth, price 6s.

SULLY (James), M.A.
Sensation and Intuition. Demy 8vo. Cloth, price 10s. 6d.

Pessimism : a History and a Criticism. Demy 8vo. Price 14s.

Sunnyland Stories.
By the Author of "Aunt Mary's Bran Pie." Illustrated. Small 8vo. Cloth, price 3s. 6d.

Sweet Silvery Sayings of Shakespeare. Crown 8vo. Cloth gilt, price 7s. 6d.

SYME (David).
Outlines of an Industrial Science. Second Edition. Crown 8vo. Cloth, price 6s.

Tales from Ariosto. Retold for Children, by a Lady. With three illustrations. Crown 8vo. Cloth, price 4s. 6d.

TAYLOR (Algernon).
Guienne. Notes of an Autumn Tour. Crown 8vo. Cloth, price 4s. 6d.

TAYLOR (Sir H.).
Works Complete. Author's Edition, in 5 vols. Crown 8vo. Cloth, price 6s. each.

Vols. I. to III. containing the Poetical Works, Vols. IV. and V. the Prose Works.

TAYLOR (Col. Meadows), C.S.I., M.R.I.A.
A Noble Queen : a Romance of Indian History. Crown 8vo. Cloth. Price 6s.

Seeta. 3 vols. Crown 8vo. Cloth.

Tippoo Sultaun : a Tale of the Mysore War. New Edition with Frontispiece. Crown 8vo. Cloth, price 6s.

TAYLOR (Col. Meadows), C.S.I., M.R.I.A.—*continued.*
Ralph Darnell. New and Cheaper Edition. With Frontispiece. Crown 8vo. Cloth, price 6s.

The Confessions of a Thug. New Edition. Crown 8vo. Cloth, price 6s.

Tara : a Mahratta Tale. New Edition. Crown 8vo. Cloth, price 6s.

TEBBITT (Charles) and Francis Lloyd.
Extension of Empire Weakness? Deficits Ruin? With a Practical Scheme for the Reconstruction of Asiatic Turkey. Small crown 8vo. Cloth, price 3s. 6d.

TENNYSON (Alfred).
The Imperial Library Edition. Complete in 7 vols. Demy 8vo. Cloth, price £3 13s. 6d. ; in Roxburgh binding, £4 7s. 6d.

Author's Edition. Complete in 6 Volumes. Post 8vo. Cloth gilt ; or half-morocco, Roxburgh style :—
VOL. I. **Early Poems, and** English Idylls. Price 6s. ; Roxburgh, 7s. 6d.
VOL. II. **Locksley Hall,** Lucretius, and other Poems. Price 6s. ; Roxburgh, 7s. 6d.
VOL. III. **The Idylls of** the King (*Complete*). Price 7s. 6d.; Roxburgh, 9s.
VOL. IV. **The Princess, and** Maud. Price 6s.; Roxburgh, 7s. 6d.
VOL. V. **Enoch Arden,** and In Memoriam. Price 6s. ; Roxburgh, 7s. 6d.
VOL. VI. **Dramas.** Price 7s. ; Roxburgh, 8s. 6d.

Cabinet Edition. 12 vols. Each with Frontispiece. Fcap. 8vo. Cloth, price 2s. 6d. each.
CABINET EDITION. 12 vols. Complete in handsome Ornamental Case. 32s.

Pocket Volume Edition. 13 vols. In neat case, 36s. Ditto, ditto. Extra cloth gilt, in case, 42s.

TENNYSON (Alfred)—*continued.*

The Royal Edition. Complete in one vol. Cloth, 16s. Cloth extra, 18s. Roxburgh, half morocco, price 20s.

The Guinea Edition. Complete in 12 vols., neatly bound and enclosed in box. Cloth, price 21s. French morocco, price 31s. 6d.

The Shilling Edition of the Poetical and Dramatic Works, in 12 vols., pocket size. Price 1s. each.

The Crown Edition. Complete in one vol., strongly bound in cloth, price 6s. Cloth, extra gilt leaves, price 7s. 6d. Roxburgh, half morocco, price 8s. 6d.

**** Can also be had in a variety of other bindings.

Original Editions :

The Lover's Tale. (Now for the first time published.) Fcap. 8vo. Cloth, 3s. 6d.

Poems. Small 8vo. Cloth, price 6s.

Maud, and other Poems. Small 8vo. Cloth, price 3s. 6d.

The Princess. Small 8vo. Cloth, price 3s. 6d.

Idylls of the King. Small 8vo. Cloth, price 5s.

Idylls of the King. Complete. Small 8vo. Cloth, price 6s.

The Holy Grail, and other Poems. Small 8vo. Cloth, price 4s. 6d.

Gareth and Lynette. Small 8vo. Cloth, price 3s.

Enoch Arden, &c. Small 8vo. Cloth, price 3s. 6d.

In Memoriam. Small 8vo. Cloth, price 4s.

Queen Mary. A Drama. New Edition. Crown 8vo. Cloth, price 6s.

Harold. A Drama. Crown 8vo. Cloth, price 6s.

Selections from Tennyson's Works. Super royal 16mo. Cloth, price 3s. 6d. Cloth gilt extra, price 4s.

TENNYSON (Alfred)—*continued.*

Songs from Tennyson's Works. Super royal 16mo. Cloth extra, price 3s. 6d.
Also a cheap edition. 16mo. Cloth, price 2s. 6d.

Idylls of the King, and other Poems. Illustrated by Julia Margaret Cameron. 2 vols. Folio. Half-bound morocco, cloth sides, price £6 6s. each.

Tennyson for the Young and for Recitation. Specially arranged. Fcap. 8vo. Price 1s. 6d.

Tennyson Birthday Book. Edited by Emily Shakespear. 32mo. Cloth limp, 2s.; cloth extra, 3s.
**** A superior edition, printed in red and black, on antique paper, specially prepared. Small crown 8vo. Cloth extra, gilt leaves, price 5s.; and in various calf and morocco bindings.

In Memoriam. A new Edition, choicely printed on hand-made paper, with a Miniature Portrait in *eau forte* by Le Rat, after a photograph by the late Mrs. Cameron. Bound in limp parchment, antique, price 6s., vellum 7s. 6d.

The Princess. A Medley. Choicely printed on hand-made paper, with a miniature frontispiece by H. M. Paget and a tail-piece in outline by Gordon Browne. Limp parchment, antique, price 6s., vellum, price 7s.

Songs Set to Music, by various Composers. Edited by W. G. Cusins. Dedicated by express permission to Her Majesty the Queen. Royal 4to. Cloth extra, gilt leaves, price 21s., or in half-morocco, price 25s.

THOMAS (Moy).
A Fight for Life. With Frontispiece. Crown 8vo. Cloth, price 3s. 6d.

THOMPSON (Alice C.).
Preludes. A Volume of Poems. Illustrated by Elizabeth Thompson (Painter of " The Roll Call "). 8vo. Cloth, price 7s. 6d.

THOMSON (J. Turnbull).
Social Problems ; or, an In-quiry into the Law of Influences. With Diagrams. Demy 8vo. Cloth, price 10s. 6d.

THRING (Rev. Godfrey), B.A.
Hymns and Sacred Lyrics. Fcap. 8vo. Cloth, price 3s. 6d.

THURSTON (Prof. R. H.).
A History of the Growth of the Steam Engine. With numerous Illustrations. Second Edition. Crown 8vo. Cloth, price 6s. 6d.

TODHUNTER (Dr. J.)
A Study of Shelley. Crown 8vo. Cloth, price 7s.

Alcestis : A Dramatic Poem. Extra fcap. 8vo. Cloth, price 5s.

Laurella ; and other Poems. Crown 8vo. Cloth, price 6s. 6d.

TOLINGSBY (Frere).
Elnora. An Indian Mythological Poem. Fcap. 8vo. Cloth, price 6s.

Translations from Dante, Petrarch, Michael Angelo, and Vittoria Colonna. Fcap. 8vo. Cloth, price 7s. 6d.

TURNER (Rev. C. Tennyson).
Sonnets, Lyrics, and Trans-lations. Crown 8vo. Cloth, price 4s. 6d.

TWINING (Louisa).
Recollections of Work-house Visiting and Management during twenty-five years. Small crown 8vo. Cloth, price 3s. 6d.

TYNDALL (John), LL.D., F.R.S
Forms of Water. A Fami-liar Exposition of the Origin and Phenomena of Glaciers. With Twenty-five Illustrations. Seventh Edition. Crown 8vo. Cloth, price 5s.
Volume I. of The International Scientific Series.

VAN BENEDEN (Mons.).
Animal Parasites and Messmates. With 83 Illustrations. Second Edition. Cloth, price 5s.
Volume XIX. of The International Scientific Series.

VAUGHAN (H. Halford), sometime Regius Professor of Modern History in Oxford University.
New Readings and Ren-derings of Shakespeare's Tragedies. Vol. I. Demy 8vo. Cloth, price 15s.

VILLARI (Prof.).
Niccolo Machiavelli and His Times. Translated by Linda Villari. 2 vols. Large post 8vo. Cloth, price 24s.

VINCENT (Capt. C. E. H.).
Elementary Military Geography, Reconnoitring, and Sketching. Compiled for Non-Commissioned Officers and Soldiers of all Arms. Square crown 8vo. Cloth, price 2s. 6d.

VOGEL (Dr. Hermann).
The Chemical Effects of Light and Photography, in their application to Art, Science, and Industry. The translation thoroughly revised. With 100 Illustrations, including some beautiful specimens of Photography. Third Edition. Crown 8vo. Cloth, price 5s.
Volume XV. of The International Scientific Series.

VYNER (Lady Mary).
Every . day a Portion. Adapted from the Bible and the Prayer Book, for the Private Devotions of those living in Widowhood. Collected and edited by Lady Mary Vyner. Square crown 8vo. Cloth extra, price 5s.

WALDSTEIN (Charles), Ph. D.
The Balance of Emotion and Intellect : An Essay Introductory to the Study of Philosophy. Crown 8vo. Cloth, price 6s.

WALLER (Rev. C. B.)
The Apocalypse, Reviewed under the Light of the Doctrine of the Unfolding Ages and the Restitution of all Things. Demy 8vo. Cloth, price 12s.

WALTERS (Sophia Lydia).
The Brook : A Poem. Small crown 8vo. Cloth, price 3s. 6d.

WALTERS (Sophia Lydia)—*continued*.
A Dreamer's Sketch Book.
With Twenty-one Illustrations by Percival Skelton, R. P. Leitch, W. H. J. Boot, and T. R. Pritchett. Engraved by J. D. Cooper. Fcap. 4to. Cloth, price 12s. 6d.

WARTENSLEBEN (Count H. von).
The Operations of the South Army in January and February, 1871. Compiled from the Official War Documents of the Head-quarters of the Southern Army. Translated by Colonel C. H. von Wright. With Maps. Demy 8vo. Cloth, price 6s.

The Operations of the First Army under Gen. von Manteuffel. Translated by Colonel C. H. von Wright. Uniform with the above. Demy 8vo. Cloth, price 9s.

WATERFIELD, W.
Hymns for Holy Days and Seasons. 32mo. Cloth, price 1s. 6d.

WATSON (William).
The Prince's Quest and other Poems. Crown 8vo. Cloth, price 5s.

WATSON (Sir Thomas), Bart., M.D.
The Abolition of Zymotic Diseases, and of other similar enemies of Mankind. Small crown 8vo. Cloth, price 3s. 6d.

WAY (A.), M.A.
The Odes of Horace Lite- rally Translated in Metre. Fcap. 8vo. Cloth, price 2s.

WEBSTER (Augusta).
Disguises. A Drama. Small crown 8vo. Cloth, price 5s.

WEDMORE (Frederick).
The Masters of Genre Painting. With sixteen illustrations. Crown 8vo. Cloth, price 7s. 6d

WELLS (Capt. John C.), R.N.
Spitzbergen—The Gate- way to the Polynia ; or, A Voyage to Spitzbergen. With numerous Illustrations by Whymper and others, and Map. New and Cheaper Edition. Demy 8vo. Cloth, price 6s.

Wet Days, by a Farmer.
Small crown 8vo. Cloth, price 6s.

WETMORE (W. S.).
Commercial Telegraphic Code. Second Edition. Post 4to. Boards, price 42s.

WHITAKER (Florence).
Christy's Inheritance. A London Story. Illustrated. Royal 16mo. Cloth, price 1s. 6d.

WHITE (A. D.), LL.D.
Warfare of Science. With Prefatory Note by Professor Tyndall. Second Edition. Crown 8vo. Cloth, price 3s. 6d.

WHITNEY (Prof. W. D.)
The Life and Growth of Language. Second Edition. Crown 8vo. Cloth, price 5s. *Copyright Edition.*
Volume XVI. of The International Scientific Series.

Essentials of English Grammar for the Use of Schools. Crown 8vo. Cloth, price 3s. 6a.

WICKHAM (Capt. E. H., R.A.)
Influence of Firearms upon Tactics : Historical and Critical Investigations. By an OFFICER OF SUPERIOR RANK (in the German Army). Translated by Captain E. H. Wickham, R.A. Demy 8vo. Cloth, price 7s. 6d.

WICKSTEED (P. H.).
Dante : Six Sermons. Crown 8vo. Cloth, price 5s.

WILLIAMS (Rowland), D.D.
Life and Letters of, with Extracts from his Note-Books. Edited by Mrs. Rowland Williams. With a Photographic Portrait. 2 vols. Large post 8vo. Cloth, price 24s.

Stray Thoughts from the Note-Books of the Late Rowland Williams, D.D. Edited by his Widow. Crown 8vo. Cloth, price 3s. 6d.

Psalms, Litanies, Coun- sels and Collects for Devout Persons. Edited by his Widow. New and Popular Edition. Crown 8vo. Cloth, price 3s. 6d.

WILLIS (R.), M.D.
Servetus and Calvin : a
Study of an Important Epoch in the
Early History of the Reformation.
8vo. Cloth, price 16s.

William Harvey. A History
of the Discovery of the Circula-
tion of the Blood. With a Portrait
of Harvey, after Faithorne. Demy
8vo. Cloth, price 14s.

WILLOUGHBY(The Hon. Mrs.).
On the North Wind —
Thistledown. A Volume of Poems.
Elegantly bound. Small crown 8vo.
Cloth, price 7s. 6d.

WILSON (H. Schütz).
The Tower and Scaffold.
A Miniature Monograph. Large
fcap. 8vo. Price 1s.

Within Sound of the Sea.
By the Author of "Blue Roses,"
"Vera," &c. Third Edition. 2 vols.
Crown 8vo. Cloth, gilt tops, price 12s.
   *** Also a cheaper edition in one
Vol. with frontispiece. Crown 8vo.
Cloth, price 6s.

WOINOVITS (Capt. I.).
Austrian Cavalry Exercise.
Translated by Captain W. S. Cooke.
Crown 8vo. Cloth, price 7s.

WOLLSTONECRAFT (Mary).
Letters to Imlay. With a
Preparatory Memoir by C. Kegan
Paul, and two Portraits in *eau forte*
by Anna Lea Merritt. Crown 8vo.
Cloth, price 6s.

**WOOD (Major-General J. Creigh-
ton).**
Doubling the Consonant.
Small crown 8vo. Cloth, price 1s. 6d.

WOODS (James Chapman).
A Child of the People,
and other poems. Small crown 8vo.
Cloth, price 5s.

WRIGHT (Rev. David), M.A.
Waiting for the Light, and
other Sermons. Crown 8vo. Cloth,
price 6s.

YOUMANS (Eliza A.).
An Essay on the Culture
of the Observing Powers of
Children, especially in connection
with the Study of Botany. Edited,
with Notes and a Supplement, by
Joseph Payne, F.C.P., Author of
"Lectures on the Science and Art of
Education," &c. Crown 8vo. Cloth,
price 2s. 6d.

First Book of Botany.
Designed to Cultivate the Observing
Powers of Children. With 300 Engravings. New and Cheaper Edition. Crown 8vo. Cloth, price 2s. 6d.

YOUMANS (Edward L.), M.D.
A Class Book of Chemistry,
on the Basis of the New System.
With 200 Illustrations. Crown 8vo.
Cloth, price 5s.

YOUNG (William).
Gottlob, etcetera. Small
crown 8vo. Cloth, price 3s. 6d.

ZIMMERN (H.).
Stories in Precious Stones.
With Six Illustrations. Third Edi-
tion. Crown 8vo. Cloth, price 5s.